I0723400

Ashfall

M.K. Martin

Dedication

To Varya,
my raison d'être

Ashfall

Prologue

Lucian twisted the green and yellow neckerchief of his Scout uniform. Overhead the sky was a perfect spring blue with shy wisps of clouds promising good weather. Only a few more weeks of school and then...

A single engine plane, a Cirrus of some kind from the design, wobbled across the sky, leaving a trail of white smoke punctuated by puffs of grey. Lucian had completed his Aviation merit badge last summer and he was confident the plane was in distress. The boy rose, shading his eyes from the sun's glare as he watched the plane's limping progress. Where was it going? The nearest airport was south in Luxembourg City, not along the banks of the sleepy Wiltz River. Was the pilot trying for the airfield at Noertrange? The way the plane was bucking, Lucian doubted it would be able to complete the trip, let alone land safely.

Unconsciously, Lucian took several running steps forward, the plane's cruciform shadow sliding over the hill and over the boy. It was growing bigger as the plane lost altitude. Lucian could actually see the pilot now. He was leaning out the open window, one arm flopping against the door. Had he suffered a heart attack or stroke? He wasn't even trying to land the plane!

The engine coughed a final sputter and stalled out. The wings wobbled. The wind screamed as the plane increased speed, half-falling, half-gliding down.

Lucian didn't think of the possible dangers as he charged over the hill following the plane. As if guided by a quest icon for a Search & Rescue merit badge in a Scout video game, his legs carried him on and down.

The plane made it past a small copse of trees in the field and then hit the ground with a crash, spraying sparks and dirt. It left a divot like giants had been golfing and bounced, propeller twisting first one way then the other. The second time the plane touched ground, it hit at an angle on the downward slope. For a second, Lucian dared hope it would settle back onto its wheels, but momentum won the battle with gravity and the plane flipped, landing with a metallic crunch as if someone had stomped on an enormous aluminum can.

Lucian panted across the field. He stumbled to a stop and braced his hands on his knees as he stared at the plane, trying to catch his breath with great gulping inhalations.

The gasoline smell of Avgas covered the scents of

earth and the hazy crop of spring weeds that had sprouted in the fertile field. Under the smell of airplane fuel, Lucian detected something else, something meaty and sweet, like a butcher's shop on a hot day.

The pilot must be hurt! Lucian took a last shuddering gasp of air and trotted forward. He should wait for adults, for proper emergency responders, but he had qualified for his first aid badge. If ever there was a time to put his skills to good use, it was now. Besides, if he waited, the pilot might succumb to his injuries or the fumes.

The pilot lay half out of the plane. Blood seeped from a cut on the man's forehead, but other than that he appeared miraculously unharmed.

Fearing that the gas might ignite, Lucian hooked his hands in the pilot's armpits and dragged the man free of the wreck. The pilot coughed and gasped, half-reached for his neck before his hands fell back. He clawed at the ground, digging into the soft soil as he twisted his body. He couldn't breathe!

Lucian fell to his knees beside the pilot. He had never performed rescue breathing in a real-life emergency. His class had concluded with a turn on the practice victim, Franny. Franny had reeked of sterile wipes and her lips had been pliant and clammy.

The pilot reeked of sweat and rotting meat and Avgas. Lucian gagged and leaned forward. He reviewed the steps in his mind and tilted the pilot's head back to clear the airway. As Lucian stuck his fingers in to swipe the pilot's throat for obstructions, the pilot's jaws snapped. Lucian nearly lost a fingertip. The pilot's eyes rolled up, showing only the whites as he kicked, his back arching impossibly so he was in an almost perfect upside-down U shape. Dark bruises stood out on either side of the pilot's neck. Had someone tried to strangle him?

"Please!" Lucian held up his hands. He wanted to restrain the pilot, to keep the man from hurting himself, but he was afraid of the man's thrashing limbs, of the strange, dog-like growl the pilot was making. Lucian scuttled back out of reach and squatted, uncertain what to do, but thrumming with the desire to do something, to help.

It seemed like forever, but suddenly the pilot jerked and fell bonelessly to the ground. Lucian tentatively crawled over to him and listened. The man wasn't breathing. Summoning his courage and relying on his training, Lucian began again. Position the head, visually check for obstructions, finger sweep the throat.

Nothing.

Lucian bent over, his lips hovering as if on the cusp of the kind of kiss he'd imagined with some as yet to be chosen girlfriend. The pilot remained still, unbreathing, dying.

Lucian pressed his mouth over the pilot's and blew. Bloody snot sprayed across his cheek from the pilot's nose. Lucian wiped his face frantically. He'd forgotten to pinch the nose closed.

He tried again. Nose closed; mouth sealed to mouth. Blow. Watch the chest.

It rose!

Lucian lifted his mouth, then gave another breath. The pilot's chest rose again. Encouraged, the boy ducked his head and focused, counting each breath, everything else falling away as he concentrated.

At seventeen breaths, the pilot coughed. Before Lucian could pull away, his mouth was filled with bloody froth. For a second the boy froze, staring at the pilot as pink spittle drooled from his open mouth. He'd heard that victims might spit or even vomit into their rescuers' mouths. Grimly, Lucian spit and spit again, wiped his tongue on the sleeve of his shirt, and spit again.

There was a wail of sirens and, from the road that curved around the field, blue lights flashed. Emergency responders rushed from the ambulance but paused at the sight of the upside-down plane, the supine pilot, and the bedraggled Scout.

Lucian didn't remember a lot of what happened next. Someone had taken him to the ambulance. He couldn't remember what he'd said, if he'd told them he wasn't hurt, but they'd wrapped him in a blanket - odd on such a warm day - and taken his pulse. When they brought the pilot on a stretcher, Lucian had tried to get into the ambulance with the man, but the medic who was with the boy tugged him gently away. She took his phone and called his mother.

Somehow, he was home, still wrapped in the blanket from the ambulance, the field dirt under his nails, the sweet, meat smell of the pilot clinging to him, the feel of bloody bubbles lingering in his mouth. Momma sent him to bed, and he went without an argument.

Lucian slept through the day and night. He woke sweating, trapped in the furnace cocoon of the ambulance blanket and his duvet. The sun had yet to rise and shadows claimed the room. Lucian's throat hurt. He reached up and felt his neck. The skin was hot and damp.

The Scout got up and tottered into the hall. Annchen,

his older sister, poked her head out of her door and screamed. "Momma. Momma! Lucian's sick."

Lucian teetered and leaned against the doorframe. "I'm not sick." His words were a croak, his throat was on fire. He was hungrier than he'd ever been. He wanted to lie down and sleep, but he wanted, he needed to eat more than he wanted to rest.

Lucian ground his teeth so hard he could hear the hinges click in the tiny bones of his ears as he shuffled down the hall, cannoning gently off the walls. Annchen paced behind him, her hands up to catch her brother should he lose his balance.

Their mother met them in the kitchen. She took one look at her son. "Go get the car, Annchen. We're going to the hospital."

In North Hospital Center, the nurses were worried. The pilot's condition had worsened. His arms were deforming as if the bone had been absorbed leaving only muscle and fat and flesh behind. The limbs were also blackening. The pilot's fever surged and ebbed like a tide, but he never regained consciousness. His tongue had shriveled. He ground his teeth and snapped his jaw hard enough to crack enamel. The bruises on his neck were echoed by spreading patches under his armpits. Clearly, something was affecting his lymph nodes. Tests were run, samples collected and sealed to be sent to labs in the morning.

Most worrying was the vomiting. The pilot seemed to have an endless supply of bloody vomit that had to be caught, contained, cleaned up, and disposed of. The biohazard bags were pressed into service to collect the bloody stew. There wasn't enough space in the storage room and the bags piled around the bottom shelves.

"We just have to get through the night," Dr. Yvea Milan-Pierre told the sober circle of staff collected outside the pilot's room. She didn't tell the staff that she had alerted the World Health Organization's (WHO) Global Outbreak Alert and Response Network (GOARN) because she didn't want to cause a panic. Near midnight, Dr. Milan-Pierre went home to catch a few hours of sleep. By the time she returned around five a.m., it was clear to her that quarantine would be unavoidable.

Dr. Milan-Pierre stood over her desk, a list of all the hospital staff and emergency responders in front of her. She would have to call everyone in. At least the plane had crashed in a field, not in the town. Thank goodness they didn't have to worry about any of the townspeople being exposed. Containment was the name of the game at this point.

She glanced at the picture of her family she kept on her desk. Her wife would see the kids off to school. With luck and good barrier nursing, they'd never even have to know about the quarantine. It would scare Kamila and she still hadn't recovered from Yvea's humanitarian trip to the refugee camp.

Annchen slammed on the brakes as the family's Fiat Panda rounded the corner into the hospital's emergency room entrance. A police officer stood in the street, waving her to stop. As the officer approached the Fiat, she yawned and stretched.

Annchen had been practicing for her driving exam and hoped to pass as soon as she was old enough to take it. As the police officer arrived, the girl's eyes widened. "Momma, I don't have my-"

The officer motioned for Annchen to roll down the window and she did.

"I'm sorry, miss, but the hospital is closed," the policewoman said. "Here is a list of clinics that will see urgent patients. If this isn't an emergency-"

"It is!" Momma shouted, making Annchen jump. In the backseat, Lucian groaned and ground his teeth. He sounded like an animal. The hairs on the back of Annchen's neck rose listening to her brother. He smelled like an animal, too, musky and sweaty, like spoiled meat.

"There is a quarantine. You'll need to go to one of the clinics on the list." The policewoman again held out a hastily printed flyer. Annchen took it, relieved the officer hadn't noticed she was too young to be driving.

"My son is very sick," Momma insisted. "He rescued the pilot. He's a hero. He needs to be in a hospital."

"I'm very sorry, but I can't let anyone in right now. It's for your own safety and your children's. Please." The policewoman held out a gloved hand as if inviting Annchen to turn the Fiat back into the narrow, cobbled roads of Wiltz.

"Let's go, Momma," the girl said softly. She felt a little dizzy and overheated, trapped in the car with the police officer staring at her.

The morning mist swirled and closed behind the car as the family drove away. The policewoman congratulated herself on saving that nice family from whatever emergency quarantine drill the hospital was undergoing.

Chapter 1 – Torres

Torres twisted her wrists, the metal handcuffs chiming together as she craned her neck to peer out the small porthole of the C-130. Strange to see the immense cargo hold so empty. Only four pallets of medical and scientific gear were strapped into a space half the size of a football field. Equally strange to see all the empty seats. The former Marine was used to seeing the Hercules filled with nearly a hundred fellow grunts. Instead, the passengers numbered only five, counting herself. Except for their custodian, all were cuffed and had been for the duration of the trip.

Below, lights in the darkness marked out a runway. The not exactly straight, not exactly even spacing of the guiding lights heralded a bumpy landing on a makeshift landing strip.

Torres reached out to shake the detainee on her left but paused. Marius was dozing, chin to chest, his dark hair falling forward to hide his handsome face. For most of the trip he had stared into space, chewing his full lower lip, and silently worrying. Seeing him softened in sleep reminded Torres of the kiss, the impulsive kiss that they had shared during the Chrysalis outbreak.

It didn't mean anything, she told herself. A spontaneous act when she no shit thought they were all going to end up tagged and bagged in a matter of hours. Not like she'd had a thing for Marius ever since she'd been detailed to bring him to Chrysalis's remote research and development site in the middle of the Arizona desert.

The landing gear lowered, and Marius jerked awake. Inside the Hercules only the running lights were on, making Marius's eyes gleam a feral red.

He's not infected. He's immune. He can't be infected. He's naturally immune.

Torres held herself still and waited for her heart to stop jittering. She hated that the virus could cause her to fear the ones she cared about the most. Stupid lizard brain. When she was confident her voice wouldn't shake, she addressed the other detainees across the aisle.

"Hey, captain, we're coming in hard and fast. Miranda, try to hold on and not get bounced out of your seat."

Former head of Chrysalis security, John Courage opened an eye, nodded, and settled back into a doze. A retired Army Special Forces officer, Courage was a veteran of many bumpy landings. In Torres's experience as a member of the Chrysalis security team, the captain was nearly unflappable.

Miranda, seated next to Courage, wasn't nearly as calm. The younger woman was much more at home in posh boutiques than in a stripped-down troop transport. She should be at college, flirting with frat boys or sorority girls or whatever she was into. Torres made it her business to not make Miranda her business. She was the boss's daughter...well, before the boss had died in the outbreak.

"Are we gonna crash or something?" Miranda leaned forward, trying to see out the porthole.

"Quiet." Their custodian, a bellicose technical sergeant, half stood as if preparing to navigate the aisle, but before he could take a step the Hercules's wheels hit the ground and the plane shuddered. The tech sergeant fell back into his seat.

A few more rolling bounces and the plane came to a reluctant stop.

The tech sergeant got up and pointed at the detainees. "Stay." He shuffled past the pallets to the tail as it lowered to open the rear of the plane.

Beyond the runway lights, a dark field spread out, sweeping up to lightly forested hills. Directly behind the plane sprouted a cluster of white tents ringed by olive drab tents like mushrooms after rain. WHO scientists swarmed around the white tents as outside the tents, UN peacekeepers and civilian contractors patrolled the gap between two rows of chain-link fencing, which were topped with rolls of razor wire. Floodlights dotted the perimeter at regular intervals. The whole area was the strange offspring of a military operation and a field hospital.

A pair of Jeeps drove onto the flight line, coming to a stop at the end of the ramp. Three soldiers sporting baby blue UN berets hopped out and hurried aboard to unload the pallets. They ignored the four Americans who waited, handcuffed and silent.

A short man in a black polo shirt and khaki pants bustled up the ramp. A security badge hung from a lanyard around the man's neck.

"Where are they?" he demanded, pushing wire-rim glasses up his nose as he squinted into the dim interior.

"This way." The tech sergeant ushered him past the hurrying soldiers and stopped in the aisle between the detainees.

"Dr. Tenartier, so glad you're here at last. We haven't a moment to lose." The short man held out a hand to shake Marius's hand.

Marius reached up, still cuffed.

"Oh, do take those off. No need for such nonsense."

"I'd keep the restraints on until they get into the camp at least," the tech sergeant said. "But your call, Dr. Mendelsen. They're in your custody now." He pulled out a key and held it up.

"Yes, yes, I accept full responsibility." Mendelsen waved impatiently. He had the same wistful, never-endingly distracted air about him that Marius often got when neck-deep in some genetics mystery. "I expect Dr. Tenartier to honor the terms of his parole."

"And the others?" The tech sergeant released Marius and glared as if the detainees might rush him. Torres curled her lip. Across the aisle, Courage adopted a relaxed, non-threatening slouch. Miranda sat up straight as if she'd just been called on by teacher.

"Yes, them, too," Mendelsen said. "They're here to help, not make a getaway into the Luxembourg countryside. Where would they even go? There's an HHV outbreak and we are the only ones with the wherewithal to address it."

After the tech sergeant released the cuffs, the former detainees followed Mendelsen down the ramp and over to one of the Jeeps. The other had already set off back to the UN encampment.

Torres paused as she stepped out from under the bird's tail, tipped her head back and breathed deep as she looked at the stars. It had been months since she'd last seen the night sky, months since she'd breathed free air.

"So, what's the situation?" Marius asked, taking the front seat beside Mendelsen. Torres hurried to catch up. She and Courage piled into the backseats with Miranda wedged between them. After all the time spent in solitary confinement in an off-the-books holding site, Torres relished the warmth of fellow humans nearby, even if those humans hadn't had a shower in over forty-eight hours. It beat orange scrubs, giving her daily blood sample, and repeatedly answering the same three thousand questions about the Chrysalis outbreak.

"What did they tell you before they let you out?" Mendelsen asked as he maneuvered the Jeep around. They bumped and jounced over the field, bracing themselves as best they could against the Jeep's frame.

"Only that there was an outbreak of a highly infectious virus in Europe and that they thought it might be related to the Harrow Hall virus," Marius said.

"We were offered the opportunity to assist and advise the UN's efforts to coordinate and contain it in exchange for our parole," Courage added dryly.

"More like a chance to be human blood banks," Torres said. Sure, the WHO needed Marius's science brain, but there was no way they were short on security, so why bring her and Courage? Why bring Miranda, for that matter? Was any situation made better by adding a 19-year-old heiress? To be fair to Miranda, she had her shit wired pretty tight for a young civilian, probably thanks to the fact that Courage had practically raised her.

"No, no," Mendelsen said. "We would never violate international law by using human test subjects. We were merely hoping that you could lend your expertise, since you were instrumental in containing the outbreak at the Chrysalis facility."

"We're not doing that again," said Miranda. "Marius nearly died."

"But I didn't," Marius said. "And if this is HHV, we need to stop it fast. Have you seen any bioformations yet?"

"Bioformations?" Mendelsen frowned.

"The meat walls," Miranda said.

"Oh, ah, yes. There have been reports of a fleshy film that grows out of contaminated biological matter. They seem to be spreading, especially through the hospital where the outbreak started."

"We'll need to access the site," Marius said.

"We'll need flamethrowers," Torres added.

"Is that supposed to be on fire?" Miranda pointed to

a glow barely visible beyond the floodlights of the UN encampment.

Mendelsen slowed the Jeep and stopped it, leaned forward to stare into the darkness. "No. Nothing should be on fire. I told them to wait. We still don't know the effects of high temperatures on the bioformations. Some types of fungi actually need fire to help them release their spores."

"But we're not talking about fungi here," Torres said. "It's a virus, right?"

Mendelsen shrugged. "Technically, yes, but some NSVs are able to incorporate fungal plasmids. They also hijack mRNA for transcription."

"Sure. What he said," Miranda said. "But mushrooms aside, what would the fire do to the Harrow Hall virus? I mean, like, can we just fry it to death or something? Cuz that would be way better than what we did last time, right Marius?" She reached forward between the seats and shook Marius's shoulder.

"We don't know, like Dr. Mendelsen said," Marius said. "Either way, we need to get into town and observe the effects of the fire on the bioformations."

"Torres and I will go," Courage said. "We don't know the status of the people in town, and we might be dealing with HHV Infected."

"But Marius is immune. So am I. They only tested us about 8,000 times in prison," Miranda said. "Besides, we shouldn't split up."

"I agree with the captain," Torres said.

"You would," Miranda muttered, crossing her arms over her chest.

Torres ignored her and continued, "Doc, we need you

safe and sound in those white tents making vaccine or whatever science thing you can do to stop this." She waved a hand at the town. Apart from the orange glow near the middle of the town, everything else looked normal, quiet, peaceful. Lights twinkled in windows and streets were illuminated by quaint-looking wrought iron streetlamps.

But there were no people on the streets. No firetrucks responding to the fire. No looky-loos rubbernecking. It reminded Torres of the way a market square in an Iraqi town looked moments before a big IED went off. As a general rule, her unit had kept an eye on the locals. If the kids weren't on the street that usually meant bad news for the Marines.

"I need to see what's going on. No offense, but you two don't know what you're looking for," Marius said.

"We'll provide them with state-of-the-art communication equipment. They'll act as your eyes and ears. Given your status, it's best to keep you out of harm's way," Mendelsen said. He shifted the Jeep back into gear and resumed their journey toward the UN encampment.

"Why two gates?" Miranda asked, leaning forward so her head was even with Mendelsen's and Marius's shoulders.

"Screening stations," Mendelsen said. "Townsfolk come in the first gate, which is locked behind them, they're screened, and then either sent into the waiting area to be evacuated or sent to the medical area for further testing and care."

"All neat and clean," Courage said. "How many have you screened so far?"

"Ah, well," Mendelsen said. "None."

"None?" Torres pressed her fingertips to her eyelids.

"General Falk wanted to wait for our experts to arrive. There's been a lot of reluctance among the non-medical personnel to let us go into the town or to let people come out."

"How long since this was reported?" Marius asked.

"There's been conflicting reports of how many were exposed, but the locals do agree that the pilot was patient zero in this case. A plane crashed four days ago."

"Any reports of HHV symptoms: bruising patterns under the arms or on the neck, extra limbs, mutations?"

"Well, the pilot, yes. That's why the GOARN's involved. The UN is supervising. After what happened with Ebola in the DRC, they've instituted a policy of military oversight for Class Four outbreaks."

"So just to be on the safe side, they've been letting a possible Class Four outbreak incubate unchecked for over 96 hours?" Marius sounded like he was talking through clenched teeth. "Has anyone read my reports? HHV is extremely fast-acting. Without a vaccine, those infected with HHV can become symptomatic within hours. Hours. Not days. And we're not just worried about human vectors. Any mammal is susceptible."

"I understand, Dr. Tenartier. I have read all your reports. As I said, as soon as we —"

"Stop!" Miranda grabbed Mendelsen's shoulder.

He slammed on the brakes. A woman staggered towards them out of the gloom. She carried a small boy on her hip. In the harsh glare of the Jeep's headlights, the swollen, purple lumps on her neck were unmistakable.

The UN guards greeted the newcomers with a barrage of commands in French, German, Italian, and several other languages Torres couldn't name. What she did understand were the raised rifles, the tense voices, the narrowed eyes, and the hand motions.

It wasn't hard to figure out what they were saying. "Get down, get down. Don't move." Or some variation of that.

Mendelsen held up his badge and spoke in German to the guards. They beckoned him forward. From a raised platform inside the encampment, a soldier kept a crew-served machine gun aimed at the infected woman and the boy. Marius moved to stand between them and the gunner. Torres heaved a deep sigh and stepped in front of the scientist.

"Stop playing hero, doc," she muttered.

"They won't shoot me," Marius said.

"Don't count on it," Courage said. He also moved a little so he was between Marius and the machine gun.

"What?" Miranda's head snapped toward the Infected woman.

"He means they don't know how valuable Marius is and they might shoot him," Torres said.

Miranda frowned, rubbed her forehead. "Yeah, I know that. Thanks, Captain Obvious."

"That's Sergeant Obvious. I work for a living." Torres grinned as Courage shook his head at the well-worn joke.

"Tell them we need to get this woman into quarantine

as quickly as possible. I'm not sure if PEPs will be effective with her since she's already symptomatic, but we should definitely try with the boy," Marius said.

"Follow me," Mendelsen said. "Do not stray or you'll be shot."

The inner gate clicked open and Mendelsen led them into the encampment. UN soldiers and security contractors fell in beside, ahead, and behind them as they passed through the drab olive-green tents and into the maze of white medical tents.

"In here." Mendelsen lifted the tent flap and ushered them inside. Inside, several chain-link cages, like large dog kennels, lined the back wall. Each kennel had a bare army-style cot and a bucket.

The rest of the tent was taken up with field tables, piled high with medical equipment. Large, hard-sided cases with medical symbols on them rested under the tables. Plastic biohazard suits and goggles hung from hooks on the walls, while paper face masks and latex gloves sat ready in cardboard boxes on shelves beneath.

Without apology, Mendelsen opened one of the kennels for the Infected woman. As she entered, he put a hand on her son's shoulder, stopping the boy. The woman tugged at the child's hand and spoke rapidly in German, tears flowing as Mendelsen shook his head. Her tears were milky white. Torres's stomach clenched. She had to look away, refused to let the memory of the sweet, meat stink of the Infected claw its way out of her nightmares.

Marius seemed to have no such negative reaction. He took the woman's free hand and patted it, speaking to her in German. After a few minutes, the woman nodded and stepped into the kennel. The door clicked behind her, a red light flashing on over it. Marius led the boy to another kennel, not next to his mother, but separated by one space.

With both mother and son locked in, most of the UN soldiers departed.

"And now, to work." Mendelsen rubbed his hands together.

"They need food, water, blankets," Marius said.

"Of course, yes. Could you see to that?" Mendelsen looked at Torres.

"Am I going to get shot if I step out of here?" Torres was accustomed to the science people taking the grunts for granted, but she wasn't prepared to tempt the already edgy security forces for some gofer work.

"Oh, no, no, no. Here. Your badges." Mendelsen opened a briefcase on one of the tables and pulled out badges similar to his own. "You have the run of the camp." Torres was surprised that the photo on hers was her old Chrysalis ID picture, from back when her hair had been long.

She draped the lanyard around her neck and handed Miranda hers. "Let's go exploring."

"I want to stay with Marius," Miranda said. She lifted her long brunette hair and slipped the badge on, letting it settle between her breasts.

"I'll stay," Courage said, donning his own badge.

"Besides," Marius said as Miranda opened her mouth. "We're just going to be doing boring science — lots of test tubes and microscopes." He gave her a half-grin, a ghost of his former cocky smile. "Plus, our patients deserve what little privacy we can give them."

Torres pushed open the tent flap and held it for Miranda.

The younger woman rolled her eyes as she exited. "Fine. Whatever. I'm not getting you coffee, though."

Torres dropped the flap and looked around, orienting herself to her new area of operations.

"This is such BS." Miranda crossed her arms over her chest and glared around at the bustling encampment. "Why'd they even bring us out here if all they wanted was for Marius to do science or whatever?"

"Would you rather be rotting in that cell, Miss Threat to National Security?"

"I would rather be talking to my lawyer about the violations of my civil liberties, but I'll settle for some Starbucks."

"If I know the military, coffee is this way." Torres headed out of the medical section and towards the biggest of the clamshell tents. Her guess that it was the morale, welfare, and recreation tent proved true. Inside the MWR tent, a bank of phones had been set up on plywood tables with folding chairs in front of each. A big screen TV showed a Dutch news program. Several UN soldiers lounged on couches watching the TV, sipping coffee.

Torres stared at the phones. She couldn't remember the last time she'd called home. Sometime before everything went sideways at Chrysalis. She'd told her mother that she wouldn't be there for Christmas. Again.

Beside her, Miranda swayed, hand to her forehead.

"Are you okay?" Torres peered at the younger woman. Miranda's pupils were pin-pointed, her gaze focused into the middle distance as she ground her teeth.

Torres glanced around. None of the soldiers seemed to be paying attention. Torres shook Miranda gently. "Hey, Miranda. What's wrong?"

Miranda shuddered all over and weakly pushed Torres away. "I'm fine."

"Are you having a freaking stroke?" Torres kept her voice low.

"We have to go." Miranda spun on her heel and bolted out of the tent.

And there he stood, not fifty feet from the outer fence, swaying in the fading light, the tents casting long shadows around him, but even the shadows seemed afraid to touch him.

"Get back! Get the fuck back! You are not to approach the perimeter," yelled one of the contractors, waving a pistol at the man. Several other contractors ran up and dropped to one knee, their own weapons out and aimed at the man. One of the UN troops turned a nearby exterior spotlight on the man.

Torres could see the swollen glands, the purpling under the man's chin. Beside her, Miranda pressed forward. Torres stuck out an arm to hold the younger woman back.

The man took a hesitant step toward the gate and safeties clicked off.

"Wait!" Miranda reached out.

"Go get Courage." Miranda shouldn't be there if this thing turned into a shitshow. Torres pushed the younger woman back toward the white tents. "And Marius. Quick."

The man clasped his hands as if in prayer and held them up as he approached the fence.

"Back away now," the contractor with the pistol yelled, aiming at the man.

"Don't shoot!" Torres shoved between two UN soldiers, knocking one's harmlessly blue beret off. One of the contractors grabbed her arm.

"Stay back, ma'am."

"We need a sample of —"

Pop!

The man fell over, curled on his side.

For a moment, less than a minute, no one reacted, frozen like naughty children who had knocked over the expensive vase; they didn't know if they were in trouble or to what degree. The air felt thin, as if everyone was inhaling at once, cringing in unison.

It was a moment where the flipped coin balanced on its edge. Torres cleared her throat, stepped into the power vacuum.

"Stand down," she barked. When no one moved, she put a hand on the barrel of a UN soldier's weapon and pushed it down. The others lowered their weapons.

This is your show now. Don't blow it.

Torres channeled her inner drill instructor, drawing up the loud, authoritative tone from deep in her belly. "Listen up!" Several heads turned, surprised. "I'm working with the head medical officer here. We need samples of the disease that man has. Now, get back and stay back until the medics get here. Do not fire on civilians, especially civilians outside the wire, you knuckleheads."

"Head medical officer, eh?"

Courage had come up behind her. He surveyed the field between the UN tents and Wiltz. Marius stood next to him, blue latex gloves still on.

"Sure, why not?" Torres said. "Glad you're here, head medical officer." She elbowed Marius.

Marius stepped into the circle and looked around, meeting the gaze of the soldiers. "What is wrong with you?"

One of the UN troops shrugged. "He wouldn't stay back. He's from town. We're protecting the base from that disease."

Torres didn't think of Marius as a violent person, but in a second he was in front of the soldier, face shoved into his. The soldier pulled his head back like a nervous dog.

Torres barely recognized the low voice that growled out of Marius. "You are not protecting anyone from anything. Do you have any idea how dangerous this virus is? You're not wearing any of your gear. You've probably got all kinds of contaminants on you. You are a walking vector." He jabbed the soldier in the chest as he spoke.

"Dr. Tenartier, let's get this cleaned up," Courage said, cool as Mamá's horchata. "The rest of you, move over there but don't leave the area. Torres, take down everyone's names."

Marius turned back to the man, his body slumping as if the anger had drained out. "I need my kit," he said.

"I'll get it and see what's keeping Mendelsen." Courage strode away.

While he was gone Torres collected names. The

guards opened the gates so Marius could perform a visual exam. One of the soldiers gave him her LED flashlight as he stepped out into the field.

After a few minutes, Courage returned with a nylon bag. Torres handed him her list of names and took the bag out to Marius.

"Can we help? Is there some protocol?" she asked.

"Ummm ...you can ..." Marius blinked and looked up. "You can start by quarantining and screening them." He pointed at the cluster of security personnel. "We need to keep them under observation for at least four days. Unless HHV is endemic to Wiltz, which I doubt, this man couldn't have been exposed more than four days ago. Let's make it five to be on the safe side." He glared at the soldiers. "This is a real cautious bunch."

While Courage made arrangements to move the soldiers to quarantine, Marius donned his protective gear. Without needing to discuss it, Courage took over as incident commander while Torres shadowed Marius. Old Chrysalis habits dictated that he needed a bodyguard. He knelt beside the body with Torres next to him, handing him slides and swabs as he wordlessly collected samples of blood and saliva.

When he was finished, Marius rose, his green eyes following the stretcher that took the body away.

"So, what now?" Torres asked, hoping to shake him out of his trance-like silence.

"Ah, now we confirm HHV. An autopsy will help us figure out how quickly it's progressing."

They put the dark field to their backs and after a few minutes were swallowed up by the warren of tents under the bright lights, surrounded by security forces and medical personnel. Courage caught up to them, having stayed to make sure the security forces followed Marius's protocols. He fell into step as they made their way to the quarantine tent.

Marius was quiet the whole way back. Torres and Courage exchanged worried glances. Marius was never quiet. He always had some bit of scientific trivia to impart.

Inside the tent, he stopped to study his gloved hands; the blood already dried on them, a few spatters on the plastic sleeves of his protective suit.

"I don't understand. Why did they shoot him? He was outside the fence." Marius yanked off the gloves and raked his long fingers through his dark hair.

"They're scared," Torres said. "Scared people do stupid things."

"But he was just trying to get help. We have the vaccine. They didn't need to shoot him," Marius said. "That's why we're here — to help people."

"Either way, he's gone now. You can't save everyone, Marius," Courage said.

"I can try." Marius's chin came down defiantly.

"Focus on what you can do, here and now," Courage said. "Save the ones you can."

The scientist turned away and pulled on a fresh pair of gloves. "Right."

Torres felt the wild urge to go to him, to put her arms around him and reassure him. They could fix everything. He was smart enough; she was strong enough. They'd been through worse.

Instead, she flipped open a binder labeled *Standard Operating Procedure - Level Four Containment,* thumbing through it randomly.

"We need to get the screenings set up so this doesn't happen again," she said.

"Sounds like a job for someone who works with the head medical officer," Courage said. "And Miranda can help spread the good word." He looked around. "Where is she?"

"I sent her to get you guys."

"Mendelsen got a radio call about an Infected by the fence, so we hightailed it over there."

Torres shook her head. With no map app to guide her, Miranda had probably gotten lost in the maze of tents.

"Well, she can't get too far." Torres dug a clipboard out of a pile of papers and tacked the screening SOP to it. "These badasses have the place puckered up tighter than a —"

The woman in the kennel screamed. She leaped off her cot and threw herself at the kennel door, shaking the frame. In his cage, her son burst into tears as his mother arched back, fingers clawing at her own ribcage.

"It's coming out," she howled. "It has to come out."

Torres scanned the room. Not a weapon in sight. She grabbed one of the first aid kits and yanked out a pair of medical shears. Courage had pushed Marius back, well out of reach of the kennel.

The woman fell forward onto all fours, growling and gurgling. She twisted her head from side to side. It was a broader range of motion than a human neck should be able to twist. Torres shuddered.

The woman went still. Drool, milky like her tears, dribbled in long threads from her lips to the floor. She raised her eyes to stare into Torres's.

"Don't. Let. Him. Watch." Her voice was a hoarse rasp, barely audible over her son's hysterical sobbing.

Marius ducked past Courage and opened the boy's kennel. He scooped him up and carried him away, the child's pudgy arms reaching for his mother as she collapsed in her cage.

Chapter 2 – Miranda

Leaving the encampment had been too easy. With all the guards crowded around the man they'd shot, Miranda simply walked out. The gates didn't lock from the inside so all she had to do was press the bar and they opened. She'd have to remember to tell John about that so he could fix it. It didn't seem safe.

The headache that had nearly blinded her earlier eased as she made her way into the field. She stepped high, feeling her way across the uneven ground. Tall grass, damp with dew, brushed against her nearly to the knee. She hardly felt the chill through the sturdy fatigue-style pants she'd been given. Not her first, second, or even twentieth choice, but with the right belt and sassy

T-shirt they might pass for grungy-cute.

Above, a few clouds rimmed the sky like set dressing on a stage. The moon was half full and there were a ton of stars. Not as many as she'd been able to see from the Chrysalis headquarters in Arizona, but still a ton.

She was going to investigate. She would get some samples or something for Marius so they could all go home.

Flimsy rationale, yes, but it was better than admitting the real reason she'd violated her parole and left the safety of the encampment. Miranda had felt the pull from the town before they'd even landed. The feeling had been growing stronger, like the need to vomit, until it was the only thing she could think of. She had to get to Wiltz.

We're waiting for you.

Miranda shuddered, tried to shake off the slick, silky touch of something simultaneously alien but also undeniably familiar. It wasn't her exactly, but it wasn't not her, either.

She pushed the invading sensation away and focused on more practical matters. If they contained the outbreak, they could all go home — free citizens with access to the internet, her late father's bank accounts, everything.

At the outskirts of Wiltz, she stopped and looked back to the island of light in the dark sea of the field. Marius was there, waiting for her. He'd be so worried. He'd wrap his arms around her, breathe a sigh of relief, pull back to gaze into her eyes, his voice low, choked with emotion. "I don't know what I'd do without you, Miranda."

Miranda smiled, smoothed her hair down, and

stepped onto the street. She couldn't have said how, but she knew exactly where she was going, as if on autopilot. Most of the buildings she passed were dark and silent. Sure, it was late, but it wasn't *that* late. But no one so much as twitched their curtains as Miranda walked down the empty street.

What if they were already infected? What if they were all dead?

Miranda's smile faltered, but she felt a swell of comfort reach out to her to enfold her, encouraging her.

This way. Join us. We're waiting for you. Come home.

The message seemed clearer, like she was tuning it in better than before. Or maybe with her headache gone she could focus better. She noticed the little details she hadn't registered upon first entering Wiltz. Broken windows — some inward, others outward — spilled sparkling shards onto the road. A few had dark stains on the glass. And then there was the smell, thick and sugary-sweet like cloying vanilla perfume.

She rounded a corner and there it was — the hospital. It was bigger than she'd imagined, but it seemed small compared to the presence she felt lurking inside. She knew it was there the same way she sometimes suddenly could tell that someone had snuck up on her in the dark.

There was definitely something in the hospital and it wanted her.

Come home. Be safe with us.

Us?

The soft hairs on Miranda's arm rose as goose bumps raced down her limbs. Her gut tightened. They were all around her, their attention pressing against her skin as if they could push her into the hospital through the force of their will alone. She should go, run away back to the safety of the camp and John and Marius.

Against her better judgment, Miranda took a step forward, then another. She didn't look at the hospital. She didn't want to see the faces of the Infected who waited for her there. During the initial outbreak at her old school, Harrow Hall Preparatory, she'd been the only student to survive unscathed.

Or had she?

Dr. Rasmussen had said her father would never have experimented on her, but someone had infected Marius with the original strain of HHV long before the Harrow Hall outbreak. What if her father had done something like that to her? What if she was going to join her classmates and become a monster after all, like a curse from a horror movie that always found its target in the end?

It might have been her imagination, but it sounded like something was breathing near her, a hitching rattle. Maybe it was just a building noise or some machine that hadn't been turned off when everyone fled the town.

No one's fled the town. You know that. We are waiting for you.

Miranda squeezed her eyes shut, clenched her fists. She hadn't survived both the Harrow Hall and Chrysalis outbreaks to walk right into the Infected's lair like some stupid virginal sacrifice from a medieval poem or epic or whatever.

The breathing sounds were unmistakable, long and deep. Whatever it was had big lungs.

My, what big lungs you have …

Miranda let out a giggle that was little more than a terrified squeak. The sound of her own voice centered her as if pinning her to herself so she couldn't be sucked into the hospital, into the thing that waited for her there.

She opened her eyes and gasped.

The face that hovered inches from her own had once been a human's. It had human features anyway: eyes, nose, mouth, but they'd been stretched over a skull that was too big for the slender neck of the creature. A tattered twist of a green and yellow Scout neckerchief fluttered from the Infected's collar. Its shoulders were still human, but the arms twisted, one branching into two thick tentacles. The other ended in a mangle of fingers and claws that might have been a hand.

The Infected drew back its lips, teeth small and sharp and gleaming under the streetlamps.

"Mir-an-da," the Infected growled.

Miranda wanted to scream, but her whole body had seized up, even her lungs. She moved her mouth, tried to remember how to coordinate exhalation with her vocal cords. Tried to deny the sensation of recognition coming from the Infected.

"We were wait —"

The Infected's eye exploded, showering Miranda with its sludgey dark purplish-red blood. It ran down her neck like warm, watery paste.

"Miranda!" Torres yelled. "Get over here."

The streets that had been empty as Miranda had come into Wiltz were not empty as she and Torres escaped. The former Marine drove a motorcycle that was barely bigger than a moped and Miranda clung to the older woman's waist, her face mashed into the space between Torres's shoulder blades, her eyes squeezed shut.

The headache was back, nearly blinding. Worse, Miranda could feel them reaching out, trying to pull her back, trying to keep her in Wiltz, to send her into the hospital. Inside her head, they buzzed and hummed like a thousand notifications. If she tried, she might be able to understand the messages they were trying to impress into her brain like it was clay.

Miranda gritted her teeth and concentrated on the putter and throb of the motorcycle's engine, the way Torres's shoulders rose and fell with each breath.

"Hang on, Miranda." The former Marine's voice and demeanor were calm, almost casual, but her pounding heartbeat gave away her anxiety. Torres swerved hard, nearly laying the motorcycle down. She kicked a couple of times, over-corrected, kicked on the other side, and got the bike vertical again.

"Freaking meat walls," she muttered.

Miranda risked a peek. They were passing what looked like the most perfectly European open-air café ever. Two-person tables with red and white checkered tablecloths, striped umbrellas, window boxes full of flowers, and a sandwich board sign decorated with whimsical designs. And the fleshy pink film shot through with purple veins that covered the windows and doors. There were shapes embedded in the meat wall, human-like shapes.

We're hungry.

The wall seemed to reach out, not for Miranda, but for Torres. It would be so easy to yank the woman off the motorcycle. It would be smart to leave the former Marine behind. The Infected would be distracted and Miranda could escape.

No!

Miranda wrapped her arms tighter around Torres. After all they'd been through, the outbreaks, the mad escape from Chrysalis, months in a secret government prison, Miranda wasn't about to turn against a fellow uninfected human so easily. Besides, Marius and John would never, ever leave someone behind. They would die first. Miranda could be at least that unselfish, at least that brave. That was the whole point of Survivors' Club, right?

"Don't look back now, but we're leading a parade," Torres said.

Miranda didn't need to look back. She could feel them like threads trailing off her.

"Finally!" Torres revved the motorcycle. Miranda peeped over the other woman's shoulder. Ahead three trucks sped towards them. Each truck had a machine gun mounted over the roof of the cab. As Torres and Miranda whipped past the trucks heading out of town, the machine guns chattered to life.

Miranda gasped as the threads snapped. Each death slapped her, way worse than electrolysis.

"You okay?" Torres yelled.

"Go. Please. Just go."

Help us. Don't leave us. Help!

Miranda clenched her hands around wads of Torres's shirt and tried not to puke. The motorcycle bounced off the road and slid, Torres braking and gunning the accelerator in turn as she fought to keep the machine up and moving forward. After a few gut-swirling fishtails, she got it back under control.

"I better get a freaking medal," Torres said.

Miranda nodded against her back. "I'll buy you ten freaking medals when we get home."

Crossing the field took only a few minutes. The headache was back with a vengeance, but the voices, the pressure dimmed as they left Wiltz behind. Miranda wanted to cry with relief but she was too tired.

John was waiting just inside the gate. He had a pistol holster on his hip - definitely a parole violation — but it looked right on him. Seeing John without a gun was like seeing your high school principal naked. Just wrong.

Torres stopped the motorcycle outside the gate and Miranda slithered off. She was trembling with fatigue and spent adrenaline. On wobbly legs, she passed through first the outer then the inner gate, thankful that the guards didn't stop her or search her. It was super hard not to throw up.

John didn't yell at her, didn't tell her how stupid she was for running off on her own. He just put an arm around her shoulder and tucked her against him. Miranda pressed the heels of her hands to her eyes and swallowed a sob. Safe against John's warm, solid body she couldn't understand what had ever possessed her to leave.

"It's HHV," Torres said as they walked through the encampment. It was full dark, probably nearly midnight, but the floodlights were on and lots of guards were to-ing and fro-ing. Faint pops and thumps from Wiltz testified that the guards there were still busy dealing with the Infected.

"Marius confirmed it from the woman," John said.

"It's everywhere in town," Torres said.

"Marius estimates that given the size of the town and the rate of infection, there are probably about 500 Infected," John said as they reached their tent.

"They're gonna torch that place bigger than shit." Torres lifted the flap and held it as John walked Miranda in. The air was warm, but not the moist heat like being around the meat walls. John sat Miranda on a folding chair and handed her a bottle of water.

"Where's Marius?" Miranda's voice was a croak. She took a swig of water and looked around. The kennel the woman had been in was empty. Marius sat on the cot in the boy's kennel with the boy curled asleep in his lap. The scientist held up a finger to his lips.

John crossed to the kennel and opened the door as Marius eased the boy off him. Marius tucked the blanket around the boy, who barely took up half the length of the cot.

"Is he infected?" John asked as Marius stepped out.

"I don't know." Marius stretched, wincing as he rolled his shoulders and twisted his torso from side to side. "After what he just went through I wasn't in a rush to start sticking him."

"There's a bigger picture here," John said.

Marius stilled, only his green eyes moving as he studied the soldier's face.

"I'm fine," Miranda said. "Thanks for asking."

Both men looked at her. She folded her arms over her chest and raised an eyebrow.

Marius gave his head a little shake and smiled at her. "Good."

"There's HHV in the town," Torres said. "I heard the Turks talking about Willy-Pete. We gotta get the evacuation moving if we're going to get anyone out."

"Willy-Pete?" Miranda asked.

"White Phosphorus. It burns really hot. I think General Falk's got the idea that cauterizing is the only way to go here," Torres said.

Marius bit his lip. "I thought that was a war crime."

"It's surprising how much international governing bodies will overlook if you save them from a deadly outbreak," John said.

"There's no evidence that it'll even work," Marius said. "It might put the bioformations into a dormant state or it might even spread the viral particles further if they're embedded in soot and ash." He went to the row of tables along the side wall and picked up a vial of blood. "We don't know enough about transmission to assume this will contain it."

"I'm not the person you need to convince," John said.

"Well, you're not helping either," Miranda snapped.

"Hey!" Torres glared at her. "Take it easy. We're all on the same side here."

Sudden rage boiled up inside Miranda. She didn't remember getting up, but she found herself inches away from Torres, hands balled into fists. "Are we?"

"Back up, Miranda," Torres put her hand flat on the center of Miranda's chest and pressed her away without shoving her.

I should kill her now. I could tear out her throat with my teeth.

Marius stepped between Torres and Miranda. "Easy. You've been through a lot of stress today. It's okay."

Miranda gulped. Why was she acting like this? She burst into tears, whirled, and rushed blindly out of the tent.

She hadn't meant to sleep and there were tons of places way more comfortable than the cold, hard bed of a pickup truck, but when Miranda awoke in the cool light of a new dawn, she felt much, much better. No headache. No weird, creepy sensation of something tickling around in her mind.

She sat up and ran her fingers through her hair, raking out the worst tangles as she looked around, trying to figure out where in the encampment she'd ended up. She heard voices from nearby and stood up to see over the tents.

A screening team, swathed in protective gear, hovered around an inner gate. They reached through an opening to take blood samples from a man and woman who waited in the space between the gates. The screeners put wristbands on the couple and pointed to a pair of guards who waited nearby. The guards escorted the couple inside and along the fencing until they arrived at a smaller enclosed area. This one was also fenced in, but rather than keeping people out, the chain-link was meant to keep them in. The guards ushered the townsfolk in and returned to the screening station.

Miranda's stomach rumbled, reminding her she'd had nothing to eat since the MRE during the flight. She climbed out of the truck bed and headed back toward the white medical tents.

"Miranda!"

She stopped.

Marius stood outside one of the screening stations, decked out in gloves and mask, but no suit. He said something to the other screener and handed off the vial of blood he'd collected before hurrying over to Miranda.

"Hi." Miranda smoothed her hair and tried not to think of how awful her morning breath must smell.

Marius smiled. "I'm glad you're okay. I was worried you'd gone back to town."

"What? No." Miranda smiled back. "I'd never do something crazy like that."

"Again." Marius winked. Even tired and scruffy, he was gorgeous, distractingly gorgeous.

"So, wow. They haven't bombed the town yet." Miranda shivered as a breeze picked up. She rubbed her arms. "I need coffee, like, yesterday. C'mon."

Marius glanced over his shoulder at the screening site and bit his lower lip. "I can't be gone too long, but we need some more supplies and I should check on the folks in containment. Care to join me?"

"As long as we get coffee at some point."

"Deal."

As they walked, Miranda could see a crowd of people in the field about halfway between the town and the encampment. Most people had backpacks or duffel bags. A few had spread out blankets and were trying to keep fussy babies and energetic toddlers entertained. Older children clustered around a man who was reading a book, while teenagers orbited the group, feigning disinterest.

"Evacuation," Marius said. "We're dividing and conquering. Anyone who's not symptomatic is welcome to come to the camp. They wait out there for a screener and then we bring them in. A couple days in containment and then they'll be moved on to a refugee site in Germany until the town's clear."

"And the Infected?" Miranda's stomach knotted. In the light of day, it was easy to dismiss the feeling of connection she'd had with the Infected as some kind of hysteria or over-tired, over-stressed hallucination.

"That's more complicated. It's possible the vaccine could be used to treat or even reverse the symptoms of HHV."

"So, why don't we give them the vaccine? Isn't there enough?"

Marius bit his lip. "No, not at the moment. After Chrysalis shut down, the FDA banned Helatek from making more vaccine until they finished with the congressional inquest. Right now, we have to save the vaccine we have for people who've been infected but haven't started to ..." He wiggled his fingers in an imitation of tentacles.

Miranda batted his hand away. "I get it. What about you? Can't you make more?"

They stopped outside the containment area so the guard could compare their access badges to her roster and open the gate. A few of the people inside looked up, their expressions hopeful or frightened or simply resigned. It reminded Miranda of being quarantined in the Submarine at Chrysalis, waiting to know if she would die in there or if she would be let out to rejoin the uninfected world or if she would spend the rest of her life trapped like Typhoid Mary on an island because she was a danger to public safety.

"I could. But not under these conditions. There's no proper lab for miles. I'm not sure what the minimum amount of direct transfusion would confer immunity, so—"

"Don't even start with that." Miranda poked Marius's ribs hard. "We're not here to be blood banks, remember?"

"I don't know if secondary immunity would be enough," Marius said, undaunted. "Until we can do further research with people like John, only my antigens are attested."

"Stop. Thinking. About. It." Miranda grabbed his arm and pulled him to a stop. "Killing yourself won't save anyone."

Marius gave her a sad smile. "That's what you said last time."

Before Miranda could respond, the guard swung the gate open. Marius squeezed her shoulder and entered the containment area. Miranda sighed and followed. Someone had to keep an eye on Marius, for his own good.

Inside the enclosure, hasty shelters had been rigged up to provide shade. Cots and folding chairs were scattered around the area. Most of the grass had been trampled down and there were already patches of dirt visible. Three port-o-potties stood in the back corner. Miranda wrinkled her nose.

"How long are they going to have to stay here?"

"Four days minimum, five to be on the safe side,"

Marius said.

The boy they'd brought in earlier ran to Marius, arms in the air. The scientist scooped him up and the boy wrapped his chubby arms around Marius's neck, burying his face against Marius's neck and shoulder.

"You remember Otto," Marius said as he patted the boy's back.

"Yeah." The boy with the dead mom. "Hi, Otto." Miranda stared at the back of the boy's head. When she'd found out about her father, she'd been alone in her room. No one had held her. No one had comforted her. In fact, she'd spent the next few hours fighting to stay alive during the Chrysalis outbreak, helping Marius with his insane-sounding but effective containment plan.

"Okay, kiddo, time for another finger stick." Marius lowered the boy to the ground and took out a sample kit from his pocket. Otto's chin trembled, but he held up his hand for Marius to swab it clean. As Marius squeezed blood onto a slide, Miranda felt something tug at her. There was nothing there, but the sensation was so real she could have sworn someone had pulled on her arm.

She looked through the chain-link fence and out into the field. The townsfolk were still gathered for their impromptu picnic, but that was not what had her interest. She could feel *them*. Many, small thems, moving through the high grass across the field, dividing around the picnic, heading for the encampment, which overflowed with the scent of humans ripe for biting and eating, humans perfect for nesting in, humans whose entrails could be spread around and-

"Hey." Marius shook Miranda's shoulder. She gasped, gagged, and stumbled away from him, her stomach roiling with the greasy taint of the Infected. She grabbed the chain-link and bent over, dry heaved. A droplet of her saliva shivered, suspended in the sun like a long bead of spider silk. It was clear, not milky white. Clear because she wasn't Infected. She wasn't one of them. She'd been vaccinated after the Harrow Hall outbreak. As soon as her father had been able to confirm that the transfusion of Marius's blood had granted John immunity to HHV, Dr. Viers had personally given her the shot.

Marius put a cool hand against Miranda's clammy forehead. The scent of him, normally an enticing combination of cardamom, sandalwood, and musk, turned her stomach worse. She pushed him away and covered her nose and mouth with both hands, trying to clear the smell from her nostrils.

"Go get Captain Courage. Medical tent 17," Marius said to someone. He didn't try to touch her again but hovered nearby. One of the people in containment asked a question in French and Marius responded. Miranda's high school French was no help in her nauseated state. She closed her eyes.

Kill it. Kill the abomination. Kill him.

They were angry. There was something in Marius that had hurt her, made her sick. She had a flash of his body, a bloody collection of limbs and viscera splayed on the churned-up ground. The Littles would kill him, a thousand bites to rip him apart, but none of the Infected would nest in his entrails.

Abomination. The idea of Marius, of his smell, of his filthy blood filled her with disgust and fear.

Someone screamed. A bite. Miranda's mouth filled

with the sensation of muscle twisting between her powerful jaws as the hot blood spilled down her throat.

No! I don't want this. I'm not part of this!

Her eyes flew open. Out in the field the picnicking families were scattering, parents scooping up children, running, screaming. A man yanked something the size of a cat off a child's back and threw it. Miranda felt the impact as the Infected hit the ground, stunned but not dead.

"It's still alive!" she shouted. She ran to the side of the fence closest to the field. "There! Right there." She pointed as unerringly as if someone had asked her to point to her own nose. She *knew* where the Infected were.

The man was too far away to hear her. He ran straight toward the Infected, which leaped up his body in two bounds and wrapped its long, thick tentacles around his neck, squeezing even as the man pushed his child away toward the dubious safety of the encampment. The girl froze, hands clenched into tiny useless fists as she screamed for her father.

The Infected trembled with glee and glut, turned from the dying man to the child pulsing with delicious life.

No. Miranda closed her eyes, pressed the idea into the Infected. *No children.*

Miranda concentrated so hard her fingernails carved bloody crescents in her palms, her lip bled where she bit it, her nose started to bleed, but she could feel it — a bigger presence, not just individual Infected. The thing from the hospital. She pushed at it, tried to force her command into it, like pressing a shape into clay.

No children.

It resisted, pushed back. Demanded that she open to it as it opened to her.

Miranda, let us in. Work with us.

Screams and gunshots. She was on her knees. Marius was close. The smell of him was nearly enough to break her concentration, but she clung to the sensation of the bigger thing, tried to match her mind to it, tried to steer it away from the children, from their sweetly soft warm bodies, too small to be turned, but perfect for feeding and nesting.

"Miranda, wake up." John's voice in her ear, his strong rough hands on her shoulders.

"I'm sorry, John. I don't know what's wrong." Marius's smell washed over her.

Abomination!

She leaped up, pushed him away, and ran. It was either that or kill him.

Chapter 3 – John

Wiltz, Luxembourg, EU - Spring, Year 1

The fast-movers streaked across the sky, trailing sonic booms. John shaded his eyes against the late morning sun and watched the munitions fall. A pop, like Fourth of July fireworks and a burst of white smoke, sparkles of golden light falling to the earth. Where they landed buildings burst into flame as if they'd been touched by an avenging angel.

John dropped his coffee cup.

Torres muttered, "Oh fu..."

The encampment was in motion, contractors and UN troops heading toward designated posts, while those who'd been on nightshift peered out of their tents, blinking in confusion.

"Where's Marius?" Torres looked around.

"The screening station." John hesitated. He should immediately move to ensure Marius was secure, but Miranda was out there, alone and scared. "Have you seen Miranda?"

"I'll go find her; you stay with him. Doc is priority number one." Torres jogged away toward the tent their quartet had been assigned.

The people waiting to be screened scattered, some trying to get into the camp, others racing back across the field toward Wiltz. Those who'd been in the field were in a panic, running in every direction. Through the tall grass, John could only catch glimpses of the small Infected creatures that attacked them.

If the white phosphorus drove the Infected out of Wiltz, a couple layers of chain-link fence wouldn't slow them long. The encampment needed to prepare for a full-on assault.

John skidded to a stop outside the screening station. Around him he could hear the chatter of gunfire, the screams and calls of the civilians, soldiers and contractors running and shouting, and faintly, above all of it, the low rumble of a plane, something big and heavy - a surveillance craft with cameras and sensors, eager to survey and record the outcome of the bombing. How effective was Willie-Pete against the Infected?

Three men had made it through the first ring of fencing and were fighting to get inside the inner one, shaking the walls. Soldiers yelled for them to get back. Screams from along the fence and that sound, the gurgling squall of the Infected. Even months after Chrysalis, that sound still stalked John's nightmares.

He grabbed one of the UN soldiers by the vest as he ran by. "Tell General Falk the Infected are in the field."

The UN soldier shook his head, "No English," and ran on.

A group charged out of the field; behind them the Infected. The outer gate was gone, torn off its hinges by the three men. In all the chaos, it was difficult to tell if the soldiers were shooting at the civilians or out into the field at the Infected. The men crashed into the small opening for the screening station, hitting the inside gate so hard several links snapped.

One of the men tried to crawl through but the opening wasn't big enough. The broken links dug into his skin, catching like fishhooks. He couldn't go forward and he couldn't go back. The metal bit into his back and shoulder, ripping him with every move as he squirmed.

"Hold still. Hold still," John commanded. The man continued to struggle. What if he was infected? John searched through the discarded medical supplies. Where was the vaccine? Marius would know how to read the labels on the different vials.

Where was he? Where was Miranda?

Infected caught the people in the field, dragged them back and down. The man in the fence screamed frantically. Infected or not, John couldn't leave him trapped like that. He grabbed a pair of medical sheers and used them to bend back some of the links. The man continued yelling, struggling. Blood ran down his flanks, pattered on and around John's boots as he leaned against the gate. The way the men had twisted it, John couldn't have opened it if he had wanted to.

"John!" Marius slid to a stop next to him, panting.

"I don't know if he's infected," John reported. "Do you have vaccine here? Where's Miranda?"

"Med station with Torres. Here." Marius drew a shot from a blue vial and jabbed the needle into the man's shoulder. "You're gonna be okay. Just hold still. We'll get you out of here. Stop moving. Everything's going to be okay."

Marius held back the links while John used the scissors to pry them out of the man's flesh. The blades of the medical shears were slick with blood and sweat and he had to keep wiping them off on his pants. Marius kept up a running commentary. John marveled at how calm and steady his voice sounded, as if there were nothing wrong, as if they had all the time in the world and the Infected weren't mere feet away. If they hadn't stopped to ravage the people in the field, the man in the fence would be dead.

White light blinded John, heat bathed the front of his body. He flew back so violently he didn't even have time to tense up.

He sat up, his ears ringing with the thumping-pop of munitions. The man in the fence hung slack, the back half of his body gone, the wound cauterized by the heat of the white phosphorus.

How dare they drop so close to us.

John shook his head at the ridiculousness of the thought and looked around.

Marius lay in a heap of medical equipment. White hot sparks had landed on his right arm. As John watched they winked out, leaving black pits in his now dirt-smeared lab coat. Other white sparks had landed on his bare hand. They were turning yellow. Yellow? Several plumes of smoke rose from the back of his hand.

He's on fire!

White phosphorus could burn through a truck's engine block. In a person it would cause second or third degree burns and could be absorbed into the body leading to heart failure. Marius's hand would be Swiss cheese.

Marius started to sit up, then screamed in pain, yanked his hand to his chest. John rushed to his side. "We have to put it out, keep it from being absorbed. Let me see." The soldier ran through his training on the recommended treatment for WP skin exposure: "Immerse affected area in cold water or cover in wet dressing."

No canteen since he wasn't wearing his gear, but the medical kits would probably have bottles of deionized water. John couldn't see any kits, but there had to be one at the screening station.

Marius shook as he held his hand out for John's inspection. He moaned and looked away as if unable to bear watching his own skin burn. Judging from Marius's reaction, he might not be able to resist the temptation to try to smother the fire on his right hand with his left. If he did, he would only succeed in transferring the burning white phosphorus to his other hand.

John yanked up handfuls of grass and plunged Marius's hand into the damp earth. He scooped dirt over it and held Marius's arm in place with both hands. Marius squeezed his eyes shut and gritted his teeth. They waited.

Hasty retreats were rarely well-organized, but given the general panic of the civilians, the unpreparedness of the security forces, and the aggressiveness of the Infected, John thought retreat might be too kind of a word for what happened. Rout was more accurate.

"Let me see the wound." A sturdy little woman arrived with a Red Cross bag and the unquestionable authority of a grandmother. Marius was shaking, already going into shock or exhausted from hunching over the grave of his right hand, John didn't know which. The soldier stepped back and scanned the area, while the medic knelt and took Marius's arm, pulling gently but firmly.

"Wait," Marius said through clenched teeth. "It's a chemical burn. White phosphorus."

"Ya." The medic's name tag said, 'Oralia'. She set a pan of water next to Marius's hand and soaked a field dressing in it. "Hurry. I have a lot of other patients."

Marius bit his lip, drew a deep breath, and looked at Oralia.

"It's going to be okay," she lied to him, just as he had lied to the man caught in the broken gate.

Marius looked away and pulled his hand out. The medic guided Marius's hand into the pan of water. John had the image of an ancient blacksmith quenching a sword, steam hissing and water bubbling.

"How bad?" the soldier asked. They were not in a very defensible situation. They needed to regroup with Torres and Miranda. At least there were no Infected close by. The white phosphorus had burned them out of the field as far as John could tell.

Oralia clicked her tongue like an indulgent parent looking over their child's scraped knee. "Oh, not so bad, ya. Not even smoking. Take it out. I clean it."

Marius shuddered as he lifted his hand and laid it flat on his knee.

"Hold still. Got to pick this out." Oralia's forceps nipped at Marius's hand, little cleaner fish seeking out the bits of white phosphorus still in the scientist's flesh. Marius dug his left hand into the ground.

"I'll be right back." Keeping the medic and Marius in sight, John circled the area. Fires burned, not just in Wiltz. There were three spots in the field, so bright John couldn't look directly at them. Several smaller white phosphorous fires burned near the walls. The guards must have been issued incendiary rounds. John knew the Americans had them, but nearly every other nation had outlawed them.

As the medic bandaged Marius's hand, John scrounged up a singed blanket and a bottle of water. No other weapons, not even a knife or a multitool. No communication equipment either.

John watched the field, alert for signs of the Infected, letting his gaze slide over the smoldering human-sized lumps, trying to skip over the child-sized ones.

Was it enough to stop the outbreak?

Back at Chrysalis with Marius dying beside him, the Infected all around, and no way out, he'd thought, "At least we kept it contained." As a soldier, John was well acquainted with Death, had flirted with it more than was wise. He'd seen it take friends and foe without regard for age or ideology. Death didn't frighten John, but pointless Death …

"He's going to need more pain medication soon and something for infection, ya." Oralia stood up, cracked her spine and brushed her hands over her knees, smudging the grass-stains and dirt. She handed Marius a pill, which he dry swallowed without even looking to see what it might be.

Oralia patted Marius's head and scooped up her medical bag. She hurried away, soon lost in the smoke that blanketed the area, an unintentional smoke screen from the white phosphorous rounds. John helped Marius to his feet and guided him through the maze of tents.

Outside medical station seven, a crowd had gathered. People on stretchers and walking wounded waited to be loaded into the back of whatever vehicles could be pressed into service. A family with a child bundled in blankets huddled in the back of a golf cart that zipped off toward the makeshift flight line.

Torres stood in the bed of a Jeep, helping to maneuver a stretcher into the back. The woman on the stretcher was missing her foot but smiled drunkenly. Morphine was a beautiful thing.

Miranda squatted next to the tent, her hair a wind-blown thistle puff, her eyes glassy and unfocused. For a second, John thought she had been given morphine as well, then her gaze shifted. She jerked to her feet and stumbled towards the men, her arms out. Marius reached her first and tucked her into an embrace as she sobbed against his chest.

"Wheels up in fifteen," Torres called to John.

"Mendelsen says that they're saving us seats, but civilians got no reservations."

"We can't leave them here," Marius said.

"Pretty sure they don't have room to take the whole town," Torres said.

Marius stared at her. What she had said was monstrous. It was also true.

"I have to get Otto," Marius said.

"No. Now is not the time to split up," John said.

Marius let go of Miranda and stepped away from her. "John, you know I respect you, but fuck off. This isn't Chrysalis and you're not in charge of anything."

Reminding Marius that he alone was naturally immune to HHV, that he alone had created the vaccine and therefore was too valuable to risk would probably not convince him, so John tried another tactic. "You're a doctor. You're needed here." He put a hand on Marius's shoulder. "You can't save everyone. Help the ones you can." He turned Marius toward the ragged line of civilians. Some were clearly injured, while others looked shellshocked. The white phosphorus had stemmed the tide of the Infected for the moment, but with a mass casualty situation bearing down on them, it was hard for John to feel gratitude.

Marius bit his lip and nodded. "I need a kit," he said.

John organized the civilians, directing the non-injured to help move the injured up to the front of the MWR tent where the security forces could ferry them to waiting aircraft. Someone had rolled up one side of the big tent and it now served as a makeshift medic station and staging area. Everyone seemed to know that there wouldn't be enough space on the planes, but no one mentioned it. After the terror of the Infected attacks and the bombings, both civilians and military, locals and foreigners seemed to be united in the simple task of caring for their fellow humans.

John paused in carrying a stack of blankets down the line to take a drink. Miranda sat in the passenger seat of a Jeep, her head hanging, shoulders hunched. There was nothing physically wrong with her and John couldn't take the time to find out what had happened.

"Last one," Torres said as she caught up to John. She handed him a tube of burn cream.

John turned it in his hands. Use it to ease the pain of the seriously injured, knowing they probably wouldn't be evacuated or use it to help the walking wounded who had better survival odds?

Torres heaved a sigh. "And he's gone."

"Who?" John looked around. Marius had been checking the wounded for obvious signs of infection and sending those without any on down the line. He was nowhere to be seen.

The line of people was collapsing into a huddle. John couldn't leave to search for Marius. Torres needed his help. Miranda needed his supervision. But if Marius was hurt or killed, it would mean no more vaccines, no hope of a cure. John believed the scientist's prediction about HHV's speed and virulence. "A pandemic," Marius had said. He'd been prepared to die to keep HHV from spreading outside Chrysalis. Now he needed to be willing to live, even if it meant doing unpleasant things, unthinkable things, like abandoning a child.

How many other children would die horribly if Marius wasn't there to fight HHV? But in the face of saving one child, here and now, John knew Marius well enough to know that he couldn't make that choice. An admirable and incredibly frustrating trait. Not for the first time, John considered how much easier it would be to simply zip-tie Marius and carry him out of danger. There was a reason most Special Forces rescue operations treated the rescuees as potential hostiles.

Damn civilians.

"I'll deal with it," John said.

"Okie-dokie, boss," Torres said. She paused, nodded, and turned to leave. "I'm taking Miranda on the next run."

"Send Mendelsen back here. I need to talk to him," John said.

Torres rubbed her shoulder and rolled it with a series of pops. "I can go look for Marius when I get back."

"We've got less than five minutes to wheels up." John smeared burn cream onto a swath of gauze and handed it to a teenager who was trying to cajole her apparently catatonic mother into keeping up with the moving line. The girl applied the bandage to the burns on her mother's neck and back.

"We're not leaving without Doc," Torres said.

"Affirmative." John moved to the next group. Over his shoulder he said, "Mendelsen, ASAP, thanks."

By the time Mendelsen arrived, John had cleared nearly half the wounded. The first of the WHO aircraft had taken off. The wind had shifted and the burning scent of the white phosphorus washed over the crowd.

"Captain Courage, Sergeant Torres said you needed to speak with me?" Mendelsen wiped his glasses on his grimy sleeve, frowned at them, and untucked a corner of his shirt to clean them.

"You'll need to detail some of the security team to find and retrieve Dr. Tenartier," John said, glancing over his shoulder. A bottleneck was forming near the landing strip as the medical personnel tried to explain to relatives why they couldn't join the wounded on the flight. Voices rose as frayed nerves snapped. After the outbreak and the bombing, few people were in the mood to listen to the UN troops as they tried to keep order. John could feel the tension growing. They needed to get out before the residents of Wiltz rioted.

"Is he in trouble? We'll send security." Mendelsen fumbled the phone from his coat's inside breast pocket.

Torres arrived a few minutes later, nearly flipping the golf cart she was driving. She scrambled out and walked away without stopping to try to fight off the civilians who piled into the cart and sped away.

"Time to grab some air, Captain." She nodded to the UN and security contractors who were now physically pushing civilians away from the two remaining Hercules on the landing strip. "Where's the Doc?"

"Mendelsen's detailed security to bring him in." John strained to see over the heads of the churning crowd, sidestepped as people pushed passed. If Mendelsen's team wasn't successful in retrieving Marius he would have to go himself and risk being stranded at the edge of an HHV outbreak. He'd have to trust that the immunity he'd gained from a transfusion of Marius's blood would still be effective. Either way, he couldn't leave. Marius was the best hope to slow and eventually contain HHV.

"There!" Torres hopped and pointed.

A pair of security contractors shouldered their way through the civilians, nearly trampling several who weren't quick enough to get out of their way. Behind them, another pair was dragging a body. A kicking, swearing body.

They had handcuffed Marius and held him under the arms. His face was swollen, one eye already blackening.

As the contractors drew even, John hurried to join them, shouting, "Make a hole. Move aside." Torres fell in behind Marius, who was trying to get his feet under him, but failing as the contractors hustled through the mass of civilians.

The Hercules's engines were already whining, the loadmaster and several armed UN soldiers arguing with Mendelsen, who stood on the tail. As the group arrived, the soldiers parted, allowing them to walk up the ramp and into the back of the aircraft. The tail started to lift and the plane taxied forward before it was fully closed. John tried not to see the desperate faces of the civilians who ran after them.

"Hey!" Torres yelled. John whirled and found the former Marine had yanked one of the contractors back by his collar. "Back the fuck off. We got him." She pushed the contractor away and stood protectively in front of Marius, who half sat in the side-facing sling seat. He looked stunned.

"Are you okay?" John grabbed the overhead cargo netting as the Hercules hobbled into the air. The big bird wobbled as it gained altitude.

"You sent them, didn't you?" Marius's voice was low,

his green eyes bright with rage as he glared at John.

"I did," John said. "I know you understand why I had to."

"You didn't *have* to, John. You made a choice. Do you know how close I was to Otto? Less than a yard away. He was fine. Not a scratch on him. He weighs sixty pounds, tops. You're telling me we couldn't have found room for one orphan?" Marius waved his cuffed hands around the dim interior. All the bunks and stretchers were full, the seats crowded with more than the usual hundred or so passengers, but with no heavy equipment John estimated they were in no danger of maxing out the Hercules's weight limit.

He put a hand on Marius's shoulder. "It's not about the space," John said gently. "We couldn't wait. We couldn't risk you to save one person."

The scientist shook his head.

"Listen, Marius, I know what it's like to have to-"

Marius shrugged him off. "To abandon a kid screaming for help? Really? You know what that's like?"

"The captain was trying to save you," Torres said. "There was no way for him to know if you would be able to find the kid or if he was even alive."

"Otto," Marius said. He slumped against the wall. "His name's Otto."

Chapter 4 – Torres

During Torres's military career and later as a civilian security specialist, she had transited through many an airport. She had never been the one being escorted past the duty-free shops, bars, restaurants, and souvenir stands. She didn't like it. How did the rich and powerful stand feeling so powerless?

National Guard soldiers met the plane as it landed. They separated the former Chrysalis personnel and took them directly to the parking garage. No chance to breathe the night air or get acquainted with the area. The price of being a critical national asset, or at least associated with one. Torres kept an eye on Marius but didn't get the chance to talk with him. The scientist seemed to have retreated into himself, staring sightlessly ahead and only speaking when prodded.

"I thought we would be released after we helped out in Wiltz." Miranda complained as the National Guard soldiers shuffled them into two black SUVs for the drive to wherever they were going next.

"The wheels of bureaucracy turn slowly," Courage said. He nodded slightly to Torres before joining Miranda in one of the SUVs. Torres returned the gesture. *I read you. I'll keep an eye on him.* She slid into the backseat of the other SUV next to Marius.

The mystery of where they were going was solved as their small convoy passed the UCLA campus. Their accommodations had been upgraded from a secret government detention facility to a La Quinta that boasted a coffeemaker, but no refrigerator. Torres was asleep in minutes, but woken a few short hours later, feeling like she was five aspirins short of a good morning.

Mendelsen had arranged for Marius to work out of UCLA's David Geffen School of Medicine under the supervision of the National Institutes of Health (NIH).

For two weeks, everyone watched and waited, combed through news reports and social media posts. They expected the Wiltz outbreak to explode, to penetrate a major metropolitan area in Europe or Asia or beyond. But it didn't.

During that time, Torres, Courage, and Miranda barely saw Marius. Anytime he was not either in his room or in the HHV war room, as John had dubbed the lab Marius had been given, he was escorted by a pair of

National Guard soldiers.

When not needed for debriefings or blood draws, Torres and Courage haunted the hotel's gym and swapped war stories with the National Guard soldiers. Miranda spent most of her time curled up on a sofa, basking in the warmth of her recently purchased tablet, purringly satisfied to be able to dive back into her social circles. Her only complaint was that her access was limited to read-only, no posting.

Headlines from Europe touted "complete containment of HHV" and "quarantine lifted in Luxembourg." The world breathed a sigh of relief and forgot that it had ever worried about HHV. Torres could feel the shift in focus as the hardworking scientists and technicians of the CDC and NIH turned their attention to other outbreaks elsewhere. For them, the work never ended, only the face of the enemy changed. Today a prion, tomorrow a mold, next week, swine flu.

At their weekly HHV briefing, Mendelsen announced he'd been recalled to Europe to handle finalizing HHV containment. "The CDC is still taking point on HHV, so they'll need your continued assistance," he added.

"Any idea how long our involuntary volunteering is likely to be extended?" Torres asked.

"Clinical trials of the mass-market vaccine should be completed in a month or two," Mendelsen said. "In the meantime, I've used what weight I have to secure you, um, less secure accommodations. Going forward, you'll be staying on campus and relatively free to move around the greater Los Angeles area."

Torres studied her hands resting on the table. Her fingers were tensed, but she hadn't balled them into fists. What would that mean? She'd joined the Marines to escape from Los Angeles and had vowed never to return. Why did she ache at the thought of the ugly lime green linoleum in the entryway or the sound of Mama's favorite telenovela's theme music?

Mendelsen continued. "You'll still be working under the supervision of the NIH."

Would Torres be allowed visitors? Would she be able to go home? Did she want to? Torres moved her hands to her lap, ignoring the way her past was about to crash into her future as Mendelsen talked on about how they'd move out of the hotel and into the dormitories.

"I always wanted to go to college," Miranda said, not glancing up from her tablet.

Mendelsen smiled. "And so you shall, young lady. Additionally, the US government has agreed to reduce the level of security and supervision around you, as long as Marius wears this." He held up a thick band of dark elastic with a small dark box on it.

"An ankle bracelet? Seriously?" Miranda frowned and crossed her arms over her chest.

"And if he doesn't agree?" Courage asked.

"He'll be restricted to his quarters and the labs. I do wish I could have done better. You've all been enormously helpful during truly trying times and I believe you deserve nothing but accolades and gratitude."

Torres caught Courage's eye and raised her eyebrows. As Beau, their former fellow security specialist, liked to say, "Stow your gratitude. I want ten percent off everything forever."

"Dr. Tenartier, you've been very quiet. What are your

thoughts about this transfer?" Mendelsen asked.

Marius looked up. "Does it change my access to the BSL-4?"

"Not at all. Your assigned times and space remain the same."

Marius gave a small half shrug. "That'll be fine."

Last day in the hotel. Torres finished her workout, showered, and took the long route to Marius's room. Even late in the day, the humidity draped itself over her, as welcome and inescapable as a sloppy drunk at a party. Despite the heat, she relished the chance to be outside. Her parole conditions had allowed her to wander freely between the hotel and the campus, unlike Marius.

Miranda was already there, sitting on the edge of Marius's bed. Since their arrival, Torres and Miranda had taken to hanging out in Marius's room in the evenings so he wouldn't be able to brood alone. As a special treat to commemorate their last night at La Quinta, Miranda had convinced one of Marius's National Guard shadows to get them iced lattes and Krispy Kreme donuts.

Torres stepped inside and shivered as the cool, dry air sent goose bumps over her limbs. The bright corridors seemed worlds away from the Chrysalis Pharmaceuticals facility where she and the others had fought for survival only a few months ago. She slid a hand into her pocket, touched the keloid scar on her thigh through the fabric. She had burned her leg while trying to save her buddy, Mac. He hadn't made it, but she'd gone on to this other, safer life. A life where all she was good for was providing blood samples as Marius struggled to fix the HHV vaccine.

"What's wrong with the vaccine?" Miranda asked as Torres opened the door. The coffee and donuts awaited her on the bedside table. She snagged one of each and sat in the room's sole chair.

Marius paced the small room, worrying his lip. Since they'd returned from Wiltz, he'd buried himself in his work. A good thing. At least he had something to do. This waiting had itched under Torres's skin like chiggers.

"There are two strains of HHV," Marius said. "One infects all mammals indiscriminately - the FOX-H strain. The other only infects people. I mean, as far as we know. I haven't been able to verify how the SAM-D strain affects higher primates, so possibly it could infect chimpanzees. And bonobos, considering how closely they're related to us. Theoretically, it might infect them, too."

"Monkeys aside, what's the problem?" Miranda twisted to watch Marius as he rounded the corner and began his trip back toward the bed.

"Apes," Marius said.

"What. Ever." Miranda flopped back on the bed.

"What's the issue with the current vaccine? Other than that there's not enough of it. What's the difference between what we've got and the 'mass market' version?" Torres tried to keep the conversation on track.

"The current vaccine was made with antigens from animals infected with the FOX-H strain. They tested it against the base strain they got from me, but they didn't use the base strain for the vaccine. I've told them."

Marius waved a hand at the door, meaning people like Mendelsen and the other clinicians, not the National Guard troops. "They keep saying they don't have permission to start researching an improved vaccine. Also, it's too costly. They want to make something that's 'good enough' instead of something that's actually effective."

"Maybe they don't need it," Miranda said, staring up at the ceiling. "They killed all the Infected at Wiltz."

"We don't know that!" Marius stopped in front of the door, then circled to head back to the corner. As he passed Torres, she resisted the urge to grab his wrist and stop his relentless patrolling.

"They did." Miranda sat up, ran her fingers through her hair so it fanned over her shoulders in hair-commercial-perfect waves.

How much does her shampoo cost? Torres gave her head a little shake and stood to block Marius's pacing. "So, what are you doing about it?"

Marius shrugged. "Nothing. I'm re-running the same tests they already ran and verifying what I already know."

"Could DARPA get away with going around proper authorizations?" The Defense Advanced Research Projects Agency had more leeway to pursue blue-sky projects than even the most highly cleared civilian organization.

"Maybe," Marius admitted. "INTERCEPT would be perfect for HHV considering how Ebola-like it is."

"So do that," Miranda said.

Marius looked at Torres, who shook her head. "I'm a glorified grunt. But you know who you could talk to if you wanted to access the movers and shakers in the Pentagon."

Marius frowned.

"Because you're both adults." Torres folded her arms. "And you can talk to each other."

"It's a good idea. Thanks." Marius said, the muscles in his jaw standing tight as he feigned a smile. "We should get some sleep. Early flight tomorrow."

Miranda hopped off the bed. "Plus, they're letting me out of social media jail! I'll be able to post and comment, not just like and upvote." She practically skipped out of the room.

Torres gave a thumbs up. She paused at the door and looked back at Marius.

"I'm fine," Marius said. "I'm not avoiding John. I'm just busy."

"Right." Torres had seen people working through trauma before and as much as they often said they wanted to be alone, that was rarely the thing they needed. She wished she knew the right things to say, how to fix what Otto's loss had broken in Marius. More than anything, she ached to see his jade eyes sparkle with the child-like joy he used to take in his work.

Instead of saying anything useful or real, she repeated, "Right. Well, sleep tight and all that."

Marius smiled and closed the door, but not before she saw the smile slide off his face.

Alone in her room, Torres pulled out her phone to call Courage, then stopped. Marius and Courage would have to patch things up themselves. She headed to the gym. At least there, she knew all the rules and didn't have to deal with Marius's righteous anger or Courage's implacable practicality.

In a previous life, or what felt like one, a young Lourdes Eliana Torres Soto had packed a bag, taken a bus, and walked a few miles to get to the Marine recruiting station. She'd been eighteen years and one day old. The El Sereno neighborhood where she'd grown up seemed to be from a different universe than the one sporting the well-manicured grounds and well-maintained buildings of the UCLA campus. Even in the height of summer, students bustled from class to class, gathered in the study rooms, or lounged on the lawns.

After the initial orientation to rooms and cafeteria, and after Marius's ankle monitor had been fitted and verified, the Chrysalis survivors were turned loose. Marius was restricted to the UCLA campus and a few blocks beyond. Torres couldn't help but feel guilty as she planned her day trip. She charted the buses. Assuming she only spent two hours with her family, she could be back by dinner time. As long as she was back before curfew and blood draw, no one would notice. Courage had set up in a teleconference room and was advising the CDC's Global Rapid Response Teams on how to update their processes and procedures for dealing with hostile locals. Miranda had vanished effortlessly into the sea of bright young things washing across campus. Marius had withdrawn back to his lab, the only place he seemed to want to be, surrounded by his Petri dishes and test tubes, the only friends he seemed to want to be around.

Still, Torres felt the need to say something, to ask for

understanding, if not forgiveness, for her defection. On the way to the lab she rehearsed her speech.

It's not that I'm leaving you. Not you you, I mean, I'm not leaving you all: you and Courage and Miranda. I am leaving, but I'll be back. It's just a few hours. You won't even notice I'm gone. Not that you'd care if you did.

Stop, she told herself. Stop trying to play martyr. You're free. You can go see your family. You aren't the one with the magic blood.

Torres pressed her hand against the reinforced glass outside the HHV lab. The 'HOT' sign was suction-cupped to the door, but considering Marius was the only person working there, she wondered why he bothered. Courage had a deep love of process and routine, but Marius's mind rarely seemed to work in straight lines. He'd plod along kicking over every metaphorical pebble and examining every theoretical twig and suddenly announce that he'd discovered the cure for cancer and it had been broccoli all along.

Marius leaned over a counter, examining the corpse of an HHV infected rat. He wore a surgical face mask, gloves, goggles, and a thin plastic apron, but not the full spacesuit of protective gear. Torres watched him, enjoying the voyeuristic thrill of knowing that he was utterly absorbed in his work. A few strands of dark hair brushed his face as he leaned forward to draw blood from the dead rat. His forehead creased, brows drawing together as he extracted a vial of gooey purplish blood. He reached for the nearby petri dish and jumped.

Torres jerked to attention. Had the rat moved? A squirming chill coursed through her at the idea of the dead rising. Living Infected were bad enough without zombies in the mix.

She reached to open the door, but stopped herself. The lab was hot. She should go get someone to help with whatever science thing was going on in there, but without Mendelsen around, she didn't know who to look for.

Marius set the rat down. It didn't move. He held up his hand and studied it, head cocked. Finger by finger, he removed his glove. Torres gasped.

A spot of red marred the inside of the glove. Marius looked at his hand, turned it back and forth. The round pink scars from the white phosphorus burns seemed to blaze against the olive tan of his skin. Torres knew enough of lab protocol to know that a needle stick should be followed by rapid decontamination.

But Marius didn't react rapidly. He squeezed his finger. A drop of blood welled, beaded bigger and bigger until it overflowed, tracing a scarlet trail down his finger. He watched unmoving, unblinking as the blood slid over his palm, collected on his wrist. A drop fell, a perfect red circle on the snow-white counter.

Torres turned away. She didn't want to admit that she'd been spying on Marius. He was immune, so he couldn't catch HHV from the needle stick. Still, as she walked down the hall, her stomach clenched at the image of his handsome face so still and passive, as uncaring as the dead rat he'd been working on.

Marius was not okay.

Which made sense. None of them were exactly well adjusted. Ever since Wiltz, Miranda had seemed distracted and irritable. Courage kept clear of Marius, giving him time to process what had happened. Torres liked to think she was handling everything all right. She'd seen her share of bad and she had methods to work through the worst of it. Running helped her escape the ghosts during the day and made her tired enough that she could fall asleep at night, even if her dreams were clogged with the twisting, grasping tentacles of the Infected, their sweet-rot stench so thick that in the mornings she had to cough and gag and nearly vomit to clear it from her nose and mouth.

But all things considered, she was doing fine.

I'm not running away, Torres told herself as she pushed open the door and stepped out into a Hollywood-perfect California summer day. Except in the movies, the heroine wasn't already sweaty and still a little shaken.

As she crossed the lawn, she saw Miranda, sitting alone under a palm tree, her hair a curtain around her as her thumbs tapped away at her screen.

Torres paused. Should she invite Miranda to accompany her?

No. This was family and family was complicated enough. Still, Torres wanted to say something, to encourage Miranda, let her know that she understood the targetless anger that simmered inside her. Miranda had lost her father, her future, everything. At the heart of it all, she was just another Chrysalis survivor.

But a bus pulled up at the stop and Torres broke into a sprint, waving to the driver. Once aboard, she settled back in the seat and turned her thoughts towards her next challenge: homecoming.

Torres hitched up her pack and turned off Hillsdale onto Academy. Not much had changed. The buildings were a little more rundown, but a new 7-11 stood on the corner. Overhead the sun had reached its zenith, pouring light and heat over LA in waves that washed up from the pavement, rippled over her feet, and hit her in the face.

The duplex looked the same, maybe a bit faded, but it hadn't been in such good shape when the Torres family had moved in, so hard to tell. Torres tried the doorbell but didn't hear anything. No one had fixed it even after all this time. She banged on the door.

"¿Quien es?"

"Mama, it's me. Lourdes," Torres said.

Mama opened the door. She stared at Torres for a second then she screamed and clasped her chest with both hands. "¡Oh Dios mio! ¡Mija!"

"English, Mama, remember. Move." Torres pushed the door and her mother stepped back. The entryway was still lime green, the linoleum still peeling. In the living room a set of three plastic chairs lined the wall facing the couch, which sagged in the middle. After Cynty had her baby, Torres had had to give up her room and sleep on that couch for three months until she left for Boot. She stared at the couch remembering that day, how she had promised herself she would never look back.

Mama hugged her, wiped tears, and hugged her again. "You don't write or call. I hear you are in jail.

Ramon just got home, too. Cynty! Your sister's home," she yelled up the stairs.

"Yeah. I need something to drink." Torres went to the kitchen. She wished she could lie on the cool floor and listen to the sink drip, but nope, Mama followed her. Torres watched her mother while the former Marine drank a glass of tap water. Alma's hair showed more grey at the roots. She was still dying it a reddish-purple color, a maroon that dreamed of being puce. She looked tired. Just being here, Torres felt tired.

Torres almost didn't recognize her little sister when Cynthia came into the kitchen. Her hair was shorter and she'd gained weight. She used to be such a fashionista, Señorita Cheerleader. Now she just looked used up. And her left eye was black.

"What the fuck happened to you?" Torres asked.

"Welcome back. Thanks for all the letters," Cynty said. She rummaged in the cupboard and cast Mama an accusing look when she came up empty handed.

"Cynty, what happened to your face?" Torres asked again. "Who hit you?" She wished her parole didn't prevent her from carrying her trusty 9mm.

"Nada. Where you been?" Cynty sat down and flipped open one of the Spanish language telenovela magazines on the table. Apparently, Ricardo had finally decided to leave Manuela for her sister, Angela.

"She was in jail," Mama explained. "But now she come back."

"Why?" Cynty asked, not looking up.

"Why was I in jail or why would I want to come back here?" Torres set her cup down with a bang. She didn't mean to, but Cynty was naturally gifted at pissing her off. "I'm on parole, so I thought I'd visit."

"Oh, we are so happy you come home." Mama hugged her again.

"Did you kill someone?" A man stood in the kitchen doorway. He wore a stained wife-beater and a pair of sagging jeans. He had wavy light brown hair and a scruffy soul patch reminiscent of Enrique Iglesias. *The infamous Ramon, I presume.*

"No, I was accused of treason," Torres said. "What did you do? Beat up some little kids or old ladies?"

"Don't be a bitch, Lourdie," Cynty said. She kicked at her sister's ankle, but Torres dodged.

"Did you hit my sister?" Torres took a step towards Ramon.

Mama giggled nervously. "Do you want some merenda? I think we have some cookies and soda."

Ramon sneered at Torres from the doorway.

The former Marine took another step. "You think that's funny? You like picking on girls? Why don't you try that shit on me? I've put chúntaros like you in the ground."

Cynty stood up. "She doesn't know what she's talking about, Ramon. She's got that crazy thing they get in Iraq. The PD thing."

"Fucking PTSD, Cynty and no, I don't have it. Why are you sticking up for him?"

"Please, girls. No fighting," Mama broke in. "Lourdie, come and sit. I have Manzanita. Remember when we went to see your abuelita and you drank so much you throw up all over her yard?"

Torres sat down and so did Cynty. The sisters drank their sodas while their mother puttered around getting cookies down and setting them in an artistic circle around the edge of a Dixie paper plate.

Ramon wandered into the living room and turned on the TV at full volume. The three women sat in the kitchen in silence.

Eventually, Torres said, "Where's Elfreda?"

"Napping," Cynty said.

"How's she doing?"

"Fine."

Torres stared at her sister. "Okay, don't talk to me." She got up and stormed out but she had forgotten how small Mama's place was. There was nowhere to storm off to. Torres stood in the living room.

Ramon looked over. "You're pretty hot." He winked at her. He spoke loud enough that Torres was sure Cynty could hear him.

"Fuck off, cabron," Torres said. She went out back and sat on the stairs, staring at the carless driveway. When she had been working at Chrysalis she had sent money home every month. While she had been at the detention facility, no money of course, but still they could have spruced up the house, gotten an old beater car. *Where did the money go? Cynty probably spent it all on clothes and that flatscreen in the living room. Or had Ramon been taking it?*

Torres watched the sun sink into the other houses. The sky turned from Iraq blue to fluorescent party girl pink then calmed down to orange before settling into dark blue. Torres watched for the first star. She really needed to make a wish.

The smog and clouds moved across the sky. The lights of Los Angeles reflected orange off their bellies. This was no place for angels. It was a hell with no stars and no wishes.

Torres had been sitting on the stoop for so long her legs were tingling when Ramon called. "Hey, who's Jimmy? He looks like a gay accountant."

Torres jumped up. She stomped through the kitchen and snatched her phone from Ramon, who grinned.

"Cállate," Torres said. She could hear Mama and Cynty moving around upstairs. She needed to head back to UCLA soon, but she also was desperate for news from her old crew. Jimmy Lennox, the former Security Team medic, had left the Arizona facility just before the outbreak - a happy accident that allowed him to spend the holidays with his family rather than in a government quarantine facility.

Jimmy's text read: *Torresita! Heard they let you all out and you're in LA. Can we get together?*

Torres sent: *Love to! Where and when?*

Jimmy replied: *Tomorrow. My office. Will put you on the roster. One mike, plz.*

Torres smiled. It would be so good to see another familiar face — especially one not tangled up with the bonds and resentments of family.

"You watching lezzie porn?" Ramon put an arm across the back of the couch, but didn't touch Torres's shoulder. She rolled her eyes and ignored him. *Maybe he'll get bored and go away.*

But he didn't. He leaned over, causing her to slide into the depression in the middle. He laughed and she glared at him.

"C'mon, mamí. I know all you chicas go gay for the stay. It's cool. I'm into three-somes. You, me, and Cynty." Ramon reached over and brushed Torres's hair away from her face. Without thinking she grabbed his hand and twisted him down on the floor in a wrist lock.

"Fuck! Lemme go you, crazy puta!" Ramon yelled.

She let go. He sat, rubbing his wrist.

"Don't touch me. Ever." Torres stood and turned to pick up her phone, which had fallen into the mid-couch trench.

She shouldn't have turned her back on him.

Ramon hit her from behind, landing a solid strike just above her left kidney. It knocked the wind out of her. She fell face first onto the couch. Ramon jumped on top of her and pressed her face into the smelly old cushion. Torres kicked, trying to get purchase on the far arm of the couch, but her feet kept slipping off the worn fabric.

Lights burst in her vision. She could taste the stale sweat, tobacco, and pot smoke that had seeped into the couch over the years. The edges of her world grayed then blacked out.

She felt herself slither off the couch. Someone was unzipping her hoodie. *CPR?*

No, Ramon was fumbling with her fly. *Are Cynty and Mama upstairs listening to this? I hope Elfreda's still asleep.*

Torres gasped, focused on getting air. Ramon had the button of her shorts undone and pulled the zipper down. She forced herself to stay still. She wasn't strong enough yet. She needed a couple more good breaths.

Ramon yanked her shorts down, lifting her legs and

letting each foot fall carelessly as he pulled her shorts off. Through her slitted eyes, Torres could see him silhouetted in the light coming through the barred windows behind him. He undid his own belt.

Now or never.

Torres rolled up, elbowing him in the crotch. Ramon doubled over and she skittered on all fours into the kitchen. She still couldn't breathe very well. All her muscles were shaky. She grabbed a knife off the counter, holding it low, blade along her forearm like she'd practiced a hundred times in training.

Ramon stumbled into the kitchen. He kicked one of the chairs at Torres. It hit her in the shins. She fell against the dishwasher. Her head bounced and she was glad it had missed the latch.

Ramon grabbed a handful of her hair and yanked, reminding her why she normally kept it pixie short. He twisted and Torres let him roll her onto her back.

For a second, he grinned down at the former Marine, triumphant. "I'm gonna teach you a lesson. Your sweet ass is —"

Torres jabbed the knife up in quick, short bursts. One, two, three - kidney, liver, lung. She felt the catch then slide of it passing through skin and muscle.

Ramon's knees gave out and he slithered down into the spreading pool of his own blood.

"¡Oh Dios mio!" Mama stood in the kitchen doorway, clutching her chest. Cynty appeared next to her. She took one look at the leaking Ramon, her bloody sister, and the dark puddle on Mama's faux tile floor and started screaming. From upstairs Torres could hear Elfreda's frightened wailing.

"Murderer!" Cynty stabbed a finger at her sister. "I'm calling the cops!"

"Mama ... He tried to rape me." Torres gasped as she stood in her torn underwear, gripping the edge of the sink in order to stay upright. But Alma turned and went into the living room. There was the creak of her weight settling on the couch. Torres stumbled into the living room.

Cynty snatched her bedazzled pink phone off the charger, fumbled it, and opened it.

Torres grabbed Cynty's hand. Her sister screamed and dropped the phone. It was flecked with blood. Torres looked down. Her own hand was covered in blood.

"Sorry," Torres said. She stared at her hand. In the light of the streetlight, it looked shiny and dark. *What if it was purple, sludgey blood like the HHV Infected?* She shook her head.

Mama was sobbing and Cynty had grabbed her phone again.

"He tried to rape me," Torres repeated, but she didn't know if either of them heard her.

"Basta ya. You were teasing him. You always like teasing and then you get mad when guys do exactly what guys do." Cynty held the phone in the tail of her nightshirt but didn't call anyone.

"So, this is my fault?" Torres stared at her sister. How could they possibly be related?

Her feet carried her away before her hands tried to slap sense into Cynty.

In the kitchen, she stepped around Ramon and the blood. She washed her hands, scrubbing with Mama's harsh lye soap until her hands smarted. She returned to the living room. Cynty sat on the couch, huddled in Mama's arms. Mama stared at the wall and stroked Cynty's hair, tangling her fingers through the knots and smoothing out the tufts.

Torres pulled on her shorts, her hands barely shaking.

"Mama, listen, escúchame, por favor." She tried again, but neither her mother nor her sister looked at her.

"Murder is a mortal sin, mica," Mama whispered. A tear trickled down her cheek.

Torres stepped out into the warm, muggy Los Angeles night. Last time she had killed a monster people had been grateful. They had thanked her after on the flight out of Chrysalis.

Torres walked down the street, headed for the bus station and she didn't look back.

Chapter 5 – Marius

Marius sat up, fumbled for the bedside lamp, knocking over a water glass. He grabbed his pad of paper, ignored the spreading wet patch and glittering shards on the floor.

I've been going at the problem all wrong, he thought.

A vaccine was a good start, but even a perfect vaccine wouldn't be enough to stop a pandemic. Not one with the potential to move as fast as HHV did. Something like smallpox, where health workers had a chance to react, to vaccinate anyone coming in contact with the infected, sure, prevention was the name of the game.

But HHV was a different beast, requiring a different

approach.

On the pad, Marius wrote 'NETWORK?'. The bioformations served as incubators and regulators, changing the environment to help the newly Infected mutate and transform from their previous selves to the monstrous Infected they would become. But what if the bioformations also served as a network? A network could be used to spread something lethal to HHV itself. Instead of fighting fire with water, why not use a different kind of fire?

Marius rolled out of bed, stepping over the broken glass. He padded over to the bathroom and flipped on the light, but didn't look in the mirror as he filled another glass with water. Since Wiltz, he couldn't help but see himself as Otto must have, as the man who'd promised to keep a desperate child safe and then abandoned him.

The nearly burning water on his hands yanked Marius's attention back to the present. He turned off the faucet and shook his head at the faint ring of black mold around the drain. Despite the aggressive air conditioning in most of the dormitories, there were some places where the mold had managed to make inroads. It spotted the ceiling in the dark corners of the basement, lurked behind the coin-operated washing machines, and slimed the communal showers.

Marius used a thumbnail to scrape the mold loose and watched it spin briefly before disappearing down the drain. He needed air, needed to move, to be in the lab. He pulled on a T-shirt and jeans and stepped out into the hall.

Normally, the walk from the dorms to UCLA's labs

would be only about fifteen minutes, but a group of protestors had gathered along Gayley, waving signs that read:

"Vax Truth"

"In ~~CDC~~ **God** We TRUST!"

"Vaccines are TOXIC. Protect our KIDS."

"Say 'NO' to CDC medical experiments."

A few police officers and campus security loitered across the road, keeping the protesters off the UCLA campus grounds. For the most part they seemed content to wave their signs and try to hand out flyers to the passersby on their side. A few shouted when they saw Marius walking on the UCLA side of the street, inviting him to join them and admonishing him to 'reject the government's lies.'

The relief Marius felt as he entered the building had little to do with the air conditioning. Inside, the halls were mostly empty. Although in theory, the HHV task force of one shared laboratory space with other projects, summer was a slow time on campus and Marius had the run of the place. The peaceful white noise hum of the equipment washed over him. Normally, the routine of the lab calmed him, but this time he couldn't seem to find the motivation to run the same tests yet again. By late afternoon, he found himself staring blankly at the now overly dehydrated sample he'd been about to put on a slide and look at under a microscope.

Something about the nature of a bionetwork nagged at him. He set the slide down. What were some examples of naturally occurring bionetworks? Superorganisms, like Pando in Utah or the Malheur honey fungus colony in Oregon. Ants were technically a superorganism, but not genetically. Were the bioformations genetic clones or individuated?

The door opened and Miranda poked her head in. "Hi Marius," she said. She strolled into the lab, casually poking at petri dishes and peeping into microscopes. She wrinkled her nose. "That mold is everywhere."

"What?" Marius joined her at the long counter on the side of the room. He had a row of Petri dishes with samples of HHV being treated by various versions of the government approved vaccine. So far, he hadn't succeeded in finding anything other than his own blood that was 100% effective against all HHV strains.

Several of the dishes had a fuzzy greenish-brown patina over them. Marius collected a sample, but he already knew what it was. The same mold from his dorm. How had it gotten in? He'd been careful about decontamination on the way out of the lab, but he must have brought in spores. And now the mold was in his lab, contaminating his experiments. How much work had he lost? Marius shook his head at his own carelessness. He pulled out a fresh slide and began mounting the mold sample as Miranda watched.

"So, Torres went into town," she said casually. "Guess she's gonna go meet her family or whatever. Must be nice."

Marius looked up at her. He couldn't help noticing the plunging neckline of her shirt, or the way her very short shorts barely clung to her hips. He could see the line where her skin went from bronze to cream over the soft ridge of her iliac crest. He bit his lip and looked away. She was an adult, and she could dress however she wanted. On the other hand, he wanted to warn her, to say the things his parents would have told his sister, Percy, if she were dressed like that. Something about not advertising something that wasn't for sale, but that was a horrible analogy. Besides, it was hot and muggy outside with the temperature gearing up for another day in the upper nineties. Of course, Miranda would want to dress in cool clothing.

Stop sexualizing your friend. Be supportive of her choice to —

"Do you like my new shirt?" Miranda smiled a slow smile, her lashes fluttering as she leaned back against the counter, resting on her elbows, her chest thrust out.

Marius blinked. For once he hadn't misread the signs. But Miranda was *Miranda*. The girl he'd saved from Harrow Hall, the friend who'd helped him through the quarantine in Chrysalis's Submarine, the survivor who'd fought the Infected alongside him at Chrysalis even though she'd just lost her father.

"I ... it's ... nice," Marius stammered.

Miranda stood up and crossed the space between them, her breasts rubbing against Marius's chest as she draped her arms around his neck. "Know what's nice?"

Marius didn't.

I'm a genius, he thought. I should be able to figure out the right thing to do here. I should—

"Us." Her voice dropped to a smoky whisper. "Alone." She gently raked her fingernails up his neck and into his hair, sending shivers through his body. "Together," she breathed so softly he barely heard it. Her red lips glistened as her pink tongue darted out to touch him. It was like fire and part of him longed to claim her, roughly and immediately. To not be alone and trapped. For just a few minutes to feel free and safe and happy, not forever rolling the Sisyphean boulder of HHV cure up the hill of governmental bureaucracy and incompetence.

Her hands found their way under his shirt, surprisingly cool against his bare skin. His nipples tightened and he gasped. She giggled, glancing from his chest to his face. "I'm glad I finally figured out how to get your ... attention." Her hand strayed downwards, hooked the waistband of his jeans.

She's just lonely. We shouldn't.

Marius gently caught her wrist and held her hand. "We shouldn't," he said, his own voice low and hoarse as he tried to focus, tried to marshal his reason and logic in the face of his body's sudden and long-neglected demands for human contact, comfort, and connection.

Miranda pouted prettily. "Why not?" She glanced down and back up with a smirk. "Everything looks like it's working fine."

Marius groaned and backed away, rearranging himself to make his erection less obvious.

Miranda put her hands on her hips—her dangerously canted hips. When had she learned to do that?

"What, Marius? I want you. You want me. We're both adults. So ...?"

"So." Marius fumbled. "So, I have work to do."

"BS!" Miranda crossed her arms over her chest. "Your samples are all moldy. You'll have to throw them all out and start over again." She lifted her chin. "If you don't want to have sex with me, be a man and tell me. Don't make up some stupid excuse. I'm not a kid, Marius. I haven't been for a long time whether you or John or Torres notice or not."

"This has nothing to do with John," Marius said. "Or Torres.

"No?" Miranda hissed. Angry tears glistened in her eyes. "This has nothing to do with *her*? The way she's always around, panting after you."

"That's her job. She's part of the security detail. And she's not panting after me," Marius said. His protectiveness surprised even him. Torres had worked tirelessly to keep him safe. There were moments when he thought she watched him with more than mere professional interest. And there had been the kiss ...

"Really?" Miranda swiped away her tears, one fist held over her chest, covering her cleavage. "She's just another stupid parolee, like me. She's not a part of any detail. Neither is John. Neither are you. No one cares about us. Not after Wiltz. They're going to burn out all the nests and kill everything and it just hurts . . . " She doubled over, holding herself.

"Miranda." Marius reached for her, but she dodged away.

"Don't you fucking touch me." Her eyes were hooded and glassy. She bared her teeth and snarled, "Abomination."

Marius drew back. "I never meant to hurt you, Miranda. I love you. You're like a sister."

Still holding her stomach, Miranda rushed to the door. She paused to look back for a moment, her lips trembling. There was no mistaking the heartbroken look on her face. "I'm sorry, Marius. I can't ..." She flung open the door and ran down the hall.

After Miranda left Marius prowled the lab, more unsettled than ever. He tried to summon his usual intense focus as he examined one of the mold contaminated samples. Instead of the usual viruses writhing and squirming, he saw a black patch, a plaque like the prions that ate away the brains of victims of kuru or Alzheimer's. He dialed back to get a wider view. Maybe it was part of a larger whole. But the entire slide seemed to be contaminated, although not uniformly. Definitely not a spill or a cleaning agent. The growth was too organic.

Marius sat back and bit his lip. There was a pattern. The viruses seemed fine in some areas, but decimated in others. Sketching out the dead zones gave him a web of destructive lines as the mold twisted its way across the bioformation sample. Wherever the mold's thread-like mycelia touched, bare patches followed. It looked like some kind of infectious biological agent.

More contamination from his blood? Or could it be the mold? Every question led not to an answer but to more questions.

Frustrated, Marius dumped the contaminated samples. He pushed his hair back and stared around the lab. He knew what he had to do: start all over again with a proper control group and completely fresh samples. No need to rush since he'd probably be spending the rest of his life here or in some other lab. He had become nothing more than a particularly helpful specimen.

The door opened with a bang. John stuck his head in.

"Get your kit and come with me."

Back at Chrysalis, John had drilled every member of the security team to always keep their go-bags packed and ready at hand. After the Harrow Hall outbreak, Marius had been accepted as a de facto member of the team, which meant he had also learned to always keep his go-bag packed and to appreciate a good pair of clean, dry socks at the end of a hard day.

Marius grabbed his go-bag from the cupboard and hurried into the hall. He didn't have time to put away his samples, so he locked the door and hoped. John was already halfway down the hall, moving fast for a man with a bum knee.

"What's up?" Marius jogged to catch up.

John's pale blue eyes flicked up at the camera above the door. "Remember what it was like when we were in the Submarine?"

Marius nodded. While quarantined after the Harrow Hall outbreak, they had been under constant surveillance—for science.

John didn't elaborate and Marius didn't press him further. He knew John wouldn't have asked him to leave the lab unless it were important. Whatever faults he had, John was not panicky. They crossed the campus, passed the restive protestors, and turned back toward the dormitories. As they drew closer, Marius caught sight of Miranda, now wearing a loose-fitting T-shirt and capri pants. She was lurking near the door, pretending to text, but for once, not actually looking at her phone.

Marius looked around and frowned at John.

"Torres is in trouble," John said. Miranda held the door open for them and fell in step with the two men.

They stopped outside the former Marine's room and John knocked.

"I'm fine, Captain." Torres's voice was muffled. Had she been crying?

"Lourdes, please open the door," John said, using his I'm-a-very-reasonable-man voice.

"I can't believe you tattled, Miranda." This time there was definitely a quaver to Torres's voice.

Miranda rolled her eyes and flapped her hands as if to say, "See what I'm dealing with!"

Marius put a hand on John's shoulder. Whatever was between them it would have to wait.

"Hey, Torres, it's me," he said. "Can I come in?"

Silence. Then the door flew open. Torres stood, hands on hips, glaring at them. She was wearing a sports bra and a pair of running shorts. Behind her, Marius could see her jean shorts and T-shirt soaking in the dorm room's sink. The water looked suspiciously red.

"WTF?" Miranda said as John stepped into the room. He beckoned Miranda to follow him. Marius joined them, closing the door behind himself.

John went to the sink and started hand washing the clothes. Miranda flipped on the overhead light and gasped.

Torres had blood on her. It was matted in her hair. Smaller drops of blood had dried on her neck and upper arms. Her hands were damp and tinged red from washing out her clothes in the sink.

Marius caught Torres's look. She was more shaken than he'd ever seen her, and he'd seen her face down hordes of Infected with nothing but a 9mm and a pocketknife.

"I'm just gonna check that you're okay, okay soldier?" Marius began checking her vitals and looking for any signs of injury. None of the blood seemed to be hers.

Torres snorted. "I'm a freaking Marine."

"You used to be," John said, taking up the inter-service teasing that had become a routine for them.

"Once a Marine, always a Marine." Torres said.

"You never get rid of it," Miranda said brightly. "Like herpes."

"Not the time," John said.

Torres swatted Marius's hand away as he reached for her neck to check her lymph nodes. "I'm not infected. Remember?" She tapped a finger on the small pale scar on her shoulder. Torres had been the first person to receive Marius's newly processed vaccine in the midst of the Chrysalis outbreak. Neither had known if it would keep her safe or turn her into a monster, but she'd trusted Marius. She'd also kissed him, but at the time he chalked it up to 'we're about to die so why not?'

But as he looked into her amber eyes, he couldn't help but read more into her expression. "I remember."

Torres's eyebrows drew down as did the corners of her mouth. Her chin came down. Whatever he thought he'd seen before, he knew what pissed off looked like.

Idiot, you've got sex on the brain because of what happened with Miranda.

Marius stepped back and busied himself rearranging his already perfectly neat and well-organized medical kit.

"She seems fine," he pronounced to the air.

"Which is why she came flying in here all freaked out and covered in blood. Cuz she's fine." Miranda perched on the edge of Torres's bed.

"I killed Ramon." Torres's voice sounded hollow, her gaze fixed on some mystery point on the wall.

"Who's Ramon?" John said without missing a beat.

"I went home. He … my sister and he … he attacked me."

"Your sister and Ramon attacked you?" Miranda pulled up her legs and crossed them, leaned forward as if watching her favorite TV show.

Torres shook her head. "No. Ramon's my sister's boyfriend. He tried to …" She trailed off, her arms held out stiffly at her sides, her fingers fluttering. "Anyway, I stabbed him. Three times."

"Are you sure he's dead?" Marius asked. In med school he'd heard plenty of stories about trauma patients who survived seemingly mortal injuries.

Torres barked a laugh.

John wrung out her T-shirt and hung it over the hand towel bar next to the sink. "If she meant to kill him, he's dead," he said. He picked up the small bar of hotel soap and scrubbed the jean shorts.

Torres went to her closet and took out her hoodie. She started to put it on, then put it back on the hanger. "I'm cold," she said softly. Her chin trembled. She balled up her fists and clamped her mouth shut. Miranda hopped off the bed and rummaged through Torres's duffle bag. She handed the other woman a windbreaker.

"Thanks," Torres muttered. She walked over to the window, which had the blinds tightly closed, and stared at it. "I'm not sorry," she said. "He deserved what he got and probably more."

Marius went to stand next to Torres. He wanted to

put his arm around her, to draw her close and make her safe in the shelter of his arms. They had all been through so much and they would get through this, too. They would stay together. They would be all right.

A phone vibrated loudly.

Miranda fished the phone out of Torres's hoodie and held it out. "It's your mom. Your sister's in the hospital."

Nurse Fernando squeaked down the hall of White Memorial Hospital in his tangerine Crocs. Outside a door marked 'Closed Ward', he stopped and turned to face the group. It was late afternoon, yearning to be evening. Outside rush hour was already underway. Drivers watched with glazed eyes as their vehicles inched down San Diego Freeway.

Marius watched Torres, who kept her face blank. Only her eyes betrayed her. He'd never known her to shy away from a challenge, but now she wouldn't meet his gaze. She's just worried about her mom. But there was the looming specter of the murdered Ramon. Could Torres be arrested at a hospital? Or were they sanctuaries like holy sites? How would being involved in a murder affect their parole?

Would he have to go back to the detention center because of this? Marius shuddered, trying to shake off the memories of the weeks and months of mind-numbing boredom and isolation coupled with the constant fear for his own health on top of the uncertainty of not knowing if his loved ones were free or prisoners, alive or dead.

"Sorry, folks. Only two visitors allowed," the nurse said. "You dudes can wait here." He waved to an alcove with two sofas, a coffee table, and a stack of out-of-date fashion and gossip magazines.

"You should go," John said to Marius. "You're the doctor."

Marius looked at Torres, who gave a jerky nod. Fernando offered them paper masks, then typed in his code and led them down the hall. In an exam room, the nurse scanned a chart and said, "They'll be back in a minute. Just getting some labs done."

"Thanks," Marius said.

After Fernando left, Torres paced the room in small circles, holding her arms tightly across her chest.

The door opened and an older woman entered, leading a young girl. The woman looked enough like Torres that Marius didn't have to ask. Torres froze upon seeing her mother, who gave a little startled shriek.

"¿Qué haces aquí?" Señora Torres asked. Torres pulled her mother aside, speaking to her in hushed tones.

Not wanting to intrude, Marius tried to blend in with the background. The little girl climbed onto the doctor's spinning stool and began kicking her way along the edge of the room.

Fernando wheeled in a young woman on a gurney. Again, the family resemblance was unmistakable. But it wasn't the uncanny similarity between the Torres sisters that caused Marius to bolt up from his spot in the corner.

Cynthia Torres was infected. He could see it from across the room. She slouched on the gurney, her brown eyes half closed, head hanging. From the doorway,

Marius could see the swollen, purple bruises on Cynthia's neck. He froze. Not long. Not even long enough for Fernando to notice. The nurse was already crossing the room, pulling his pen light out of his pocket.

"Is she the only one presenting with this?" Marius asked, stepping forward. He angled himself between the nurse and the infected woman. Imagining how quickly HHV could spread through a clinical setting chilled Marius to his core.

"Nope," Fernando said. "We've got two kids like this checked in this afternoon. We called the CDC and they said they'll send a team to evaluate when they can free up some resources." He shook his head. "Budget cuts, am I right? So, you're a doctor? Does this look like HHV to you?"

"Oh hell yeah," Torres muttered.

"Are you a doctor, too?" Fernando asked.

"No. I'm her sister." Torres said.

Fernando gave Marius a quizzical look.

"Listen, this definitely looks like the early stages of HHV to me," the scientist explained. "I've seen this kind of thing before. You need to isolate anyone with these symptoms and contact the WHO. I can give you the direct line for their HHV task force coordinator. They should be able to get some vaccine here by..." Marius trailed off. What if Cynthia didn't have the strain of HHV that the vaccine would affect? Would Torres have to watch her sister turn into a monster who would infect others? Would she have to kill her?

"A bit above my pay grade, doc," Fernando said. Marius was relieved the nurse made no further attempts to examine Cynthia.

"Go get your administrator. Make sure the kids are isolated. Treat them like they have Ebola — it's blood borne and highly contagious." Marius knew he might sound alarmist, but he didn't care. If this really was HHV and they didn't get taken care of, they'd have a lot bigger problems.

"Fu ... fudge," Fernando said. He looked from Cynthia to Marius to the little girl giggling as she twirled the stool between the bed and the wall. If I was him, I'd be getting my family out of LA, Marius thought. He could see the nurse shared his assessment.

Fernando backed up to the door. "I'll go get Dr. Gausman. You dudes stay here, okay?" He left without waiting for anyone to agree that they would stay put. Marius didn't blame him.

"They're not gonna get the vaccine here in time," Torres said, squeezing herself so hard Marius could see pale fingermarks against her light brown skin.

"I know it was an accident with Ramon," Señora Torres put a hand on her older daughter's arm. "You didn't mean to hurt nobody, did you?"

"He got what he deserved," Torres said, not breaking eye contact with Cynthia. "Didn't he?"

"I can't believe you got me sick, you puta. You're a fucking curse," Cynthia rasped. "Bruja."

Torres flinched.

"I didn't get you sick," she said. "Did you get bitten today or yesterday? Cut yourself? Trade needles?"

"I'm not a junkie!" Cynthia snapped. She took several deep breaths. Marius could hear the phlegmy rattle in her lungs. "I'm tired. Can you leave so I can rest? Please?"

"We need to stay here until we figure out the best way to handle this situation. Do you understand what's happening?" Marius asked. Regardless of what was going on between the sisters, Cynthia was sick and he needed to help her.

"I have a cold or something and she's freaking out because she's a drama queen." Cynthia's eyes narrowed. "And a murderer."

The little girl stopped her scooting and looked from her mother to her aunt. "What happened, Tia Lourdie?"

"Nada," Torres said. She patted the child's head. "Your mama's sick, but my friend can help her." She looked at Marius, the asking naked in her face. "You can help her, right?"

"I don't know if they even have any HHV vaccine at this hospital. We could get some from campus but those are experimental batches." Marius hated telling her these hard truths, watching her hope crumble and collapse under the weight of his words.

Tears glinted in Torres's eyes, and she let them fall unremarked. "So, what can we do?"

The little girl started toward her mother, but Torres caught her and picked her up. "Hey, how's my favorite sobrina?"

"I'm your only niece," the child said, squirming to be free. "Put me down. I want my mamá."

"She's sick," Torres said.

"I should have called the cops," Cynthia said. "Give me my phone. You should be in jail!" She struggled to sit up. Marius assisted her, using their proximity to more thoroughly examine Cynthia's external symptoms. Given the size and color of the nodal swellings, he was not surprised she was already exhibiting aggressive tendencies. She'd probably been infected for a day or more.

"Can you lift your arm?" he asked.

"Get off me, perv," Cynthia snapped. "I'm in mourning. I'm bereaved." She grinned as she spoke, her eyes glittering as she focused on her sister.

Marius stepped in front of her and half turned to speak to Torres without taking his eyes off Cynthia. "You should take your mom and your niece and go wait with John and Miranda. I'll stay with her until we get this figured out."

"You're not taking my daughter anywhere, pato." Cynthia held out her arms again, giving Marius a chance to see her purple, swollen axillary lymph nodes. Either she'd been infected longer than he'd originally guessed or the HHV was progressing faster in her than he'd seen in previous outbreaks. Faster symptom expression could be a good thing in that it would alert the general public to the severity of the issue. He hoped.

Torres turned away from her sister, the child wriggling on her hip. She took Marius's hand, squeezed it, and looked deeply into his eyes. "If there are three Infected in the hospital, how many didn't come in?"

Marius didn't want to think of it, but he knew the statistics. "For every patient who presented, there were probably fifteen to twenty who were home with what they thought was a really bad flu."

"We have to get out of LA. Now. Tonight," Torres said.

"Okay, we need a plan," Marius said. *We need John.* He could see Torres was thinking the same thing. "We can't take your sister with us like this."

Torres nodded and spoke to her mother in Spanish. Cynthia joined in the discussion, her tone growing louder by the moment.

The door burst open and a flushed nurse's aide poked her head in. "This is a hospital! You need to keep it down in here or I'm going to have security remove you." She left, nearly slamming the door, but she didn't because it was a hospital.

Cynthia and Torres exchanged a look and both burst out laughing. Their mother smiled and shook her head, muttering and shaking her finger at her daughters. Even Elfy stopped trying to escape from her aunt, resting her head against the former Marine's shoulder.

"Ms. Torres?" Marius said and was pleased when Cynthia responded immediately. He didn't know where in the disease progression she was, but he had to act as if she still might be saved.

"Mr. Tall Dark and Handsome?" Cynthia batted her eyelashes.

"Do you know a lot about HHV?"

"Like AIDS?"

"No, HHV—Harrow Hall Virus."

She shook her head.

"There's a vaccine, a cure." That was a little white lie, but Marius didn't think it would do harm. "But we don't know if we can get it in time. I've already been vaccinated and if I give you some of my blood it will basically vaccinate you."

Cynthia sat up straighter, coughed, and spit into a tissue. Her phlegm was tinged dark reddish purple. "Um, no. Thanks, but no. I'm not getting blood transfusions from a random dude my sister's been boffing."

Torres flushed. "We're not ..."

"If you don't get a transfusion soon, as in within the next few hours, you'll probably die." Marius hated to scare his patient, but they were running out of time and options.

"Cynty, él tiene razón. You should do what this nice doctor says," Señora Torres said.

"Ay, Mamá, okay. Basta ya," Cynthia complained. "But I don't need an audience, okay?"

Torres drew Marius away from her sister's gurney a few steps. "I'll take my mom and Elfy home and let John know what's up. Jimmy's in town, so we can coordinate with him to get some bug-out supplies. Can you stay with her until I get back? Do you think that'll be enough time for the transfusion?"

"Should be. We'll be fine. I won't leave your sister alone," Marius promised.

Torres took her mother and Elfy away, promising Cynthia they would return with some clothes and toiletries from home. Cynthia dozed off while Marius plundered the cupboards for a hypodermic needle and syringe. One of the maddening things about the moratorium on new HHV vaccine research was that it prevented him from nailing down how much of his own antigens were needed to confer immunity. He'd given John a transfusion of his blood after the soldier had been injured during the Harrow Hall outbreak, which was how they'd first learned that Marius's blood would halt and even reverse an active HHV infection. But that transfusion had hardly been under ideal clinical conditions. Marius estimated he'd given about a pint.

If he wanted to ensure Cynthia's recovery, would he need that much? The biggest hypodermic syringe in the room held 45 mL. In order to get a pint, he'd have to inject Cynthia around a hundred times. Marius doubted she would agree. He needed a way to either concentrate his antigens—and lacking a BSL-4 lab that was a nonstarter—or a way to transfuse his blood, which could be done by repurposing the IV drip already in Cynthia's arm.

From the gurney Cynthia coughed, a wet rattle. She gagged and then launched into a coughing fit, struggling to sit up. Marius rushed over to assist her. Pinkish-purple drool bubbled from her lips and fell onto her chest as she fought for air.

Marius helped her sit up and supported her. With his free hand, he pressed the red alarm button to call the nurse's station. He clicked it over and over until the fit passed and Cynthia leaned exhaustedly against him. He gently wiped her mouth, murmuring that she'd be okay and other lies.

The door burst open. "What?" demanded the nurse's aide.

"She needs a doctor," Marius said.

"Everyone's busy. We're dealing with patients coming in from Cedars-Sinai's total divert."

"What's going on at Cedars?" Marius asked.

"I don't know. All we were told was to get ready. They had a code triage," the aide said. She took a deep breath.

"I'm sorry. She'll have to wait." She hurried away.

Marius's gut twisted. Three Infected at White Memorial and something was going on at Cedars that caused them to send patients elsewhere. It could be any number of things. An earthquake. It was Los Angeles, after all. Or a twelve-car pileup. Or a school shooting. Or …

But he knew it wasn't.

It was HHV, twining its tentacles through the heart of the second largest city in the US. Los Angeles was infected as surely as Cynthia was. While he might be able to spare a pint of blood to save Torres's sister's life, he did not have 4 million pints to save everyone in Los Angeles.

"We save the ones we can," Marius echoed John's words. Otto could have been saved. John had made the wrong call to leave the boy. Marius studied Cynthia as the woman gasped and sputtered. It's not too late. It's not too late. I can save her. I can't save everyone, but I can save her.

He slammed the doorstop behind the door. The last thing he needed was the nurse's aide interrupting him mid-transfusion. Fernando was probably long gone, and Marius wished him all the luck in the world as he prepared the tubing and needles. He smiled ruefully as he slid the needle into his arm. He'd never imagined he'd become so adept at finding his own veins.

Cynthia drifted into an exhausted slumber. Marius hesitated before connecting to her IV bag. She hadn't agreed to this treatment, but he'd promised Torres to take care of her. This was life or death. Better she be alive and angry with him than dead or worse, a monstrous

Infected spreading HHV.

Marius sat back, watching the blood drip into the IV bag where it swirled crimson to pink before vanishing in the saline. He checked the clock on the wall. He couldn't measure his blood, but by now, he had a pretty good idea of how long it took him to bleed a pint.

Feet slapped along the corridor outside. Several sets of feet. Marius had been around enough security teams to know the sound of tactical shoes when he heard them. He stood up, wobbled against the head rush of sudden blood pressure drop, and pushed Cynthia's gurney back away from the door.

"Dr. Tenart, are you in there?" A man's voice. Not someone from the usual team. Marius had trained them all how to properly pronounce his family's French last name. He had expected they would come looking, given that he had left the campus. Took them long enough to find him, considering he still wore the ankle tracker.

"Yes," Marius called back. He needed more time. Cynthia needed more time. "Who's that?"

"Back away from the door."

"It's not locked, you goons." Marius couldn't keep the near hysterical chuckle from his voice. "Just wait a sec. I'll open it." He stalled, checking the clock. Maybe three-fourths of a pint. Would that be enough?

The door handle jiggled and the door opened a crack, caught on the doorstop, and stopped.

"Dr. Tenart, what's going on in there?" The opening to the hall vanished as someone peered in through the crack.

"Nothing. I'm fine. Here, I'll open the door now." Marius held up a hand and moved toward the door.

"Step back, sir!"

Ah, shit, the now-we're-gonna-bust-some-heads voice.

The door crashed open, spilling what seemed like an infinite number of commandos into the small hospital room. Marius had a wild image of the nurse's assistant speeding down the hall to demand they quiet down and then he was on his belly, his arms jerked painfully back and zip-tied behind him. They hauled him up, yanked the IV out, and practically carried him out of the room. He tried to turn, tried to get a final glimpse of Cynthia. Her eyes were half open. Were they all black, like a shark's? Had he made any difference?

A bag went over his head and he was breathing his own near-panicked breaths. Down the hall, up some stairs. Hands on him, pushing him this way and that. The National Guard soldiers had never been this rough with him before.

"We'll get him to the car." A man's voice. The first one? A different one? He couldn't tell.

They're here to rescue me, Marius thought. Giggles bubbled up and he fought them off. He could neither laugh nor scream. Be calm. Be calm. Keep your feet under you. Keep your head clear. He recited John's pearls of wisdom. Be in the Now. All you need to do is survive Now. There are no consequences in Now.

An elevator dinged. In they went. Only two now, one on either side.

The click of a button.

"Hey, the car is on B4. What—"

Pft!

A silenced pistol isn't really silent. It should be called

a quieted pistol, but to Marius the sound was shockingly loud. It was the sound of bad going to worse, the sound of bidding the sweet frying pan a fond adieu before being engulfed in the raging inferno of I'm being kidnapped in the middle of an outbreak.

Chapter 6 – Miranda

Big Sur, CA, U.S.A. - Summer, Year 1

Miranda had seen her fair share of hotels, ranging from five-star luxury resorts to European hostels that charged for single-ply toilet paper by the square. All things considered, there were worse places to be than the Rodeway Inn off I-5. At least the Wi-Fi was free, even if it was slow. Miranda curled into a chair near the window.

Once in the hotel, Mrs. Torres had tried to call the hospital to check on Cynthia. After nearly fifteen minutes on hold, Torres had insisted she hang up.

"Marius will take care of Cynty, Mamá," she said, holding out the TV remote to her mother.

Mrs. Torres replied in rapid Spanish and Torres said something back about John, her voice overly patient.

"No te importa nuestra familia," Mrs. Torres muttered, half turned away. Miranda's high school Spanish was good enough that she could figure out what that meant.

Torres jerked back as if her mother had slapped her. "How can you say I don't care about our family? I came back, didn't I? After everything that happened, I'm still freaking here, still trying to help you."

The older woman picked up the remote and strenuously ignored her daughter. Torres stood, hands on hips, glaring at her mother for a few long minutes before she turned away with a loud sigh.

Miranda hated the tension. It reminded her of being on family getaways with her parents before Mom had left. Both Albert and Cecilia had tried to bury themselves in work and act like the other wasn't even there.

I'm not playing go-between for Torres and her mom. I don't even speak Spanish.

Mrs. Torres flipped through all the Spanish-language channels and the two kids' channels in a slow but unrelenting cycle. Elfy lay on her belly on the floor between the two beds in the room. Miranda checked her phone again. No texts, no calls, no notifications other than her usual social media notices.

Torres rummaged through the items on the bed. She'd collected all the complementaries and was making little piles for everyone, like having three showers worth of gel or a teeny bar of soap was going to save anyone.

During the ride up here from Los Angeles proper, Torres had been on the phone to Jimmy. Miranda vaguely remembered the medic from her time at Chrysalis's Arizona facility. Torres had given him a list of gear and equipment and arranged to meet him at a place called Mike's Diner near the Pilot Travel Center in Castaic.

"It's far out enough that we'll be ahead of the surge." Torres had explained after she hung up from talking to Jimmy. "John's grabbing our stuff from the dorm, then he's gonna swing by the hospital and get Marius and my sister. Jimmy's bringing cash and supplies. That should be enough to get a head start."

Miranda wasn't sure how John intended to get a car to bring Marius and Cynthia to meet them, but the soldier seemed to have friends who owed him favors everywhere they went.

"We're out of the twenty-mile range," Miranda observed. They passed Santa Clarita with its green flanked hills and orderly housing developments. What would breaking parole mean? A fine? Back to some secret government detention center? Or worse, being sent to some over-crowded, corporate-run prison?

"By the time they figure out we're gone, they'll have bigger problems," Torres said.

Was it wrong to hope for an outbreak? Just a tiny one, just enough to keep the government busy and remind them how much they needed Marius, his magic blood, and his trusty sidekicks.

Torres checked her phone. "Jimmy will be here in five minutes. I'm gonna head over to Mike's. We can pick up anything we need that he couldn't get from the truck stop."

"Okay," Miranda said, not looking up as Torres shut

the door behind her.

Things would be better when John and Marius joined them, although the thought of facing Marius after what had happened in the lab sent a hot rush of shame and anger coursing through her body. She'd thrown herself at him and he'd treated her like she was a dumb kid. Or a virgin, which she definitely was not, thank you.

The only good thing about being on the run, which is what they were whether Torres wanted to admit it or not, was that the further from downtown Los Angeles they got, the less Miranda felt the sticky-soft strands of the Infected across her brain. It was like telepathic spiderwebs and she did not like being a fly. The feeling had been growing ever since they'd arrived in Los Angeles, but what could she say? Who could she tell?

"Oh, hi, John. I'm kinda hearing voices or whatever and I think the Infected want me to kill Marius."

Yep, that would totally fly with John. The only thing he cared about more than following the rules was keeping Marius safe.

Miranda wracked her brain, trying to figure out why she felt connected to the Infected. Had she gotten exposed to something in Harrow Hall? Or was she really hearing them at all? Perhaps it was a psychological side effect of trauma. Maybe it would go away. She hoped.

The bed creaked as Mrs. Torres stood up. She smiled at Miranda and headed for the door.

"Hey." Miranda set her phone down. "Um . . . donde . . . going?"

Mrs. Torres held out her hands. Hesitantly, Miranda put her hands into the older woman's palms. Mrs. Torres squeezed her hands gently.

"Lourdes is very strong and brave. She will take good care of you. Cynthia is not so strong or brave. She needs me."

Miranda blinked, surprised at how clearly Mrs. Torres spoke English.

"I think they'll be right back," Miranda said, but Mrs. Torres let go of her hands and went to Elfy. She tried to pick the girl up, but Elfy grumbled, and Mrs. Torres settled for hugging and kissing her.

"They'll be right back," Miranda repeated. She didn't want to be left alone with the kid.

Mrs. Torres smiled. "Yes," she said. "Don't worry. She watch TV and go to sleep."

"You shouldn't go back to LA," Miranda said. The tickling of the Infected was like the scent of death in a field on a windy day. Sometimes she could feel their pressure against her head and other times she was sure she had imagined it. But she wasn't and she hadn't imagined it in Wiltz, either. Los Angeles had more Infected in it than anyone realized, other than her.

A swell of hunger and anticipation set her mouth watering. She licked her lips. Los Angeles was ripe like a bloated corpse. So many bodies. So many nests.

Miranda rubbed her head, tried to shut out the sensations. She needed to warn someone. John could alert the Army and Marius would get the scientists involved.

The door closed and Miranda jerked up, startled. Mrs. Torres had gone. She'd actually gone and left her granddaughter with some random stranger who was in the middle of some kind of mental health crisis because what else could it be?

I think I can communicate with the Infected. I think they want me to help them. I'm pretty messed up.

Maybe they would give her drugs that would make her feel safe and floaty. She wouldn't have to think about Elfy watching *Kitty Cat Compadres* or Mrs. Torres going back to Los Angeles to be with her daughter or Marius and the look of horror and pity on his face when he'd rejected her.

From the floor the child's round face peered up at her. "Do you wanna watch something else? Sponge Bob is on." Elfy waggled the remote, apparently totally fine that her grandmother had abandoned her in a hotel room with a woman who thought she could speak to the Infected.

Stupid kid. The thought was so strong and sudden that it took her breath away. The hatred wasn't hers, but it rattled in her head all the same. Miranda squeezed her eyes shut and leaned forward, pressed her forehead against the cool, damp window. Outside, the heat of the day was finally giving way to evening's offshore breezes. Palm trees rattled their fronds. A stray dog trotted along the edge of the parking lot with a purposefulness Miranda envied.

"Uh, no," she said. "No Sponge Bob." She stood up and checked her phone again. Still nothing. "We better go catch your grandma." She pictured the older woman trying to hitchhike back into town and snorted a laugh. Who would stop for her? *Foolish, foolish person. Better to be useful, to be consumed and remade. Better to serve the Enlightened.*

"The Enlightened?"

"What?" Elfy looked over her shoulder, kicking her

small feet.

"Nothing." Miranda leaned out the door and looked around. No sign of Mrs. Torres. How could someone that old move so fast? More importantly, who or what were the Enlightened? Why did she know that term?

A silver Audi pulled into the parking lot. Torres was riding shotgun. Miranda barely recognized Jimmy. He'd traded his fatigues for a corporate polo shirt and khakis. The sun shone on his mostly bald head.

Torres stepped out of the car and turned back to pull out a light, but sturdy high-tech backpack like serious hikers or rock climbers wore.

"So," Miranda stumbled over the words, unsure how to tell Torres her mom had abandoned her. Again. And saddled them all with a kid.

"Abuela went back to the hospital to get Mama," Elfy piped, not bothering to even come to the door to deliver her news.

They drove north, heading for Jimmy's vacation house in Big Sur.

"One of the perks of selling your soul to the big bad pharma folks, no offense, Miss Viers," he'd said when explaining how he'd come to work for her father's biggest competitors.

"Once a mercenary, always a mercenary, right? Tigers, stripes or something like that," Miranda said. She watched the stars, considered her profile in the black mirror of the window. She hadn't seen the night sky since Wiltz.

"Sure enough," Jimmy said, his voice overly cheery. He was in the backseat, theoretically resting while Torres drove. Also in the backseat, Elfy slept the deep boneless sleep of the very young, the very old, or the very exhausted. Torres had stopped glaring at Miranda in the rearview mirror. Finally. And seriously, had Torres expected her to tackle an old woman and force her to stay?

"I left John directions to get to the place. They shouldn't be more than a couple of hours behind us." Jimmy leaned forward to catch Torres's narrow-eyed gaze in the mirror, and then sat back, studying the passing scenery. This far out, Los Angeles was only an orange stain on the southern horizon. With Bakersfield behind them, they turned west into Los Padres National Forest, passing through towns of decreasing size and increasing quaintness. The bustle and glitz of Hollywood was replaced by artisanal hippies and the wealthy tourists who enjoyed their sanitized brand of enlightenment.

"How are they gonna move my sister?" Torres whipped around a slower car with no regard for the double yellow line. Miranda resisted the urge to clutch the dash or the oh-shit handle above the door. She refused to give Torres the satisfaction.

"Well, if she's not in serious condition, they can just bring her in a car." Jimmy's cheer was wearing thin, but he persisted in being upbeat. Brave little fellow.

"What if the hospital won't let her go?"

"They can't hold people prisoners in hospitals."

Torres snorted. "Right. We spent how long in detention being poked and prodded and tested over and over again after what happened at Chrysalis?"

"A while," Miranda said. Torres was speaking to her again. Progress. Not that Miranda cared what Torres thought of her. It was just so annoying to have her sulking about her mom the whole trip. And if Torres stopped sulking it might mean that Miranda letting Mrs. Torres leave wasn't that big a deal. Mrs. Torres was a grown woman. She could go wherever she wanted.

"What did the captain say?" Torres asked. The road turned north, winding along the coast. Hills rose to the east with strips of beaches and coves between the scenic route and the Pacific to the west. A parade of vacation homes blocked the view, but over their roofs, the water stretched away black and mysterious into forever.

Miranda checked her phone. Still no texts.

"I'll call him again, but they might be busy." She kept her voice peppy and light. No need to poke this particular bear or Marine—basically the same thing as far as she could tell.

The phone rang and then John's quiet, steady voice announced that he was 'um, busy at the ah, moment.' Before she could record her message, the phone buzzed. John was trying to call her. She shook her head, smiling a little. He'd never learned how to use any technology more complicated than an Army radio.

She accepted the call.

"Miranda, this is John."

She suppressed a grin. "I know, John. Where are you guys?" She looked at Torres, who raised a hand in a 'go on' motion. "How's Cynthia?"

"There's an issue. Can everyone hear me?"

"Just a sec." Miranda synced the phone to the car's

audio system. "Okay, go for it."

"Hello?" John said.

"Hey, Captain. Torres here. We can hear you loud and clear. Go ahead."

"Is Marius with you?" John asked.

"What?" The women exchanged puzzled looks and Jimmy sat forward.

"He removed his geo-locator and left the hospital," John said. Miranda frowned. That did not sound like something Marius would do.

"He's not with us," Torres said. "Did my mom find you? How's Cynthia?"

There was a pause, punctuated by a whoosh and roar in the background, then John said, "I didn't go back to the hospital, Torres. Mendelsen alerted me that Marius had deactivated his tracker and asked if I had seen him while I was still on campus. He's pulling the logs now. I was hoping Marius had arranged to meet up with you."

"He doesn't have a phone, remember?" Miranda said. Marius's parole conditions included a ban on all communications platforms. The government didn't trust him not to leak actual information on HHV when their story was that it was totally contained.

"I was afraid of this," John said. "I'm at the airport. Got a buddy standing by in case we need to head to Crossroads to intercept him."

Miranda frowned. "Crossroads?"

"That's where his family lives—Crossroads, Montana on the Morning Star ranch," Torres said. Of course, she knew where his family lived. She probably fell asleep every night reading his dossier or whatever.

"What about my mom and sister?" Torres asked. Her

knuckles showed white against the dark brown steering wheel.

"As I said, I didn't go back to the hospital."

No one spoke. Torres stared ahead, her jaw clenched. Miranda glanced at Jimmy, who lifted a shoulder in a half shrug.

"We can go back," Miranda said softly.

"We can't go back." Torres looked in the rearview mirror at her niece. "Marius knows enough to get out of the city. He'll borrow a phone and call us when he can."

"What?" Miranda couldn't believe Torres of all people was considering abandoning Marius.

"Torres is right," Jimmy said. "By the time we got back, he'd be long gone."

"What about your mo—" Miranda started, but Torres slapped the turn signal and pulled onto the shoulder, sending a shower of gravel rattling over the sea figs and highway ice plants that had overrun the ditch. She wrenched the gear shift into Park and shot out of the seat, leaving the car still running. Miranda turned on the hazards as the former Marine strode away, spotlit in rave-like bursts of red.

"We'll call you back, John," Miranda said and hung up.

Elfreda grabbed Miranda's headrest with her grubby little hands. "I have to tinkle." The child's breath was hot on the back of Miranda's neck. She leaned forward and twisted to look at Torres. The former Marine had been dozing in the backseat but had one eye open.

"I'm sorry, kiddo, but I don't think there are any bathrooms around here," Jimmy said. It was his turn to drive.

Morning had arrived sluggish and draped in clouds, resentful of having to get up so early. Miranda could relate. They'd made it three and a half hours into the five-hour trip to Jimmy's hideaway home. The slithering feeling of the Infected or the Enlightened or whatever they were trying to squeeze into Miranda's brain lessened with every mile away from Los Angeles. She remembered a story about a girl who'd fought off mind-control by imagining the multiplications tables. It was better than nothing.

Neither Cynthia nor Mrs. Torres had answered the flood of texts and calls Torres had sent them. Miranda hadn't even bothered to suggest that the best thing would have been to drop everyone off at Jimmy's vacation house and Torres could go back alone. No point. Torres was a snappish ball of tension. Miranda wasn't sure what she was most worried about—Marius running away, her mom going back into an HHV outbreak, her sick sister, or her cranky niece. Whatever was going on with Torres, Miranda didn't want to be on her radar.

"Mama says you're not 'posed to hold *it*," Elfy said. Her voice dropped to a loud whisper. "You get befections in your cha-cha."

"There's a rest stop just ahead," Miranda said. "I saw the sign a few minutes ago."

"I think we could all use the break." Jimmy's eyes flicked to the mirror, gauging Torres's reaction. "Plus, we need gas."

"Sounds like a plan," Torres said, staring out the window.

Jimmy turned on the radio. *What a Friend We Have in Jee-zus* radio was in full swing, complete with Pastor Pat Pendergast's fire and brimstone denunciation of the wickedness and sins of those Godless idolaters in Los Angeles. "Once more All Mighty God has chosen to punish the sin of pride. His eye is ever watchful. The stench of their abominations has finally grown too much. Man marrying man, unwed mothers, academics exulting their science over the inspired Word of the Lord. Yes, brothers and sisters, God is smiting that wicked city like He did to Sodom and Gomorrah in the old days."

Miranda rolled her eyes and flipped through the stations. It was the top of the hour and Pastor Pat wasn't the only one preaching fire and damnation for Los Angeles.

On the news station, a professionally urgent voice intoned. "We interrupt this program to bring you breaking news in the Los Angeles outbreak. Sources at Cedars-Sinai Hospital, who must remain anonymous, have confirmed that at least five patients with advanced symptoms of the disease known as HHV have been identified and quarantined. Local officials fear there may be dozens more infected who have not sought medical help."

And there it was, all over Miranda's social media feeds. The LA Outbreak. She held up her phone. "They're telling everyone to be calm and go to the doctor if they have any symptoms. Otherwise, they should stay home."

"They're not gonna firebomb LA," Torres said.

A shudder of relief from the Infected rippled across Miranda's mind. Were there Infected at the roadside rest? The feeling of them seemed to be growing stronger. *Leave me alone!* She tried to push them away and for once, they seemed to heed her.

"Firebomb LA? What?" Jimmy guided the Audi onto the exit ramp, passing signs that promised gas and several restaurants.

"Like in Wiltz," Miranda said. Without the Infected battering at her, it was easier to keep track of what was going on around her.

"They can't evacuate LA and they can't lock it down," Torres said. "All those people are just fresh meat for the Infected."

Miranda's stomach grumbled. She wanted a steak. A nice bloody, juicy steak.

"Well, looks like a lot of folks are already trying to get out," Jimmy said. The parking lot was full, with several cars and pickups circling like vultures ready to pounce on an open spot.

"Tia Lourdie, I'm gonna have an accident," Elfy whined.

Jimmy slowed to wait for a car with its brake lights lit, and the pickup behind them blared its horn and flashed its ultra-bright headlights.

"This mother-fu...fudger," Torres said. "You got your lady gun?"

"Don't mock the lady gun," Jimmy said. He popped open the center armrest and handed Torres a holstered pistol. "This isn't the OK Corral, sis."

"I know." Torres tucked the pistol away under her clothes. "We're going to scout ahead while you park. The kid has to go pronto."

"Mmm-hmm, I do." Elfy wriggled, doing a seated pee-pee dance.

Torres stepped out of the car as the truck gave another long blast. She waved both middle fingers at the driver and bent to help Elfy crawl across the seat and out.

"I better go with them," Miranda said.

"Thanks. I'll be right in," Jimmy said.

Torres lifted Elfy and settled the child on her hip before shouldering her way into the crowd that milled around in the parking lot. People were camping on the lawns around the rest stop. A handmade sign posted above the Arco gas station's pumps announced: NO GAS. NO DISEL. NO <u>CASH</u> IN ATM. SORRY! Fast food wrappers crunched underfoot. Miranda kicked a couple of beer cans and liquor bottles before stepping into the strip of fast-food joints and souvenir shops.

At the door, she hesitated. The crowd was worse inside, packed shoulder to shoulder, clamoring. The counter jockeys had a stunned, overwhelmed look. One barista, a kid barely sixteen, was crying openly as a woman with a huge lopsided pile of platinum blond hair screamed at him and jabbed her hand toward the menu board. Above the din from the other would-be customers, all Miranda could make out of her shrieks was "...soy, not coconut. Soy!"

"Lourdie." Elfy squirmed on Torres's hip. "I gotta go!"

"Okay, kid." Torres patted her and then dove into the mass of bodies. Miranda glanced back, hoping to see Jimmy's shiny pink head with its wisps of thinning brown hair. No way he would be able to find them, if he'd even found a parking space.

The bathroom was a nasty mess. One of the toilets had overflowed and a stinking puddle had spread onto the floors of the adjacent stalls. As Miranda waited, she saw several women plug their noses and, careful not to step in the puddles, they ventured into the flooded stalls.

Torres set Elfy down between herself and the wall, sheltering the girl from the jostle of bodies while she danced the pee-pee dance and whimpered. When it was their turn, Torres joined her in the stall and Miranda stood guard outside.

As Miranda took her turn, shivering in relief, Elfy's piping voice rose above the low din. "Tia Lourdie, there's no soap."

"Here." Torres grunted. "At least rinse your mitts."

Miranda opened the stall and stepped out as another woman practically pushed her way in.

"Excuse you!" She joined Torres and Elfy by the sinks.

Gunshots rang out. They sounded like flat handclaps, barely discernible above the babble of voices, but gunshots were something Miranda's ears were unfortunately well-tuned to. She froze. Torres looked around. They were at the end of the trough sink, farthest from the door. That was good. None of the other women or kids seemed to have noticed the noise, except one.

The woman wore a floral print hijab and clutched two boys by their wrists. The boys looked to be about six and eight. A little too old to be in the women's bathroom, but if Miranda were their mother, she wouldn't have let them out of her sight, either. At the sound of gunfire, the woman's head came up, her dark eyes wide, lips parted. She knew. She looked around and focused on Torres.

The former Marine waved the other woman to join them in the back corner. She pushed through the crowd, the boys trailing in her wake.

"They're shooting," the woman said. She maneuvered her boys into the corner next to Elfy. Both boys were thin with high, delicate cheekbones and thick, dark lashes. They looked like someone had made up their eyes. They stood silently, holding hands, worried eyes darting around. Elfy glared at the boys, adjusted her Dora backpack, and looked at Torres.

"No boys in the girls' bathroom," she said, crossing her arms tightly over her chest.

"Elfy, shh," Torres said. She held up a hand, seeming to listen. So did Miranda and the other woman.

Just when Miranda had almost convinced herself that she had imagined the gunshots, she heard another volley, this time accompanied by a change in the rumble of the crowd. The voices were angry or afraid or both.

The other woman started muttering in an Arabic-sounding language. It sounded like a prayer.

"Hey." Torres grabbed her shoulder. "Don't." She held a finger to her lips. "Take that off." Torres pointed to the woman's headscarf. She started to shake her head, but a scream pierced the tumult near the door. Miranda stood on tiptoe. She could see the top of a shiny black helmet. Police in riot gear? Motorcycle club members? Some kind of local militia?

The woman yanked the scarf off. "I'll take it." Miranda held out a hand and the woman handed it to her. She wound it around her neck like one of those war correspondents. The woman snatched the prayer caps off the boys' heads and looked around.

124

"How's your English?" Torres asked.

"Quite good," the woman said. "My name is Soraya. These are my sons, Wahid and Meraj." Her accent was a mix of clipped, posh British and throaty Middle Eastern.

"I'm Lourdes. This is my niece, Elfreda, and Miranda. You're my sister. Your name is Maria and the boys are José and Juan, okay?" Her words tumbled around as more helmets joined the one in the doorway.

Soraya nodded. "Thank you. We are in your debt."

"Don't talk. If they ask you anything just say, 'No English.'"

"I'll do the talking," Miranda said. She stepped forward, shaking out her hands to try to rid them of their nervous trembling.

"Shut up. Shut up. Shut the fuck up!" bellowed a man's voice from the door. Elfy ducked behind Torres.

"This stop is closed. You're all trespassing in the sovereign territory of the state of California." The speaker was a short, middle-aged man. He sported a large silver and gold inlaid belt buckle with the word DUKE on it. Duke, and the two others Miranda could see with him, wore police riot gear ominously devoid of the word POLICE. "The governor's declared a state of emergency and closed the border. We're checking that there's no illegals here. ICE is on the way to pick you guys up."

Soraya hugged her boys to her. Miranda hated the resigned fear in their little faces. Elfy seemed to pick up on their emotions and started to cry. "I wanna go home. I want Mama." She pounded her little fist against Torres's thigh. "You're a bad aunt!"

"Get your IDs out. Americans line up on this wall. The

rest of you over here." Duke waved around. "We gotta search you." Miranda could see the barely concealed smirks on the faces of the other men.

Several women hurried over, flashed their IDs and were shuffled out with a brisk pat down.

"This is illegal," Soraya hissed.

"I don't think they care," Miranda said.

Torres wrapped her arms around Elfy and fumbled to stuff the pistol into the bottom of the girl's Dora backpack. To Miranda, she said, "Can't let the local bubbas take Jimmy's gun. We'll need it later."

"What if we need it now?" Miranda hissed back. A gun would make her feel better. Well, Torres having a gun would make her feel better. She had no desire to shoot anyone, but it would be nice to know someone was willing to do it if it came to that.

"They're not gonna search a kid," Torres said.

"What if they —" Miranda started, but Torres pointed toward the door. Most of the other women and kids had left. The restroom was nearly empty. The grinning militia turned to the first of the remaining people.

At worst they'll grope. They're not going to rape anyone in here with everyone else. Better humiliated than hurt. Miranda hated herself for thinking like that. She glanced at Torres. No way the former Marine would put up with that kind of thing. She'd figure a way out. Wouldn't she?

"Don't fight them," Soraya murmured, echoing Miranda's thoughts.

"Just don't let them get you alone," Torres said. "Stay with me, no matter what."

They joined the other women and kids heading out of

the bathroom. Miranda went first when they got to the men at the door. They were bantering openly with each other, loudly rating the women one-to-ten as they patted them down or, more accurately, felt them up.

Miranda gritted her teeth as hands roamed her body.

"Thanks, honey," a twiggley blond rail of a man said. He had the nerve to wink at Miranda. "Go ahead, miss."

Shaking from equal parts fear and rage, Miranda shuffled forward. Behind her, Torres adopted a thick Tex-Mex accent. "My sister don't speak good English, señores."

"Man," Twiggler winked at his companion, a sleaze-ball with a porn stash. "I'm feeling really into sisters, even illegals. How bad you girls wanna stay in America?" He reached out and, with no pretext of a security pat down, fondled Torres's breast.

Miranda held her breath, as Torres's whole body seemed to shrink away. Her fists were clenched tight and her legs trembled. Miranda had no doubt that if Torres had been alone, she would have risked it. She would have shot Twiggler right in his horny, nasty crotch and run like hell.

But she wasn't alone. What Torres did would affect all of them.

Elfy stared up at the man leering at her aunt.

"What a pretty little girl." His face split into a jack-o-lantern smile. Elfy burst into fresh tears.

"Shut up," Twiggler snarled. Elfy only cried harder. He reached for her, but she dodged behind Torres. "Little bitch. Get over here."

"Don't touch her." Miranda's voice was ice in her own ears as if coming down a tunnel.

"Go on, sweetie. You're cleared." Twiggler turned his attention back to Miranda. "We're just making sure we protect our nation from disease-spreading foreigners."

Behind his back, Miranda could see Torres heft Elfy's Dora backpack, her hand slipping inside. Torres was a good shot, but even if she killed both men, how many more were outside? Torres's narrowed eyes and lowered chin had a last-stand kind of vibe Miranda didn't like at all. Maybe going out in a blood-soaked blaze of glory was Torres's idea of a good time, but Miranda had plans for her life, a future.

Let us help. The thought wrapped around her like a comforting quilt and she drew it close, pulled it towards her tugging in the threads of the shabby network of Infected that surrounded the rest stop. There were people already infected, but she couldn't quite compel them. What she could do was summon all the small lives, the Littles whose immune systems had already fallen even while their owners packed them into their travel crates and cooed about how poor Fluffy or Bingo just hated car trips.

The unholy cacophony of infected pets' howls and screeches rose from the parking lot.

"Hey, stop fucking around and get out here!" a man yelled from outside the bathroom.

"Later, señoritas." Twiggler made a kissy face at Torres. "You want to stay here, you know who to pay for the privilege."

A smile curled Miranda's lips. *Him first.*

Being able to communicate with the Infected had its upside.

Chapter 7 – Torres

As the self-appointed border guards pushed their way out of the bathroom, Torres heaved a sigh of relief. She pulled Jimmy's HK45 out of Elfy's Dora bag and slipped it back into her jacket pocket. Beyond the bathroom the crowd was surging, some of the people trying to push out into the parking lot, while others tried to get deeper inside. Torres couldn't see what was happening outside, but she should hear the rising cries. She knew the sound of fear.

"Okay, we need to get out of here and find Jimmy," she said, still straining on her toes to peer over people's heads. No use. She braced her feet against the bathroom doorframe and her back against the other side and shimmied up until she was nearly at the top. From there she could follow the helmeted heads of Duke's militia carving through the anxious travelers. Several of the baristas abandoned their posts, ducking into the back of their storefront, which meant there was probably a way out there. A backdoor for deliveries.

"We can get out through there." Torres pointed. Below her, Soraya held her younger child close. Miranda stood in the corner staring into the sink.

"Hey." Torres slid-walked down the doorframe. "Miranda, did you hear me?"

Miranda leaned forward, her forehead nearly touching the grimy mirror. She was making a low moaning-growling sound.

Soraya reached towards her shoulder but stopped short. She looked at Torres. "Does your friend suffer from epilepsy?"

"Not that I know of."

Gunshots from the parking lot and several screams. They needed to be moving. Staying still made them easier targets of whatever was happening outside.

Torres gently shook Miranda's shoulder. Without even looking at her, Miranda shoved her away. A few drops of blood rimmed Miranda's nostrils.

"We should go," Soraya said.

"Yeah." Torres tried to turn Miranda to get a better look at her, but again the young woman pushed her off.

"Leave. Me. Alone," the younger woman snarled.

A volley of shots rang out. They reminded Torres of the celebratory gunfire she'd witnessed in Iraq. Cheers rose from the din. Then the squall of a bullhorn: "This is the U.S. Customs and Border Patrol. You have been exposed to a highly contagious infection. Do not attempt to leave the area.”

Torres caught flashes of the rapidly emptying parking lot. It looked like a high school house party about when the police arrived.

A pair of buses were parked at the far end of the parking area. Cars and trucks raced away, some driving over the shoulder, a few going across the grass itself as they headed back to the highway. A camper had gotten stuck in the ditch and its driver and passengers burst out, scattering as they dodged past the militia, who’d been joined by agents wearing ICE windbreakers.

“They’re gone,” Miranda said, her voice low and strained. She sagged into a squat and folded forward, her head hanging between her knees.

“Who are gone?” Torres demanded.

“The Infected.” Miranda teetered and Torres put a hand on her shoulder to steady her.

“Allow me,” Soraya said. She knelt next to Miranda and pressed the back of her hand against the younger woman’s forehead. Miranda groaned. Dried blood covered her upper lip. When she opened her eyes, Torres gasped. They were bloodshot and fever bright.

“Is she sick?” Soraya asked.

“No,” Torres said. “No. She’s immune. We’re immune. We were vaccinated.” *Am I trying to convince Soraya or myself?*

“Lie down, miss.” Soraya coaxed and Miranda did. She lay down, without complaint, on the filthy floor of a public bathroom at a roadside rest stop. Miranda was not all right.

From the window of the ICE bus, Torres strained to catch a glimpse of Jimmy, but in the milling mass of angry and confused people, it was impossible.

As they had excited the bathroom, the ICE agents had directed them to the buses, their invitations backed up by batons and pepper spray. Between trying to keep Miranda upright and moving and keep hold of Elfy, Torres was not in a good position for any evasive maneuvers. Soraya trailed behind her, shadowed by her wraithlike boys.

The women and children had been jammed into the bus, with Miranda and Torres sharing a seat. Torres held Elfy on her lap. Soraya's youngest sat on hers, while the older boy huddled next to the window. From the rear of the bus, Torres could hear sobbing. Outside, one of the ICE agents tased a man who refused to get on the bus. When the woman he was with protested, the agent maced her in the face. Several groups broke away from the bus and bolted across the parking lot. Two of Duke's militia members took a couple shots at them before Duke screamed at them to stop. Luckily, the militia members were poor marksmen and the runners all escaped clean.

The last of the escaping vehicles had made it to the highway and taken off, likely spreading HHV in both directions.

"We need to get out of here," Torres muttered. Her chin rested on Elfy's sweaty head. The girl's hair still smelled like the baby shampoo Cynthia had last washed it with. After two days on the road, sleeping in the backseat of Jimmy's Audi, Elfy's hair no longer fell in shiny black waves. It clumped in ratty, oily knots.

"Undoubtedly," Soraya said. She turned Wahid's head so the younger boy couldn't watch what was happening outside.

Miranda slumped against the window, her eyes half-closed. Every few minutes, she wiped at her nose, which had already stopped bleeding.

The bus maneuvered through the mostly empty parking lot. Torres saw Jimmy's Audi parked in the grass along the exit. No sign of Jimmy. She patted her pocket, confirming the HK was still tucked safely inside.

The bus rejoined I-5, heading north.

Torres leaned forward and pulled out her phone. Half battery. She should have charged it in Jimmy's car. She looked around. Besides the driver there were four ICE agents on the bus. The two in back were chatting and laughing, while one of the ones in front talked on her phone and the other seemed to be asleep, his chin burrowed deep into his jacket, arms crossed over his chest. Torres held her phone low in her lap and sent John a text: *In ICE custody, heading N on I-5. How's Doc?* She didn't expect an immediate response. John was probably still in the air on the way to Montana. She turned the phone off and settled in to rest. There was no point wasting her energy until they had a better chance to escape.

Soraya shared sesame seed cakes and granola with Torres and Elfy. Miranda had fallen into a deep sleep.

After a couple of hours, the bus exited near a sign that read   GRANT'S   PASS   NATIONAL   FOREST

REVITALIZATION AREA. NO OVERNIGHT CAMPING. A makeshift camp was in the process of being built as they arrived. People in ICE windbreakers waved the bus to a rucked up grassy area that they seemed to be using as a parking lot. A few other buses had already parked and discharged their bewildered and angry passengers.

Torres shook Miranda awake. She blinked groggily and looked around. "Where are we?"

"Oregon." Torres said.

"Um, what?" Miranda pushed her hair back and wiped her nose.

"Everybody out, let's go!" yelled one of the ICE agents from the rear of the bus.

Torres, Soraya, Miranda, and the children shuffled out and joined the others from their bus. The guards herded them behind hastily erected metal barriers. They milled around for a few minutes. People were getting more and more frightened and angry. A rumor ran through the crowd that ICE intended to separate the children and deport the adults immediately.

"Nah, they going to shoot us," said a tall thin man with a fuzz of graying hair. He glared around nervously, his long neck extending and retracting like a bird's. "I been in the camps in Texas. They kept us all locked in and just let them young bucks have their way with the womens. You ladies should stay with me. You need a good man to take care of you, güera." He reached out to touch Miranda's hair. Torres slapped his hand away.

"No violence!" A booming voice squalled from a bullhorn. "Assault will not be tolerated." A pinch faced woman in an ICE jacket glared directly at Torres.

She stepped away from the man, pulled Elfy and Miranda with her so there were a few people between him and their group. Soraya followed, flitting through the crowd, her boys trailing after.

"First chance we get, we're gone," Torres told Soraya.

"Most definitely." She nodded, reached to adjust her hijab and realized it wasn't there. "In the meanwhile, shall we remove temptation?"

"Huh?"

Soraya waved at Miranda's long, brunette hair. Torres's normally shaggy bob cut, the same one she'd sported since Boot, had grown out to nearly shoulder length.

"What about you?" Torres asked. Soraya's hair was a thick, glossy dark mane.

"Regrettably, this will all have to go." She drew a pair of scissors out of her bag and offered it. Torres took it and gathered Soraya's hair. It felt like heavy silk. She cut it at the base of the other woman's head, leaving her with long bangs. Then she scooped Soraya's hair into fistfuls and cut off any that stuck out over her hand.

"I'm afraid to ask, but how do I look?" Soraya tried to smile as she brushed prickly strands out of her face.

"Less fuckable?" Torres handed her the scissors. "Exact your revenge."

"I shall."

Torres bent her head and listened to the snipping, watched clumps of her own hair fall like black rain.

When Soraya was done, Torres turned to Elfy. "Your turn."

"No!" Elfy wrapped her arms around her head. "Mama's going to get me pink stripes."

"Too bad. Turn around." Torres pushed the girl's shoulder.

"No! I don't wanna." Elfy tried to wrench away. There was no safe way to cut her hair with her squirming.

"Hold still, you ..." By force of will, Torres unclenched her jaw. "Elfy, this is to keep you safe. Hold still."

Soraya squatted in front of Elfy and reached out to stroke back her bangs. "My, your hair is lovely." Elfy froze. "Do you know, it reminds me of my daughters' hair. So long and pretty."

"Yeah, and my mama's gonna let me get pink stripes." Elfy beamed, then she frowned. "Where are your girls, Mrs. Soraya?"

"Here." Soraya reached out and touched Wahid and Meraj. Torres looked more closely at the 'boys.' She'd taken their delicate features as something related to their Middle Eastern ancestry. Now, she could see they were girls, the older one hiding the beginnings of her womanly features in shapeless male attire. The younger one still had the coltish androgyny of childhood.

"This is Mirzha." Soraya touched her older daughter's shoulder. "And Wahida." She patted the smaller girl's head.

"Hello," Wahida smiled, revealing she had lost her two front teeth.

"Salam," Mirzha said solemnly.

"You're girls?" Elfy blinked.

"Yes, they are," Soraya said. "We cut their hair so they would be safe. May I cut your hair? I'm quite certain your mother can still get you pink stripes later."

Elfy frowned, looked from Soraya to Torres and back. "Fine," she said.

When Torres held up the scissor to Miranda, the younger woman shook her head. "I'll find a baseball cap or something."

"Seriously?" Torres half-snapped, half-laughed. Of all the hills to die on.

"Seriously." Miranda twisted her hair up and stabbed a pen through the bun to hold it in place. "Honestly, it's super messed up that you think *we* should have to do this. Like, don't expect men to not rape or anything. Just cut your hair and if you don't, it must be your fault, right?"

"What?" Torres blinked in confusion.

"It's victim-blaming and it's bullshit," Miranda said. "I'm not cutting my hair. Don't like it? Feel free to leave me."

Torres gave her head a little shake and stared at her feet. The ground was dry, the grass a green so faint it barely qualified. Miranda was as terrified as she was, if not more so. It was easier to be angry than scared, but blaming the younger woman for her mother's decision to pick Cynthia—again ... as always—wasn't fair and it wouldn't help either of them.

"It's fine. It's not a big deal." Torres forced a light, reassuring tone. What would Courage have done? He always knew how to handle Miranda.

Soraya patted the younger woman's shoulder and Miranda gave a tight-lipped smile. Progress—of a sort.

After the haircuts, Torres turned Elfy's Dora backpack inside out to hide its bright girly pink. She agreed with Miranda in principle, but she also believed in being a hard target in practicality. She slipped the HK into her waistband, ignoring the captain's voice in her head. He'd never let them do something as stupid as carrying their weapons 'movie style.' But Courage wasn't here and she had nowhere else to hide the piece.

Afternoon turned to evening. The girls were hungry, thirsty, and tired. So were the women. So was everyone else. They heard more and more fights, saw a couple. As more and more people arrived, they had to keep moving to stay near the edge of the crowd.

Torres and Soraya took turns watching the girls and napping. Miranda traded her Chapstick for a wool beanie cap that made her look like she was trying out to be a pro skateboarder. Mirzha and Wahida taught Elfy a Persian game that involved a song with specific hand gestures, claps, and little dance steps.

Torres was dozing when she heard the scream. It was different from the shouts of previous fights. Someone was genuinely panicked. She scrambled up, hand at the small of her back, finger on the HK's reassuring grip.

They only had to wait a few minutes before the rumor mill of the crowd brought the news.

"They found someone who's infected." An aging hippy with dreads to her waist leaned over her shoulder to pass the message.

"Infected? What are their symptoms?" Torres demanded.

The hippy shrugged and held up a jar of dark brownish liquid. "Chai?"

"No ..." Torres wasn't sure what was in that jar and didn't want to gamble it was free of all natural 'extras.'

"If the Infected are here, we need to make a run for it," Torres said. "You can't believe how freaking fast they are. Don't let them bite you. That's how HHV's spreads."

"They're here," Miranda said softly. She stared out over the crowd.

Their group was already near the edge of the camp. The ICE teams were still working to rig up flood lights and flimsy chain-link fences. Border guards clustered near the unfenced areas.

"I have a plan." Torres shook Elfy awake, ignored her hungry grumbling, and hoisted the child onto her hip.

Torres remembered riot training. She had stood in the line with her fellow grunts, sweating and straining under the weight of their gear, waiting for the "mob" of professional role-players to get unruly. The funny thing about mobs was that a pretty small number of organized, trained and armed people could keep a really big number of rioters in check. During training she had learned about deploying large scale suppression resources, a fancy way of saying the water cannons and strobe lights equipped with sounds to make people nauseated. The ICE camp didn't seem to have any anti-riot gear, or at least none at the ready. Their bad.

Torres carried Elfy, followed by Miranda, Soraya and her girls, into the middle of the crowd. There was a set of bleachers, already piled with the trash people leave when they don't care about who has to pick it up. Used diapers, food wrappers, broken flip-flops, hats, sunglasses, even a used condom.

Seriously? At a time like this? Gross! Well, at least they're using protection.

"Keep the girls under the bleachers." Torres set Elfy

down and pointed to the space sheltered by metal struts. "If this works, there'll be a crowd surge." Unless the bleachers got tipped over, they were in the best partial cover she could find.

"What are you doing?" Miranda asked as Soraya herded the girls inside the bleachers.

"Getting us out of here," Torres said. She started to climb to the top, but Miranda grabbed her wrist.

"I'm not a kid." *Like them,* she didn't say, but both women knew what she meant.

"I know, which is why we're going to have a serious grown-up talk about what the fuck happened back at the rest stop."

Miranda's mouth clamped shut hard.

"That's what I thought," Torres said. "Can you just hang out with Soraya and don't let any more of my family members wander off this time?" As soon as she said it, Torres regretted it, regretted the gut-punched look on Miranda's face. "Miranda, I —"

"Fuck you." Miranda ducked below the bleachers and stalked away.

Briefly, Torres considered going after her. No. Around them the crowd washed back and forth in uneasy eddies, crashing against the gates, the guards, and each other. People were scared. The guards were nervous. There wasn't time for the kind of intense showdown that she needed to have with Miranda.

The former Marine climbed up to the top of the bleachers, threading her way between the tired, sweaty, angry, dehydrated internees. Neither Doc Marius nor Captain Courage would agree with what she was about to do. Marius would come up with some elegant, brainy solution that ended with the guards shaking his hand and thanking him. Courage would find some means to recruit until they could either fight or sneak their way out. But neither of them were there. It was just Torres, Miranda, Soraya, and the girls. Torres did a few tactical breaths.

"They can't hold us," she yelled. Heads turned in her direction. People shaded their eyes from the late afternoon sun's glare. "This is a violation of our rights. We're Americans!" More people were staring at her. Normally, she hated to be the center of attention, but there was no stopping now.

"They're going to keep us locked in here with the Infected. They're going to let us all die." Torres could see people relaying her words to the folks in the cheap seats. At the edge of the camp, the guards had started to cluster up, pointing at her. *Let's hope they don't have a sniper.*

"Shut up! Stop trying to scare people, you bitch!" a man yelled from the crowd.

"They should be scared. I've seen HHV. We have to get out of here."

"You'll spread it," called a woman.

"This isn't a quarantine. Open your eyes. There are no medical people here. They're just rounding everyone up, like Nazis," Torres screamed back, her voice nearly breaking. "If we stay, we die."

A group of guards had donned their helmets and pushed their way into the crowd, headed her way, batons ready for the ass whipping they planned to administer.

"Let us out! Let us out! Let us out!" Torres pumped her fist in the air in time with her words. With her other hand, she waved at the people on the bleachers to join in. At first no one moved. *I'm going to look butt-stupid.* Then a woman jumped to her feet. "Let us out!" she yelled.

Another man, two more. A group of teenagers. An old couple with matching baseball caps. More and more people rose, fists in the air, yelling.

Torres pointed, a big, overly dramatic telenovela stab of arm and quivering finger at the approaching guards. "They're coming to silence me. Free speech! Free speech!"

The crowd took up her chant. As the guards tried to shove their way towards the former Marine, people started pushing back. The guards were getting broken up, separated. A big no-go in riot suppression. Never let yourself get cut off from your team. Retreat if necessary. Don't let them drag you out, drag you down. You won't get up.

Torres's stomach knotted. Most of those guards were probably just people doing what they thought they had to in order to protect their homes and families. On the other hand, they'd made it into an either-you-or-me scenario and she wasn't going to just tap out.

"They brought us here with no food, no water, no bathrooms. They don't care about us." Torres wished she could take a swig from the canteen in the Dora bag. Her throat ached. Below the crowd was roiling, boiling, looking for a target for their fear and anger.

"They're trying to fence us in like animals. We need to escape. Scatter. Get the hell out." A group of men pushed past several ICE officials and started shaking the chain-link fencing. Soon other people joined them. The whole fence swayed back and forth, bucking and twisting like a pinned snake. The guards in the crowd had realized too late they were in trouble. People were yanking and shoving them, spitting and swearing and kicking at them.

Then the inevitable. One of the guards pulled his weapon. The sound of the shot was muffled by the chants of *Get out! Get out!* Torres could see an opening around the guard. A woman lay on the ground, clutching her leg. Her mouth was open in a scream Torres couldn't hear. *I'm sorry. I caused this. I had to.*

Like water rushing back in after a wave breaks, the crowd around the guard surged forward. Torres didn't know how many more shots he fired before he disappeared. The chanting was breaking down into screams, yells, gunshots, the mad roar of a mob.

Something punched Torres's shoulder. She turned with the impact, lost her footing on the metal bleachers and sat down hard. She looked down and saw a hole, black, about half the size of the ball of her thumb. As she watched a bubble of red appeared, swelled and popped. The blood flowed down over her chest. It wasn't gushing, but it was enough to soak her shirt in a matter of seconds. She pressed her hand to the wound and smiled. *All those deployments and I get shot in freaking Oregon.*

Soraya and Miranda were under the bleachers. They probably hadn't seen Torres get shot. She scooted sideways to put the metal railing strut between herself and the shooter.

"Here, let me look." A woman in a pastel pink polo shirt squatted next to Torres. Her expensively dyed hair, pink pearl earrings and matching necklace, and complete lack of concern for personal space screamed, 'Doctor!'

Voices blasted from bullhorns. The ICE guards tried to reestablish order to no avail. Torres was too good of an agent of chaos. The crowd howled, a rolling wave of panic and rage that crashed through the fence and washed out into the mountains.

Dr. Okeke pushed open the door to the ICE aid station. Torres and Miranda nearly tumbled inside. Soraya reached to catch the former Marine, but Miranda hooked her arm around Torres's ribs and pushed her back against the door. Soraya beckoned for Mirzha to bring her a chair, which she wedged under the doorknob. Wahida and Elfy held hands, their eyes wide. For once, Elfy seemed speechless. Torres skinned back her lips in a grin of humor and pain.

"Sit." Dr. Okeke pointed to the canvas cot, probably intended to treat people with heat exhaustion, not gunshot victims, even if they had brought it on themselves. Miranda helped Torres lower herself onto the cot. She tried to hold her left side completely still. The pain struck like lightning through her body whenever she moved too much.

Dr. Okeke ransacked the aid station, collection tools and bandages, ointments, and painkillers. "Take these." Torres took them. "They'll kick in soon, but we shouldn't wait." Dr. Okeke poked at the hole in Torres's shoulder with merciless curiosity. She barely kept herself from punching the woman in the throat.

"Torres?"

The former Marine turned slowly, babying her side.

Jimmy stood up from behind a stack of boxes and crates. He had a black eye, but otherwise looked okay.

"Jimmy! Where the fuck have you been, you asshole?" Torres winced as a crackle of pain shot through her.

"The bullet is still in there. Looks like a .22, so good luck there, eh?" Dr. Okeke said. *Don't hit the doctor.* "We need to get it out before it does more damage. You should lie down."

"Jimmy's a medic. He can help," Torres said. She leaned back and Miranda helped her position herself on her side.

"No," Jimmy said. He hadn't moved from his spot.

"Why the hell not? You're our medic, brother. Get over here." Torres was about to make a joke about how he could finally get inside her but looked at Elfy and Wahida. *Nope. Be good.*

Jimmy pushed up the sleeve of his shirt, revealing his forearm. Two red crescent moon wounds, haloed by tendrils of black veins, like some evil corona.

"Shit," Torres hissed. Not Jimmy. Jimmy was one of them. One of the survivors. "But you got vaccinated!" She hurled it at him like an accusation. How dare he get infected!

He nodded. "Yeah ... The Helatek vaccine isn't based on Marius's antibodies. They couldn't risk using it while it was still under investigation, so they used a different one, something they got from Carmine."

"But everyone knows Carmine's an idiot. Why didn't they use the good vaccine?" Torres struggled to understand. Jimmy was infected. He'd been on Christmas leave when the Chrysalis outbreak happened.

"Yeah," Jimmy said. He looked around, blinked fast a couple of times.

"Hey, we need to do this," Dr. Okeke said. She snipped away part of Torres's shirt. *I probably look like some redneck with a homemade wife-beater sleeveless shirt.* Dr. Okeke pushed and prodded at Torres' shoulder. The former Marine grabbed the cot frame with her good hand and hung on, squeezing so hard she could feel the metal edges dig into her skin. She focused on the pain in her hand.

Finally, Dr. Okeke stopped. Torres drew a shuddering breath. Her lip was bleeding. She didn't remember biting it.

"And now the painful part," Dr. Okeke said in a bright, chippy voice. *Don't hit the doctor!*

"That wasn't the painful part?" Torres grunted.

"Nope, just assessing where the bullet is. I'm pretty sure I can get it out without tearing any major arteries."

"Pretty sure?" Torres closed her eyes.

"Or we could do nothing and hope it stays put." Dr. Okeke leaned back.

"No," Jimmy said. "Lourdes, it needs to come out."

"I know. Just a sec." Torres took a couple breaths. "Jimmy, tell me about Carmine. How did he come up with a vaccine? How did they not test it to be sure it worked?" She needed to be pissed. She wanted to ride her anger through the pain.

She barely heard Jimmy as he started to explain. After a couple seconds she couldn't help it. She screamed. Dr. Okeke froze. Elfy burst into tears. Torres grabbed the tail of her shirt and stuffed it into her mouth. She nodded to Dr. Okeke. Miranda knelt next to the cot and held out a hand. Torres took it and squeezed. Hard.

Chapter 8

SHIT!

OK, got that out of my system. My hands are shaking. I can hear the guards yelling inside. The patient we were trying to help is dead, and so am I. He bit me.

I've thought about this a lot, ever since I heard of Dr. Samuel Katz. He developed the measles vaccine and tested it on himself. He was willing to die because he thought it would save lives. Would I be willing to risk my life for a patient's?

The worst thing is, my contracting HHV won't save the patient. He's dead. The guards shot him after he bit me. Great timing, guys. They left one guard to watch me, to shoot me when ... yeah.

I don't feel afraid. I feel detached. I must be in denial. No, I'm not!

I wanted to do so much. I wanted my life and my death to mean something. Which brings me to the journal. Although I never would have wanted my contribution to medicine to take this form, here it is. I can document step by step, the symptoms of HHV.

Time since exposure: 15 minutes. Symptoms: None.

TSE: 30 min. Symptoms: Fever, hunger, dehydration, mild anxiety. What if I can't properly describe my symptoms? What if no one finds my journal?

TSE: 1 hour. Symptoms: Fever, hunger, dehydration, agitation and

NOTE: The following was written by L. Torres, on behalf of J. Lennox.

I found Jimmy about an hour after he was bitten. I was traveling with others, who are waiting in one of the abandoned buses. Jimmy has a fever, he's hungry, but refuses to eat. He said, "According to Marius's observation, HHV uses the body's energy to fuel mutation. Maybe I can slow it down by not eating." He paces, looks at my pack. There's no food in it. He looks at me.

Jimmy fell asleep for about 45 minutes. He tossed and turned, mumbled, sweated, and farted a lot. It reeks in here! He woke up and asked for food, but then said,

"Don't give me any food. What the fuck is wrong with you?" I didn't have any food and I hadn't said I would give him any. He sits on the edge of his cot and glares at me, grinding his teeth. I lean against my corner, Jimmy's own HK in my hand. He won't take me with him.

Jimmy tried to escape, so I shot him in the leg. I should have killed him. If I was a nice person, I would have, but before he went crazy, he made me promise to keep him alive as long as he could talk. He can still talk, but I wonder how helpful anything he says now will be. Most of it is just swearing and calling me names.

Jimmy's GSW is healing ... kind of. There's a big purple bruise on his leg. I can see it because he ripped his pants off below the knee to show me what I did to him. It looks like a kid traced dark purple lightning lines on his leg. I guess those are his veins or arteries or vessels. The wound is closed, which is amazing, since my shoulder GSW still hurts like a motherfucker. I bet you future science people will edit that out.

Jimmy has grown a weird mini-leg from his GSW. He went back to sleep for about 15 minutes and when he woke up, it was there. His face looks thin, like he's sucking in his cheeks.

Jimmy said, "I feel better. I think I'm over the worst of it." I tossed him a thermometer. His temperature is 107.5. I asked him if that's normal. "Nope. It's boiling my brain." He smiled at me. His gums are bleeding. The whites of his eyes are red. "It's like Ebola but the blood stays in," Jimmy says. "My whole body is a sack of viral plague, liquifying from the inside. I can feel my pancreas." He kneads his right side. From my combat training, I know this is his kidney. "It's squishy. Come feel it." I stay put. Jimmy tries to get up, falls off his cot. I hear a snap. He sits up on the floor. He holds out his left arm. It has two elbow bends now. He smiles. "See, it doesn't even hurt." I tell him to stay back.

It's been about three hours since I found Jimmy. He wants to sleep. I wake him every five minutes. "Hey. Jimmy?" I yell until I get a response. I ask him about his symptoms. Here's what he said: "I'm not afraid anymore. I know we'll be together. They're waiting for me to join them."

Jimmy hasn't said anything for 30 minutes. I've yelled and screamed. I've thrown things at him. He lies on the ground. I think he pissed and shitted (shat?) himself. It smells like a camel's ass in here. Will have to burn my clothes. There's a pool of goo on the floor around Jimmy. Some is his blood from his broken arm and his GSW.

Jimmy tried to attack me. I shot him in the shoulder and the gut.

There's only his head and chest left. His arms are boneless tentacles, but they're not strong enough to lift him. He's still got one leg, but the other is splitting from the GSW entry point up toward his crotch. He stares at the ceiling. He's humming. It's fucking freaky!

It's been five hours. Jimmy turned his head to look at me. His teeth are broken and bloody from snapping and grinding them. His eyes have a pinkish film over them. One of his ears fell off. Just plop, there it went. He didn't even notice. The floor is covered in that pink slime. It smells like a butcher's shop.

I recorded this on my phone. Here's what Jimmy said: We had a good run. It doesn't hurt anymore.

Torres, I'll miss you. Did you write it all down? (I say "Yes") Good. We have to find him. Do you know where he is? (I say "Who?") Marius. He can fix this, can't he? (I say "Yes, but he's probably in Montana with his family") We knew it. (He's quiet for a few minutes. I think he's dead) Hey! Look at that!

He cries. His tears are white with flecks of reddish purple, like blood in milk. He seizes. After a while he's still. No breathing. I watch and count to thirty, sixty, ninety. I get up and go over, weapon ready. He opens his eyes. They're completely black.

"I see you, Torres."

I shoot him in the face.

Torres and the others buried Jimmy on an Oregon hillside, overlooking a hazelnut orchard.

The only grave maker Torres could find was a faded STOP sign, which she stuck on top of his grave:

JAMES LENNOX

Medic, Team Member, Friend

He died as he lived, trying to make the world a better place.

Chapter 9 – Marius

The car had stopped moving. Marius blinked. Inside the hood, it was dark and so humid the air felt like a damp cloth draped over his face. His own respirations crashed around him as he strained to hear the sound of footsteps outside the trunk. Last time they had stopped, the man hadn't let him out of the trunk. He'd opened it and lifted the hood enough for Marius to gulp too little water.

From the few words the man had spoken, Marius had been able to gather that he had an Irish accent and sounded middle aged. Not much to go on, considering the scientist had long ago lost track of time, distance, and direction of travel. No point trying to contact the cavalry; he wouldn't have been able to tell them where to look.

Before shoving Marius into the trunk, the kidnapper had snipped off his ankle monitor. He figured that by the time anyone got around to triangulating the monitor in the hospital's parking garage, he was already hundreds of miles away.

It didn't help that the kidnapper had laced the water with something. A sweetish tang that clung to Marius's tongue and settled deep in his belly. It was probably nothing stronger than an over-the-counter sleep-aid, but it was enough to keep him asleep for most of the trip. When he did manage to wake up, he felt dazed and hungover. He'd been able to discover that his feet were zip-tied together, as were his hands, but other than that he'd been left to his own devices in the trunk of a car speeding ... somewhere.

The trunk latch gave with a soft *click* and the hinges and springs creaked as the lid opened. Marius pushed himself into a half upright position. His body ached from being coiled in the trunk, especially his back and legs.

"And here he is. A sight to behold, eh?" The kidnapper sounded jovial. He grabbed Marius under the arms and hoisted him out of the trunk, holding him steady until he could stand to put weight on his legs and feet. Marius groaned, biting his lip to keep back the sobs of pain as the blood rushed back into his legs and feet. Two people picked him up and carried him out of the echoey space into one that was quieter. Out of a garage? Must be, he thought.

The hood was yanked off. Marius gasped, squeezed

his eyes shut against the stabbing light. They were in a bright room, probably an office, but he couldn't see for the tears. Through squinted eyes, he glimpsed the guards as they half-carried, half-dragged him to an exam table.

"What did you do to him? This isn't a 'dead or alive' kind of thing, Liam. Helatek wants him fully functional. They're not paying for him to be chemically lobotomized." The voice sounded like a woman's, with the tone of command Marius had come to associate with C-level people and their direct underlings.

"Whist," Liam said. He ruffled Marius's hair and chuckled when the scientist raised clumsy hands to bat at him. "He's grand. Just needs a bit of sleep and he'll be right as rain."

"We'll see," the woman said. She wore a lab coat over a red blouse and charcoal skirt. Next to her, Liam looked like a goon in his T-shirt and dark tracksuit. As Marius had suspected, Liam had a pasty complexion with hair the color of blood tinted urine. The guards who had brought Marius in lounged near the door. They wore identical black and grey mottled fatigues with the red and white Helatek eagle patch on their shoulders.

The place looked enough like Chrysalis's old facility that Marius had no trouble believing his former employers' former greatest rival corporation was behind his extraordinary recruitment. The walls and ceiling were medical grade off-white, the countertops thermoformed nonporous slabs with integrated sinks in an unassuming palette of ash grey and gunmetal blue. Cabinets were marked and each displayed a list of their contents. It was the kind of doctor's office that was often toured by key investors, but rarely used for the actual practice of medicine.

"You can wait over there." The woman waved toward two chairs in the far corner of the room.

"Yes, mam. I mean, yes, em ... Now is it Chan-Juan or just Chan?"

"It's doctor and Chan is fine."

Chan gave Marius a quick once over. "Well," she said with a deep frown, "he seems to be in decent shape. We had planned to sedate him for transport. I'm told it's disturbing. However, we won't be able to do that now because we can't risk a detrimental drug interaction, can we?"

Liam gave a half shrug. "Not my problem, my girl."

"I'm not your girl," Chan said. "I'm sure you can find your own way out. Good night, Mr. Trimble."

"I'm not going anywhere with you," Marius announced. He was trying to keep up, he really was, but all he wanted to do was lie down on the soft exam table, stretch out, and sleep. He knew he should be trying to escape. John would have already escaped. Probably five or six times just because he wanted the practice.

"I'll be after my money and then he's all yours." Liam ignored Marius.

Chan put her hands on her hips. "Do I look like Accounts Receivable?"

A slow leer split Liam's face as he looked her up and down. "Wouldn't rule it out. I'd love to see your dividends."

"Get out," Chan said. Her voice was soft and perfectly controlled, but her eyes sparked. The guards pushed themselves off the wall.

Liam held up his hands. "Come off it. Just a bit of fun, eh. No need for this whole thing to get banjaxed up over a little misunderstanding then."

Chan strode across the room until she was almost nose to nose with Liam, a feat considering she was nearly a foot shorter than him. Slowly, she looked him up and down. She reached out and drew a cigarette out of the pack in Liam's breast pocket and held out a hand to the guards, never taking her eyes off the kidnapper.

"Would I be wrong in surmising that if I asked either of these fine folks to put a bullet in your brain that not only would no one miss you," she lit the cigarette, "but there's a good chance more than a few people would send me 'Thank You' notes?"

"Calm yourself, woman," Liam said with a forced grin. "T'was only a joke for which I'm eternally sorry."

Chan blew smoke in his face. "Even though I'm not Accounts Receivable, it occurs to me that the cost of a bullet and discrete burial would be better for Helatek's bottom line than your finder's fee."

Liam narrowed his eyes, glancing from one guard to the other. Again, he held up his hands in a Don't Shoot gesture. "Why don't I just leave on my own steam, then? I can contact Carmine about setting all the pretty paperwork to rights at a later date. No need to trouble yourself further."

Before Chan could respond, Liam ducked out the door. The guards started after him but she coughed and shook her head and they returned to their previous positions.

"What a delightful man," Chan said. She turned back to Marius. "So, you're him, huh? Marius Tenartier of the natural immunity. Dr. Anino is very excited to renew your collaboration. He thinks there's a lot you can do to help Helatek with the HHV vaccine."

The last time Marius had seen Dr. Carmine Anino, he'd chased him down a hall and shot a flare gun at him. From the smirk on Carmine's face, nothing had been forgotten, let alone forgiven.

As Carmine opened his mouth to speak, Marius said, "I'm not sure what you think kidnapping me is going to accomplish. Take all the blood you want. It's never going to transform you into a decent virologist."

Carmine's eyes narrowed. "Get the bats ready."

Chan started and glared at him. "He's a company asset, not your personal ..." She trailed off.

"Your concerns are noted, Dr. Chan." Carmine opened the door leading deeper into the facility. "Have a good evening."

Chan paused in the doorway. "I don't like to repeat myself, but as I told that mercenary fellow, Viers wants Dr. Tenartier alive. When I left, he was alive. I suggest you don't alter that state."

Carmine pantomimed a salute and waved. Chan shook her head and walked out.

Viers? Viers was still alive? Marius had left his former boss trapped in the Chrysalis quarantine unit. He had assumed Viers had died along with the rest of the Infected when the National Guard firebombed the site. But he hadn't.

Carmine shut the door and turned to Marius,

smirking.

"How did Viers survive?" Marius blurted out. Carmine liked to brag and show off. Maybe he would start talking and Marius could —

Carmine hit him. An open hand strike to the ear. It wasn't hard, but Marius hadn't expected it. He was still groggy from whatever Liam had given him. He fell off the exam table, more out of shock than pain.

Carmine tipped his head, pouting his lower lip. "Aww, are we sorry now, bro?"

Neither of the guards looked keen to interfere. How badly would Carmine hurt him? Would he kill him? Marius wished he'd paid more attention to John and Torres when they'd talked about surviving capture and resisting torture. He'd always thought it was pointless paranoia. Until they'd been held by the US government. But even that hadn't been awful. Mostly, his time in detention had been incredibly boring, which had been its own form of torture.

The next while was a haze of trying to curl into a protective ball as Carmine hit, kicked, elbowed, kneed, and spit on him. Whenever Marius tried to do more than passively defend himself, the guards would push him down or hold him back.

At some point they dragged Marius out of the room, into an elevator, and then out onto a rooftop. The night was cool and the air sagged with the moisture it had picked up from the Pacific. Mist curled around the low hills and licked through the folds and valleys of what looked like wine country.

Through his split lip, Marius smiled. As John might say, a good place to die. At least the view was nice.

The guards dropped him into a pile of pain and wandered off to smoke and grunt.

Carmine squatted in front of Marius. He shaded his eyes as if it were bright out and looked around. "Any minute now, bro. Just wait. It's a sight."

Something moved in the sky, shapes heaving and twisting against the wind toward the building. Marius tried to lean back on his heels to get a clear view. One eye was swollen shut and he had to keep blinking blood out of the other.

The creatures loomed larger, like gargoyles out of a dusty old medieval legend. Before Marius could get a clear view, they dropped below the level of the roof's parapet. The wall shook with the impact of them hitting it.

Had they crashed?

Marius suppressed a hysterical bark of laughter. All Carmine's big talk, and his Infected had smashed into the side of a building like a pair of befuddled pigeons.

The Infected could move shockingly fast, their bodies awash in adrenalin. Two of them burst up and over the edge of the roof, like a pair of Olympic pole vaulters, but covered in cankerous sores, tentacles, and teeth. They were about four feet tall with huge, leathery, bat-like wings, which snapped open spanning 25-30 feet. They hooked their clawed feet around the railing and used their momentum to swing over.

Carmine scrambled back, then stopped. He held out a trembling hand toward the bat Infecteds. One reached a tentacle and wrapped it over his hand, wrist, and up his arm. Carmine shuddered and whimpered. Beside Marius, the guards hadn't actually retreated, but they were leaning as far away as they could without moving their feet.

The bat Infected waddled forward, using its forelimbs to support it as it advanced. Its head swung back and forth, giving Marius a view of its empty eye sockets. It paused to sniff the guards, then Marius. The bat peeled back its lips, revealing at least three rows of needle sharp teeth. It pulled back its upper lip, lifted its tongue and sniffed, again. A deep, resonating sound rumbled in its chest. The other bat Infected gave a high-pitched squeal and skittered forward. This one had fever-bright eyes, red rimmed and staring. Ulcerated patches of flesh showed through its matted fur where it must have scratched itself raw, under its wings, along its neck. It gave a high-pitched series of sharp clicks and squeaks. The other responded in kind.

The bat in front of Marius grabbed him so fast that his head snapped back. His shins hit the railing. The Infected wrapped several tentacles, each about a foot or so thick, around Marius's upper torso. It squeezed so hard Marius was sure his ribs would pop or break completely. He tried going limp. That worked with some predators.

The bat carrying Marius flapped its wings a few times, as if testing the air. Through all their maneuvering and smashing around, Marius managed to wiggle an arm free. He jabbed at the Infected's face, aiming for the eye. It hissed and yanked its head back. Again, it opened its mouth, and this time Marius could see a long, flexing spike, like a prehensile tongue. The bat reared back its head and then flashed forward, driving the spike into his shoulder.

Bursts of pain followed by numbness spread from the wound. Marius could hear Carmine and the guards yelling, but the sound seemed to be getting fainter and fainter. He fell back onto the roof, unable to move, staring up at the dusky sky, at the low clouds.

The bat took a couple of hopping steps and squatted over Marius. It was actually purring, then it began to gag and hump its shoulders, like a cat working on a hairball.

It was going to puke on him and he couldn't move.

The vomit was steaming and sticky, more viscous than honey, with bloody fibrous ropes mixed into it. As soon as it hit the air it began to harden. The bat Infected was cocooning him!

Far away, he heard a woman yell, maybe Dr. Chan. A piercing high-pitched screech filled the air from the other Infected bat.

Marius tried to yell, to move, to breathe, to think, to do something, anything. The numbness became paralysis. Then it was greyness turning to blackness. He lost consciousness.

They flew, at least Marius thought they did. He rocked in the grip of the cocoon, each breath a struggle to force his chest to move. There were a few thin places where the outside air reached his skin. It felt moist and cold; thin. High altitude. The motion, up and down, up and down, he could interpret as beating wings. Sometimes the motion was smoother, wide circling climbs and long glides as the bat Infected used thermals to speed their passage along.

He passed out a couple times as the air got too thin. How high were they flying? Over the Sierra Nevadas? The Klamath Mountains? The Cascades? Marius wished he'd paid more attention to orology or geology or, at least, geography.

Sometime late the next night, the bat Infected carrying Marius circled lower and lower. With a bone-jarring impact it dropped him. He rolled a couple of times and then hit something. Whatever venom the bat had injected him with had started to wear off. Tingling was replacing the numbness that had spread through his body. Marius tried to move his fingers, his hands.

Something grabbed him and ripped open the back of the cocoon. A sudden stabbing pain at the back of his neck. Had it bitten him? No, the pain was a sharp jab, not a tearing sensation. A needle?

Sure enough, Marius felt himself falling again. The last thing he was aware of was the sound of guttural speech, gravelly harsh consonants and nasal vowels mixed with clicks and grunts. The Infected were talking. That couldn't be a good sign.

Pain. Pain was what Marius knew. It raced up and down his nerves, gripped his heart and squeezed his lungs. Pain throbbed and pounded his brain to mush inside his skull. It made every movement into screaming agony and every moment of stillness into the maddening need to move, to struggle, to escape the pain.

Sometimes they came to look at him. Marius couldn't be sure of anything about them. They might have had odd numbers of eyes and limbs, or he might have been delirious. They might have talked to him or only about him. He tried to beg, but mostly he made small whimpering sounds or gasps. Marius was not one of John's stone-cold killers capable of resisting terrorist torture. He knew without a doubt that he would have sold out anyone if only they'd asked him to.

They didn't. They didn't seem to want anything from him other than to make him suffer.

And so Marius suffered until one day he didn't. He didn't really sleep, more passed out and woke up, then passed out again. Finally, there came a time where he woke without every fiber of his being trying to twist itself free of his husk.

He hung, trembling with relief and fear. Having the pain gone was blissful and terrifying. What if they started again? He would do anything they wanted if only they wouldn't hurt him again. Please, please, don't start again.

A sound, something other than ragged breathing — that was him. That and the soft mindless moaning. Marius realized he had been making that sound, too, and stopped. His head was clearing. His body shook as tensed muscles relaxed. His lungs filled to capacity and his heart slowed its frantic pace.

Marius opened his eyes and immediately closed them. The room he was in was dimly lit, but even that weak light was too much.

How long had he been there?

"Marius." The voice was soft, feminine, halfway between a growl and purr. *Marius.* His name. He was Marius. He was something more than a vessel of agony.

Marius tried to speak, coughed, spit. The drool ran down his chin. He didn't mind. To feel something, anything other than the torment, was its own kind of salvation. He had nearly forgotten that other sensations existed.

"You shouldn't fight them. You can't win." The voice was closer.

Marius slit his eyes and made out the wavery figure in front of him. She had long filament strands growing out of her head in place of hair. They shifted and moved gently around her as if she was underwater. Several reached out and brushed his face so lightly he could hardly perceive their touch.

Taking stock of his situation, the scientist found he was in a cocoon on a wall. As Marius flexed his body, reacquainting himself with parts that had previously been only sources of misery, he realized there were things inserted into his spine. They ran from the base of his skull to his tailbone, tiny tubes like IVs had bored into his spinal column or into the joining spots for major nerves. No wonder he had been in so much pain.

"Can you speak? It's important you speak." The woman sounded frightened. "They want you alive. I am to get you ready. You must speak!"

Marius cleared my throat. "Where …?" It was a croak, but his vocal cords were his own once again. Little victories.

"Portland." Something soft and damp touched his neck. Marius shuddered. "I'm Reyka," she said. "I work for the Enlightened."

"The Enlightened?" He squinted around. The room was small and circular. Several cocoons hung from the wall. One held a desiccated corpse. The others were empty. One looked like it had been torn apart from the outside. Blood and viscera decorated the walls around it. There was no evidence of any effort to clean up the mess.

"Yes, they came to us. Some of us have joined them. Others need to be purified before we can join. They know when we are ready." Reyka lowered her voice. "They knew everything. There are *no* secrets, there is no escape."

"There's a vaccine —" Marius started. She slapped him.

"No. There is nothing that can fight them." Reyka sank back onto her heels, her eyes darting around the ceiling. Marius followed her gaze.

The ceiling was covered with a fleshy pink membrane. Long tendrils sprouted from the membrane. They were almost clear, with ribbing of grayish material, resembling human trachea. Most ran horizontally across the ceiling, while others dangled from strands of pinkish tissue, raising and lowering themselves seemingly at will.

"What the ...?" Marius frowned as one of the tendrils reached towards Reyka. It moved with slow deliberation, turning this way and that as if tracking her by scent. As it got closer, he could see there was a small mouth, for lack of a better word, in the end of the tendril. It was more like a lamprey's sucker, filled with needle teeth.

The tendril touched Reyka's shoulder. She let out a long sob but otherwise didn't move or react. With frightening speed, the tendril whipped around and clamped its mouth onto the back of Reyka's neck. She screamed and dropped to the floor, writhing. Small black stains radiated up and down Reyka's spine, as if some invisible tattoo artist was creating fractal patterns along her nerves.

After a few interminable minutes of Reyka's suffering, the tendril withdrew. It was bloated. As it rejoined the membrane on the ceiling a flush of red suffused the pink and the tendril deflated.

Marius tried not to move, acutely aware of the tiny tubes in his spine. They could wrack him with anguish or paralyze him at a moment's notice.

Reyka curled into a ball, or nearly. There was something wrong with her legs. Marius had initially thought she was wearing black boots, but looking at her, he realized the black was in her skin, stripes like the marks on the back of her neck. Her feet were twisted into a mockery of someone standing on their toes. Also, her knees seemed to be permanently bent at a slight angle. The Enlightened must have shortened her tendons. To walk she had to tip-toe and balance on knees that couldn't bend or unbend.

Slowly, Reyka pushed herself up, staggered to her feet. She wiped her face with the backs of her hands. "I'm going to take you down. You should know if you resist in any way, we will both be punished. The Enlightened are very wise to use me to show you punishment."

"And two plus two equals five," Marius muttered. She either didn't hear or chose to ignore him as she reached down to pull apart the cocoon at his feet. While she worked on freeing his legs and torso, Marius endured the pins and needles of standing after so long suspended.

"There." Reyka pulled the last strands loose. She put a hand on Marius's chest to prevent him from moving forward. "Wait."

He frowned, then felt the bone scraping withdrawal of tubes from his spine. Marius bit his lip and held his breath until it was over.

"This way." The pink membrane covering the door irised open. Reyka tugged him toward the doorway. "Dr. Viers is eager for you to get to work."

As a kid, Marius had imagined being shrunk so small he could fly up someone's nose and travel through their body, investigating veins and tracts, various organs, watching food liquify in the stomach, lying on his back behind the eye and trying to understand the upside-down images projected on the retina.

His daydreams had not included the cloying meat smell, the warm, humid air, the pulsing veins or the jittering muscular twitches of the passage walls. Every surface of the hallway was coated in the bioforming membrane. It made each step feel treacherous, sinking into the springy, slick surface.

Reyka guided him out into what had once been a laboratory. Marius could tell from the equipment, the layout of the room with cabinets and fume hoods for chemicals. After the chamber he had been in and the hallways, the lab was shockingly devoid of bioformations. There was a military style cot in one corner. Near the cot was an open doorway leading to a small bathroom. No shower, just a toilet and sink. The frame of a mirror still hung on the wall, but all the glass was gone.

"This is where you'll work," Reyka said.

"Work?"

"Yes, the Enlightened know that you are special. Dr. Viers told them about you. You should be honored they sent messengers to find you and bring you here." She smiled in a strangely doll-like manner.

"What kind of work do the Enlightened want me to do?" Marius asked. It was like a nightmare where things just kept going from bad to worse, but everyone acted like it was normal.

"I cannot possibly know their mind," Reyka said. "You are to wait here for instructions." She turned to leave, then paused at the door. "You should know the Enlightened do not want to hurt your family. They want to be reasonable with you. I hope you are reasonable with them. Working together is to all our benefits."

Marius watched her hobble away. The passageway closed behind her, and he was alone in an empty lab. He gingerly ran his fingertips up and down his spine as best he could. There were swollen puncture wounds. He could feel raised welts across his back. Without a mirror, he had no way of knowing, but he suspected his back was marred with the same tattoo-like patterns that covered Reyka's calves and spidered out from the back of her neck.

A wetly soft sucking sound brought Marius's attention back to the door. The bioformation irised open revealing a man.

"Carmine!" Marius gasped.

"I bet my flight was a lot more comfy than yours, bro."

Carmine swaggered into the laboratory. "Did I forget to mention I get to be your supervisor?"

"What the hell is going on?" Marius demanded. "Reyka said Dr. Viers was here. How? I thought he died at Chrysalis."

"What? You don't know about the resurrection and the life? How is that possible, Marius the genius?" Carmine smirked. "You know, They think about you a lot — the Enlightened. The doctor thinks you've had the virus since you were a teeny-tiny baby. All these years you carried it around, kept it safe."

"That's not what happened." Marius glared at the other man. "Rasmussen injected me with two strains of HHV at the school over a year ago."

"Cálmate, bro," Carmine said. "I'm not the one who spread the virus all over." He winked. "We all know who that was, don't we? Probably the only reason They don't kill you. We owe you so much. Couldn't have done it without you."

Marius resisted the urge to punch Carmine in his face. "What do They want?" he said through gritted teeth.

Carmine raised a shoulder. "Just for you to fix the virus."

"Fix it? You mean make it worse. Spread it further and faster than it could on its own. You know that will never happen."

All teasing left Carmine's face. "Then I'll let them know to take you back, hook you in, and drain you. Do you know what it will be like?" He smiled slowly, watching Marius's face. "Yes, they can make you feel anything, heaven and hell. You'd rip out your heart to make it stop beating, but you see, bro, that won't stop them. They'll fill your veins with blood like fire and make your body a funhouse of pain."

"No," Marius whispered. He couldn't go back there. Just thinking about the cocoon made him nauseated and light-headed. He stumbled away from Carmine and grabbed one of the counters for support. His legs buckled and he slid to the floor.

"No?" Carmine echoed.

"Please ... I can't ..." Marius pulled his knees up and rocked.

"Then you'll help us." Carmine bared his teeth in a smile.

John would never cooperate. John would nobly go to his death, shouting curses or in stoic silence. If John were here, he would throw himself out the window, rather than aid the enemy.

Marius looked around, but the room was windowless. The only way out was back the way he had come, back toward the cocoons. There was no way he could will himself to go there.

"They're killing people. It's a pandemic. It's in Europe, Canada, major cities in the U.S.," Marius said, from behind the barrier of his knees.

"We know," Carmine said. "There are a few, a very few, like Reyka who have some natural resistance to one strain or another. Then there are the ones you vaccinated. They are completely immune. Plus, the ones that got the Helatek vaccine have about a 50-50 chance of being immune."

Marius closed his eyes. If he helped them, everyone he loved would be infected, probably everyone in the world.

"And you want me to find a way around that? Engineer a strain so no one's immune." The scientist took a couple quick breaths to keep from passing out at the thought of being dragged back to the cocoon. This was worth dying hard over. "Never. I'd rather die screaming."

"And your family?"

Marius clenched his fists, tried to block the image of his mom wrapped in a cocoon, howling in pain. What kind of monster would let his family suffer when he could save them?

He shook his head. If he helped the Infected no one, not his family, not anyone's family would have a chance.

"Oh, come on." Carmine's tone took on a wheedling note. "We're not asking you to create a new strain, just fix the SAM-D strain."

"What's wrong with it? Apart from the obvious tentacliness." Marius forced himself to meet Carmine's dark eyes, trying to channel John's steely-eyed killer look. He didn't want Carmine to see the wash of gratitude that surged through him. Carmine was offering a compromise, a way out.

"The Sammys are the more intelligent ones. They're the Enlightened. They can communicate, like a hive mind. The problem is they only last for a few months before the virus becomes unstable. It degrades into the FOX-H strain, the animal one. They become irrational, aggressive, suggestible. None of them want to lose their minds like that."

"And you? What strain do you have?" Marius uncoiled and stood up, proud that he wasn't shaking.

"Me? Bro, because of you, I have nothing. I took one of your vaccines. I can never be one of the Enlightened." Carmine bared his teeth again. "I'm so grateful to you."

"Consider it karma for a life spent as an asshole."

"Look who's all badass now. You're not going to curl up and cry again? Maybe piss your panties for me?"

Marius smiled. He had the beginnings of a plan. "No, Carmine. I've got a lab to get running, remember."

Chapter 10 – Torres

Grant's Pass, OR, U.S.A. - Autumn, Year 1

There was a hillside in the Siskiyou Mountains of Oregon near a plot of land where a riot destroyed an ICE camp. On the hillside stood a Stop sign, marking the grave of James Lennox.

Soraya had said a prayer in Farsi and Torres managed the rosary, even after all the years. To cover all the Christian bases, Miranda stumbled through the Lord's Prayer.

Jimmy didn't have tags, so Torres didn't know who might show up to collect his soul. It bothered her, not because she was religiously minded, but because she didn't know if Jimmy had been. It felt wrong to leave him rotting in a barely marked grave without even his gods to watch over him.

Dr. Okeke had vanished sometime during the night that Jimmy spent dying while Torres had watched him, useless as a nature photographer on those Wild Wherever shows. There was always some adorable baby animal being hunted or starving or about to wander off a cliff. You scream at the TV, at the camera people. Do something! You're right there. They never listen. The babies die, their eyes wide and terrified and their anxious parents watching, helpless and baffled. How did that happen? How did we get here?

"Tia Lourdie?" Elfy tugged at Torres's pant leg. She looked at the girl, looked around. They stood at the edge of a gravel parking lot, a pull-off from the winding scenic byway that offered a spectacular view of a valley full of pine trees. How far had they driven last night in their stolen Subaru Forester?

Miranda sat half in, half out of the driver's seat, studying her phone. There had been no signal all day, rendering the phones nothing more than flashlights and music players. The GPS was spotty at best. At least the car had a charger, so the phone's batteries were topped up.

"Hey, kid. What's up?" Torres's voice sounded creaky, like it had rusted in the wet of autumn in Oregon.

"Can I go play with Wahida?"

The Forester's backdoor was open, and Wahida sat inside kicking her feet. Soraya and Mirzha stood next to the car, examining a road atlas. Luckily for their little band, the car's former owners had been Triple A members who believed in paper maps.

A truck, pulling a travel trailer type RV, drove past. Behind it was a Suburban and behind that a Geo Metro. The Suburban honked and flashed its headlights, turned into the pull out. The Geo followed it. The truck stopped after a few seconds. The driver of the truck hopped out and walked back to the parking lot.

He was a middle-aged Black man with a bundle of dreadlocks and a goatee. Coupled with his blazer over a yellow roll-neck shirt and black slacks, he looked like the second coming of the beat poets. As he headed towards the Forester, Miranda stood up, one hand on the wheel, one on the door. Torres cut a path to intercept the truck's driver as Soraya gathered the girls and herded them back toward the Forester. None of the other people got out of their vehicles.

"Go get in the car. Close the door." Soraya pointed for Mirzha to get in the car as well. She walked around to the passenger's side, not hurrying, but not slowly either. Just casually, as if the women weren't terrified of strangers. They might be Infected. They might be members of some militia or other. They might just be strangers.

The beatnik stopped and held up a hand. "Good afternoon, ma'am." His voice was warm and deep, like he talked smiling.

"Afternoon," Torres said. She clasped her hands behind herself, like a general out for a stroll, except her fingers were hooked under her jacket's hem, touching the HK's cool and reassuringly solid pistol grip. Would she be able to shoot with her shoulder? She tried not to picture all of Dr. Okeke's careful stitches being torn out from the recoil. They'd held so far, but that had only been one shot, well braced and stabilized.

"My name is Phineas Maxwell." The beatnik let his hands drop but kept them in sight.

"Torres."

"We saw you in the camp."

Torres glanced at the road, the cars, the passengers, the surrounding hills, waiting for Phineas to get to his point. Let him do the conversational heavy lifting.

"You seem to know what's going on."

Torres didn't try to hide her sneer.

"We were hoping …" He rubbed his hands together as if to warm them. His fingers were long and thin. He looked at the other cars. "Are you going someplace safe? Can we go with you?"

"What makes you think we're doing any better than you?" Torres put her hands on her hips, tucked back her jacket. Phineas didn't strike her as dangerous. He had the calm good humor of a professor, one still young enough to love his work and his students. In another life, Torres felt sure he and Marius would have had very long and very earnest discussions about things like philosophy or early Renaissance poetry or why killer whales were misnamed.

"That's the thing, Ms. Torres," Phineas said. "None of us are doing particularly well. I don't think we stand much of a chance alone. We've heard the reports. The Infection's spread through pretty much all the major metropolitan areas. They're saying to stay out of cities. To—" he paused.

"Shelter in place," Miranda recited.

Phineas bobbed his head. "Exactly. Thank you, miss. But we can't really shelter here. We heard there's a cure in Montana, but no one seems to know anything for sure. So now we're just," he shrugged, "going."

Torres wished they were going. She drew in a deep breath. The air was cool and filled with the smell of dirt and leaves and rain.

"That doesn't answer my question," she said. "Why do you want to go with us?"

"Safety in numbers."

"What makes you think I can keep you safe?" Torres said. She tried not to picture Jimmy's last moments, his eyes totally black, like a shark's, the crash of the HK in her hand, the puff of smoke and pink mist from the hole in Jimmy's forehead. Her ears had rung and if she listened, she was pretty sure she could still hear the high-pitched, tinny 'Eeeeeee,' the echo of the shot that killed her friend and brother-in-arms.

"We're not looking to you to keep us safe, ma'am." Phineas soft, sure voice broke through her thoughts. "Just to give us a direction, to be a guide. Right now, we're wasting gas."

"If I may," Soraya said. As if she needed Torres's permission. *I'm not in charge.*

"Yeah, go ahead," Torres said. She tried not to sound impatient. *Don't let them see division in our ranks.*

"Mr. Maxwell has a good point. If we encounter any more militias it would be good to have ... others with us." She didn't say 'men,' but she might as well have.

Torres looked over at the Forester, at Mirzha who was within spitting distance of womanhood, at Wahida, all wide-eyed and wondering, at Elfy, who was probably an orphan and definitely her responsibility.

"Who else is with you?" the former Marine asked.

Phineas smiled. He seemed to sense Torres would agree. He waved for the people in the Suburban and Geo to exit their vehicles.

A middle-aged white couple and sons, one college age, one late teens, exited the Suburban. From the Geo tumbled a trio of sorority girls, two white, one Black, like the cast of some TV drama.

Last out of the RV was a mixed boy about ten, Torres guessed. She wasn't good with kids' ages.

Phineas introduced everyone. From the Suburban, Art and Patty, their boys, Henry and Greg. From the Geo, Sandra, Becca, and LaTaya. And from the RV, Washington.

"A friend we met along the way." Phineas put a hand lightly on the boy's slender shoulder. "His foster parents accidentally left him at an RV campground in California and we offered him a ride."

Washington scuffed the toe of his battered sneaker through the moldy leaves and gravel. He stared at the patch of damp brown earth his shoe had turned up. Poor kid had already been left once.

Torres didn't want to be in command of a band of civilians. She couldn't trust any of them to know what to do if they ran into the Infected, or a militia. But without guidance, they might end up dead or worse, infected. "You can follow us. We're going to Montana."

"Montana? We heard that's where the cure is," Patty the soccer mom called. She had blond stripe highlights through her brown hair. It made her look like a stick of butterscotch candy.

"There's a guy there I used to work with. He—"

"He's a scientist," Miranda interrupted. She took a

couple of steps away from the Forester, poised between the car and Torres. She shot the former Marine a significant look. Yes, Marius could make the vaccine, but more importantly, he was the vaccine. What would people do if they knew that Marius's blood could save their kids' lives? Considering the traffic jam out of LA, the Oregon militia, and the ICE camp riot, Miranda was probably right. No need to risk telling a bunch of strangers.

"He can help us," Miranda added.

"Maybe." Torres rolled her good shoulder, let her body relax, and straightened up. She took a breath, channeled her inner drill instructor. "Listen up. You want to travel with us? Fine, as long as you follow the rules."

As if on cue, the college boy, Henry demanded, "The rules?" He was a big guy, with meaty round shoulders that screamed football. Torres hid a smile. He was perfect.

"Yeah." She turned and marched over to him. Fast. Henry took a step back as Torres stopped less than arm's reach away from him. The former Marine had to look up to make eye contact, but there were lots of ways to loom and she'd learned most of them in the Corps.

"The rules, Henry, are as follows. We go where I say, when I say. We get weapons and supplies where and when I say. We keep our vehicles and our gear in good working order, and we don't mess with each other."

Torres took two steps back and looked around, made eye contact with each of their new recruits in turn.

"If that doesn't work for you, no problem. Keep going. Good luck to you. I got kids to watch out for. I'm not going to let them get hurt because one of you didn't want to listen."

"May we have a moment?" Phineas said.

"Sure." Torres took it as a good sign that he was asking her permission.

While the others huddled together, Torres walked over to lean against the driver's side of the Forester.

"I'm liking feisty-pants Torres," Miranda said. She dropped into the driver's seat, glancing at her phone. Still no bars.

Soraya stood near the rear passenger's side door. She tapped her lips with a finger. "Do you know, our stories of Moses are quite similar to yours?"

"Shush, you," Torres growled. "I'm not Moses."

Soraya smiled. "Not yet."

Torres winced as she pressed her palm against the furnace of her shoulder, tried to steady herself against the rocking of the RV. They were somewhere in northern Oregon or maybe western Wyoming. Another day or so and they'd be in Montana. They'd have to figure out how to find Marius's house. He'd mentioned it was in the middle of nowhere and from what Torres had heard about Montana, that could describe the whole freaking state.

She had set up a driver rotation that allowed everyone to get some honest sleep in the RV. There was a fold-out bed in the back and a bunk over the front area. Elfy, Wahida, and Mirzha were sleeping in the bunk while Soraya and Torres shared the bed. Phineas was driving the truck with Miranda riding shotgun. One of the blonds had taken over the Forester so the women could get some rest.

The pain in Torres's shoulder had snapped her out of sleep. She fumbled out of the blankets, tried not to kick Soraya in the head, and escaped the bed. She wavered to the bathroom, pushed back the little accordion door and stepped inside.

The light was yellow and harsh. Her face looked sweaty and waxy. The wound was outlined with reddish pink. When she put pressure on it, a little stream of thin, pale-yellow pus trickled out. That couldn't be good.

She wasn't Infected. She had gotten Marius's vaccine. All the tests they did in prison had confirmed. Torres was immune to HHV. Still, she remembered Jimmy's arm, the bite mark and its halo of infection.

Torres washed the wound as best she could in the rocking rolling RV bathroom. She hadn't thought to bring the first aid bag with her. When she opened the door to head back for it, Soraya was waiting, bag in hand.

"Let me see," she said.

"I'm okay. Just need to change the dressing." There was nothing Soraya could do. She needed antibiotics.

"Lourdes, there are a lot of people who are counting on you." She handed the former Marine the bag.

"I know. If you can help, I'll let you know."

"I accept your promise."

Torres narrowed her eyes. She hadn't promised anything.

"You should get some rest."

Torres frowned. Wasn't she supposed to be in charge? But Soraya was right. She couldn't allow pain to cloud her judgment. Torres cleaned and dressed the wound, took some more pain killers, got back into bed, and tried to ignore the throbbing in her shoulder until she fell asleep.

They must have been stopped for a while. That was Torres's first clear thought as she lay in her nest of sweaty blankets. They must have been stopped for a while because the folks in the tailing vehicles had had time to get out and gather up outside the RV. The hum of excited voices carried in through the cracked window.

Torres sat up slowly. Her head swam and her stomach was trying out for a gymnastics contest. Other than that, she was fine. She swung her legs over the side of the bed, shoved her feet into her boots, her toes catching on the cool metal of the HK. She lifted it with her good arm and popped the magazine. Only eight rounds.

A swell of voices caught the former Marine's attention. It was still dark outside, but she could see the bob and weave of cell phone screens as the group milled around. Not an ounce of noise and light discipline among the lot of them. Torres bent to tie her boots. The world looped and whirled. She let the pistol drop to the floor and braced herself, closed her eyes until things stilled. Okay, no shoe tying.

She picked up the HK and tucked it into the waistband of her jeans. Before she opened the RV door, she wiped her sleeve across her forehead and cheeks.

"Tia Lourdie!" Elfy squealed and launched herself at

her aunt. Torres barely managed to catch the child with her good arm and hold her off as the girl wriggled with the enthusiasm of a Labrador.

The others paused at Torres's appearance.

Miranda held up her phone, eyes shining. "I got a signal!"

"What part of 'Stay in the vehicles' was unclear to you knuckleheads?" Torres glared at the group.

"Um, rude," said one of the white college girls. Sandra or Becca. Torres couldn't tell them apart with their long straight blond hair, matching leggings, oversized sweaters, and expensive hand-knit scarves. LaTaya dressed the same, but at least she was a different color.

"So, like, what does she say about the vaccine?" The girls clustered around Miranda. They could have started a band.

"'Sexy scientist' is trending. I follow this freelancer, Phoebe Allen Poe. She just posted an update." Miranda turned her phone toward Torres as if that would somehow clarify events for the former Marine.

It did not.

Torres shook her head. "It's not hard, is it?" she asked no one in particular. "I said, 'When we stop, stay in the vehicles until I give the all clear.' That's not hard."

"How are you feeling?" Soraya asked.

"Hungry." Torres was pretending the sheen of sweat on her face was due to RV's excellent heating system, not a fever.

"You promised."

Torres ignored her and scanned the area. The wind muttered through the trees, the branches grumbling as they shook off the leftover rain drops from the night's shower. A carpet of wet leaves along the road's shoulder deadened the group's footfalls.

"It's about Marius," Miranda said, earning her Torres's full attention.

"What is? The trending thing?" Torres squinted over Miranda's shoulder trying to make sense of the tags, emojis, links, and GIFs as Miranda scrolled through her feeds. How did she have so many things running at once?

"Yeah." Miranda tapped her screen, bringing up an image of Marius, smiling. Torres recognized the photo. It was from his Chrysalis ID badge. She'd been sitting across from him when the picture was taken. He looked so young and hopeful.

Under the photo was a clip explaining that "The noted virologist and the architect of the government's HHV response, Dr. Tenartier, was believed to be in Montana, although so far, no official sources would confirm that information on the record."

"That's your friend, right?" Phineas asked. "Good friend to have right about now."

A chill ran over Torres. The sweat from earlier suddenly felt like ice water. She shivered but held her jaw open enough that her teeth didn't chatter. She had to get through this and then she could go back to sleep. If she slept, she would feel better. She just needed to sleep.

"At least we know we're on the right track," Art said.

"Um, about that," Miranda said.

"What?" Torres said. She wanted to lean against the RV, but it seemed so far away. She held herself upright, careful not to lock her knees so she wouldn't pass out.

Soraya handed her a bottle of water, and she gulped down a few swigs gratefully.

"It's for you." Miranda extended the phone, showing Torres a text from John, which read: *Need to speak to T ASAP. M not in MT.*

"He said you weren't answering your phone and I said I wasn't your secretary or whatever and he said it was urgent, so we stopped, but she said you should probably rest." Miranda nodded toward Soraya. "How's your shoulder?"

"It hurts but I'll live." Fingers crossed that wasn't a lie.

Torres took Miranda's phone and texted back: *T here CPT.*

They waited a few minutes. The college girls wandered back to their car to see if their phones would also get a signal. Patty fussed with Greg's hair until he waved her off with the gusty sigh of the offended adolescent.

Miranda's phone buzzed. *How close are you to Portland, OR?*

Torres frowned and handed the phone back to Miranda. "Can you pull up the GPS?"

Miranda swiped and tapped and handed the phone back. It showed a route from their current location in central Wyoming to Portland, Oregon.

Torres sent back: *16 hours approx. Why?*

John replied: *Per operator buddy, M taken to Portland by unk hostiles. Am grounded in Helena. Hoping for a flight tomorrow. May have to try private skies.*

Torres frowned and typed: *No need. We are closer.*

Will secure M. Where RP?

John's message was a ten-digit grid coordinate. That would be the rally point when they found Marius. Torres copied it and put it into the map app.

"Wow. He really does come from BFE Montana," Miranda said, peering over Torres's shoulder. A tiny blue flag marked a spot southeast of Great Falls, and northeast of Helena, near the town of Crossroads.

Torres returned the other woman's phone. Phineas and Washington loitered a few feet away, not exactly eavesdropping, but definitely within easy hearing distance.

"So," Torres said. "Marius, our scientist friend, isn't in Montana. Looks like we're going to Oregon."

"Oh, well, the thing is," Art started, but Patty cut in. "We're going to Montana. They have a cure."

"We don't know that, hon," Art said.

Patty flapped a hand at Miranda. "She said that scientist was in Montana. They probably took him to one of those bunkers to keep him safe."

"He's not in Montana," Torres said.

Patty put her hands on her hips. "How do you know? You have no proof that he's not."

Torres shook her head. She was too tired to deal with Patty. "I don't care where you go, ma'am. We are going to Oregon." She trudged back to the RV.

Behind her, Soraya and Phineas began talking quietly.

Torres crawled into the bed and closed her eyes. The fever beat against the backs of her eyeballs. She had forgotten to take off her boots. She kicked at them a couple times. One fell off. She decided to rest, only for a few minutes, before trying the other boot.

Chapter 11 – Miranda

Prairie City, OR, U.S.A. - Autumn, Year 1

A wooden cutout of a drunken stag stood beside the road, grinning at the oncoming traffic. In his right hoof he held a sign that said, "Ernie's Emporium – The Best of the West!". In his left, he held a can of sudsy beer. Miranda had probably seen tackier places, but she couldn't think of any.

About half a mile ahead, Miranda could see the parking lot of Ernie's. It was early morning. Ernie's sat in a depression and a low fog swirled around the area. The building itself was hidden by a windbreak of tall skinny pines all huddled together like college kids around a free pizza.

Miranda slowed the Forester and pulled onto the shoulder. Soraya, riding shotgun, opened her dark eyes and sat up, her hand going up to adjust her missing head scarf.

"We need gas," Miranda said. She watched in the mirror as the truck, Suburban, and Geo also pulled over. Sandra, or possibly Becca, opened the driver's door and started to get out, paused as if listening and rolled her eyes.

"Torres will lose her shit," Miranda said. But Sand-Becca got back in before the grumpy former Marine could react.

Not waiting for Torres to appear from the RV, Miranda got out of the car and stretched. Her phone had lost coverage again, not totally unexpected in the mountains of wherever they were. Western Wyoming? Eastern Oregon? Someplace where the only plants taller than her knee were disgruntled looking pine trees. Miranda couldn't blame them. She wouldn't want to be rooted in a high desert, either. Besides, she needed to get to Portland. The feeling had been growing with every passing mile. Her phone might not have a signal, but she felt like she did.

The RV door banged as Torres stepped out. Were her boots untied?

The former Marine waved to let the others know they could exit their vehicles. She beckoned Miranda to follow and walked back towards the Suburban. From Patty's tightly crossed arms, it didn't look like she had any plans of giving another inch. She'd agreed to go with them to Portland, but had complained every mile of the way there. Miranda wondered if Art might be deaf. Or maybe he was the most zen person ever.

Torres stopped and leaned a hip against the Suburban. "Gather round," she said.

They gathered. Around them, in the thin forest and across the dry hills, something else was moving, a slow tide, drawn north with a force that felt as elemental as the tides. Miranda had to keep consciously turning so she faced the group instead of Portland.

She'd never been great with directions. Not as bad as Marius, who could get lost in a mall food court, but certainly not blessed with the inner compasses John and Torres seemed to have. Regardless, Miranda was sure that if blindfolded, spun around, put in a box, and buried, she could still have pointed directly at Portland from wherever she was.

Whatever the source of the feeling, she knew it was the reason the Infected kept moving, hadn't tried to nest in this area. She felt them brush her mind and move on, the way women at clubs glanced at each other now and then, checking in, checking up. "You okay?" "Yep, you?" "All good." And back to dancing. It was nice to know she wasn't alone, that something noticed, that someone cared.

"Here's the deal," Torres said. "Looks like a little general store/gas station type place. Let me talk to the folks running the store." Most of the others stared at her, but Phineas nodded. "If no one's there, here's what we need — Food, stuff that can travel, like canned stuff and jerky. We need weapons, guns, knives, hell, bows and arrows."

Patty wrinkled her nose but didn't say anything. Art put an arm around her.

"We also need medicine. Especially stuff like Neosporin and aspirin. Just grab all the medicine and we'll sort it out later."

Torres pointed at one of the blonds and LaTaya. "You two, get the medicine." She pointed at Greg, Washington, and Mirzha. "You kids are on food detail. Art and Patty, weapons. Drivers, see if there's any gas in the pumps." The drivers were Miranda, Henry, Phineas, and the other blond.

"Why don't I get gas and you can go with Torres?" Soraya murmured to Miranda. The younger woman nodded. Torres looked like she could use someone to watch out for her. She looked sick.

She's not Infected. Even if Miranda hadn't known Torres had been vaccinated, she would have known the former Marine wasn't infected with HHV. Miranda could sense the disease in others. It wasn't quite a feeling or a smell, but something like that. Something not quite there, but definitely there.

The group dispersed back to their vehicles and drove the remaining distance to the wide gravel parking area in front of Ernie's. Miranda waited in the car for Torres to get out, check her pistol, and wave to the others to follow her. There were no lights on inside the place. Half of it was a bar, and the other half a general store. Three Harleys were parked in the front.

"There's no one here," LaTaya said.

I'm here. An Infected brushed Miranda's mind. She pushed it away. *Stay quiet. Stay away from us.*

"Hey, Torres —" she started, but Torres was busy with directing their little raid.

"Make sure you check the bar and the bikes for

weapons." The former Marine pointed Art and Patty back out toward the motorcycles in the parking lot.

Miranda stepped inside and looked around, waiting for her eyes to adjust to the nearly black interior. A free-standing book rack was lying on the floor near the counter. Cheap paperbacks, mostly romances and Westerns, were scattered across the floor. Some had muddy bootprints on them. The cash register on the counter had been smashed open. A spray of coins glimmered on the counter and floor.

"Hello?" Miranda called. Torres drew her pistol and fumbled it, nearly dropped it. She winced and switched it to her other hand. Her shoulder must still be really sore, Miranda thought. She should probably wait in the car, but she'd never agree to that.

"You got this?" Miranda asked.

"I'm fine." Torres said. "We gotta clear this place." She stalked forward like they were in a combat zone rather than an empty general store. Other than the Infected that Miranda was ignoring hard, there were no other Infected in the store. The ones outside weren't interested in them. They were moving north and west. Miranda resisted the urge to join them. She needed to help Torres clear the store or whatever.

There were four aisles with everything from jerky to kitty-litter and baby diapers. A walk-in beverage cooler stood against the back wall. The door of the case nearest the windows was ajar and the light inside the cooler was a soft blue beacon. Across the room from the windows, on the counter side was a door leading into the bar area. Faint red, blue, and yellow neon lights cycled from some sign in the bar. Nothing else moved.

"Okay, let's do this." Torres tipped her chin, and the others came in. Sand-Becca actually picked up a little shopping basket and rested its handles in the crook of her elbow, like she was waltzing down 5th Avenue with this season's most stylish purse. "Meds." Torres said to her.

She rolled her eyes. "Yeah, okay." She and LaTaya headed down the closest aisle.

The others spread out, Patty and Art going down the furthest aisle, near the windows. Patty brushed a hand across Greg's back and he headed down the aisle next to his parents, followed by Washington and Mirzha.

Torres headed for the counter and Miranda followed. "There's bound to be a weapon close to the cash register," Torres said. She stepped around the counter and froze.

A man's body lay face down on the floor. The top of his head was missing, his brains a puddle of cranberry jelly on the floor. He wore a leather biker vest emblazoned with four patches. At the top, arched letters read 'Cossacks' and at the bottom, 'Nevada.' In the middle was a skeletal rider on a fiery horse, waving a sword. Next to the insignia was a smaller patch that said 'MC' — motorcycle club. Well, that explained the bikes outside.

Miranda looked around. No one had noticed them, or the body. Torres squatted and patted down the man.

"Eww." Miranda wrinkled her nose.

Torres shrugged and held up a Zippo. "He's not gonna miss it." The dead man's pockets also yielded a half pack of Lucky Strikes, a wallet belonging to one Clarence W. Burns, which contained $53.00, and a .38

snub-nosed revolver. Torres put the revolver in her pocket.

"Check for other weapons." She pointed to the counter. Miranda dutifully bent and looked under the counter and in the drawers.

From the third aisle, where the youngsters had gone looking for food, came a loud rustling and then a squealing, gargling sound. Someone screamed and someone else yelled. Torres bolted from behind the counter and tore across the few feet to the end of the aisle. Patty was clutching a plastic shopping basket full of food and staring at her son. Greg squatted on the floor, his hands around the neck of a raccoon. It twisted and hissed, its freakishly human hands pinching and clawing at Greg. He had scratches and bites all over his hands and forearms.

Miranda recognized the Infected's mind.

"Stop! What are you doing?" She reached out a hand as if she could stop what was happening, as if she could explain that the Infected had only been frightened, that it had been trying to escape.

"It attacked my mom."

"Get off it." Torres leveled her pistol.

Get it off me! The Infected twisted, sinking its teeth into Greg's hand again.

"Let it go!" Miranda shouted.

"It attacked my mom."

"Dumbass, I'm gonna shoot it. Now let go and step away."

Greg looked up, registered the pistol, and let go of the Infected raccoon. It rolled over in a ball of limbs and came up growling. Even in the dim light of the store,

Miranda could see the bruises and patches of missing hair. The others would know it was Infected.

Torres's pistol went off and Miranda jerked as if the bullet had pierced her own chest. Torres made a strangled cry of pain and dropped the pistol. She grabbed her shoulder.

The Infected raccoon charged her.

No, no. Miranda tried to turn it away, tried to get it to go for the open door, rather than attacking the woman who'd shot it, but her influence wasn't strong enough. She could feel the raccoon push off her will, following its rage and hunger toward Torres.

The former Marine stumbled back, clutching her arm. The raccoon leapt at her and managed to bite the toe of her boot.

Torres half-fell, bracing herself against the front windows. She fumbled in her pocket for the biker's gun.

Please stop, Miranda begged, but she knew the raccoon wouldn't listen. With tears in her eyes, she grabbed a metal shovel and swung it overhead, like some old-timey lumberjack splitting a log. The blade severed the raccoon's spine and its two halves flopped and twisted. Miranda could feel its little life, all hot rage and gnawing hunger. It was still fighting, still trying to get back to the nest where the web could give it strength, where the others could help it rebuild.

Sobbing, Miranda brought the flat of the shovel head down on the raccoon's head until it finally stopped twitching.

For a moment, all was still and silent in the store. Greg stared up at Miranda, his eyes wide, but his lips drawn tight, teeth clenched. She blinked back tears, looked at her arms, speckled with purplish-red blood and bits of raccoon fur.

Then LaTaya screamed.

Torres managed to draw the biker's revolver. Miranda held out a hand to get the former Marine back on her feet. The two women hurried over to the first aisle. LaTaya and Sand-Becca stood near the front of the store, a basket of medicine at their feet. They clutched each other's hands and stared at the biker's body behind the counter.

"Oh, for fuck's sake," Torres muttered.

Miranda managed not to laugh. Dead people weren't even scary anymore.

"Why don't you go outside?" Miranda set the shovel down in the second aisle where they wouldn't see its gory head, dripping raccoon guts and little gobs of fur.

"Should we, like, call the police or something?" Sand-Becca said.

"There are no police," LaTaya said and burst into tears.

"Go. Out. Side," Torres said.

"You don't have to be such a bitch!" Sand-Becca glared at her. She grabbed LaTaya's arm and pulled the other college student toward the door.

"Are they all right?" Patty stood at the end of her aisle, next to Greg. He was examining his injured hands—where he'd been bitten. He'd been bitten by an Infected raccoon. He was Infected. Miranda could feel it.

From the look of horror on Torres's face, she'd figured it out too, or at least strongly suspected. She stared at Patty and her doomed son. Art stood uncertainly in doorway, his gaze skipping from his wife and son to the parking lot where the students had gone and back to his family.

Phineas pushed in past Art. "Torres?" He looked from the former Marine to Greg to Miranda and back. "What happened?"

From outside Miranda heard the sound of the Geo's engine, barely louder than a lawn mower and then the squeal of tires and the crunch of gravel.

"Hey! They're leaving!" Greg started for the door.

Torres put the revolver back in her pocket and turned to the basket of medicine. She picked out a bottle of aspirin and held it out to Miranda, who opened it and poured four into her outstretched palm. Torres downed them, crunching the bitter powdery pills on her molars and swallowing the chokey mass dry.

"Miranda, you're with me," Torres said. "We'll check for anything they missed. Patty, Art, Greg, finish your aisles. You, too." She nodded to Washington and Mirzha, who had watched the whole thing in silent, wide-eyed wonder. "Let's get out of here." The former Marine trudged over to the body of the raccoon and scooped up Jimmy's pistol.

The group looted in strained silence for a few minutes, then Art opened the walk-in freezer in the back.

"Oh holy ..." He stepped back, hand on his chest.

"Dad!" Greg started forward but Torres caught him with her good arm.

"Wait here." She drew Jimmy's pistol and went to see what Art had found.

The little red light over the door to the walk-in freezer blinked on and off, warning the freezer had no power. Art leaned against the wall, rubbing his chest.

He better not have a heart attack. That's the last thing we—

Miranda's train of thought crashed to a stop.

The floor of the freezer was strewn with beer cans, some smashed open. A grey-brown froth coated the lower interior of the freezer like dirty seafoam. Industrial sized bags of ketchup and mustard had fallen off one of the lower shelves, adding swirls of yellow and red to the mess.

In the far corner, huddled in a naked ball, was a woman, barely more than a girl. All Miranda could see of her was her skin, pale, almost blue and mottled with yellow and green bruises. Miranda shuddered. She wished she could believe the red spatters on the woman's legs and butt were from the spilled ketchup.

"Oh god …" Torres actually seemed shocked for once.

"Is she dead?" Art muttered. He was still backed against the wall, looking away.

If she's lucky.

But Miranda didn't say it. She couldn't tell Art that some things weren't worth surviving. She knew it was true, but she didn't want those words loose in the world, working their evil magic on other people. Let them keep whatever faith or hope they had. It would be wrong to take that from them.

Torres stepped forward, her feet leaving long streaks

in the slime on the floor. "Ma'am?"

No response.

"Ma'am, can you hear me?"

Nothing.

Torres squatted down and reached out, touched the sole of one bare foot.

"No!"

The woman exploded from the floor in a frenzy of flailing limbs and wordless screams. She slapped at Torres, her ragged nails catching on the former Marine's jacket and hair. Torres lunged forward and wrapped her arms and legs around the woman. She held the woman as she struggled, held her until her body went limp and she started sobbing.

"Please. I'll be good. I'm sorry. I'll be good."

Miranda's guts twisted at the thought of what she must think of them. "Let her go."

Torres ignored her. To the woman she said, "I'm not going to hurt you, ma'am, but I need you not to hurt me or my crew, okay?"

"Hey! She's freaked the fuck out. Let her go." Miranda stepped forward, not sure if she meant to try to wrestle the woman away from Torres or not. After what had happened with the raccoon, she couldn't stand the idea of the woman feeling helpless and terrified.

The light from the door dimmed and Miranda looked over to see Phineas. He covered his mouth and held up a hand to stop someone behind him.

"We're okay," Torres said, like it was totally normal for her to be grappling a naked, hysterical woman. She added, "Get everyone out front. Whoever left her here might come back."

"Right. Get everyone out front. Right." Phineas disappeared.

The woman didn't move.

"I'm gonna let you go now," Torres said. "Stay still, okay? We're going to help you."

"Yeah, choking her out is, like, the perfect way to earn her trust and stuff," Miranda snapped.

Torres glared at her over the woman's head.

The woman didn't respond. Miranda could see her breathing, but her eyes were fixed and staring ahead. Dead eyes.

Miranda tried the reasonable approach. "Torres, c'mon. We got this. She's not like a threat or anything."

Torres relaxed her grip, let the woman's body slide to the floor in a wet squish of condiments and semi-frozen beer slime. Her body looked like a modern art masterpiece of color slashes.

Torres stood up and stepped away. Phineas reappeared, standing outside the doorway. At the sight of him, the woman moaned and pawed at her body, as if trying to cover herself.

"Back off." Miranda pointed and Phineas ducked out of sight. She took off her jacket and held it out. After a few minutes, she dropped it over the woman.

"He's gone. You're safe now." Miranda squatted near the woman. "I'm Miranda and this is Torres. What's your name?"

The woman closed her eyes tight.

"Hey!" Torres snapped her fingers. In her Marine voice, she barked, "Ma'am, what's your name?"

"Alice," the woman whispered.

Miranda patted Alice's arm. "Good. You're doing

good, Alice. We're gonna help you, but we gotta go. Can you walk?"

Alice finally opened her eyes and looked around. No Phineas or Art in the doorway.

"They're gone. It's just us. Can you take my hand?" Miranda held out her hand.

Shakily, Alice took Miranda's hand. Good, Miranda thought. She still has the will to live. Miranda pulled her up, tried not to look at her naked body as she limped to the door. Alice pulled Miranda's jacket around her. Torres shepherded them, keeping Alice moving down the aisle, past the counter, careful to stay between her and dead Clarence.

Phineas waited near the door. Art and Patty clustered around Greg in the parking lot. They were examining his raccoon wounds. Mirzha and Washington had taken the food to the RV and had several gas canisters lined up next to one of the pumps. Soraya stood near the truck and the girls peered out the RV's windows. Of course, the Sand-Beccas, LaTaya, and their Geo were long gone. Miranda almost wished that they would meet up with the people who'd left Alice to die in a freezer. No. That was wrong. Sure, they'd been annoying, but no one deserved that.

Alice pulled back when she saw Phineas.

"Guys, can you send Soraya in with some wipes and clothes?" Miranda tipped her head to get him to leave. A gust of wind lifted the few remaining wet leaves on the trees and sent scattered drops of water down. The sun took refuge behind ranks of clouds. The store smelled of stale booze and old sweat. The strangling scent of gas rose from a slick spilled near the pumps, making

Miranda's head spin. All she wanted was to be back on the road, heading northwest, heading to Portland along with the other Infected.

Reaching out to the surrounding area, she could feel most of them hadn't noticed the raccoon's passing, but some felt more anxious, angry, aggressive. They pushed a strange sort of self-loathing at Miranda. *How could you hurt us? How could you do that to us?*

"Hey, focus." Torres nudged Miranda and put her good arm around Alice, shielding her from the wind through the door while they waited for Soraya, who hurried in with the first aid bag and quilt from the RV. When Soraya got a good look at Alice, her face tightened, her jaw clenched, even as tears glimmered in her eyes.

"This is Alice," Miranda said.

Traitor. Abomination. You're supposed to be one of us.

Miranda's head swirled. She sagged against the door frame.

Torres grabbed her wrist. "Pull it together."

"Nah ... nothing. It's nothing." Miranda fought to get the Infected out of her mind. "The ... the gas fumes are really getting to me. I gotta go outside in the fresh air."

"Me too." Torres's face was sweaty and her eyes looked glassy. How long had she been this sick?

"Alice." Soraya held up the quilt. Alice nodded mutely. Soraya handed Miranda back her jacket. She draped the quilt gently around Alice's shoulders. There was a hand shaped bruise around her throat.

"I have to —" Torres stumbled forward, barely cleared the threshold and vomited into the butt can that stood next to the door.

"Tia Lourdie!" Elfy burst out of the RV.

Torres waved at her. "Get back in —" Another bout of vomiting.

Miranda fought her own gag reflex, tried not to stare at the chunks spattered across the sidewalk. When had they eaten hotdogs? They still looked the same. Gross.

She drew a deep breath. Mistake. Shouldn't breathe in through the nose. Her stomach clenched.

Torres leaned her head against the plate glass of Ernie's front windows. Elfy grabbed her leg. She jerked and yanked the pistol out, dropped it. Splat! Right into her own sick. She spewed again. They'd hardly eaten anything in the last few days. How could Torres have so much to throw up?

"Elfy, leave her for a minute." Miranda pulled her shirt over her nose and mouth and herded the girl a few steps away.

Something was growling, getting louder and louder. Miranda looked around. Three more Harleys were stopped, spread out across the exit to the highway. The men on the Harleys wore jackets with the Cossack patch on them, like dead Clarence from the store.

Alice screamed.

"Get her —" Torres yelled, stopping as if fighting down nausea. "RV." She pointed.

Soraya pulled Alice to the RV where Mirzha and Washington waited. Elfy stood next to Miranda, her wide dark eyes flickering from her to the bikers to the hysterical naked woman to her sick aunt.

"Hey!" yelled one of the bikers, the one on the red accented Harley. "That's ours." The other two grinned. They were barely twenty yards away. The wind had died down. The light was dim. Any other day, Miranda would have been confident in Torres's ability to shoot them dead. In her current, feverish state, it was probably good she was leaning against the wall, not doing anything aggressive.

Phineas stepped forward, hands up, palms out. "Gentlemen, I'm sure —"

Torres drew Clarence's revolver and fired. For a split second nothing moved. The shot echoed around the parking lot, sound rippling out over the quiet forest and surrounding hills.

Red straddled his bike. He looked down at the small hole in his chest. "You bitch," he said.

Then everything seemed to happen at once.

Torres squeezed the trigger again, but this time her rage didn't seem to be enough to overcome her shoulder. The shot went wide and her target, the one on the blue accented bike, dove for cover behind his hog. The bike wobbled and fell over, and Mr. Blue crawled behind it, using it for cover.

The two remaining bikers started shooting. Behind Miranda, the window exploded as a shot whipped past her head. Elfy squealed and covered her ears. Phineas crouched behind the Suburban. Soraya shoved Alice inside the RV and sprinted to the truck.

Art grabbed his chest and because it was the worst possible thing he could do at that moment, he crumpled to the ground. Patty fell to her knees beside him, leaving poor infected Greg standing all alone in the middle of the parking lot, like a pine tree on a hill in a lightning storm. Henry scrambled out of the Suburban's driver's seat and ran toward his parents and brother. Mr. Black poked his head out. Torres pointed her revolver at him, just as he took another shot at Miranda. This one was close enough that she could feel the concussion as it hit the doorway next to her head.

Miranda pushed Elfy into the store. Outside, Torres was shooting at Mr. Blue and Mr. Black. They ducked behind their motorcycles, cursing and firing wildly. Henry lay in a pool of blood in the middle of the parking lot. Greg stood, staring down at him.

"Greg, get the fuck down!" Torres shouted. Greg blinked and turned one way then the other as if trying to figure out what to do. He slowly sank down to a squat next to Henry and reached towards his brother.

Among the scrubby trees and droopy bushes, the Infected paused. The pull was as strong as ever. Miranda half turned northwest herself as she hid behind the gas station's doorframe. Still, fresh blood rode the wind with the promise of more to come. Excitement, bordering on ecstasy, shivered through Miranda's body.

We are so hungry. Always hungry. Let's eat.

Miranda leaned forward, parted the blinds with trembling fingers, and pressed her eye to the glass. She opened herself to the Infected, let them see what she saw. *Kill them. Mr. Black. Mr. Blue. Feast and move on. Leave the others.*

Mr. Black raised a crumpled white paper napkin. "Truce. You don't want more dead folks, right? Let's deal."

"We don't need to deal. We got you outnumbered." Torres flicked the revolver open. Miranda could see there were only two bullets left. Two didn't seem like "outnumbered" to her.

"We got you outgunned, honey. And —" Mr. Black's head appeared for a second. He shot out the tires of the truck. "Now you're trapped here."

Torres snapped the revolver closed, fumbled it with her bad hand. She tried to aim for Mr. Black, but couldn't get the shot off before he ducked down. The former Marine muttered a number of things Elfy was way too young to hear. Miranda covered the girl's ears.

"You wanna deal?" Mr. Blue called.

Torres was going to get them all killed if she kept up taunting the bikers. What they needed was a distraction until the Infected could arrive. Miranda guided Elfy behind the counter and held up a hand to signal that she should stay.

"I wouldn't worry about us, my dude." Miranda leaned out of the doorway. "You are about to learn some sorry lessons about the food chain." She peered around, hoping for rustling or something in the bushes. There were some Littles close, but the nearest Infected who could handle one of the bikers alone was a good ten or fifteen minutes away. *Hurry! I know you're hungry. See. You can have these ones.* Miranda pressed the image of the bikers on the Infected's minds.

"Listen, sweetheart," Mr. Blue leaned up a little to grin at Miranda. "You send that pretty little girl over and we'll be on our way. Think of it as a toll for using our highway." Miranda flipped him off and he laughed.

"You're never going to see Alice again." Torres yelled. She looked around, her gaze resting on the pistol she'd dropped in her own vomit.

Oh no. No way.

But the former Marine started edging toward it.

Miranda didn't think either Mr. Blue or Mr. Black could see the pistol. If Torres could get it, she could probably kill them both.

"Alice?" Mr. Black was doing something with the saddlebags on his bike.

"Who the fuck is Alice?" Both Mr. Black and Mr. Blue crowed together.

We will have them.

Miranda shuddered at the collective hunger of the Infected. Her mouth filled with drool. She could practically taste the fresh, juicy muscle, the delicious fat pulled in strips from around stomach, butt, thighs.

Only those two and the dead ones. Remember.

"We're tired of Alice. We want that girl with her in the RV." They were talking about Mirzha. Miranda glanced over at Soraya, hunkered down in the truck's driver seat. Her face was bloodlessly pale.

"Not happening." Torres flexed the fingers of her good hand.

There was a muffled scream from the RV. Soraya bolted from the truck. Mr. Black leaned up to throw something. Torres's shot took him in the shoulder and the grenade he meant to lob under the truck fell about halfway between the bikes and the truck. Miranda ducked. The hot flash of the grenade's explosion brushed her cheek, singed her hair. Rocks and gravel from the parking lot whizzed around from the little crater in the middle of a six-foot-wide space of cleared asphalt. A small fire burned at the center, the remains of the grenade.

Another scream from inside the RV, this time cut off in a gurgle. Only Mirzha, Washington, and Alice were inside the RV. What would Alice do to save Mirzha from the bikers? What would she do to save herself?

"You got thirty seconds, bitch, then we're killing all of you." Mr. Blue held up a military looking rifle.

Soraya yanked at the door of the RV. "It's locked!" she screamed.

Torres froze. Her eyes flickered around as if taking in the situation. She looked at the revolver in her good hand. Miranda knew she had one shot left. She could probably kill Mr. Blue with it.

Instead, Torres slung the revolver toward Soraya like she was bowling a strike.

We're almost there.

Miranda imagined what the Infected would find when they arrived. The bodies of everyone lucky enough to have been killed, rather than taken by the bikers.

But Torres kept moving, walking toward the bikers like some Wild West sheriff. In her hand was the pistol. She pointed it and squeezed the trigger.

In the movies, the shot sets off an explosion, a massive fiery orange popcorn ball of heat and force. The bad guys are blown to unrecognizable bits and the good guys jump out of the way at the last second. Occasionally, they're thrown into each other, landing in a tangle of singed bodies if there's a romantic angle to the story.

Nothing happened. No explosion. No fire. Nothing.

In real life, a motorcycle's tank, if full, holds about two and a half to three gallons of gas. Maybe, if the bike's frame were packed with C4, there might be a Hollywood boom from shooting it.

Miranda shrank back, reaching for the Infected. *Hurry. Hurry!*

"You stupid—" Mr. Blue started.

But then the fire from Mr. Black's grenade caught the spilled gas from his motorcycle. A flickering file of blue and yellow flames licked and jumped across the parking lot. Mr. Blue scrambled up and ran back up the exit ramp towards the highway. He was almost there when his bike caught fire. There was a small pop as the expanding fumes cracked the bike's gas tank open, spilling the remaining fuel across the parking lot. It flowed out in a widening fan, the fire dancing along behind it.

Torres grinned ghoulishly as she watched the flames tickling Mr. Black's boots. He levered himself up, and scooted away from his bike, following Mr. Blue's lead toward the road.

They're trying to run. Chase the prey! Miranda couldn't be sure the thought was hers or the Infected's.

The puddle of motorcycle gas was heading toward the puddle of spilled gas from the pumps.

"Torres, get back!" Miranda yelled. She ran a few steps toward the other woman. Torres followed Miranda's gaze, a look of horror replacing her manic grin. She bolted for the store. The women tumbled inside, nearly falling over dead Clarence.

Torres pushed herself up on her good elbow. "Well, that —"

Outside, the massive explosion finally made its debut. Ernie's remaining windows shattered, spraying shards of glass across the store. A flash of light and heat followed, a burst of sound, then an instant of silence as if the fire were drawing a deep breath. In that moment, Miranda looked at Elfy, huddling behind a counter in a general store with a dead biker in BFE Oregon. Hard to say that Torres bringing her niece with had been in the girl's best interest.

The second blast from the pumps tore the door off. It sent a wave of fire in through the windows. The pile of books from the overturned rack caught. Miranda scrambled up and grabbed a woven blanket, the kind rustic places tried to pass off as "authentic Native American Indian," but which were mass produced somewhere in China. She smothered the flames, before sinking to her knees, then sitting back on her heels.

"We are some lucky fuckers, aren't we?" Torres said hoarsely. She sat up slowly and leaned against the counter.

"You said a swear," Elfy whispered.

"And I played with fire. It's good to be a grownup." Torres grinned and tried to get up, but her arm gave out. She would have fallen, but Miranda caught her.

"Thanks."

Miranda helped the former Marine brace herself against the counter. Most of the shattered glass had fallen out of the window frames, but a few shards hung on like rotten teeth. The air was thick with the smoke from the fire Miranda had put out. She didn't know if they were in danger of lung damage from smoke inhalation, but it seemed about right for the kind of day they were having.

A pillar of fire shot into the sky. It rose higher than the store. The tops of the surrounding trees were on fire and flaming branches were dropping to the forest floor below.

The bikers were nowhere to be seen. Small mercies. *Where's our meal?*

Miranda blinked. What would happen if a big group of the Infected arrived and there was no food at the buffet she'd invited them to? They needed to get moving, and fast!

"C'mon." She waved for Elfy and Torres to go out.

Elfy shook her head, so Torres hooked the girl around the waist with her good arm and carried her out. The pistol dropped from her fingers. She barely missed a step, but Miranda could guess how much Jimmy's gun must mean to her. She crouched and refusing to imagine the gun in a pool of vomit, scooped it up. Torres would thank her later.

Then she was out and into the raging inferno of the gas station.

"Looks like Kuwait after Saddam paid his respects," Torres said, like this was a totally normal whatever day of the week it was.

"Oh shit — Alice!" Miranda turned toward the RV. Elfy thrashed in Torres's arms, her little hands connecting with the former Marine's injured shoulder. Torres's eyes rolled back in her eye like a cartoon — just the whites showing. She dropped to her knees, gasping. Elfy tottered free as Torres crumpled forward, her head against the asphalt of the parking lot.

Miranda ran back and dropped next to Torres. She was muttering, "I can't, I can't, I can't ..."

Where was the stupid first aid bag? In the RV? Miranda looked around. The parking lot seemed to waver, as the Infected tried to reach into her mind. *Let us see. Let us see. Show us what you see.*

No! Miranda pushed them back with more force than she knew she possessed. *Get out. Leave me alone.*

"Who are you talking to?" Torres's voice was a croak. Miranda opened her eyes. Torres lay on her side, her shoulder dark with blood. The wound must have reopened. Elfy hovered near Torres, tears streaking lines through the soot on her face. Phineas ran toward them from the far side of the parking lot.

"Na ... no one." Miranda stammered. She could still feel the Infected, like a migraine about to strike. They were moving north again, brushing against her mind, but not part of her. They'd found something else, some other prey. A town? A Geo Metro full of sorority sisters? But she was cut off from their communication and their community. For the time being, her mind was her own.

Miranda shook her head. No bikers. Only their burning bikes remained. The pump fires burned steadily, maybe like oil wells. Miranda would take Torres's word for it. Around the parking lot, the blackened trees still smoldered, but no forest fire had started. Probably because everything was soaked from the rain.

"Please get up. I'm sorry. I'll be good." Elfy held out a hand to Torres, paused to rub snot from under her nose.

I'm sorry. I'll be good. That's what Alice had said.

Alice.

Miranda and Torres exchanged a look. Torres stumbled up and Miranda helped her. They limped toward the RV. Torres had to lean on Miranda a little. The former Marine's balance seemed to be off, but the women made it to the RV before Phineas did.

Someone was muttering, a low droning chant. A prayer in Arabic, Miranda guessed. She climbed the steps.

Soraya knelt on the floor, rocking back and forth, cradling Mirzha. Alice lay on the bed. The top of her head was gone and her eyes stared blankly at the ceiling. Washington stood in the doorway of the bathroom, with Wahida peeking out from behind him.

"Is she?" Miranda stopped. How could she ask a mother to admit her child was dead?

Soraya paused rocking. She turned her head, her eyes wide and dry. There was blood sprayed across the lower half of her face. Her teeth gleamed white against her light brown skin and the darkening mask of blood.

"No. Praise be to Allah, the Merciful. I am a happy murderess."

Mirzha raised her head from her mother's chest. Her throat was chaffed and red. She reached to touch it and shook her head, then lay back against Soraya.

"She killed Alice," Washington said. "Shot that lady in the face. I saw it." He still hadn't moved from the bathroom.

"She tried to kill my sister," Wahida said.

"Miranda?" Phineas called from outside. "What's going on in there? Do you need help?"

Soraya bent down and laid her cheek along Mirzha's. She took up her rocking and chanting again.

"Hang on," Miranda called. She turned to Washington and Wahida. "You kids okay?"

"She hit me. Busted my wrist cause I tried to help that girl," Washington said.

"Um, yikes," Miranda said. What was she supposed to do about a broken wrist? Was it even broken? "Wahida?" She waved at the girl.

Wahida waved back. "I'm fine. Where's Elfy?"

"I'm fine, too," Elfy called from outside.

Miranda did a quick roll call in her head. Soraya and her girls. Phineas and Washington. The sorority girls were gone. The Suburbans. Art and his heart attack. Henry had been shot. Greg was infected. Shit. There was still all of that to deal with.

She stepped out of the RV and watched the flames dance in the rising wind. Another shower was moving in. Sparks flew up into the sky. The black smoke vanished into the clouds. It blended and bled like watercolor paint. It was turning the whole sky, the whole world, dark.

Chapter 12 – Torres

Portland, OR, U.S.A. - Autumn, Year 1

"She needs a doctor or a pharmacist or drugs or something."

Torres clawed her way out of fever dreams. The RV wasn't moving. The window near her was cracked open and she could hear Miranda's voice from outside. Trees surrounded the RV. Had they stopped in the woods? Torres couldn't remember where they were. They'd been going to Portland to get Marius. She knew that.

"I fear we have more pressing issues," Soraya said.

"Greg?"

"Indeed. It's clear he's not well."

Greg. He'd been bitten by an infected raccoon. Why

didn't we leave him? Why didn't I make us leave him, Torres wondered. They'd left Ernie's in a terrified rush. Miranda had been frantic, insisting the Infected were coming. Soraya had worried the bikers would return. Torres had been too tired to do anything besides trace out the route to Portland and crash into bed. How long had she slept?

The first aid bag lay next to the bed. Torres took a few aspirins and some Motrin for good measure. She drank the rest of the water in her bottle and wiped her face. As she opened the RV door, the conversation stopped. Miranda, Soraya, and Phineas were gathered near the RV, which was in a mostly empty RV park. Patty and Greg sat on the open tailgate of the Suburban. The girls were climbing a tree while Washington, arm in a sling, and Mirzha watched them.

"We need to find Marius," Torres announced. "He's the best chance we've got to help Greg."

"Do we even know where he is? Portland's not, like, small or anything," Miranda said.

"Any word from John?" Torres scanned the area. Through the trees, she could see the rooftops of single-family dwellings. A residential area. They must be in the suburbs.

"Nope." Miranda held up her phone. "And rumor has it they're going to be shutting down social media sites soon. Here, you gotta see these posts from LA."

The posts showed a city in chaos. The streets were filled with barriers. Some were clearly military, while others looked like a bunch of locals had collected anything they could find from picnic tables to couches and surf boards and piled them together. Several videos were of terrified people who whispered their final farewells to family and friends while hiding under desks or in closets. A few videos were of the Infected, usually taken from a far distance or from above as if the camera people had been afraid to get closer.

"The government's advising everyone to get to evacuation points if you can," Phineas said. "And if not—"

"Shelter in place," Torres and Miranda chorused.

"So, nothing useful." Torres handed Miranda back her phone.

"Might check with those folks at the checkpoint," Phineas said.

"Ah, no." Miranda didn't look up from scrolling. "We don't need the same line of BS or to get rounded up again for our own protection."

Phineas looked at Torres, but before the former Marine could respond, Soraya said, "I'm afraid I must agree with Miranda. I know very few tense situations which are improved by adding armed strangers."

"Besides, we know more about what's going on than they do," Miranda said.

"She's not wrong," Torres said. "But we're going to need to get into the city to get Marius, so 'being rounded up' might work in this instance."

In the gloaming, a wind set the trees to swaying, shaking off leaves. Elfy and Wahida collected armloads, heaping them up to make a pile about up to the girls' knees. They ran back and forth through it, squealing and whooping.

"Whatever we do we're gonna have to do it super fast." Miranda tipped her chin towards Greg. "He's

Infected and gonna turn soon."

"How do you know?" Torres frowned. Since when had Miranda become such an expert in the speed and severity of HHV infections?

"Because ... I ... look at him!" Miranda waved a hand at the Suburban. Patty and Greg looked up from their conversation. Patty glared, but Greg looked scared. Scared and sick. Miranda had an undeniable point. Torres didn't know exactly how long it might take someone to turn, but Marius had mentioned some strains were worse than others. Her mind flashed back to Jimmy lunging toward her, all recognition gone. No humanity, only hunger and rage.

Soraya held out an energy bar, which Torres accepted. She wasn't hungry, but she knew she needed to eat.

"Okay, let's game this out. We have two problems— Marius and Greg. But if we find Marius, he can help Greg." Like he helped Cynty? Torres tried not to think about her sister and mother still in Los Angeles. Or what if Cynthia had turned and infected Mama? What if the only family she had left was Elfy?

"Except that we have three problems," Soraya said. "I don't need to be a doctor to know your shoulder needs care and soon."

But if my infection spreads, I won't grow extra teeth or tentacles or try to kill all of you and nest in your guts, Torres thought. She missed John and Jimmy and the other former military folks from the security team. They understood that the needs of the many always outweighed the needs of the few. They would try to save her if they could, but they also understood the main objective was—had to be—Marius.

Miranda paced a small circle. "We need to go."

"We will. We need a plan." Torres bit off a chewy chunk of energy bar.

"We can figure it out once we're in town."

"It's pointless and a waste of gas to go until we know where we're going and why."

Miranda stopped, stared over the treetops as if she could see into Portland. She started forward as if she meant to walk into town by herself.

"Hey, where are you going?" Torres grabbed her arm. Miranda whirled around, teeth bared, eyes narrowed. Torres held up her hands. "What the fuck?"

"Don't touch us," Miranda snarled.

"Miranda—" Soraya took a step toward the young woman, but Torres waved her back.

"Who are you?" the former Marine asked.

"We are the Enlightened." Miranda's voice was low, rasping. All the hairs on Torres's arms rose. The chill calm of combat washed through her, chasing away the fever. At least for the next few minutes, she would be clear and focused.

"Why do you want to go to Portland?" Torres concentrated on getting the information, while the back of her brain screamed for her to destroy whatever this Miranda-shaped threat was. It was Infected and worse, it had infiltrated their group. It was a spy.

"Don't want to be disconnected any longer. We ... I ..." Miranda stopped, squeezed her eyes shut and shuddered, a full-body shake, like a dog shedding water. "Torres?" Her hazel eyes looked confused, frightened even. The usual veneer of perkiness and snark vanished.

Tears slid down her cheeks. "I'm so sorry. I didn't mean to!"

"You didn't mean to what?" The warm fever haze was creeping back in. Torres put a hand on the truck's hood to keep from swaying.

Miranda crumpled to her knees, her hair curtaining her face. In a whisper, she said, "I told them to kill people. I didn't mean to. At first, I tried to get them to leave everyone alone, but they're so hungry. I'm so hungry. And they wanted to help me. They want me to come home. They want to take care of me." She looked up. "They don't want me to ever be scared again."

"How long ...?" Torres blinked, unsure what she meant to ask, unsure how to process what Miranda was saying, what it meant for their group, for her friend.

"Since Wiltz," Miranda said. Her voice was still soft, but not the raspy growl of the Infected. "I'm sorry. They wanted me to hurt Marius. They say he's an abomination. They hate that they need him. They don't want him here. They're ... we're afraid of him." She pressed her palms against her eyes.

"Fuuuuuck." Torres bent over the truck's hood, stared at the small patch of silver paint enclosed within the borders of her arms. As long as she didn't put any weight on her bad shoulder, the pain was bearable. Barely.

"But they do know he's here?" Phineas spoke softly from behind her. "I mean, for sure they know?"

"Mmm-hmmm." Miranda pointed. "He's over there."

"How do you know?" Torres asked.

"I can feel them. There's like a hub or something."

"A hub? That sounds more than slightly dangerous,"

Soraya said.

"We're not all going." Torres pushed herself up and looked around at the little band. "Listen up, you lot!"

Torres and Miranda took the interstate into Portland, following the Columbia River. The plan was that once downtown, they would rely on Miranda's Infection-sense to pinpoint where Marius was. While they were gone, Soraya suggested that Patty and Greg could stay in the RV. He'd be more comfortable there, she'd said. And easier to contain. But she didn't say that part.

"Get everyone's stuff and pack up the truck," Torres had told Phineas and Soraya. "You girls listen to Soraya and do what she says. Stay close. Especialmente tu, Elfy."

Patty had shuffled Greg into the RV, her furious eyes blazing as if she meant to mark each of them through the power of her will alone. Miranda had driven the Forester and much to her own surprise, Torres had dozed off. The soft hush of the wheels on the interstate lulled her, as did the warm comfort of the truck's cab.

"There's a sign for the VA hospital. Should we go that way?"

Torres blinked awake, disoriented. The last rays of the sun were fading blue in a darker sky spangled with stars. A crescent moon rode the ridges, as if pleased to have their company. Torres rubbed her eyes and pushed herself up with her good arm. Even that motion jarred her shoulder and she hissed against her teeth.

"Too late," Miranda said. "I had to make a choice.

We're committed now."

They were climbing a ramp up onto a curving bridge. It had multiple levels, which split off in different directions at either end of the bridge. Below the Willamette River drowsed in its bed, smooth and dark, dreaming of the waters of the Pacific.

"Wait," Torres said. She braced herself, craned her neck, looked over the edge of the bridge. "What is that?"

"What?" Miranda said, her tone almost comedically casual.

Torres studied the younger woman for a long moment. Would she have to kill Miranda to get rid of whatever Infected influence clung to her? No. That was not an option. No friendly frags. Marius would be able to help. Miranda was part of the team.

Miranda heaved a sigh. "It's a nest."

"A nest?" Torres shuddered, picturing something like a spider's egg sac bulging with squirming, writhing Infected, eager for a nibble of human flesh. "Why are there nests under a bridge in a major city?"

"Don't look now, but we're, like, surrounded," Miranda intoned as they descended from the bridge.

Torres peered out the window, searching the darkened homes and offices for signs of the Infected. She sat up further. It wasn't only the houses and buildings that were dark. The streetlights were out. Parking lots were shrouded in shadows. Anything beyond the light of the Forester's headlight beams was a mystery.

"There's no power," Torres said. But where were the generators, the camping lanterns and candles for emergencies?

"They don't know we're here."

Torres shivered. It was weird hearing Miranda speak so flatly, so factually. No emotion, no internet speak. On top of that, it was deeply unsettling for Torres to have to rely on Miranda and her Infected-sense to navigate the city. She thought she could do it, but that had been with the assumption that the lights would be on and people, non-infected people, would be hunkered in their homes. Where was everyone? Had they all evacuated? How had they had time?

Miranda pulled the Forester over and parked. Torres exited the vehicle, scanning the area. The avenue was lined with weeping willows and quaking aspens. The houses appeared abandoned, but a closer look revealed broken windows, doors hanging askew from their hinges. A suitcase lay open in one yard and in another, an adult's bike and a child's bike, complete with training wheels, were jumbled together.

Miranda walked into the middle of the street and stopped, turning her head slowly one way and then the other. "This way," she said, and set off at a near jog. Any other time, Torres would have been confident of her ability to outrun and outlast Miranda. With the fever clenched at the base of her skull and the pain throbbing from her shoulder, it was a struggle to keep up. Torres gritted her teeth. She would die before she asked the younger woman to slow down for her.

The street wound up a hill. About halfway up a hairpin curve, Miranda turned aside into the scrubby woods. A stairway of weathered four-by-four boards led up the hill at an even steeper angle than the street. Despite the evening's chill, Torres was slick with sweat.

At least, she hoped it was sweat. Now was not the time for her stitches to let go.

At the top of the hill, they emerged from the trees onto another road, which continued up and around toward the MAIN ENTRANCE as a sign announced. On the side of the building a plaque designated the place they'd arrived at as The Portland VA Medical Center. As they crossed the road, Torres realized what she'd first taken to be ivy or moss on the building's exterior was not any plant, vining or otherwise. They were like the fleshy bioformations she'd seen before in Chrysalis and Wiltz. Was this what Miranda meant when she said they were nesting?

"Hold up," Torres reached to grab Miranda's arm, but misjudged the distance, her hand swinging uselessly through the air. The younger woman didn't seem to hear her, her pace steady as she marched toward the hospital's rear entrance. "Miranda, that's a meat wall."

"They don't like that term," Miranda said over her shoulder. "He was right about it. He was right about most things."

"Right about what?" Torres hurried to catch up.

"That it's bioforming. They use it to help the newly turned. They share strength and information." Miranda stopped in the doorway, her hand hovering over a dark mass where several thick veins knotted together.

"Don't." Torres didn't know what she thought might happen if Miranda touched the meat wall, but she knew deep in her guts that it would be bad. Catastrophic, even.

Miranda stared at her hand, shivered, let it fall. "This way." She pushed open the automatic door. With no power to the building it took a lot of muscle power to lever the door open wide enough that the women could squeeze through.

Inside the sweet stench of the Infected hit Torres full force. She gagged and pulled her shirt up over her nose and mouth. Miranda turned on her phone's flashlight app and led the way down the hall and up the stairs. As they pushed deeper into the hospital, the bioformations grew thicker, making the corridors feel tighter and tighter.

"Oy!" A voice hissed from out of the dark of one of the side offices. Torres yanked out Jimmy's HK. Only five rounds remaining. "Don't shoot."

"Don't jump out of the dark like a freaking popup target," Torres snapped.

"You can't go up there." A short, wiry man stepped into the dim light Miranda's phone cast in the hall. He had an Irish accent.

"You're not in charge here," Miranda said. Again, her emotionless voice sent chills through Torres. How long had Miranda been like this? Was this person even Miranda or was she merely a vehicle for the Infected or the Enlightened? Torres wasn't clear on what the difference was.

"Don't I know it, girl?" the man said. He held out a hand. "Name's Liam."

Torres lifted the pistol. "Back off, buddy."

"Calm yourselves. We're on the same side, eh?"

"Now he knows which side we're on," Torres said. She adjusted her stance to keep herself between the man and Miranda.

"Namajaysus." Liam fumbled in his jacket pocket and pulled out a pack of cigarettes. He put one in his lips but didn't light it. "Course we're on the same side. You don't have feelers and such growing out the tops of your heads. Is the way out clear, so?"

"Clear enough for us to walk in," Torres said. "No guards or scouts or anything."

"And why would there be?" Liam waved his unlit cigarette at the ceiling. Torres looked up.

The ceiling writhed.

"What the ..." Torres caught Miranda's hand and turned her phone-flashlight upwards. The ceiling was covered in tentacles, tubes, and veins in a horrific upside-down spaghetti splatter.

"The world's most shite internet hub, that's what that is." Liam tucked his cigarette behind his ear.

"What are you doing here? You shouldn't be here," Miranda said.

"Not a one of us should be here, my girl," Liam said.

"Your condescension is not nearly as endearing as you may think," Miranda said. She turned back toward the hall that led deeper into the dark, Infected-filled hospital.

"There's no one up there," Liam hissed. "You're gonna get yourself killed. I'm just after exploring this whole place. There's only the old man in the tower and no one's getting nowhere near him."

"Hold up," Torres said. She wasn't trying to stall, she told herself. They needed to find out why this man was here alone. That was it. She definitely wasn't afraid of the Infected or some old guy in a tower. "You never answered our question. Why are you here?"

The dim light of Miranda's phone-flashlight wavered in time with her breathing. Or was it that the light was reflecting off the slimy, pink-purple flesh walls? Were the walls breathing?

After this I'm going to do a deep dive into an Olympic sized pool of bleach, Torres decided.

"Came to see a man about some money I was owed. Got into town right enough, even with all the checkpoints and such. But don't you know, Carmine couldn't bother himself to finish the job. After all the trouble I went through, lugging his precious man hither and yon ..." Liam snorted. "Sends him off with the Infected quick as you please."

"Carmine Anino?" Torres stared at Liam. "I thought he was dead."

"Not unless that Chinese lady murdered him."

"What Chinese lady?"

"Torres." Miranda had walked away without Torres noticing. In the gloom, only her hands and legs were visible in the light from her phone. "We should go. They're hurting Marius."

Torres kept a hand on Miranda as the women made their way through the bioformation choked hallways. The light from Miranda's phone bounced off the slimy walls, revealing mottled hues of pink, red, and purple. Not sure where to find Marius, Torres had suggested they keep heading upwards. Liam had decided to try his luck outside alone rather than risking another trip into the hospital.

The only sound, besides the disgusting gurgles and whooshes of the bioformations, was Torres's labored breathing. And the patter of approaching footsteps.

Torres squeezed Miranda's shoulder and pulled her back. The younger woman quickly turned off her phone's flashlight app. Torres covered her lower face with her elbow, hoping to muffle the sound of her panting.

Ahead of them was an intersection where their hallway met another passageway. A figure moved across the opening. It looked like a person, but not quite. The legs were wrong, with back bent knees like some nightmare creature from a fairytale. They were carrying a tray that rattled and chimed gently. Even Torres recognized the unmistakable sound of test tubes.

The figure shuffled away down the hall and paused before a knot of twisted tentacles. The person touched the knot and the tentacles retracted. Behind them was a door marked STAIRWELL 4 - EAST.

As soon as the person had gone and the tentacles reformed their knot, Torres burst out with the coughs she'd been holding.

"We should follow her," Miranda said as Torres wiped her eyes and caught her breath.

"Do you think that's where Marius is?" Torres wheezed.

"Maybe Marius is the man in the tower that dude was talking about." Miranda started forward. "Whoever's up there is important. I can feel the Infected. They're all paying attention to him."

At the bioformation, the women paused. It was a twisted tangle with no obvious way through. Miranda pressed her hand to it and froze.

"What?" Torres looked around, half-expecting the

walls themselves to attack them.

Miranda held up her other hand, which trembled. "He … he's here." She looked at Torres. "He's alive. He's here. He was waiting for me."

"Good," Torres said. "Let's get going before the Infected figure out what we're up to."

Miranda closed her eyes and put her other hand on the bioformation, which opened for her. The door was covered in sludge and slime. Torres was grateful for the poor lighting, so she didn't have to see it all that clearly as the women wriggled through the opening and doorway into the stairwell.

They climbed two flights of stairs. At the third landing, Miranda pulled open the door and stepped inside. Torres didn't even have a chance to ask how she knew they were at the right floor.

A short hall led to a row of offices. Judging by the size of the offices, with their banks of windows and expensive furnishings, they were in the rarified air of upper management. Or what used to be upper management.

Miranda's light glanced off couches covered with biofilm, desks half drowned in puddles of sludge, big screen TVs entangled in forests of veins.

And Albert Viers.

He was almost human. At least the part of him Torres could see over the top of the desk he sat behind was.

She had last seen the doctor at the fateful holiday party the night everything had gone to hell back at Chrysalis. He'd had the vitality of a person who was lucky enough to spend their life doing exactly what they wanted and getting paid very well for it. His current appearance was a stark contrast. His skin was sallow and looked slightly damp like a frog's. He had lost all his hair and his glasses. His eyes shone eerily as Miranda's light reflected off them. Dark veins pulsed just below his skin, which was pocked with small, ulcerous sores and dry patches of flakey eczema.

"I knew you would find me." The voice didn't seem to come from Viers as much as from everything around them, as if every tentacle vibrated along with his vocal cords.

"Dad." The phone tumbled from Miranda's hand, but otherwise she didn't move. Torres picked up the phone. She shook the worst of the sludge off it and wiped it on her pants.

"Don't cry, Miranda. We have the problem in hand. We can be together again and —"

A scream, wild and wailing, echoed through the room. Torres whirled to keep the door in sight. She stuffed the phone in her pocket. She needed both hands to have any chance of keeping Jimmy's HK steady if it came to that.

A small explosion.

"We have to go." Viers rose from behind the desk. The bottom half of him looked like the sea witch in that kids' movie about the mermaid. Long, thick tentacles supported Viers, moving him in a smooth glide as they writhed across the floor. A second set of withered-looking arms sprouted from just below his ribcage. They reached toward the women.

Miranda recoiled, but then, fists clenched, stepped forward. "Dad, I have to ask you something about the Enlightened."

A second, louder explosion rattled the room. The

door from the hallway slammed open. Carmine burst in. He was carrying a flashlight and decked out in the kind of ostentatiously tactic-cool outfit that Torres and the rest of the security team had mockingly referred to as 'Walmart warcore.' Between the embedded-journalist vest and the cargo pants, he probably had twenty pockets on his outfit.

Torres snapped the HK's sights onto Carmine's center mass.

"No!" Miranda grabbed the pistol's barrel. Torres nearly squeezed the trigger out of shock but managed to stop herself in time.

Carmine dashed across the room and pushed open a door that had been hidden in the gloom behind Viers's desk. Through the door, Torres could see the slightly lighter sky and building silhouettes. A flat rooftop with the markings of a helipad waited outside.

Two more explosions rocked the building.

"Kill him," Viers said to Carmine. He glided out the door as a chopper settled onto the landing pad.

"Reyka already did," Carmine said. He dodged out the door and bellyflopped into the chopper.

Viers paused to look back at Miranda.

"Find me," he said, then boarded the chopper, which was hovering. The whole building rocked as if they were having an earthquake.

"Wait!" Miranda charged the door. "Dad, wait!"

The chopper lifted away as the roof collapsed. Torres grabbed Miranda by her jacket and hauled her back from the edge.

"Don't leave me." Miranda's voice was so faint Torres could have imagined it, but the tears on the younger woman's face were very real.

Chapter 13 – Marius

Portland, OR, U.S.A. - Autumn, Year 1

It was a cat that saved the world. A cat and some mushrooms.

Most of the wildlife in Portland had either been eaten or infected. According to Reyka, the city had been 'cleansed.' Marius did not want to imagine what that might mean. He kept his focus on two tasks: observing and cataloging the devolution process from the SAM-D strain to the FOX-H strain and finding a way to destroy the base HHV strain.

The Enlightened could provide him all the Fox samples he needed. They were less accommodating with the Sammies. For the base strain, Marius had only himself to sample. With the Enlightened's limited genetic sequencing capabilities, he still couldn't determine where his own immunity had come from. The idea that he'd been deliberately infected or that his genes had been altered rustled around in the back of his brain, but he pushed it aside in favor of the task at hand.

In order to have any chance at destroying HHV, he had to understand it, track how it changed and mutated. The same research the Enlightened demanded of him brought him closer to finding their weak points and vulnerabilities.

Marius stood at the counter, peering into a microscope, studying a slide of cat blood. He couldn't use his own to see how his latest efforts to modify the SAM-D strain would affect the Enlightened. After all, he was immune.

The donor of the blood lay in a cage on the counter. Marius rubbed his eyes. Without windows or clocks, the only way he could gauge time's passage was by how often Reyka arrived to bring food and demand updates. He was allowed a stopwatch to keep his experiments on track, but it didn't tell him if it was day or night or three weeks from when he'd been relatively safe and comfortable in the lab in Los Angeles. Ah, the wonderful days when an ankle bracelet had been the height of hardship.

"Dr. Viers will only be with us for a few more days," Reyka said. She had been collecting the medical-waste containers. "It would be wise to have a solution for him to take back with him." One of the bags had a leak, but she didn't acknowledge the bloody fluids that seeped from it to snake down her forearm and drip from her elbow.

"I'm working on it," Marius said.

"Work faster. There will come a point where you're no longer useful to them." Reyka tottered out without elaborating.

So, Marius pushed himself. If the Enlightened killed him, no one with the skills, knowledge, and yes, the immunity to HHV would remain to fight it.

In lieu of sleep, he braced himself against the counter and watched the microscopic drama unfold. Healthy cells were attacked, red saturated with purple, all defenses swept aside as if the immune system was nothing. Marius checked the cat. It was in the late stages of infection. So far HHV's mortality rate hovered around 60%. The tally sheet he kept hanging from the wall above the counter didn't bode well for Fluffy's chances.

Better not waste the specimen. Marius drew a fresh vial and prepared another slide. The devastation in the cat's cells had advanced significantly since the last batch he'd drawn two hours ago. All the little mechanisms of the cells were shutting down. Some of the cell membranes had thickened as if trying to protect the inside from the infected blood outside. This had caused waste buildup in the cells, and some had ruptured. Others had surrendered to the infection. Marius could see nuclei, no longer discrete bundles, now stretched, twisted. The virus was busy trying to rewrite the cat's DNA.

Fluffy coughed weakly. Marius hated having to hurt animals. The right thing to do with a suffering animal was to end its pain. His parents had brought him up with an understanding of the necessities of life. Yes, they occasionally slaughtered animals for various reasons, but it was never something frivolous or fun. Experimenting on cats was not fun, especially the ones that reminded Marius of the numerous tribe of barn cats back home.

He stared at the slide, trying to shut out the last raspy breaths of Fluffy's life. Finally, they stopped. He sagged against the counter, closed his eyes, dreamed of sleeping, of lying down on the cold, hard tile and escaping into unconsciousness.

Pop.

The sound was so soft, Marius almost doubted he'd heard it. He opened his eyes and looked around. He knew all the lab sounds, the click and whir of the centrifuge, the hiccupping burble of the Bunsen burners, the hiss of gas, the clatter and roll of the spectrometer.

But this sound was different. Organic, not mechanical. He listened, head tilting this way and that. Maybe I'm finally losing it, he thought.

Pop. Pop.

It was close. Quiet, but close.

Marius looked around. Fluffy's corpse lay on a large piece of butcher block paper, ready for her necropsy. But she was moving.

Marius jerked back instinctively.

In her death throes, Fluffy's lips had drawn back, revealing very pale gums. He'd seen that before. As the Infected neared death, their organs shut down and most of their blood pooled in their bellies and lower digestive tract.

Something dark threaded through Fluffy's tissues. A bubble, so small it was nearly invisible, rose and, with a gentle pop, burst. Marius grabbed a face shield and bent closer. What looked like movement along the dark thread, was really the bubbles rising and bursting like tiny puffball mushrooms.

Was HHV airborne?

Marius frowned. There was no evidence that it was. Small mercies. Virulent, yes. But it could only survive in the liquid media of the body.

Quickly, Marius collected samples. Under the microscope, he found mycelia and spores. At some point, before the cat had been brought to the lab, some enterprising mushroom had colonized it and started the decomposition process. Marius walked a slow circuit of the lab, chewing his lower lip. He knew that, like bacteria, viruses could fall victim to fungi. The mold that had contaminated his specimens in Los Angeles provided evidence that HHV infected media were susceptible to multiple kinds of fungi, not just saprophytic mushrooms.

If fungi could infect HHV, it might be used as a delivery system to introduce a stabilizer to the SAM-D strain. A spore could also contain an inhibitor that would prevent the virus from replicating outside its original host. Or even in the original host. What if the virus lost the power of mutation? Each virus would be effective only against the specific genetic code of its host at the moment the stabilizer was introduced. Any further mutation of HHV would trigger the inhibitor. It would prevent any further infections, definitely. It would slow or stop the course of HHV in the current host. It might even cure the Infected.

Marius stopped in front of Fluffy. He didn't have time

to reinvent the mushroom's DNA, nor did he have the resources. But the bioformation network might do the trick for him. A super-massive organism like that could do millions, if not billions, of replications a second, leading to thousands, if not millions, of chances for mutation. All he had to do was introduce the right copying error and the bioformations would propagate the fungal infection itself.

For the first time since Wiltz, Marius felt a surge of hope. Yes, the Enlightened would likely torture and kill him, but if he was correct, they would be dead before they could get to his family.

It worked.

Marius stared at the vial in his hand. Under the naked bulbs of the lab, it gleamed like Eärendil. Inside, curled within the spores was a blessing and curse. As the fungus infected the virus, it would stabilize it, slow the devolution from SAM-D to FOX-H strain. Once the fungus had fully saturated the bioformations, it would enter the spore-producing phase of its lifecycle. The spores would spread the genetically modified fungus, even as the original host bioformations withered and died, victims of the parasitic fungus.

"Good."

Marius started. He'd completely forgotten Reyka, crouched silently in a corner, watching him work.

She unfolded and joined the scientist at the table. "Of course, this will be tested thoroughly before we consider what comes next."

Marius had no illusions as to what would come next. The Enlightened would kill him once they believed they had what they needed. How long would it take for the spores to develop? What if it happened too fast? What if the spores needed some specific environmental cue or set of conditions, like jack pines that needed fire to open their cones?

After the hours ... days? ... of work, Marius was suddenly wracked with doubt. This was his only chance.

"I'm not sure it's done." Marius reached for the vial, but Reyka stepped away. She laid a hand on the bioformation that closed the hallway and several tentacles pried themselves away from the door, twisting and slithering towards Marius.

"Let's hope it is. Imagine what might happen if you tried to harm the Enlightened."

The tentacles shot forward, two of them wrapping around Marius's arms and legs, while the third latched onto his neck. The shock of the pain was so immediate and intense that at first all Marius could perceive was a blinding whiteness. No sound, no physical sensation. His nerves overloaded his brain, and it interpreted it all as a haze.

In seconds that haze dissolved into individual sensations. Rolling cramps, which felt like they would tear his muscles from his bones, surged through Marius's body. Nerve pain that would put even the worst anesthetic-free dental procedure to shame flicked from the crown of his head to the soles of his feet, from the tips of his fingers to his toes.

At some point, he pissed himself. At some other point, or maybe the same one, he vomited. Moments or hours later, he lay in a puddle of his own filth, shivering and twitching with the aftershocks, utterly exhausted. A curling fractal pattern of corruption spread, following the nerves across his shoulders, marking him.

"Preliminary results are promising." Reyka's voice, smooth and unconcerned as if she floated miles above him.

Marius grunted. Uncurling his seized-up hands was proving tricky.

"Dr. Viers is concerned about the fungus. Why use it?"

Marius grunted again. Reyka toed him in the ribs. It wasn't hard, barely more than a touch, but the sensation was nearly overwhelming. Marius shuddered, tears tracking down his face.

"Why?"

Marius gritted his teeth. "Because the spores can spread the cure faster than anything else. There's no environment that they can't be modified for. Arid, damp, even underwater. The mycelia will work with the bioformation, reinforce the connections between Infected—"

Reyka toed him harder, and he cried out. His body wanted to curl into a fetal position, but his muscles were too tired, too full of lactic acid. He twitched uselessly.

"The Enlightened don't like that term."

Marius let his head sink into the muck and closed his eyes.

"Dr. Viers wants a demonstration of what the Enlightened can expect once your cure is implemented."

For better or for worse, the spores had to get out in the world. He only hoped that Reyka would decide to make his end fast. Painless would be asking too much.

"Fire," Marius said. "The spores need fire. I would need a sample from one of the SAM-D...from the Enlightened. I introduce the cure and use fire to cause the spores to explode so I can measure the rate of spread."

"I'll be back. Get yourself cleaned up. This is a laboratory, not a latrine." Reyka limped to the door, which irised open for her, the tentacles that rimmed it coiling out of the way.

Marius levered himself up on one elbow, then backed into a kneeling position, and finally, with the aid of the counter, pulled himself up to his feet.

He was going to die soon. Within hours, if not minutes. He wished he could call his family, tell them he loved them, apologize for failing them, for failing the world so spectacularly. The spores wouldn't work. They couldn't. It had been a fever dream, a last frantic clutch at a solution as he sank into the Infected.

Was this how people felt as they mutated? Did they know they were dying or at least becoming so other that the person they used to be would never again exist? Marius hoped not. He hoped HHV disabled higher brain functioning—all evidence strongly suggested it did.

So, he was alone in knowing his own death was toddling towards him on crippled legs.

"Fuck your canoe," he muttered, remembering a joke John had told him. Viers would be careful of anything he produced, would test it, would probably discover the not-so-well-hidden inhibitor and never implement the cure.

But Viers didn't have all of it. Marius wiped his face

and hands as clean as he could get them and, leaning his elbows on the counter for support, got back to work.

Marius stood in the center of a ring of spores. The powder was nearly translucent, glimmering ever so slightly. He held a lighter up, watching the small golden flicker dancing. Was this how humanity's ancient ancestors had felt when they first realized they could harness the power of fire to do their bidding?

The spores were designed to affect the SAM-D and FOX-H strains through the bioformation, but Marius had no guarantees they wouldn't also affect the base strain that slept within his own body.

"Better to be ashes than dust," he murmured. His mother had always loved Jack London. Better not to think of home, of his parents, Philippe and Annette, or his sister and brother. He might be sentencing them to horrific deaths. Would they understand? Forgive him?

The bioformation in the doorway shuddered, opening to reveal Reyka.

"What do you think—" Her question turned into a shriek as Marius dropped the lighter. The ring of spores burst like tiny fireworks. The heat of the fire spread them throughout the laboratory. A faint sizzle erupted from the bioformation in the doorway as the spores embedded themselves in it.

"They're going to kill you," Reyka howled. She had fallen to her knees. Marius caught a glimpse of her crawling away as the doorway closed behind her.

Woof! The membrane caught. There was a faint

sucking sensation as the air moved through the room toward the door. Reyka screamed. Marius stared at his handiwork. He had hated Reyka, and now she was going to burn to death because of him. He tried to feel guilty. A good person would have. He only felt vague curiosity. Would she explode too, like the spores?

The fire raced over the membrane in a spray of orange and gold and then another explosion. The force was much greater than the one from the ring of spores. It knocked Marius back against the counter. He shook his head to clear it. His ears keened a high-pitched whine. The doorway was devoid of membrane, only swirling dust and the misshapen lump of Reyka. The charred remnants of her mouth moved, but Marius couldn't understand what she was saying for the ringing in his ears.

Following Reyka's gaze, through the open doorway, he saw a spangle of tiny flashes spread across the membrane in the hallway. It exploded with even greater force than the one in the doorway had. The impact flattened Marius against the counter. His head cracked and everything blurred out for a few seconds.

Ashes fell around him as if he sat in the center of a dirty snow-globe. All around, in an expanding wave, Marius could hear explosions. It sounded as if the whole of Portland had been set up for demolition. The closer impacts rattled the building, but as his head cleared and the ring of destruction moved outward, the shaking decreased.

Marius staggered to his feet, levering himself up by grabbing the edge of the counter. His ears throbbed and his fingers, when he reached to tentatively touch them, came away bloody. His nose was also bleeding; he noticed from the bloodstain on the front of his shirt.

As his hearing returned, Marius registered the pitiful mewling from the hallway. Reyka.

The first flash had destroyed the doorway.

Marius's already nearly empty stomach heaved. He bit back his gorge and reminded himself Reyka was a collaborator. From the first, she had worked with the Infected and later with the Enlightened. She had helped keep him prisoner, threatened, and tortured him, and planned to do the same to his family.

Still, it was hard to watch her writhing in pain, her eyes closed, the lids slack. The flash seemed to have destroyed her eyeballs.

"I don't know if you can hear me, or if you understand." Marius squatted over the woman. "I'm not doing this for you. I'm doing this because it's what a decent person would do." He took hold of Reyka's head. Her only response was a shuddering whine. Marius gently turned her head from side to side, testing the tension of her neck muscles. They felt slack, relaxed, as if she knew what he intended and welcomed it.

Snap!

Marius broke her neck as quickly and cleanly as he would have done for any buck he might have killed on a hunt back home. Reyka gave a final jerk and stilled.

Marius stood and surveyed the lab. All the infected animals were gone, small piles of ash the only sign they'd ever been. A few living cats squatted, hissing in the backs of their cages. He opened the doors and they fled.

The floor trembled. Marius looked up in time to see the hallway, now devoid of membrane, nothing more than a honeycomb of disconnected support beams, collapse. Without the bioformations holding the place together, the building was falling apart around him, like a wall where decades of vines had been removed.

The empty space where the hall had been gave the scientist his first glimpse of the outside world. The building he was in stood near the edge of a cliff. Below a wide highway ran parallel to a river with a bridge off to the north. To his left a tram hung from its wire tracks. The bioformations didn't appear to have damaged the wires or the tram car, but Marius didn't trust it. The fall would be significant.

Not knowing how long the building he was in might stand, he gathered his meager possessions and rolled them up into the blanket from his cot. He stuffed this into the pillowcase and made his way to the edge of the lab. Marius was on the second floor, so he swung down, hung for a second and dropped.

Portland was dead. From the expensive houses climbing the hillsides, to the downtown office buildings, to the husks of food carts, nothing moved but the ash. Soft clouds of it kicked up by the warm pre-dawn wind twisted along the streets, reaching up towards the sky as they encountered updrafts near the taller buildings of the city's heart.

Marius stood outside the remains of the hospital where he'd been held. It looked like something from a documentary on what the world would look like absent humans for a hundred years. The outer walls were pocked and riddled with deep channels and grooves where the bioformations had burrowed into the structure.

"Marius!"

The scientist jumped at the sound of his name. Two figures dislodged themselves from the shadows of the hospital and headed his direction. One carried a cell phone, which they used as a flashlight.

"We thought you were dead," Torres said. She looked a little unsteady, but that could be from navigating through the hospital debris. "We came to rescue you. Are you okay?"

The wave of relief Marius felt nearly took his legs out. He wrapped his arms around Torres and Miranda and for a few moments they all simply clung to each other. Marius had expected to die but had escaped alive. As if that wasn't enough, Torres was in his arms, safe and warm.

"Okay, okay," Torres said. Her voice was muffled against Marius's shoulder, but it sounded like she was sniffing back a tear. "Now, what the hell happened here?"

The three of them huddled together around Miranda's phone and caught each other up.

"So, that Irish dude took off and we came to find you," Miranda finished.

"You gonna tell him about the rest of it, or am I?" Torres asked the younger woman.

Behind them, the building groaned and something heavy crashed. A plume of dust and ash rose from the hospital, which the wind drew toward the three people.

Miranda glared at Torres. Whatever was going on,

Marius didn't want to discuss it so near the collapsing hospital. It seemed like tempting fate to have escaped the place and then loiter in the parking lot.

"Let's talk and walk," he suggested. They wound their way down Marquam Hill, angling towards the bridge. Around them, buildings stared sightlessly, many with gaping holes where bioformations had exploded during what Marius had started calling 'The Flash.' They kept to the middle of the road, avoiding rubble as unstable structures collapsed.

The only sound, apart from the soft hush of the wind swirling the ash around, was the occasional grumble and roar of a building as it gave up the fight against gravity. Ash drifted through the air, falling from the higher hills that rimmed the city's river heart. It coated everything, the travelers included, in a soft gray blanket, dulling the edges of the destruction.

"How long has it been like this?" Marius asked. He kept his voice low, careful not to break the cemeterial atmosphere of the morning.

"It wasn't like this last night," Torres said. "It was freaking abandoned. Seems like a lot of folks evaced, but probably a lot didn't." She shivered and pressed her hand to her neck. Marius looked at her, glanced at Miranda who lifted a shoulder as if to say 'don't ask me,' and looked back at the former Marine.

"Are you sick?" Marius reached to touch her forehead, but Torres waved him off.

"I'm not infected. I mean, yes, I am infected, but not Infected. Freaking ... here." She peeled back her T-shirt's sleeve to reveal a dirty bandage. Marius didn't need to get very close to recognize the signs.

"You need antibiotics. Now."

"And a month of leave and a raise, thank you, sir." Torres forced a grin, but her sarcasm sounded tired and weak.

"How much further to the car?" Marius looked at Miranda, who stood, head tilted like a dog listening to some mystery sound beyond human perception.

"Not far."

From their vantage point on the hillside, they could see clouds of ash forming, moving with the wind like small storms. Some fell into the Willamette River, creating wide gray slicks. At first these rafts of ash were broken up by the current, but soon there was so much ash that it began to collect in shallows, along the riverbanks, in eddies and against bridge pilings. If Portland's river dwellers had escaped the infection, they now faced death in the form of a choking rain of ash falling into their homes.

"What did you need to tell me, Miranda?" Marius shortened his step to match Torres's pace. Normally, she left him puffing in her wake.

Miranda stopped, her eyes narrowing. She turned back, facing uphill. "Who else was there?"

"What?"

"Who else was there with the Enlightened?" Her eyes flicked to him, but her head didn't move. It was predatory, unsettling.

"She can communicate with them," Torres said. "Ever since Wiltz, right, Miranda? Maybe earlier. It's like telepathy or something, a voice or a feeling in her head."

"You lied to me." Miranda glared at Marius.

"What?" he asked again.

"About my dad." Miranda closed her eyes. A tear slid down her cheek, leaving a pale streak through the grey ash that coated her skin in a layer so fine Marius hadn't noticed it until it was disrupted.

"Miranda, I didn't ... I didn't know anything. No one knew anything for sure."

"You knew." Miranda spoke in a low tone, her voice choked with pain. "You saw him alive at Chrysalis and you let me think that he was dead. All this time, Marius. I thought he was dead and he's not. He's been looking for me."

Marius opened his mouth. But what could he say? It was true. He had left Viers trapped in the submarine, assumed that he had died with the rest of the Infected when the National Guard had sanitized the site. He hadn't told Miranda because he'd thought it would be easier for her not to think of her father dying that way.

"Don't!" Miranda snapped. Marius closed his mouth. "Don't say anything. I don't want any more of your lies. The all-knowing-Marius come to save us all. Except my father. And that kid, what was his name? Otto."

"Miranda, stop." Torres stepped between them.

Marius stared at Miranda, too shocked to reply. Her rage seemed to radiate off her. He imagined that if he had a thermal scanner, he'd be able to see it licking towards him like fire. Miranda held his gaze for a moment longer, then sank into a squat. She wrapped her arms around her knees and pressed her face into them and sobbed. It was a wrenching sound as if her soul were trying to tear free of her body and escape through her breath in ragged bits and pieces.

Instinctively, Marius started to go to her, but Torres

shook her head. She crouched next to Miranda, not touching her, but simply a warm and human presence next to the bereft young woman.

As they approached the bridge, Marius got a better view of the scope of the Flash. It looked like a bomb had gone off and riddled the town with strangely organic shaped shrapnel. He had succeeded in ridding Portland of the Infected, but in no way had that saved the town. All he had done was finish what the Enlightened had started.

From the chunks missing, he was able to imagine what the city must have looked like before the Flash. Membranes spreading out, crawling from one building to the next, creating a living network for the Infected to access from anywhere.

They drove past block after block of deserted buildings, their empty spaces filling with ash. With all the blocked and damaged streets, it took several hours to make their way down the hill and through downtown.

They stopped at every pharmacy, clinic, and animal hospital they passed until Marius found enough of the correct antibiotics. He gave Torres an injection and a bottle of pills to be taken three times daily for the next ten days.

It was late afternoon by the time they reached the bridge. There were holes where the bioformations had taken away chunks of concrete and rebar. Marius and Miranda got out of the Forester and stood at the edge of the land, studying the remaining structure.

"We can't take the car across that," Marius said.

Miranda nodded without looking at him.

"How far is it to the RV?"

Miranda shrugged.

"I'm not looking for exact mileage, but in general. An hour? Fifteen minutes?"

Miranda shrugged again. "IDK. Probably half an hour or so."

"She's not walking that far."

"So, let's get some bikes. It's Portland. They're, like, everywhere."

They left Torres dozing in the Forester and walked back through downtown. At an REI, they helped themselves to sturdy hiking boots, cargo pants, undershirts, Henley long sleeve shirts, several pairs of socks, and coats. Marius loaded a backpack with a flashlight, batteries, a first aid kit, water purifiers, fire starters, a camp stove, and gas canisters. Miranda collected the most high-tech sleeping bags she could find. They got a small tent and a waterproof tarp.

As they bundled their loot onto a mountain bike, Marius said, "How did you know about your dad?"

Miranda was silent for several minutes and Marius had nearly given up when she said, "I felt him. I didn't know who it was, but I knew there was someone here. It was like a pull or something. All the Infected felt it. When I got into the hospital and I touched the network there, I knew it was him. He recognized me." Tears welled in her eyes, but she swiped them away. "I never thought I'd get a chance to talk to my dad again and when I did you took that away from me, too."

"Miranda, I didn't ever mean to hurt you like that."

The young woman guided two bikes out of the store and turned back up toward the bridge. Dusk had fallen. The swirls of ash made the day seem even darker.

"That's the problem, Marius," Miranda said. "You never mean to hurt anyone, do you? But you knew my dad was here. You knew what you were doing would probably kill him. And you did it anyway."

"He's not your dad," Marius said. "Not like that. He's Infected or Enlightened or whatever they are. He's not himself anymore."

Miranda stopped and faced Marius squarely. Rage and grief twisted her face, and her voice was something between a snarl and a sob. "You don't get to talk about him. Not to me. Not ever."

"But you know I'm right. You know they're not—"

"Not ever. I mean it. If you can't respect that, I'll leave right now."

Marius bit his lip, studying his friend, a woman who had once claimed to be in love with him or at least, to like him enough to want to have sex with him. With the coming of dusk, the wind fell briefly. The ashfall slowed, the soft grayish flakes hovering in the air as if they'd lost their nerve to touch the ground.

"You can't go alone." Marius shook his head. "It's too dangerous."

"Not for me." Miranda grinned. "I'm Viers's daughter, remember?"

"I thought we weren't going to talk about it anymore," Marius said.

"So, you get it? Good." Miranda pushed her bikes forward. "Let's go get your Marine."

By the time they arrived back at the Forester, it was

nearly full dark. They kept the hoods of their jackets up and wore scarves to keep the ash from getting in their ears, eyes, noses, and mouths.

Torres sat on the Forester's hood, swinging her feet as she watched them approach. "You look like those street performers but covered in ash, not silver body paint." She slid gingerly to the ground, looked from Marius to Miranda and back and wisely didn't say anything.

They repacked their gear and pedaled over the bridge. When it got too dark to see, they camped outside of a Costco. Miranda's phone still had no signal and none of the pay phones they were able to find had service either.

In the morning, they were up with the sun and ventured inside the cavernous store. The inside was dark, except for an ominously open patch where the ceiling was missing. From the ransacked state of the aisles, Marius deduced they were certainly not the first people to loot the store. They trudged through the aisles, hunting high and low for canned or dried food. A half an hour's work yielded three cans of soup, a flat of ramen noodles and a box of assorted candy bars, which had slid under a cashier station. They also picked up several cans of soda.

Fueled by sugar and salt, the trio continued on. A map, swiped from a gas station, told them they could take I-84 to Troutdale where the women had left the RV. From there, they could connect to 395, which would eventually become I-90 and take them to Montana.

Chapter 14 – Torres

The RV park was empty. Not empty. Abandoned.

Torres braked at the top of the short incline that led into the RV park. Where was Elfy? She scanned the area, searching for a child-sized Infected or a pile of viscera that would be all that was left of her niece. Her throat seized and she forgot to breathe. She'd left Elfy alone and unprotected and now the girl was gone.

Marius propped his bike against a tree and drew the hunting knife he'd picked up.

"There's no Infected here," Miranda said. She put a hand out as if to pat Torres's arm but didn't, let her hand fall. "They're all dead."

Torres dropped her bike.

"The people, too?" Marius asked. "Are you sure?"

"How would I know about them? It only works for the Infected. And there are no Infected here. At all."

Both the RV, and the truck that had towed it were gone. The Suburban remained, the driver's door and driver's side rear sliding door open.

Torres stumbled forward.

"I'll go check it out," Marius said, but the former Marine held up a hand, waved him back. "I have to see."

The inside of the Suburban was spattered with blood. It was impossible for Torres to tell if the dried blood had once been the bright red of normal blood or the sludgy purplish-maroon of infected blood. Ash had mixed in with the blood in a red-grey paste. Had Greg turned far enough to be killed with the rest of the Infected? Or had he survived long enough to take the others with him? Torres picked up a pearl earring. Patty's. Somehow, it had escaped the blood. The white gleamed like the sun, easy to find. Easy to rescue. She set it in the cupholder, as if the woman might return and want her jewelry.

Torres scrambled out of the Suburban and looked around. She didn't know what she expected. A note tacked to a tree saying, "Gone to LA. Be back soon!" or something like that.

"We left them alone with Greg," Torres hugged herself with her good arm. Her fever wasn't as bad after a day on the antibiotics, but the gunshot wound was far from healed. It ached as if it had chewed through her muscles and into her bones.

"Greg?" Marius stood nearby, tensed and ready as if he yearned to do something. Torres could relate. She needed to act, to fix what had happened, to get away from the empty RV park with its lack of Elfy and Soraya, the girls, Phineas, and Washington. She wanted to run, the long mindless run from boot camp that would leave her wrung out and drop her mind into survival mode, where she hadn't failed her mother and her sister.

And her niece.

"Greg was infected. He got bitten." Torres stopped. She couldn't remember how long it had been. A day, two, four? "He had started to show signs. We were hoping you could help." She pounded her good fist on a picnic table. "We should have killed him. We never should have left him with Soraya and the kids."

"Blaming yourself won't help," Marius said. Torres glared at him. "We don't know the rest of the group is dead. You said you all were planning to go to Montana before. They're probably going there now. They might be a few hours down the road, but we're never going to catch up to them if we stay here playing 'Who Fucked Up the Most' and trust me, I'd win."

"ENTERING IDAHO PANHANDLE National Forest". The large brown Forest Service sign stood watch over a sloping curve of road. On the right, the pines trooped downhill as if on their way to vacation in the foothills. On the left, the side of the hill was terraced from the initial excavation. Seedlings clung to the lower hillside, fighting shrubs for their space in the light. Higher up, a wall of pines reached skyward, old soldiers calmly watching the world.

Torres glanced up. Ever since the Flash, the sun had been hidden behind a curtain of darkness. Marius said that his grandpa had talked about the way the sky had turned gray and ashy for days after the Mount Saint Helens eruption. How much ash had come from one volcano? Could there be more than that from the Infected in Portland? What if it was enough to cause local weather changes? What if it spread around the world, like the Saint Helens ash had?

They abandoned the Suburban after it ran out of gas miles from anywhere. Fortunately, they had been smart enough to strap the bikes on top. Pushing her bike up the hill, Torres tried to keep her mind occupied, rather than letting it linger over the eternal throb from her shoulder. A couple days of antibiotics had the infection under control. All that remained was the pain, tenderness, and a growing itch. She considered the irony of a bunch of scientists in Asia trying to backtrack ash from Portland, sent back to them in exchange for the long-ago Krakatoa eruption. Assuming, of course, that Asia still had scientists, that against all odds, HHV hadn't made its way to their shores.

A rumbling sound jarred Torres back to the present moment. A landslide? She and Marius exchanged a look. Miranda was trailing them. For the past few days, she'd made it plain that she wasn't interested in talking about anything other than the basics of survival. Where and when to camp. How much food and water to consume. Should we stop at that gas station and look for toilet paper?

Marius pushed his bike towards the middle of the road. No traffic since they had left the greater Portland area, so no cause to be worried about getting hit. On their right, the slope was traitorously steep. On the left, the mountain at a twenty-degree incline, and not surprising that a creature might send rocks tumbling. Even so, Torres cocked her head back and forth, trying to tune in to the sound she had heard.

It was a steady, sharp noise, growing slowly louder. After a few seconds, Torres could make out the individual sounds. Hoofbeats. The former Marine didn't know a lot about horses, but she suspected they would rather head for the lovely pasturage in the valleys below than climb up a paved road.

Marius held up a hand. "Riders," he said. He looked back at Miranda. "Infected?"

"Not on the horses." Miranda shrugged. "They're kinda always," she waved a hand broadly, "around."

Torres glanced at the bikes, at their packs strapped to the backs. All they had was their gear, a few cans of soda, canteens of warm water, and two Pop-Tarts each. Hardly worth the energy for someone to steal. Still, the bullet holes they had found in some of the places they had scavenged for supplies made the former Marine cautious.

"We gotta get under cover," Torres said. "We can't haul these bikes up that hill." She scanned the slope to their left; they might be able to get down it, but they couldn't afford to spend the last few hours of daylight struggling back up a near vertical rock face.

Marius bit his lip, his jade eyes flashing as if weighing their options, too. Behind them, the hoofbeats rang off the surrounding mountains as if the entire Mongol horde was headed in their direction.

"No time." Torres yanked her pack free, dropped her bike in the median strip and hightailed it up into the tree line, fighting her way past the ash-coated seedlings and shrubs. Miranda followed a few steps behind. Marius squinted back the way they'd come and then followed the women.

"It's definitely riders," he said. "Three, maybe four."

Under cover of the pines the ground was nearly ash free, just a light dusting like a layer of grey powdered sugar over the bed of thick needles carpeting every horizontal surface. A few birds eyed the trio curiously. Still no small woodland creatures.

"We should get away from the road more," Torres said. She started walking up the hill, but the slope was too steep, so she settled for scuttling crablike. She hoped it would give her a low profile from the road. She moved diagonally away from the highway below. There wasn't a lot of underbrush so when the first of the riders crested the ridge and came into view, Torres hid behind a wide pine tree and motioned Marius and Miranda to duck down.

The first of the riders rounded the hairpin turn. Torres guessed he was a little younger than her, mid- to late twenties. He had an AR-15 in a scabbard hanging near his right thigh. Two other riders, similar enough to be brothers, followed closely behind the first. Behind them, a heavyset older man with a salt and pepper beard brought up the rear.

When Torres had been deployed to the Middle East she'd seen camels festooned with tassels and bells. At first glance, she thought that the string of swaying bunches hanging across the last horse's chest were something similar. Tassels or maybe ribbons. But as the group ascended the mountainside, she got a better look at the old fellow and his horse. Acid burned down her throat.

Hanging on the string was nothing so benign as tassels. They were human scalps. At least five.

The first rider held up his hand and the others reined in, hands going to their various weapons. They each had a rifle of some sort and a pistol. Torres didn't need to check to know they were vastly outgunned. Their only advantage was that the riders didn't know they were there.

"Looks like we got more hippies on the run," called the lead rider. He waved his AR at the pile of abandoned bikes in the road.

Why hadn't they thrown those down the mountain instead of leaving them for any fool to find? Torres gritted her teeth.

The brothers grinned at each other. "I like hippies," the younger brother said.

"You see anything?" the older brother asked the leader, who was moving out in a slowly widening spiral.

Torres waited, timing his circuit to when he would be looking away from their side of the mountain, then she signaled Marius and Miranda to retreat up the slope.

"Nothing." The younger brother kicked Miranda's bike, sending it scraping across the median.

"What you think?" the old man addressed the leader. "Worth tracking? Don't look like much of a trail, but we wait, wind'll blow all that away." He pointed at the road. Torres's stomach dropped. The marauders could see the soft dimpled impressions their footsteps had left in the ash. Another ten or fifteen minutes and the wind would have brushed them out.

The leader paused his circling at the edge of the highway shoulder, peering past the shrubs and seedlings into the pines. Torres closed her eyes. People could feel when they were being stared at. She'd learned that in combat zones around the world.

"Don't matter to me," he said. "You got thoughts one way or the other?"

The older brother furiously scratched his head, inspected something he'd found there, and crushed it between finger and thumbnails. "Can't have gone far. Bikes ain't dusty yet. I say we have some fun."

The hillside was pretty steep, but a good rider might get their mount up it. They couldn't wait for the marauders to find them. Torres glanced over her shoulder. Miranda was bear-walking up the mountainside. Marius crouched behind a bush and beckoned for Torres to follow. She waved for him to keep going, but he shook his head and beckoned her again. Torres narrowed her eyes at his stubborn idiocy. There was no choice. She backed up the hill. Each breath crashed in her ears, each rustle of branch against her clothes sounded like a screaming alarm.

Below, the younger brother led his horse over to the edge of the highway and glanced at the leader, who waved at the hillside. "Go on, scout. Time to earn your keep."

The younger brother squatted down and poked at the ground. "Got 'em," he said, way too quickly.

If they could get to the saddle at the top of this ridge, they would have more options. Every fiber of Torres's being screamed at her to sprint, but if she did, they would spot her immediately. She half-ran, half-crawled, moving from tree to tree, following Marius and Miranda's path.

A branch just above and to the right of Torres head splintered, raining shards of pulped wood down on her. A second later she heard the reverberating crack of a rifle. No point in stealth now. The former Marine charged up the hill.

Behind her rang the clatter of hooves against asphalt and then the heavier thump as the horses moved onto the duff and shrub covered hillside. Torres didn't spare a look back. The hillside grew steeper, and she scrabbled, sometimes dropping forward to grab tree trunks or boulders with her good hand. Despite being down an arm, she could easily hit the marauders at this range. But even with one shot-one kill accuracy, she didn't have enough rounds for all of them. Best save the ammo.

"Run, rabbit, run!" one of the marauders whooped. Another shot smashed into the ground just in front of Miranda, who froze. "Cute lil bunny, ain't she?" The others laughed.

"Fuck you!" Miranda yelled.

"Go!" Torres had almost caught up to Marius, who reached back from the top of the ridge to help her up. Below the mountain swooped steeply downward. If they went over, they would be committed to a one-way trip. No horse, no matter how surefooted, would be able to follow, Torres hoped. Any pursuit would have to be on foot.

She looked back, judging the amount of cover

between them and the marauders. The leader and the older man waited on the shoulder, shouting directions to the brothers as they flailed their horses up the slope. Miranda hesitated at the precipice. The longer they waited to cross the saddle, the closer the brothers got.

"We gotta go over," Torres said.

"Yep." Marius cinched his pack tight and gave Miranda a thumbs-up, then he rolled over the ridge.

"Marius!" She started forward to grab him and slipped, sliding after him with a startled grunt.

Zing!

A shot pinged off the rock in front of Torres. The adrenaline buzzed through her. She jumped down the hill, pinwheeling her good arm to keep her balance. Her feet churned, each step an inch away from completely losing control, but somehow she didn't.

Torres stumbled into something out of a fantasy movie. Fuzzy green plants huddled along the base of the rock walls, which were covered in soft moss. A narrow stream cut through rocks and over sandbars along the bottom of the narrow valley. Water crashed somewhere in the distance. The air was cool and full of the earthy scents of an autumn forest. Above, the wind knocked the last leaves clinging to the branches to the forest floor. The sun was dipping toward the west, probably only an hour or two left of daylight.

Marius and Miranda picked their way upstream toward where the ravine made a sharp bend.

"Think we lost them?" Miranda pushed her hair out

of her face.

Torres shaded her eyes and searched the ridge for any sign of the marauders.

"Over there!" one of the marauders yelled.

"I see 'em," replied another.

Torres spun, trying to pinpoint the source of the voices but the steep rocky mountains that ringed the ravine sent the echoes bouncing and crashing around, making it sound like they were surrounded.

"Hold up," Torres called. "We don't know where they're coming down. We might be moving directly towards them." She scanned the trees. Over her shoulder she picked out a patch of dusty red plaid, the old man's coat.

"Okay, go on." Torres waved for Marius and Miranda to keep going. Marius was leading them in the opposite direction, but she had no idea how much of a head start they had. It didn't look or sound like the horses were going to be coming over the ridge, so that was one thing in their favor at least.

A shot snapped past Torres's shoulder. She dodged and twisted, trying to keep as much cover between herself and the marauders.

"Don't kill 'em!" One of the brothers yelled.

"Yeah, we ain't gonna kill you," shouted the other. "Just wanna play for a bit. C'mon back, bunnies."

Torres caught up to the others, positioning herself behind Marius. Old habits, she told herself. That's all it was. Once around the bend, they would be clear of the marauders' line of fire. They crossed an open patch, Torres's shoulders hunched, anticipating the impact. Her foot slipped on a rock and she tumbled and slid, like a runner stealing home. Her slide took her around the corner.

Safe!

Then she looked up. Three Infected elk creatures stood staring at them, their multiple eyes blinking out of sync. The bull of the trio opened its snaggle-toothed maw and brayed a high-pitched call. Torres froze. The bull pawed the ground, all the small tentacles along its neck and back standing on end, a waving field of shiny strands like a lion's mane.

Miranda held out a hand, her eyelids fluttering closed. Marius reached out, but Torres grabbed his ankle before he could touch Miranda.

"No." Torres mouthed, shaking her head.

Marius bit his lip, but let his hands fall to his sides. He looked away from the Infected elk, watching it out of the corner of his eye.

The bull Infected was a little larger than a normal elk, probably close to 900 pounds. As it lowered its head, presenting its gnarled rack of antlers, the brothers burst out of the trees. The bull paused, backed up, as if to get all the humans in his sights.

The Infected elk charged. Torres braced for impact, but it didn't come. The Infected split around them as if they were a boulder and went after the marauders. The bull snorted, then threw up his head, bugling again as he jumped back, kicking his feet out in what would have been a comically agile display under other circumstances. One of his hind hooves hit the older man in the chest, knocking him to the ground. The cows danced like they were on fire, leaping and then charging the remaining marauders.

"Go." Miranda's eyes were still tightly closed. A sheen of sweat covered her in spite of the coolness of the late afternoon.

Torres edged back further down the ravine. She grabbed Marius's arm and pulled him away, leaving the sounds of the enraged bull's screams, gunshots, and the cries of the marauders behind them. She had no idea where they were going, but the priority was putting distance between them, the marauders, and the Infected. Pine branches slapped at her face and hands. Rocks and roots clutched at her feet, hoping to twist an ankle or knee. Still better than listening to the slurping crunching of the Infected elk or the gurgling whimpers of the dying men.

After a few yards, the former Marine paused to check that Miranda was following.

She wasn't.

The younger woman stood, head cocked to the side, a smile twitching her lips as she watched the Infected tromp through the disemboweled remains of one of the marauders.

Torres shuddered. This was not the time to dwell on the morality of how they'd escaped the marauders. They had been rapists and murderers. The world was a better place without them.

But that wasn't the point. The point was the look of pleasure on Miranda's face as the Infected tore into human flesh.

Miranda did that. Miranda sent the Infected to kill people.

They were lost.

The last Pop-Tarts were gone.

Torres flopped down on a flat rock that stuck out of the hillside they'd been angling across all afternoon. She pulled out the foldable, laminated Idaho road atlas she had taken from a gas station. It was worthless. While the map showed the main roads, it was largely blank on the wilderness areas. Since escaping from the marauders and Infected, they had headed generally eastward for two days.

Marius handed out bunches of purple chanterelle and penny bun mushrooms he had scavenged. They still hadn't seen any woodland creatures, other than the Infected elk. The ashfall had tapered off, but the sky remained overcast. The wind whipped across the mountains, pulling the chill off the peaks and jabbing the travelers with it.

Miranda took several sips from her canteen, wiped her mouth with finger and thumb as if she might smudge her lipstick, and heaved a deep sigh. "Worst field trip ever."

"We gotta get off this mountain before dark," Torres said. She rolled her shoulder, trying to work the muscle back into strength and flexibility. The skin pulled and itched and the deep ache seemed to have settled into her bones.

Marius stood and held out a hand to help Torres up. His hand was strong and warm. Heat raced through Torres at his touch. For a moment, she was back in the dark hallway in Chrysalis, facing what she believed was certain death. She had pressed her lips against his and breathed him in one last time. The memory sent tingles through her. She glanced at their hands, still clasped together, then up into Marius's bright green eyes. With a cough, she pulled her hand out of his and walked away before he could see the flush heating her neck.

As they descended into the valley, the ashfall lightened and the blackberry bushes thickened. Torres could make out flashes of deep reddish brown, flecked with the burnt yellow of fallen needles. A dirt road, most likely a Forest Service maintenance trail. She resisted the impulse to run, leaping and bounding down the hillside. She nudged Marius and pointed out the road. He nodded. Over the past few days, they'd fallen into the habit of keeping their talk limited. Part of it was worry that some group like the marauders would hear them; mostly it was that they were too tired to talk and tired of repeating the same things.

Yes, we're still lost.

No, we don't have any more food.

Torres trotted the last few steps onto level ground. The sides of the trail were overgrown with ferns and tall grasses, recently gone to seed. A patch of weeds rose nearly waist high along the middle of the trail. If the Forest Service did use this road, it wasn't often and certainly not recently.

None of that mattered. It was a trail, a human trail and it would lead to some sort of civilization. Torres grinned and raised her canteen. Marius and Miranda clinked their canteens, and the trio took a celebratory swig of the tepid water. Torres checked her compass.

"Northeast." She pointed up the trail.

"Why not?" Miranda said.

They made much better time moving along the trail than climbing through the mountains. That evening, they camped uphill from the trail and set off at first light, hungry and tired, but hopeful.

By noon, Torres had fallen into a mindless plod, watching her feet scuffing through the reddish dirt, when to her surprise her foot landed on crunching gravel. She stopped and looked up. The trail widened, now two gravel lanes. A good sign. They were definitely headed toward civilization.

The gravel road wound its way upwards in lazy, looping hairpins. Torres tried not to look back as they climbed. Seeing the valley floor still so close was depressing. Another day of walking and a cold camp on the western side of a low pass. Marius didn't waste energy on snares.

"No sign of game," he said before burrowing into his sleeping bag.

Torres lay next to him, staring up at the scudding clouds. What if the Flash had dumped enough ash into the atmosphere to change the weather? How big of an area could it affect? Torres rolled onto her side to ask Marius, but he'd pulled his sleeping bag over his head. She didn't think he was asleep, but hesitated. How to ask, 'Do you think we doomed the Pacific Northwest to nuclear winter?' Yeah, that would help his freaking guilt complex. Torres scrunched down in her own sleeping bag, focused on the feeling of her own body heat warming the air around her. As long as she didn't sniff too deeply, it was all good.

Morning and Torres's breath steamed out in a cloud. The chill air, as she poked her head out of her sleeping bag burrito, stung her nostrils. Miranda was still cocooned in her sleeping bag, but Marius was up, packing his gear. His exhalations were freezing in the stubble on his cheeks.

Torres wriggled out of her sleeping back and into her coat and shoes. "You look like a skinny Santa Claus." She brushed a hand over Marius's cheek, leaving a dark patch where her heat had melted the frost.

"Ho ho ho." He grinned, then blushed.

"Lame," Miranda muttered. Only a tuft of her brunette hair peeped out of her sleeping bag.

Torres winked at Marius, feeling a renewed strength for the day that had nothing to do with food.

"Yeah, so lame," she said, stirring more than a little Valley Girl into her voice. "I mean, like, where are even the cookies or whatevs?"

"Je ne parle pas cette langue," Marius said. He scrubbed both hands over his face, defrosting it.

With a loud huff, Miranda sat up, flipping down her sleeping bag. "Fine. I'm up. Just stop, you two."

Torres pointed two fingers at her eyes then one at Marius signaling 'I'm watching you.' Marius held up both hands in the 'I surrender' gesture.

"I'm ready already." Miranda put on her pack and cinched down the straps.

Marius waved a hand for Torres to proceed. "Fearless leader."

"Oh no. After you. Can't wait to get to ranch, sweet ranch," Torres said with a smile.

"Gah, flirt harder." Miranda rolled her eyes and

stomped off down the trail.

Torres froze, staring at Marius. Had she overstepped? She couldn't believe she'd dropped her guard like that. She'd been practically giggling, not watching out for Infected or marauders, or mountain lions, or any of the other million and ten things that would love to kill Marius.

Marius bit his lip and turned to follow Miranda, but as he passed Torres he grabbed her hand and squeezed it before letting go. In a low voice, he murmured, "Flirt harder."

Chapter 15 – Miranda

Running Rabbit, Idaho, U.S.A. - Autumn, Year 1

Sometime in the late afternoon Miranda, Marius, and Torres had crossed the pass and were headed down and east. A soft clanging sound jerked Miranda out of her trudging stupor, halfway through an imagined trip to an Italian restaurant. She stopped, pushed back her sweaty hair, letting the cool wind run its fingers through it. Although the nights in the mountains were cold, the days had turned hot and humid. The last of summer, Miranda guessed. Would that make it late September or early October? They'd been traveling for four days since Portland, give or take a day. It was hard to keep track.

Clang. Ting, ting.

The sound came from over her left shoulder. Without thinking, she reached out for the Infected. Since the elk, she'd found them more and more often. Like herself, Marius, and Torres, the Infected were moving away from Portland. They were confused, looking for a new hive, for the Enlightened to give them direction. It was easy enough for Miranda to push them away, make sure they knew her group was not for eating.

Torres had stopped and stood staring at the source of the clanging noise, head cocked to one side like a baffled spaniel. A flagpole, the flag at half-mast. Its clips tapped and clanged gently against the metal pole. Behind the flagpole, a small, graveled parking lot fronted a little building made of whitewashed cinderblocks. Men's and women's restrooms were attached like parentheses on either end of the building. The sign above the door said, "Welcome to the Vardis Fisher Memorial Campground and Trailhead." Next to the door was a glorious vending machine, fully stocked.

It took only a few minutes and a couple of large rocks to smash open the vending machine. Miranda guzzled a can of V8, then practically inhaled a Snickers bar. Marius and Torres did the same. They all filled their packs with candy bars, chips, gum, packs of trail mix, and cans of soda.

After her gorging, Miranda's intestines twisted.

Marius stood up, a hand on his stomach and headed to the restrooms.

"You gonna be okay in there all by your lonesome?" Torres asked Marius as they stacked their packs along the wall.

"I'm confident in my capabilities." Marius grinned.

Miranda rolled her eyes and ducked into the women's restroom. There were no lights inside, just panels of semi-transparent plastic near the ceiling. It was eerily similar to the one at the Shandon rest area—the cinderblock walls, trough sink, two stalls with no doors and toilet paper.

Toilet paper!

Miranda had never imagined she would be so thrilled by government-issue single ply and a dimly lit, overly warm and musty bathroom. It was heaven.

Miranda emerged first, happy to take in a deep breath of the warm woodsy smell. She closed her eyes and tipped her head back, listening to the bird calls. A woman's voice cut through the quiet.

"Get away from me."

Miranda's eyes flew open. She looked around. Only trees and bushes.

"Struggle all you want." A man's voice, young, mocking. "You'll never escape." The voice carried from the forest on Miranda's left, probably not far beyond the cinderblock structure.

"Do your worst," the woman's voice was softer now.

Miranda squatted next to the gear pile and rummaged through Torres's pack, looking for the gun.

"What are you doing?" The former Marine stared down at Miranda, hands on hips.

"Shhh!" Miranda held up a hand. Torres frowned, but dropped into a crouch beside her, angling herself so she could watch the men's restroom.

"What's up?" she whispered.

"There are people in the woods," Miranda muttered back just as Marius stepped out of the bathroom.

"I feel a million —"

"SHHH!" both Miranda and Torres hissed.

"I'll never submit," the woman's voice rang out. Marius jumped as if he'd been shot.

"See?" Miranda whispered. "Where's the gun?" Her search had turned up nothing.

"I have it." Torres stood up, pulling the gun from the back of her waistband. Of course, she had it. Of course, she didn't trust anyone else with it.

She's not one of us.

Not now. Miranda pushed the Infected out of her thoughts. More and more they intruded and more and more she'd let them, grateful for the company. They were always willing to listen when she fought the drowning grief for her father, for her future, the rage at Marius and his betrayal, even the embarrassing schoolgirl crush she still nursed for him despite everything that had happened.

Torres pulled on her pack and Marius followed suit.

"C'mon," Torres said to Miranda. Without waiting, the former Marine headed towards the woods. She held out a hand to signal Marius and Miranda to follow at a distance.

As they made their way through the trees, Miranda could hear a murmur of voices. A woman and at least two men. Miranda trembled, flashing back the bikers at Ernie's.

This time, let us feed.

Not now!

Marius patted Miranda's shoulder, which startled her. She nearly screamed.

"You're safe," Marius whispered. He smiled

reassuringly. For just a moment, Miranda remembered what it had been like when she had trusted him. What it had been like to know that Marius and John were protecting her. She had believed they always would. Had believed their promises never to abandon her. They were the Survivors' Club. But John was gone, and Marius didn't care about her.

"Me first," a man said. He sounded gleeful.

Torres pushed through the final line of trees, emerging into a small clearing. In the center, the remains of a huge, gnarled tree stood. A young Asian woman was bound to the tree. She'd been stripped to the waist. Her long blue-black hair fell loose around her face, covering her bare breasts.

Two young white men crowded close to her. They both wore military fatigue pants and T-shirts. One had dark hair and horn-rimmed tortoise shell glasses. The other had ginger hair and a fuzz of mustache.

The young woman raised her chin defiantly. "You wouldn't dare, you low born—" Her attention shifted to Torres. "Who the fuck are you?" She yanked her hands out of the restraints and covered herself.

"Back the fuck away." Torres pointed the gun at the men. Both held their hands up.

"Don't shoot!" the ginger yelled, his voice rising several octaves from his previously menacing tone.

"There seems to have been a significant misapprehension," the dark-haired man said.

"Yeah, called 'I think gang rape is fun and now I'm gonna get my sack shot off.'" Torres tipped her head. "Over there. On your knees."

"Are you gonna kill us?" The ginger's voice squeaked

even higher, his pale blue eyes wide, tears gathering.

"Are you okay?" Marius asked the woman. He kept back from her, turned half away. "Miranda ...?"

"Yeah, I got her." Miranda hurried over to the woman who was fumbling to put on her shirt and pull up the straps of a pair of bib overall shorts she was wearing.

"Madam, please allow us to explain," the dark-haired man said. He knelt, keeping his hands clasped behind his head.

"Shut up." Torres stepped forward and pressed the muzzle of the gun against his forehead. The front of his fatigues darkened as the smell of urine wafted through the clearing.

"Stop. Please," the woman said. She pushed Miranda out of the way, her bibs still undone, and lunged at Torres. Marius grabbed her before she reached the Torres. Ever the hero.

"What the actual fuck is going on here?" Miranda demanded.

"They're my boyfriends!" the woman yelled. "We were ... you know."

"So, this was what? Role playing?" Torres frowned.

"Ah, yeah," the woman said. "This is Bailey." She pointed to the dark-haired man then at the ginger. "And that's Toby. I'm Dawn."

"You're, like, a throuple?" Miranda asked.

Marius let go of Dawn like she was on fire.

"I guess," said Toby. "Um, can we get up now?"

Torres shrugged. "Sure. We don't have any freaking bullets anyway."

"We have bullets," Toby said brightly as he scrambled up.

"They don't even have bullets. As if urinating on myself in front of strangers isn't humiliating enough," Bailey said. He lumbered to his feet, holding his fatigues away from himself with dainty thumb and forefinger.

"You have bullets?" Torres ignored Bailey. "Where? Can we trade for some? Why don't you have weapons?"

"Um, because we're Regency highwaymen from *The Delicate Matter of Lady Charlotte*," Toby said.

"Obviously." Miranda couldn't help laughing, but no one joined her. "Oh, c'mon. It's hilarious."

"I don't find it at all hilarious. This entire thing has been humiliating from beginning to end," Bailey said. "I'm going to change." He stalked away following a faint game trail that ran up and out of the valley to the northeast.

"He's Lord George," Toby said. "I'm William. Technically also a lord, but I don't know I'm actually the bastard son of—"

"TMI, Toby," Dawn interrupted. Miranda caught a glimpse of Torres's shocked face and snickered harder.

"I'm Marius. Not a lord or bastard son of anyone that I know of." Marius shook hands with Dawn and Toby. "This is Torres, our head of security, and Miranda."

"Nice to meet you," Dawn said. "We'd better catch up. Bailey's not great with directions. We'll end up at the radio tower if he keeps going that way."

Bailey led the way up the winding pathway and into a small gravel parking lot. A Humvee hunkered below an awning of camouflage netting, which sagged under the weight of pine needles and ash. The only other sign of human habitation was a heavy, metal door that was set directly into the rocky mountainside.

"Welcome to Running Rabbit Launch Control Center!" Toby swept out an arm indicating the parking lot and door.

"Wow. I can see why we're a superpower or whatever," Miranda said.

"Pretty sweet, huh?" Toby hurried over to the door and entered a combination into the keypad next to it. An LED light on the keypad flashed green twice. "If we ever launched our baby, she'd take the whole top of the mountain with her, I bet."

"Wait!" Bailey pushed the door shut. The light flashed red twice.

"Here we go again." Dawn folded her arms and leaned against the Humvee. "Get comfy," she said to Miranda.

"What?" Toby looked from Bailey, who stood in front of the door, to Miranda and Dawn by the Humvee, to Marius and Torres in the parking lot.

"They don't have clearances," Bailey said. "They're civilians. For all we know, they're FIS or Mossad or KGB."

"Is he serious?" Miranda muttered to Dawn.

She shrugged. "He made me wait out here for two days."

Torres held up a hand. "We're not trying to infiltrate. If we were, we wouldn't have told you we didn't have any bullets, would we?"

Bailey shook his head. "I suppose that would sacrifice a significant advantage, but regardless we are duty-bound to defend our post—"

"Until properly relieved," Torres finished with him. At the confused look on Bailey's face, she said, "Marines. Did a couple of trips down range. I'm not seeing any patches, Zoomy, but I'm not seeing a proper uniform, either."

"Um, we weren't expecting an inspection, ma'am," Toby said.

"She's not an officer," Miranda said. "She works for a living."

"Hey, I got an idea," Dawn said. "Let's go inside and get something to eat and you can catch us up on what's going on out there."

"Agreed. They're cleared to enter the facility," Toby said grandly. "Plus, we don't wanna be out here too much later. Those weird animals might come back. Have you seen them? They're mutated or something. We've only seen a couple small ones from far away."

"The Infected," Marius said.

"Fine." Bailey re-entered the code to open the door. "But for the record, I think this is a bad idea and I was overruled."

"Outranked," Toby muttered, a mischievous grin on his face.

"By two months!" Bailey snapped. He threw open the heavy door and stormed into the dark, narrow hallway.

"He's so sore about that," Toby said, following Bailey in.

Miranda wondered how two men who both looked not a day over eighteen could have different dates of ranking. Toby must have joined earlier than Bailey. From what Miranda knew of the military, the first few promotions were pretty automatic.

The ceilings and walls were concrete, painted a pale robin's egg blue. The hallway branched. Off to the left, Miranda could see a kitchen, dining area, and pantry. To the right, she caught a glimpse of several bunkbeds strewn with candy wrappers, handheld video game consoles, and magazines. Ahead the hall descended several steps and opened into a control room with banks of old computers that faced a wall of screens. One of the screens had a continuous scroll of bright green letters and numbers on a dark background, something straight out of the dinosaur days of the internet. The two center screens showed a go-kart racing game paused with characters in mid-collision. A mattress lay in the center of the room, piled with blankets and pillows and surrounded by books.

Toby showed them the showers, which were four showerheads coming out of the wall, two on either side of an open tiled room barely bigger than Miranda's old walk-in closet.

"There's not a ton of hot water, but we've got enough soap and shampoo for an army, or squadron, I guess." Dawn smiled as she opened a cupboard. Bars of soap were stacked high inside along with several rows of shampoo bottles, tubes of toothpaste, and boxed toothbrushes.

"Shouldn't we get debriefed or whatever first?" Miranda asked as Dawn headed towards the living quarters.

"He's already halfway there." Dawn pointed at Marius, who was shedding his layers of outer jacket followed by his hoodie, T-shirt, and undershirt. He had always been lean, but now he looked starved. She could see every rib and every ripple of muscle as he moved. A black tattoo spread from the nape of his neck down his back. It looked like feathery ferns.

Torres stepped closer to Marius and ran her fingers over it. "Is that from the Enlightened ...?" She trailed off, looking into his eyes. "Does it hurt?"

Marius shivered and Miranda could see Torres had his attention.

"It's nerve damage," Miranda said. She yanked off her clothes. Let them be embarrassed by her nakedness.

"How do you ... right." Torres took off her own clothes, folding each article and setting them in a neat stack. She was thin, too. Her hair spiked out in tufts from Soraya's amateur barbering.

Miranda was suddenly self-conscious and turned toward the wall. She refused to try to cover herself after making such a display of getting naked. She focused on the glorious lather in her hair. It felt like it might take a year of scrubbing to get clean. When had her last shower been? Los Angeles. How long ago had that been? A week. No. At least two or three. Maybe more.

All too soon, the water started to cool. Miranda wrapped a towel around herself. It was so short she had to half squat to cover everything.

"When you're done, I set out some clothes, if you don't mind Air Force casual," Toby called from the control room.

"Like the Air Force is ever not casual," Torres said. But John wasn't there for their super special military insider jokes and Miranda let her remark shrivel up and die.

After Miranda, Torres, and Marius had dressed, they

gathered with Bailey, Dawn, and Toby in the dining area. Toby presented them BLTs, potato chips, and an assortment of juice boxes. While they ate, the airmen and Dawn caught the newcomers up on what had brought them to Running Rabbit.

Bailey and Toby were both Senior Airmen, newly assigned to their post. They had been left behind when everyone else had been summoned away for an emergency. Comparing notes, Marius and Torres estimated that the emergency must have been the beginning of the Los Angeles outbreak or shortly thereafter.

Dawn said she'd been on a camping trip with some friends. She was vague about what happened to them or why she'd been alone, simply ending with, "And then I walked up the driveway and found these guys sunbathing on the Jeep."

"It's not a Jeep. I feel we've been quite clear on this point," Bailey said.

"Anyway, there they are. Two legit snacks, making out like they were getting paid to do it. I was still freaked out from those monster-zombie things in the woods, but I think I scared them more. They ran into the bunker and locked the door."

"We were being cautious," Bailey said.

"We let you in eventually," Toby said.

"I had to sleep in the Jeep overnight."

"It's not a Jeep."

Torres cleared her throat. "And you've had no communication from your higher since then?"

"Nope," said Toby, wrinkling his freckled nose. "We're like *Y The Last Man*."

"Except there are three of us and two of those three are men, but yeah, basically the same," Dawn said. She kissed the top of Toby's head as she got up to throw away her trash.

"I mean, we're isolated and don't know what's going on out there," Toby said.

"Meh, you didn't miss much," Miranda said. All eyes turned to her. "I mean, other than the collapse of Western civilization, but other than that everything's totes fab."

"We used to work for this bio-pharma corporation," Torres began. It took nearly an hour, but eventually, they had filled the throuple in on how the world was falling apart.

Toby and Bailey sat on either side of Dawn, their hands and fingers interlinked. Toby had sniffed back tears a few times, and Dawn pressed her face against Bailey's shoulder. For his part, the dark-haired airman sat stiffly, nodding occasionally, but not interrupting or visibly reacting. As Marius finished explaining about the Flash and ashfall in Portland, Bailey stood and walked out of the living area. Marius had conveniently left out that he was the cause of the Flash, and, oh yeah, that the virus was created from his blood. In the dormitory, Bailey fell into his bunk fully clothed and still wearing his boots. After a few seconds, he pulled the green woolen blanket over him.

"We should go to bed," Dawn said. Toby sniffled and followed her. Muffled voices and sobs filtered down the hall.

"I'm gonna go check on the Humvee," Torres said.

Marius and Miranda joined her outside. They

propped the door open since they still didn't know the code. The sun had already set and twilight lay heavy over the mountainside. The wind caught Miranda's hair and tugged it back from her face, lifting it from her neck and flicking it over her cheeks. She tuned out Marius and Torres's vehicle discussion and reached out for the Infected.

A few Littles here and there at the edge of her perception, but they felt distant, distracted, hard to connect with. Miranda pulled one closer, trying to get a clearer idea of what was happening. Ever since Wiltz, her ability to enter into the Infected's consciousness while still maintaining her sense of self had gotten stronger and finer. She could tell from the Infected's senses that it was low to the ground. The rocks, sharp and cooling, scraped against the pads of its feet. Its sensory tentacles waved through the air, tested the wind. A storm coming from the pressure drop. It stopped, snorted, backed up. It was filled with a disgusted horror.

Abomination?

Had it crossed Marius's path? The Infected usually didn't react to anything else the way they did to him. But this wasn't quite the same. Similar. It was afraid, instinctively afraid of something that was hidden among the clast and mud of a stream bank.

What is it? Go closer. Miranda urged the Little. It resisted. She pushed harder. For a moment, she thought it would close off its mind from her, but she pushed harder, breaking through like piercing a bubble's skin. Inside the Little's mind, there was no resistance. It was hers in the way her hand was hers. It would do what she wanted and what she wanted was for it to investigate the stream bank.

As the Infected approached, it could smell and even see it—*Danger, abomination, corruption*—but her Little did as she commanded and moved forward, reaching out a tentacle to touch it.

Black mold.

The Little spit and spit again as its mouth filled with saliva. Part of Miranda wondered what Marius's science-y explanation would be.

"Interesting. Observe how the virus uses the Infected to try to spread. As the host is dying, the virus causes it to spit and cough in an attempt to find a new host."

Or something like that.

"Hey." A hand on her arm—her human arm. The real touch stressed her tenuous connection to the dying Infected. Miranda's consciousness snapped back to her own body. She gasped, wiped the drool from her mouth.

Marius peered at her, his intense green eyes only a few inches from hers. He smelled blandly clean, fresh-scrubbed, but under that she caught his own scent, warm and spicy. She shuddered as part of her recoiled from him like the Infected would. But another part of her, maybe also influenced by the Infected, yearned to take him, consume him, make him hers forever.

"I'm fine." Miranda yanked her arm away. She couldn't trust herself with Marius. The Infected meant to hurt him, meant to kill him. When she let herself dip into their minds, let her consciousness swirl away with the flow of information that washed through the network of bioformations and Infected, she understood. Marius was a danger, an abomination. She understood why he had to be destroyed with his full lips, his dark hair softly falling into his eyes, his collarbones standing out in his olive skin, his strong and dexterous wrists, his agile and delicate fingers, his …

"C'mon, you two," Torres called. She stood in the doorway, her shadow reaching across the long rectangle of light from the bunker as if to swallow Marius.

If we can't have him, no one can.

Miranda shook her head. *That's not who I am.*

Isn't it?

At first waking, Miranda thought she was back in the government detention center. She'd never been able to confirm her suspicion that they'd been held in New Jersey after they'd been rescued from Chrysalis.

Between the hard bunk, the bleach-smelling, cheap sheet, and itchy blanket, it was like she'd never left that off-the-books detention site. Above her was another bunk, the mattress slightly sagging. The springs groaned and a person groaned as they sat up.

Torres's feet came over the side, dangled for a second, then she hopped down.

It was almost like a sorority, with them both wearing matching Air Force uniform, shorts and a T-shirt. Torres gave Miranda a tight smile. Yep, exactly like a sorority sister.

I'll have to kill her. She'll never let me hurt Marius.

Miranda shoved the thought away and rolled out of bed. Dawn and Toby were in the kitchen. He smiled and took Miranda's omelet order. Dawn handed her a glass of chilled orange juice. Marius and Bailey sat at the table, hunched over a notebook that was already covered with Marius's notes, diagrams, and mathematical equations. It was weird because it was all so normal, as if HHV had never happened, as if her father wasn't dead—*not dead, Enlightened*—as if any minute she would grab her carry-on and fly off to her gap year of backpacking around Europe with her besties.

"… so you want in?" Toby was looking at her, wide-eyed and hopeful. If he were a dog, he would have been a corgi.

"In?" Miranda perched on a stool and probed her omelet.

"On the mold operation." Toby grinned and pointed at Marius. "We got a ton of mold around here. Marius says he thinks it can mess up the Infected's network. That's what you guys did in Portland, right?"

"Something like that," Miranda said. Marius had said something about infusing the mold with an HHV inhibitor. She didn't totally understand the science, but she knew the Infected viscerally understood the danger Marius and, to a lesser degree, the mold posed.

Torres walked past on her way to the coffee maker. Actual brewed coffee, not just what grounds they could find swirled in a canteen of lukewarm water. The former Marine took the seat next to Bailey, smiled at Marius as he held up his notes and diagrams.

"Mold isn't my thing," Miranda said. "I'm going for a hike." She waved at the shorts and T-shirt. "I'm already dressed for it."

"You can't go out there alone." Toby looked like she'd suggested she was going to go chop off her foot.

"Why not?" Miranda stood and stretched, enjoyed

Toby's blushing appreciation and Bailey's uncomfortable shifting. Marius was oblivious, lost in his mold project.

The only thing that excites him is killing the ones close to you.

"Because of the zombie-mutants," Dawn said. "I can go with if you gotta go. I know how it is. Sometimes you just need to be on-the-go."

Miranda shook her head. They'd been on-the-go since Portland, since Wiltz, since Chrysalis, since Harrow Hall really. "Nah, thanks though. I need the me time."

"But —" Toby started.

Torres interrupted him. "She doesn't have to worry about the Infected. It's fine, Zoomy."

Miranda didn't wait to hear how Torres would explain her connection with the Infected. She didn't need to see Toby's curious friendly face close down in disgust or to watch Dawn edge away from her or hear the suspicion in Bailey's nasally pronouncements.

Outside, it was almost noon. Miranda was surprised at how late they'd all slept. They must have been more exhausted than they'd realized. It was also hard to keep track of time in a bunker with no source of outside light. Not that outside had much light. The grey clouds still choked the sky.

At first, Miranda trudged down the trail, but gradually she picked up the pace. In high school she'd been a cross country runner. As she warmed up, the urge to go faster grew. Without any means of tracking her time, speed, or distance, Miranda simply started running.

The gravel road curved and curved back as it slalomed lazily down the mountain. She pictured running the trails near the international school she'd been at the year she'd lived with her mom outside of Paris. On the weekends they would take the car into town and spend hours strolling from one boutique to the next, only stopping for coffee and pastries. At the end of the day, they would settle down to unpack all their treasures.

How many trendy outfits, cute clutches, and designer jewelry had Miranda modeled to the adoration of her social media followers? What had happened to them? What had happened to her mother, for that matter? Miranda had always assumed Cecilia, her Swiss husband, and their creepy litter of ultra-blond children were in some bunker in the Alps. But what if they weren't? What if—

As Miranda rounded the final curve where the road met the asphalt of some county road or other, she skidded to a stop.

A Ford Taurus was parked in the middle of the road. Liam leaned against the hood, a lit cigarette in mid-smolder pursed between his thin lips.

"Easy there." He held up both hands. "I come in peace."

Miranda narrowed her eyes, reached out for the Infected. There were only a few nearby. They were avoiding the area because of Marius and because of the black mold that had found its way into nearly all the bunker's plumbing. She found a pair of deer and brought them closer — on standby as John would have said.

"You made it out of Portland." Miranda put a hand on

her hip, timed her words with her panting. At least the cool air had taken away her sweat, but a rash of goosebumps spread over her arms and legs. Her nipples tightened in the cold and if Liam stared, she would straight up murder him.

He didn't. He took out his pack of cigarettes and offered her one. She shook her head. She didn't need to score cool-kid points with anyone. Certainly not with some weird Irish stalker guy.

"So, what are you doing here, then?" Liam said in a falsetto. Dropping his voice, he went on. "Glad you asked. Kind of you to care and all that. I'm here for Marius. Again."

"And you're telling me this why? So, we all know why you're dead?"

"Nah, love. I've been through a rough patch or two and I've learned a bit about the human condition, is all. I saw how they done you and yours. Your man there left your da for dead and tried to murder him flat out in Portland, didn't he?"

And yet you're still with him.

But Liam didn't say it. He didn't need to. What kind of daughter would stay with Marius after everything he'd done? She'd been following him out of habit, out of a lack of options, but staring at Liam, she realized she could take a different path, her own path.

After the Harrow Hall outbreak when she and John and Marius had been struggling with their traumas, they'd promised to stay together, to look out for each other. But where was John? And Marius was too busy smiling at Torres and actively scheming to kill her father instead of trying to save him. What did she owe either man? The same amount of loyalty they'd shown her? That was a tragic-comic joke.

Liam drew deeply. The tip of his cigarette glowed, lighting tiny fires in his eyes. "The way I sees it, you want him gone, eh? Punished so to speak? But not given over to Them." He flapped his hands at the surrounding area. "They'd kill him and if killing were what you had in mind, well." He smiled a slow cocky grin as his gaze traveled from Miranda's shoes to her face. "You don't need the likes of me for murder, do you?"

Miranda crossed her arms, tucked her fists against her sides. She should deny it. Good girls didn't feel a swell of savage pride at being recognized for being dangerous. But she liked it. Around Liam she didn't have to be the doe-eyed high school nymphet Marius and Torres persisted in seeing her as.

"Go on."

"I'm here with an offer to solve two of your problems," Liam said.

"Gosh, my hero." Miranda fanned herself like a swooning Southern belle.

"I know where your da is," Liam said. "And I'm of a mind to trade that information. I get Marius and you get a happy family reunion, eh? After Carmine double-crossed me in Portland, I got to wondering how much would Marius go for on the open market, so to speak. I give a tinker's dam which fat cat gets his blood or which secret luxury bunker they stash him in. I do care that I got a way home. I don't know about you, my girl, but I'm not planning on dying in America."

Miranda blew her bangs out of her eyes and crossed her arms. "That's super great for you, but why hang out here so you can monologue your evil scheme, Mr. Bond? What do you want from me?"

"Bond is the spy," Liam said.

"Literally no one cares."

One of the Infected deer stepped out of the forest onto the road about a quarter mile away. It didn't charge, simply stood with its head up, all eyes focused on Liam, its tentacles waving gently around it like a gorgon's mane.

Liam stiffened but didn't back down. He looked from Miranda, to the Infected and back. Miranda smirked.

Yes, you underestimated us.

"Oy, I'm looking to help you. Call off your dogs."

"Tell me exactly what you're planning to do to Marius and if I don't totally hate it ..." Miranda lifted an eyebrow. Playing the villain was fun.

Chapter 16 – Torres

Torres wriggled out from under the Humvee. It wasn't exactly a helicopter, but military vehicles were designed to be Private Snuffy-proof and easy to repair. Plus, she had the manual, so it was only a matter of time.

Earlier she had glowered at Toby as he sheepishly showed her the pristine tool kit that had come with the vehicle. "You didn't even try some basic maintenance?"

"Um, no. We don't know anything about trucks."

"It's not a truck."

"We weren't planning on leaving. We thought the rest of the squadron would be back soon."

Torres shook her head. "Whether you plan to use the

vehicle or not, you need to be doing proper PMCS daily and keep it in working condition. Freaking flyers."

Toby grinned. "Think you can fix it, sarge?"

"Torres. And yeah, give me the time and tools and I'll get her running again."

Oh, she'd been so confident two days ago when she'd started this project. She'd spent nearly every waking minute working on the Humvee. If she could get it up and running, they could be in Montana within hours, rather than days or even weeks.

Elfy would be at Marius's family ranch. There was no other option. That was how things would be, during the day. But at night, when she was too tired to chase away the fears, they hunted her through her dreams. Mama, her face melted like wax, lurched after her demanding to know why she'd abandoned la familia. Cynthia screamed insults and accusations from the heart of an Infected nest, her grotesque offspring skittering in the surrounding darkness.

Worse were the dreams of Elfy. Torres never saw her niece as an Infected, but when she closed her eyes to rest for even a moment, images of the Infected chasing Elfy assaulted her. Elfy would be crying, calling her name, screaming for help that Torres was never in time to give.

Torres stood and cracked her back, squinting in the grey day. The light on the keypad next to the door blinked yellow, alerting her that someone was coming out. Probably Miranda going for another run. She'd suddenly developed a desire to be a marathoner, disappearing for hours at a time. Torres considered another lecture on how Miranda needed to build up her endurance or she'd hurt herself, but why bother? The younger woman would roll her eyes and ignore Torres's advice like she had the last few times the former Marine had tried to talk to her about anything beyond 'Hey how are ya? Pass me the peas, please' type conversations.

Marius walked out of the bunker. He wore a backpack and carried another over his stomach.

"Any idea who the father is?" Torres grinned.

Marius returned her smile. "Some Marine, I think. Probably already shipped out. It never would have worked anyway."

Torres hooked the second backpack's straps and lifted it off Marius. She slid it over her good shoulder easily. With a silent sigh, she held out her arm. She hated asking for help, but she also didn't want to stand there struggling to put on a freaking backpack for five minutes.

Marius situated the strap over her shoulder and tightened it a little. Torres could feel the heat from his body. He could wrap his arms around her, pull her close. She shivered, feeling suddenly both feverish and chilled.

"You okay?" His voice was low and soft, his breath tickling the nape of her neck.

"Fine, fine. I'm fine." She practically sprinted out of the gravel parking lot. Much as she wanted to, she didn't exactly know how to flirt. All that giggling, batting eyelashes, and listening in rapture to stories about e-sports. Not for this Marine, no sir.

Marius caught up and with a secretive smile, waved her toward a dim trail that led up rather than down toward the road.

"Where are we going?" She couldn't help but smile back.

"The radio tower," Marius said. "The airmen say there's no way to get the antenna working, but I'm not sure those kids know as much about radios as they claim, which is why I'm glad you came." He winked. How long had it been since he'd seemed so carefree? A few days in the bunker trying to find and infuse mold seemed to be doing him good. Maybe I shouldn't rush the repairs, Torres thought. A few more days of safety, of hot running water, electricity, and plenty to eat would do them all good. But balanced on the other end of those quiet peaceful days were Elfy and Mama and even Cynthia.

"We'll find her," Marius said. He wasn't looking at her and she was grateful. His calm certainty allowed her to believe, even for only a moment, that it was true. Elfy was alive and healthy and safe. She swiped at her eyes. Weird how the sun through the blanket of clouds was still bright enough to make her tear up.

The trail wound up the mountainside and over a narrow saddle between lumpy peaks, not yet snowcapped, but definitely making plans in that direction. The wind was stronger, sharper, colder. Good thing their body heat kept them warm. As long as they were moving, they were reasonably comfortable.

The antenna stood on a long, broad ledge. Marius shed his pack and without waiting for her to ask, assisted Torres off with hers. They walked around the antenna a few times, studying it. Torres had helped erect and tear down her share of antennas as a Marine, but beyond the basics that every grunt had drilled into them in Boot, she didn't know much about the finer points of communications equipment. There were a few things that caught her eye immediately, but those were mostly structural things, like missing or misplaced guide wires, which wouldn't prevent the antenna from functioning.

"Are we sure it's not working?" Torres shaded her eye against the diffuse sunlight as she peered up.

"The boys say it's not." Marius stood next to her. She could have leaned against his chest, only a few degrees and she'd be nestled under his arm.

"Based on what?" Torres spoke quickly, focusing her mind on the current issue, not the way her stomach fluttered or how she kept smiling for no freaking reason at all. "The boys have been sending out messages, haven't gotten a response, but all that means is there's no one responding. It doesn't mean the antenna's not working."

Marius smiled at her. "See, that's why I need you."

"That's me, trusty Ms. Fixit." Torres tried to smile. She wasn't trusty. She failed the ones who needed her most. She'd lost Elfy, abandoned Cynthia, even Mama had left her.

"You're trusty to me," Marius said. "You're still here, I mean." He rubbed the back of his neck as he looked away. Was he blushing?

"Of course, I'm still here. We're all still here. We're a team. We look out for each other." Torres stared at him, tried to read the look on his face. Was he picturing Otto the way she pictured Elfy? Or was he thinking about all the people in Los Angeles who were infected by now? Or was he worrying about his own family?

Marius nodded and squatted to dig though the backpacks for tools. "We should run diagnostics. I brought the manuals."

"I love you."

He stopped, the manual half extended, pages falling open to a section on weather-proofing the A-474-10 series antenna.

Torres froze, too. It was a joke, as in 'I love you for bringing the manuals,' but that wasn't what she'd said. How had she been so stupid, so unguarded?

"Torres." He reached up and took her hand, tugged her to squat beside him. At that level, the mountain sheltered them from the wind and Torres found herself in stillness and warmth.

"Marius, I—"

He kissed her. "Me too."

She kissed him back, nearly lunging at him. He sat back on his butt, grinning, and she followed him down, straddling his hips. He was hot and solid under her. He held her hips and guided her as she ground herself against his rapidly hardening erection.

Torres shut out all thoughts of Elfy, her family, the Infected. In Marius's arms, she could escape what she couldn't control. Even just for a short time. She needed a few minutes of bliss in her life. She buried her face in Marius's neck, breathing in his scent from the soft place where his neck and collarbone met, the hollow of his throat where his pulse thudded, and the warm space behind his earlobe that smelled of him and only of him.

He slid his hands under her clothes, pressing them against her sides until they were warm, then exploring upwards, slipping over her bra. He reached behind her, fumbled at the clasps.

"I feel like I'm in high school." His voice was a low rumble, half a purr, half a growl. With his bright green eyes and dark hair, Torres could easily picture him as a panther set to pounce.

Torres pulled his hands out of her shirt and scooted back a few inches. "Race you." She yanked off her layers in a mass. It would be a freaking nightmare to untangle the various arms of the various shirts, but that was a problem for Future Torres. Present Torres had a topless Marius to play with.

She ran her hands across his chest as he explored hers. She followed the scars, old and new, and traced the fractal tattoo-like markings the Enlightened had left on his back. He was gentle with her bad shoulder as he pushed her back onto the pile of their shirts. He bent to nip and suck her nipples and she groaned deeply. He teased her mercilessly, an impish grin on his face as she arched her hips, rubbing herself against him. She reached down, but he stretched back to keep himself away. All her fingers caught was the tops of his jeans.

"Rude." She pouted.

"I have a plan," he said.

"This is no time for plans!" Torres levered herself up on her elbows to find Marius was undoing her pants. For a second the memory of Ramon unbuttoning her shorts flashed into her mind. She yanked her legs up and away, curling into the fetal position.

Marius stopped, held up his hands and rocked back on his heels away from her.

"I'm sorry, Torres. I wasn't thinking. I should have checked that you were," he bit his lip, "ready?"

"I am!" She pounded the shirts in frustration. She had fantasized about being with Marius for so long and now all she could think of was Ramon, the weight of him on top of her as he pinned her to the cheap linoleum of Mama's front room floor.

"We don't have to ..." Marius started to re-button his pants. Torres caught his wrist.

"No. I want to. I want you. I've wanted you for ..." She took a deep breath. "I've wanted to fuck your cute little brains out since that first day in the helicopter."

"Hey now." Marius forced a jolly tone. "My brain is a national treasure. It's not little."

"Look, I really appreciate what you were going to do there," Torres said. "Believe me, I love a cunning linguist." He shook his head at the pun. "It's just that Ramon ..." She looked away, hating how the dead man had the power to make her feel small and scared.

"Lourdes." Marius knee-walked to her, pressed his forehead to hers. "We can go as fast or as slow as you're comfortable. Maybe we could try a different position?"

Torres sagged against him. She loved the delicious way their bodies fit together.

"How do you feel about me being on top?"

Marius kissed her and lay back, stretching his arms up and over his head, pulling his already flat belly even tighter. Torres reached into his jeans to find he was still very much at attention.

"All aboard, sailor," he said.

"Oh, you're gonna pay for that one." Torres straddled him.

His impish smile widened. "I'm counting on it."

A former Marine, her lover, their friend, two airmen,

and their lover huddled together in the middle of the shower room, all staring at the drain.

"Um, what's it supposed to do?" Toby whispered.

"Just wait," Marius said. His mischievous smile was back. Not arrogant, Torres decided. He seemed genuinely delighted to share his science with them, like he was a stage magician pulling off a particularly baffling illusion.

Black mold rimmed the shiny metal of the drain cover. As they watched, a silver haze moved through the mold then faded to a faint glow.

"Is that it?" Dawn leaned over Toby's shoulder. Bailey kept a hand on Toby's back. They always seemed to want to be in physical contact with each other. Maybe they were becoming one of those super organisms Marius had suggested the Infected's bioformations were. Torres smiled grimly at the comparison.

"That's the infusion," Marius said. "I added a phenotypical expression to coincide with the genotypical change because I figured I might not always have access to a lab to be able to run a sequencing challenge. Better safe than sorry, right?"

"I thought you said he spoke English." Dawn elbowed Miranda and smiled at her.

Miranda had been staring fixedly at the mold, her lip curled. When Dawn touched her, she shrank back. Her face twisted into a mask of rage, but it was gone so quickly, Torres almost doubted what she'd seen. What was going on between Miranda and Dawn? she wondered.

"Sorry," Marius said. "I'll try to E-L-I-G. Torres taught me that: Explain It Like I'm a Grunt." He winked at her. How had she not noticed how long and thick his eyelashes were? He could be a mascara model.

"Back in Portland, I added a bioluminescence to the inhibitor so that when it had successfully infused the mold, it would glow. That way even if we can't test the mold, we can look at it and know it'll work to spread the inhibitor."

"Fascinating," Bailey said. "I suppose the next logical step would be to administer the modified fungi to a suitable test subject, although happily we have a dearth of Infected in our bunker."

"English, huh?" Miranda quipped and Dawn grinned. Okay, so maybe they weren't best buddies, but they seemed to be on friendly terms. Torres put this newest mystery at the end of the long list of things to worry about, after survive, keep Marius safe, find Elfy, and get toilet paper.

"I got the street smarts and socializing covered, so Bailey gets to be the book smart one," Dawn said.

"Um, what about me?" Toby half turned to look at her over his shoulder. "What kind of smart am I?"

"You're the cute one." Dawn lightly scratched her fingers through his buzzcut.

"And I know first aid," Toby said.

"We don't have Infected here, but we do have a way to find them," Torres said, trying to get everyone back on mission. She turned to Miranda. "How long would it take to get one of the Infected?"

The younger woman closed her eyes and breathed deeply for a few seconds. She opened her eyes and shrugged. "I'm not really finding any around here."

"None at all?" Toby looked like someone had

suggested Christmas might be canceled. "There's usually tons of them. I mean, like when we go to … um … go on nature walks and stuff we were always seeing them around. Could we go find one?"

"Don't see why not," Torres said. She tapped Marius's shoulder. "You got everything you need, doc?"

He shook his head. "Not quite. I've got a couple more things to finish up to make this mobile if that's the new plan, sarge."

Torres frowned. Whether she liked it or not, Toby's nickname, as unoriginal as it was, seemed to have stuck.

"Miranda, you take point. Scout around and send up a flare if you find any Infected. I'll keep an eye on Marius."

"My hero." Marius scraped the faintly glowing mold onto a glass slide. "I'm the one who's immune, remember?"

"Me and Miranda are also immune. We got vaccinated directly from you, remember?"

"I didn't," Miranda said.

Torres blinked. "Yes, you did. You got vaccinated at Chrysalis, right?"

"Yeah, but not like you did." Miranda stood up and stretched, twisting back and forth as her spine popped. "I got the first batch of Chrysalis's special formula in the Submarine right after Harrow Hall. My dad gave me the vaccine as soon as they confirmed that Marius's antibodies were what saved John."

"The point is, Marius isn't the only one who's freaking immune." Why did Miranda feel the need to argue about every trifling issue?

"Whatev. See you out there." Miranda breezed away,

leaving Torres to do some breathing and counting exercises, while Marius finished taking samples. Dawn and the airmen followed Miranda out to start looking for Infected as well.

As Torres finished gathering her gear, Marius caught her wrist and pulled her in for a quick kiss. She loved the feel of his lips, warm and soft, yet insistent. He seemed to want her as much, if not more, than she wanted him.

The kiss turned into necking and before Torres could think better of it, Marius had his hands in her shirt and she had hers in his pants. They were breathing so heavily neither heard the footsteps.

"On second thought, I think I can —" Miranda stood in the hall, staring as Torres and Marius separated. Despite not being a teenager, Torres felt her face grow hot and had to fight down the urge to launch a barrage of explanations and excuses for their behavior. They were freaking adults in the middle of a freaking apocalypse. A little making out was the least of their worries.

"Miranda." Marius stepped forward, tucking his shirt in.

"It's fine." Miranda held up a hand. "Clears things up." She hurried away before either Torres or Marius could react.

"Okay, we need a come-to-Jesus talk," Torres said.

"Must we?" Marius zipped up his jacket and held out Torres's backpack. "We're late already ... for some reason." He tried to hide his impish and slightly smug smile. They'd been caught being naughty, but more importantly, they'd been being naughty.

"Here's what I'm gonna say," Torres held out her arm

as Marius positioned her backpack strap on her shoulder. "Whoever you were with before doesn't matter to me, but going forward, I need to know. And that includes complications like Miranda. Did you two ever ...?"

"No!" Marius blushed. "No, but she ..." He bit his lip. "In LA, she kinda came on to me. I turned her down and I think it hurt her feelings."

"That makes sense." Torres took the lead as they moved out down the hall. "No wonder she's been treating me like I'm the evil stepsister in a telenovela. I wish I'd known that before. We could have been more covert."

"I can be covert," Marius said.

"Really?" Torres laughed.

"We could have a secret hand signal. They have a lot of hand signals in the Coast Guard, right?"

Torres pushed open the bunker door. "You know, for someone so freaking smart, you sure are a slow learner."

Miranda was nowhere in sight as they emerged. Dawn and Toby leaned against the Humvee while Bailey walked around it, his hands clasped behind him like an aspiring Napoleon. The plan was to spiral out from the bunker and try to find and capture one of the smaller Infected—a Little, as Miranda referred to them — then return to the parking lot. Dawn and Toby had rigged up a cage using the bottoms of unused cots and several miles of 550 cord.

The temperature had fallen, and the low, dark clouds threatened rain or possibly snow. It was nearly October. That wasn't too early for snow in the Rocky Mountains from what Marius had told them. Torres tucked her outer windbreaker close around her neck and picked her way out along the western curve of the mountainside.

Her mind drifted back to the Humvee as she hunted. She'd figured out what was wrong with the vehicle as she'd been trying to fall asleep. Once this mold challenge was done, she could finish the job.

She hadn't told anyone and wouldn't. Not until she was sure. But if she was right, they could be in Montana by night or at least early the next morning. A large part of her wanted to leave immediately, but another part of her was afraid of what the ranch wouldn't have. Elfy. She reminded herself that Marius's work was critical. The world shouldn't suffer because her guilt and worry caused him to rush his tests.

Something moved through the underbrush. Torres held up a hand to sign STOP. Marius stopped, but Bailey must not have been watching. He kept moving, taking long downhill strides that put him well out in front.

"Freaking Zoomy," Torres started running. She heard the thump of Marius's pack as he dropped it, then he was behind her, his longer legs working to make up her head start.

The Infected was small, a Little. Torres wasn't great at identifying runty critters moving at high rates of speed, but she thought it might once have been a badger or a wolverine or something. Now it was a snarling ball of teeth and tentacles.

Bailey jerked back and froze in a pose that any other time would have been hilarious. One foot up, arm out for balance, looking toward the onrushing Infected, like he'd been tagged in a game of Freeze Tag and couldn't move.

Torres dove for the Infected. Her gloved hands caught its back ankles. It shrieked and twisted, spinelessly flexible. It bit down on her forearm. If not for all the layers, Torres might have lost the arm, or at least been skinned.

The Infected badger snarled and crunched down harder. It was like having her arm in a vice. Torres instinctively grabbed its mouth, trying to pry it off her. It didn't seem to even notice, much less let go. The pressure increased. Her fingers were going numb. It was going to crush her arm since it had failed to snap it off with the first bite. The teeth sawed back and forth as the Infected badger worked its jaws.

"I got it. I got it!" Toby came loping into Torres's view, a length of pipe cocked and ready to strike.

"Wait!" Dawn yelled.

Torres rolled over, shielding the Infected, which took the opportunity to start kicking her belly with its rear feet. The thick claws raked against her, shredding her windbreaker.

"Hold it." Marius dropped to his knees beside her. The Infected badger screeched again, louder this time. Marius tried to grab it by the scruff, but it whipped its head back and forth even more violently.

"Allow me," Bailey said. He joined Marius and the two pinned the Infected badger against Torres. Crimson seeped from her forearm through the layers of her clothing, warmth spreading. She wasn't sure if she'd been bitten or if the skin had simply been ripped off.

"Do it, doc," Torres said. She didn't know how much longer her arm would hold before the badger snapped it off. "I trust you." She caught Marius's eye, remembering when she'd told him the same thing back at Chrysalis before he injected her with the only batch of vaccine made from an unmodified sample of his own antibodies.

It seemed impossible, ridiculous even, that a dropper of liquid could stop a ball of muscles, teeth, and rage. Marius put the tip of the cheap plastic dropper against the neck of the creature. A glow so faint as to be almost imperceptible moved across the Infected from where Marius applied the inhibitor-treated mold. The glow didn't cover everywhere but flickered and jumped.

The Infected badger screamed and wrenched itself away, finally letting go of Torres's arm. It bolted away up the mountainside.

Marius jumped up to follow, looked back at Torres on the ground in the tatters of her windbreaker.

"Go!" She waved him off. No way she did all that to lose the experiment.

"You two go with Marius." Torres tipped her chin at Bailey and Dawn. They hurried away.

"Are you okay?" Toby asked.

"Let's find out." Torres held out her arm. "Who's got the medic bag?"

"Um, I do." Toby fumbled the satchel over his head and held it out to her.

"Can you peel back the material?"

He did so, revealing three shallow puncture holes and one of the worst friction burns Torres hoped to ever experience. She pressed the already clotting wounds.

"Would you do the honors?"

"Sure." Toby smiled sheepishly. He carefully dressed her arm and assessed her for shock.

"Not bad," Torres said. "I think we should promote

you from the cute one to junior medic. Thanks."

"The world is a poop-show," Toby said as he gathered up the gauze wrappers and stuffed everything back into the first aid bag. "If I can save the world by saving the mold-genius's protector, I'd call that a good day."

They had spent the remainder of the daylight hours and much of the twilight searching for the Infected badger, but the creature seemed to have vanished completely. Torres could feel the disappointment and frustration bubbling up among the others.

As the first stinging drops of rain fell, she shepherded the dejected airmen, a brooding scientist, and an overly cheery former cheerleader back to the bunker. Miranda was waiting in the parking lot.

"Where have you been?" Torres snapped. "The Infected escaped. We needed you."

"I've been here, waiting for you," Miranda snapped back. "Like you said to."

"Convenient how you're never able to communicate with the Infected when it would be useful." Torres yanked off the remains of her windbreaker and threw it into the Humvee's empty bed.

"You got something you wanna say to me, say it." Miranda stepped forward, hands on hips. Torres was aware of the others watching from near the bunker door. Despite the drizzle, they weren't going to miss the only entertainment available these days.

"I said it." Torres grabbed her tools and popped the Humvee's hood. She was too keyed up to go inside, so she figured she'd work on the vehicle. Mechanical devices, while frequently baffling, were never deceitful. If she couldn't figure out what was wrong, it wasn't because the Humvee was lying to her, only that she hadn't understood the problem yet.

"You think I'm, like, a spy or something for the Infected?" Miranda circled the vehicle to stand across from Torres in front of the engine.

"No, I don't think you're a spy." Torres reached in and began loosening a nut. "I know you are."

Miranda stormed into the bunker. The others followed her more slowly. Marius came over to Torres as the door closed behind Dawn.

"She's not a spy," he said.

Torres looked at him. All the weeks of helplessness and fear, anxiety and desperation rose in the urge to scream in his beautiful freaking face.

But he was right and she knew it, even if she would die before admitting it.

"We should be able to get on the road in the morning," she said as a peace offering.

"That's incredible!" His entire face lit up. She wanted to throw her arms around his neck, but she awkwardly stuffed her hands in her pockets.

"I'm not taking sides." Marius looked towards the bunker, then back at her. "But if I were, I'd be on your side."

"Always side with the nookie," Torres recited. She knew that wasn't fair. She wasn't even angry with him.

Marius frowned and shoved his hands in his pockets, too. "I'd like to think you know me better than that."

"Okay, that was a cheap shot."

"I accept your apology," Marius said. Before she could argue that she hadn't actually apologized he kissed her, which was clearly unfair. Then he kissed her again, which was nice. Then he kissed her neck and her shoulder and lifted her arm to kiss the inside of her wrist, which was diabolical.

"Do you want me to throw you in the back of this truck and ravish you?" Torres gasped.

"It's not a truck," Marius said and skipped back. "I have to get these samples back inside before they get too wet, but speaking of wet." He leaned in and whispered, his lips brushing her neck and ear. "I'll be right back."

Torres cradled the clipboard to her chest, checking off supplies as Toby and Bailey brought them out. Dawn was packing the things Torres had cleared into the Humvee's bed, leaving space for four people to ride. The rain had set in as if it meant to stay, so Torres and Dawn were wearing Class A raincoats taken from the colonel's office.

Marius had taken the colonel's cap. Setting it at a jaunty angle, he'd said, "I'm king of the birds," and pointed at the silver eagle insignia.

Torres had shaken her head and muttered, "Freaking civilians."

"Speaking of civilians, Miranda wants me to take a walk with her," Marius said. "Look, it's not her fault that the Infected can connect with her. She never asked for it. She's doing the best she can. Give her some credit, okay?"

Torres caught Marius's chin and looked deep into his jade eyes. "She's not the only one who didn't ask for their connection with the Infected and who's doing the best they can and who should be given some credit. Okay?"

Marius paused. Torres could see the withdrawing in his face.

"It's not the same and you know it." He stepped away from her.

"It basically is and you know it." She crossed her arms.

Marius walked to the door, stopped, and without turning to look back said, "Nothing would have ever happened to her if it weren't for me. It's not the same."

Torres tried to keep her focus on getting everything prepared for the trip to Montana. Convincing the reluctant airmen to abandon their post had taken some work, but she'd assured them that once they checked in with Marius's family on their ranch, they could return and make sure the bunker was still fine.

It helped that Dawn told them flat out, "I'm leaving. I'd love it if you'd come with me."

Ah, the power of the shag, Torres thought.

She watched Marius and Miranda stroll down the drive, ostensibly to look for any sign of the missing Infected badger. Torres reminded herself that she didn't do jealousy and that she trusted Marius. She tried to believe truth into those ideas as she checked off boxes of rations, gallons of water, first aid kits, cases of ammunition, and packages of single-ply, government issue, special extra slick toilet paper. Of all the things for the Air Force to cut costs on!

"That's the last of it," Toby declared as he waddled

out carrying a box jumbled full of video games, controllers, batteries, and cords.

"Are you seriously taking that?" Torres picked up one of the shooter games. "We can go shoot Infected anytime we like."

"Yeah, but we might be able to use the parts," Toby said. "It's vital equipment or something." He tucked the box under the Humvee's cover to keep it away from the steady rainfall.

"Or something," Torres said. She raised her voice so that Bailey and Dawn could hear. "Go do a final sweep. We've got enough room for one more backpack. One. Uno. Un. One. Got it?"

"Understood," Bailey said.

Torres did final checks. The Humvee wasn't in perfect condition, but it would run reliably. She suspected a slow oil leak, but that would have to wait until she could raid an auto parts store for rubber hoses and gaskets. In the meantime, they had plenty of oil. They'd just have to stop every few hours to check the levels.

The throuple returned. Bailey was carrying a bulging rucksack. Torres shook her head as they clambered into the back and wedged themselves in amongst the gear.

Torres checked her watch. Marius and Miranda should have been back at least a half an hour ago.

Chapter 17 – Marius

Running Rabbit, Idaho, U.S.A. - Autumn, Year 1

"We'll have to keep this short." Marius pushed the colonel's patrol cap back and frowned at the rain. His dad could read the weather signs like a mountain man, but Marius hadn't inherited his father's gift. Philippe would have known how long the downpour would last and probably been able to guess how much precipitation it would dump on them.

Miranda tucked her hands deep in the pockets of the Air Force-issue cold weather coat she wore. She pursed her lips and puffed out a ring of breath, then grinned proudly.

"Shouldn't take too long. I can kinda feel where she

went." She slowed and Marius matched her pace. Here it comes. The Talk. He'd been having a lot of Talks lately. Small price to pay if it meant Torres finally opened up to him and not just physically, although that was amazing. He bit his lip to hide his smile. Whatever Miranda had to say, he needed to listen and take it seriously.

"What'll happen to the Infected if this works?"

Marius cocked his head, surprised. That wasn't at all where he thought the conversation would go.

"It's hard to say precisely. I've only been able to do the most rudimentary tests on the mold, but if I'm right, the inhibitor will destroy the virus. I don't know if that'll cure the Infected or kill them, but either way, it solves our problem."

"What about the Flash? Will that happen again?"

They reached the bottom of the gravel drive and stepped out onto the asphalt. The wind sailed down the corridor of the roadway, tugging at their clothes, the rain seeking warm, tender flesh. Marius studied his hands. The white phosphorus burns had left him with four perfectly circular scars, pale against his olive tan skin. It was hard to remember that barely a year ago he'd started working at Chrysalis, believing he'd be part of advancing the fight against pathogens. Now instead of curing the sick, the best he could hope for was that he could destroy them before they destroyed what was left of humanity.

"I don't know about the Flash. I think it happened because Portland was almost totally bioformed. The bioformations seem to act like network hubs or nodes or something. I'm not a computer person, but anyway, when the inhibitor got into the Portland 'network' it spread fast."

Miranda stared down the road.

"Does that make sense?" Marius was accustomed to having to re-explain himself. He didn't mind as it helped him consider the issue from other angles in order to reword it.

"Yeah." Miranda turned to face him. "This will kill my dad, won't it?"

"Miranda," he reached to touch her shoulder, but she stepped back.

"Tell me the truth. You owe me that much."

"I get that you're upset about your dad, but—"

"But nothing!" Miranda's face twisted. She brushed back angry tears. "Am I upset about my dad? Hell yeah, Marius. Fucking Christ! You've been moaning and whining for weeks about a stupid kid you met once for like an hour and you're surprised that I haven't just gotten over what happened to my dad?"

She walked away a few yards, then came back. "I thought he was dead. You let me think he was dead. For months. You knew he survived Chrysalis and you didn't say anything." She jabbed her finger into his chest. "You had no fucking right. None."

"I was trying to protect you." Marius winced as the words left his mouth. Mistake. But he couldn't seem to stop himself. Miranda had things to say? Well, so did he. "I was trying to protect everyone and I'm sorry. But, no, I didn't prioritize you or your dad. He knew what Carmine was doing the whole time and did nothing, I might add. HHV would never have happened without my blood, sure, but it never would have happened without your dad and Rasmussen tinkering around with a highly dangerous virus. I never asked for this either, but I'm still here, Miranda. I'm still trying to fix things. Your dad had me kidnapped and tortured, threatened my family and you know why?"

Miranda glared at him. Her lips were pressed together so hard they were nearly white. "Why?"

But he stopped. Miranda was his friend. They'd saved each other's lives. They'd comforted each other during the long nights in the Submarine and afterwards when the memories of Harrow Hall had dogged them. Miranda was tough and brave, but she was barely more than a child. She'd lost her father and her future and if she needed a target for her rage, Marius decided he was strong enough to be that for her.

"I'm sorry." Marius forced his hunched shoulders to relax. "What I should have said was—"

"Don't fecking move." Liam's unmistakable Irish accent sent a burst of fear through the scientist.

Liam had been concealed behind some pines. He pushed his way onto the road, a pistol aimed at Miranda. Marius lifted his hands, as did Miranda.

"Get on your knees," Liam commanded. They did. Liam tossed a pair of zip cuffs at Miranda. They hit her chest and fell to the road. Liam smirked, his gaze traveling up and down Miranda's body.

"How did you find us?" Marius asked. He had to keep Liam focused on him.

"Oh, no grand mystery there, boy-o. I followed you out of Portland."

"Why were you in Portland?" Marius couldn't think of a better question.

Liam snorted and waved the pistol. Miranda picked up the zip cuffs and slipped them over Marius's wrists.

"I'm sorry about all this," she whispered.

"Don't be. It's not your fault, Miranda," Marius looked over his shoulder, caught her red-rimmed hazel eyes. "It's gonna be okay. We've gotten through worse than this."

Liam lit a cigarette and pushed Marius back with the toe of his boot, pinning the scientist's hands under his body. "I'd be saving me breath, were I you. The trunk just wasn't the same without you."

"Not the sharpest scalpel, are you?" Marius forced a cocky grin. "Portland's gone. The Enlightened are gone. There's some Infected still around, but I'm betting you can't sell me to Helatek twice. Dr. Chan will just kill you."

Liam put more of his weight into his foot, pressing against Marius's chest, increasing the pressure with each of Marius's exhalations.

"Sure I'm not gonna sell you to Helatek. They gyppied me once." He leaned down. Marius had to focus on taking shallow breaths, trying to hold his ribs up to keep enough space to get air in. "This time you're going up for auction. Highest bidder gets the elixir of life itself straight from the vine. Or the vein, eh?" He ran the pistol barrel along Marius's jaw and tipped up his chin. Marius wheezed. The first of the black spots were popping in his vision. Liam was going to suffocate him. He pushed his feet under himself, but Liam kicked his knees. Marius barely noticed the pain as the sweet relief of air rushed into his lungs.

"Aw shite."

Marius curled onto his side, gasping. Miranda was running down the road. She was nearly to the gravel turn off. Liam raised the pistol and took aim. Marius kicked the backs of the mercenary's knees. Liam staggered and the shot went wild. Miranda skipped a step, looked back, then bolted around the corner and up the hill.

Marius lay on the road and laughed.

Liam dragged Marius down the road. He'd given up trying to force the scientist to walk. Every time he got Marius on his feet, he collapsed into a boneless heap.

"You're not going to shoot me, and we both know it," Marius said. "You're going to have to drag me."

So Liam did, swearing and muttering the whole way to his Ford Taurus. He pushed Marius up against the wheel well and went to open the trunk. As he turned away, Torres leaned out from behind a tree. She waved some hand and arm signals, which she had probably explained at some point. Marius had no idea what she was trying to communicate. He shook his head. Liam was actually whistling as he rearranged whatever he had in the trunk. Marius pushed himself up on his knees and started heel-toe walking his feet under himself. Torres waved some more, frowning deeply.

What? Wait for rescue?

"Ahhh!" Someone screamed from the far side of the car. Marius turned as best he was able.

Toby flung himself out from behind a juniper bush and grabbed Liam. The mercenary pulled an arm free and elbowed Toby in the ear. To his credit, the kid tucked his chin and hung on. Liam couldn't get a clean hit in, but he pummeled Toby's head and shoulders.

Marius levered himself up and charged around the car's rear bumper. He drove his shoulder into Liam's side, nearly knocking him and Toby into the ditch. Liam backhanded Marius, which normally wouldn't have slowed him much. He'd never been a brawler, but he'd been in a few fights in high school and gotten mixed martial arts lessons from the members of John's security team, whether he wanted them or not.

On the cold backcountry road in eastern Idaho his training simply wasn't enough. The zip cuffs made it so he couldn't keep his balance. He staggered away, stumbled down to a knee. The road peeled away the already distressed fabric of his jeans and took some skin for good measure.

He could hear yelling. Torres was yelling. Something about "— should have waited for the signal, damn it!" And Bailey was yelling, but a sound cut through everything else.

The crash of a gunshot.

Marius got to his feet again. Liam had Toby by the back of the neck. He shook the kid, like a dog trying to snap a rat's neck, then threw him into the ditch.

As Liam started to get into the car, the mirror exploded. Torres strode down the middle of the road, Jimmy's pistol in hand. She fired again. The only thing that saved Liam's life was the metal of the car's open door frame. Still the shot shattered the window and peppered the mercenary's face with shards of broken glass.

Torres stopped, adjusted her stance. Liam gunned the engine. Torres took aim.

Marius ran. He knew he'd never beat the car to

Torres. He didn't care.

But Liam wasn't trying to run the former Marine over. The car jerked and squealed away in reverse, barely missing Marius, who dove into the ditch, narrowly avoiding the crush of the wheels.

Torres let her arms fall, the pistol dangling. "Fuck."

Liam's car disappeared down the road, still in reverse. Marius kicked and twisted his way out of the ditch.

Across the road, in the other ditch, Dawn and Torres were crouching over Toby. Bailey ran down the road to join them. He took one look at Toby and yelled, "Medic! We need a medic."

Marius floundered upright. "That's me," he said. He turned around so Bailey could cut the zip cuffs. He winced as the airman nicked his wrists a few times but didn't complain.

As soon as Bailey had cut Marius loose, he pointed back towards the bunker. "Go get the aid bag."

"It's in the Humvee," Torres said.

"I'll go," Dawn said, stopping Bailey. She kissed the top of Toby's head. "I'll be right back." She sprinted away.

"She went to state in track," Bailey said as he grabbed Toby's hand. "I failed my last three PT tests. For the run."

Marius pushed aside the brush and saplings in the ditch. Before he even looked at Toby, he could tell Torres wasn't hopeful. Her face was drawn and her eyes glittered. She pressed a wad of cloth over Toby's chest.

"We need something to keep out the rain," Marius said. Bailey stood, pulled off his coat, and held it over

Toby as best he could. It didn't cover the young man completely, but it did protect his head and torso.

Once Marius had prided himself on his scientific objectivity. As he knelt to examine the gasping airman, he wished he could simply exist in the moment, that his mind hadn't already jumped to a future where Toby's eyes were blank and glassy, his reddened cheeks pale, his hands, so tightly clenched, limp.

Toby's eyes were wide, his breath coming in rapid puffs.

"Let me see," Marius said to Torres.

She gave a half head shake. "It's bad. I need to keep pressure on it."

"I trust you, but I still need to see it," Marius said. In medical school, he had learned to do minor surgeries, mostly just stitches. At Chrysalis, he had practiced with the medics and learned combat life-saving skills. ABC's—Airways, Breathing, Circulation. He had no doubt that Torres might have had more real-world experience with gunshot wounds, but he had more technical knowledge—technically.

"You got three seconds, then the pressure needs to go back on," Torres said. She lifted her hand, taking the soaking cloth with her.

Toby's chest heaved, his mouth opened and closed, his fingers clenching and unclenching. Okay, breathing was a problem.

"Give me your knife," Marius said, and Bailey handed over his Leatherman multitool. Marius flicked out a blade. He forced what he hoped was a confident, calming smile for Toby as he said, "Sorry, this is gonna be cold, buddy." He sliced Toby's shirt, peeled it away from the kid's pale chest. The shirt was already soaked with blood.

Only one entry wound, not too big, just above and to the right of the xyphoid process. In the lung. Marius laid his ear against Toby's chest, listened to the hitching gurgle and hiss of a collapsing lung.

Marius looked at Torres. "It's the lung. You know what that means?"

She closed her eyes. Yes, she knew.

Marius looked down the road, trying to will the Humvee to arrive. Toby didn't have much time. The Rule of Threes was in effect: three minutes without air, three hours without shelter, three days without water, three months without food.

They needed to operate not within hours, but within minutes. All they had was a pocketknife. Toby would almost certainly die of infection, assuming the pocket-knife surgery didn't kill him.

Torres's gaze followed Marius's. The road was maniacally empty. "Can we get him prepped?" she asked. Marius bit his lip, nodded. It would keep everyone busy and save time when the Humvee arrived. Which had to be soon.

Bailey sat next to Toby and smoothed back the soft fuzz of hair just growing out from the latest buzzcut. Marius ignored Bailey's soft reassurances and lies.

He put a hand on the kid's shoulder. "Listen, Toby, I'm going to get you all patched up and you'll be okay."

Toby grabbed Marius's wrist, stared into his eyes. "Liam?" he panted.

"He's gone."

"Dawn?"

"She's fine. She'll be right back." Marius forced a smile. "Now, we gotta get you ready, okay?"

Toby winced and gave a thumbs-up.

Marius and Torres rolled the kid onto his side and tugged the remainder of his shirt free. The exit wound was just below his shoulder blade. Marius wadded up Toby's shirt and pressed it against the wound then settled him back down, his head in Bailey's lap.

"You okay?" The young airman patted Marius's arm weakly.

"You saved him," Torres said. "And everyone else. After all this, I'm awarding you a damn purple heart and freaking court martial for disobeying orders during combat, you knucklehead."

Toby tried to laugh but started coughing. Flecks of blood sprayed from his mouth. "Don't. Feel. Good. Sarge."

Marius scanned the area, searching for something to seal the wound.

"Hang in there," Torres said, helping to steady the airman's head. "Doc's gonna get you fixed up so I can knock some sense into you."

Marius's head jerked up as he picked up the rumble of the Humvee. Torres leapt up and ran. She was back in moments with the first aid bag. Marius spread his coat and dumped the bag onto it. Gauze, tape, scissors, band-aids, aspirin. Nothing big enough to cover the whole exit wound.

"Ohmygodohmygodohmygod." Miranda stood on the road, her hands covered her mouth. "I'm sorry. I'm so sorry."

Dawn scrambled into the ditch and Torres directed

her to join Bailey holding up the coat. "Try to keep him talking," she encouraged them.

"I need a ..." Marius grasped the empty air above the guts of the aid bag.

"What?" Torres took a few steps towards the Humvee.

"Plastic. About this big." Marius framed the dimensions.

She dove into the back.

Toby clutched at his chest. "Can't. Breathe." His trachea was deviated to the right. Marius groaned. He'd been worried about a tension pneumothorax. Without being able to seal the wound, Toby's lung would collapse, taking the other with it. The pressure would mount around his heart and ...

"Here!" Torres thrust an MRE's outer plastic case into Marius's hands.

Toby twisted, eye bulging, lips cyanotic. Bailey was sobbing. Dawn dropped the coat and reached out, but didn't try to hold Toby down. Marius leaned on Toby's shoulder, tried to cover the wound, but the kid's thrashing prevented him from getting a good seal.

"Hold him still," Marius ordered Torres.

"Help me." Torres showed Dawn where to position her hands. "Like this."

Marius slapped the plastic against Toby's exit wound and taped it in place. He took the second half of the plastic and taped the edges, leaving a corner open for the air to escape, and watched the jerky rise of Toby's chest.

"Waiting to exhale. Waiting to exhale," Marius whispered the phrase Jimmy had taught him back at Chrysalis during combat medic drills.

Toby's chest fell and Marius covered the hole. He sat back and watched the kid, felt his pulse. Tachycardia, but the rhythm was improving with each lungful of air. Toby's lips were pinker, his breaths less wheezy.

He smiled up at Marius. "Where's my purple heart?"

While Marius tended Toby, the others rearranged the baggage in the Humvee and rigged up a stretcher. Torres, Dawn, and Bailey helped lift Toby in. Miranda hovered around them like a distraught moth. Marius climbed in the back with Toby. Dawn and Bailey both tried to, but Torres made Dawn come with her to ride up front. There wasn't a lot of room.

Marius and Bailey braced Toby as Torres drove slowly and carefully back up the gravel road toward the bunker. Toby wheezed, each breath hard won. Marius put an ear to the young airman's chest. The breath sounds were better. When he tapped on the kid, the sound didn't have the hollow thump it had before. Progress.

Bailey held on tightly, his gaze fixed on Toby. How long had they been stranded out at the bunker together before Dawn arrived? Marius knew what it was like to be so utterly alone you thought you'd never hear another voice besides your own. After all that time Bailey was now watching his only friend dying.

Dying?

Marius checked Toby's vitals. He should be stabilizing. Instead, his skin was pale and clammy, his heart rate elevated—weak and rapid, fluttering and stuttering like a trapped bird trying to escape the young man's chest.

He's going to die. The thought sent a spike of freezing pain through Marius. Toby's going to die because he left the bunker, because he tried to save me. I told him I could stop the outbreaks. It's my fault.

"No," Marius whispered. He bent over the semi-conscious airman. I have to save him. Just work the problem. What's the problem? ABC's. Airway. Airway is open. I patched up the wound, so his lung is functioning. Breathing. He's breathing. A little gurgley, but breathing. Circulation. Marius checked the pulse points in Toby's ankles and wrists, and in his throat. He detected a pulse in each. No disruption to circulation. But the pulse was weak, rapid. That meant …

The Humvee screeched to a stop. Doors opened and Torres appeared at the opening of the back, pistol in hand.

"The bunker's on fire," she said. "He's destroyed it." She stared at Toby and Marius, both covered in blood. "How bad?"

"I don't know." Marius shook his head. "It's bad."

"But you patched up the wound, right?" Torres's brows knit.

"He needs to be in an ER, not the back of a truck." Rage at his own helplessness boiled up. It was all Marius could do to keep from screaming and punching the side of the Humvee, but that wouldn't help. He had to figure this out. Weak, rapid pulse. That meant …

"What can we do?" Torres asked.

"Should we get him out? Lay him down on the ground?" Bailey sniffed.

"Probably best not to move him," Torres said.

Weak, rapid pulse. That meant …

"Blood loss!" Marius yelled. He lifted Toby's shoulder and sure enough, a puddle of blood soaked the coats they'd piled under him. The gauze from the first aid kit hadn't been enough to stop the bleeding. Marius tore off his flannel shirt and Henley undershirt. He ripped the sleeve off and wadded it up, pressed it to the wound. The blood soaked the shirt but didn't drip. Because the wound was on Toby's chest and due to the danger of collapsing his injured lung, Marius couldn't risk a pressure dressing. He had to hold the dressing himself, monitor it.

"We need to move away from the fire," Torres said.

"Okay, fine." Marius snapped.

Torres put an arm around Dawn's shoulders and guided the younger woman back to the front of the Humvee.

Marius pressed his index finger to Toby's carotid and counted the seconds between the fluttery beats. Still not good. Marius gently laid the kid back, keeping one hand under him to steady him and keep pressure on the wound. He ran the other hand over the front of Toby's body, checking for wounds he'd missed. None, other than the entry wound.

The Humvee shuddered into motion. Toby flopped against Marius. The dressing jarred loose. Marius clutched the kid to him, pressed the wad of cloth to the wound. It was soaked and the blood ran through his fingers like wringing out a dish towel. He grabbed the other sleeve of his shirt and added it to the packing.

The Humvee trundled down a steep incline. With

both of his hands occupied by steadying Toby, Marius couldn't stop his slide. He turned so his back would hit the Humvee's cab. Bailey positioned himself between Marius and the metal frame.

The road flattened out and Bailey wiggled out of the way, crouching beside Toby, holding one of his limp hands and rubbing it.

"Not today. Not today," Marius muttered.

Toby's pulse was so weak Marius could hardly find it. If he didn't get a transfusion, he'd die. Marius wracked his brain for anything they could use to transfuse his blood to the kid. They had no medical tubing, but they did have wider tubes from the Camelbak drinking packs. What about hypodermic needles? None. Could they make one? Did they need one? Marius remembered reading about the first transfusions—vein to vein. Direct transfusions. That could work. It had to work.

The Humvee stopped. Torres came back around, Dawn leaning against her.

"We're far enough away from the bunker I figured it would be safe to stop," Torres said. "How can we help?"

"He needs a transfusion," Marius said, keeping his voice low so as not to disturb Toby. "I stopped the hemorrhaging, but he's lost too much blood already. I can give him some of my blood. I need your help. I'm going to cut my wrist and when we're done, you'll need to sew it up."

"What?" Torres blinked.

"Can you sew, like with a needle and thread? There's a sewing kit in Bailey's bag. I saw it earlier. Get everything prepped ahead of time."

"This is crazy," Torres said. "No way."

"He's going to die," Marius hissed. "We have to save him."

Torres looked at Toby then up at Marius, back to Toby. She reached over the tailgate and pressed her fingers to Toby's neck, waited and shook her head.

"No." Marius pushed Torres's hand away, felt for the pulse himself. It was just faint. He waited. It would be there. He waited.

"Marius?" Torres put a cool hand over his. "You did everything—"

"No!"

"You did everything you could."

Marius gently laid Toby back on the pile of blood-soaked clothes. He moved away as Dawn scrambled into the back. She and Bailey knelt on either side of Toby, their heads pressed together, one holding each of Toby's hands.

Marius didn't remember getting out of the Humvee or washing up or changing his shirt. He remembered standing in the middle of the road, watching smoke tumble out of the mountainside, taking the mold and his inhibitors with it. He remembered Dawn and Bailey's keening wails and Miranda's stunned silence. He remembered Torres, who took his hand and pulled him out of the fast-falling snow back into the Humvee's warmth. He remembered leaning his face against the thick, cool glass and that sleep had been unstoppable.

Chapter 18 – Courage

The air was crisp and clear as John stepped out of the Crossroad's town hall. Night had flung handfuls of stars across the enormous upturned bowl of the sky. He hadn't seen so many stars since his last trip to Mongolia. The scent of woodsmoke and diesel fuel hung in the air, mingled with the cooling smell of baked prairie grass and earth. The first snow of the year had come and gone, leaving a false autumn to tease them with promises of warmer days and clearer skies.

John rubbed his bad knee. It had been a good meeting, a productive one, but sitting so long had been hard for him. With the changing weather, the lack of proper physical therapy, and anything resembling cortisol shots, the knee was locking up more and more these days.

The townsfolk parted ways, calling their goodbyes, promises of dropping by for this or that reason, and reminders to drive safe. The roads would be icy and the deer frisky.

John scanned the nearby rooftops. There were only a few buildings in this snowy land that had roofs flat enough for lookout posts, but he insisted they be staffed at all times, especially when folks gathered for the weekly meeting of New Avalon community council.

Crossroads was the biggest town of the four cities that made up the new council. Anoheka was the site of the main water reservoir for the whole valley. Point Zebulon had the granary and feed store. Esmerelda boasted talented siblings—the only glassblower and blacksmith in several hundred miles.

The brother-sister team spent their summers on the Renaissance festival circuit, but had come home early from a gig in Oregon. They'd brought tales of local militias and outbreaks that would have been hard for most of the locals to take seriously without John backing them up. He'd seen such things and worse and if they didn't want those things coming to their town, they needed to prepare.

It had been Percy, Marius's younger sister, who'd proposed the name New Avalon to encompass their extended community. And it was increasingly Percy who was John's reason for staying at the Morning Star ranch. At first, he'd waited there because he believed Marius would show up soon. Where else would he go?

As if summoned by his thoughts, Percy walked up, her arms crossed tightly under her breasts. John tried not to notice. She was at least ten years younger than him, not to mention Marius's sister. Marius was the mission, John reminded himself. He needed to stay focused. He'd allowed himself to get sucked into the whirlwind of trying to prepare four small towns for an onrushing pandemic, rather than trying to find and guard the one person who could stop it all.

"About time they got their butts in gear about those solar panels," Percy said. "We're gonna need more heat in the bunkhouse soon." She rubbed her upper arms and blew a puff of foggy breath.

"And more lighting for Marius's lab," John said. "And the perimeter, of course."

"Perimeter, huh?" Percy grinned, flashing the dimples in each of her cheeks. "Here I always just called it the property line."

John found himself grinning too. "Whatever y'all call it." He added a long twang to 'y'all.'

"We're lucky to have you looking out for us," Percy said. She patted his back and set off across the street to where her old Toyota pickup was parked. John tried to keep the limp to a minimum as he followed. Percy hopped into the driver's seat while he settled gratefully into the passenger's side. The way his leg felt, driving would have been torturous.

As Percy drove, John reviewed the endless task list that started with security for the ranch. More lights, clean out the water sources on the allotment in case the well went dry, could the windmill be repaired, could a new one be built, how many people could fit in the bunkhouse, where else could they put the refugees? They had been flocking to Crossroads, chasing the rumor of a cure or a vaccine linked to Marius.

Percy cleared her throat. "Anatole said there was a recall for the military. Are you gonna go report in?"

A year ago, John would never have imagined even hesitating to answer, 'Yes, of course.' But now, studying Percy's profile in the soft glow of the dashboard's lights, he paused. He'd sworn his life and his honor to protect and defend his country, but what sort of country would there be if HHV continued unchecked? Without Marius, would there be a USA to protect and defend? Was he really staying at the ranch for Marius?

"I mean, do you have to report in? I'm not sure how that works." Percy glanced at him. In the faint light, her dark blue eyes appeared black, mysterious. What did she want him to say, expect him to say? She was a test he'd never prepared for.

Before he could form a coherent response, she added. "I ... we would miss you. If you had to go." She turned her gaze back to the road. Was she blushing or was it just his wishful thinking?

Stick to the mission, John reminded himself. Marius was the mission.

"The situation is complex," John fell back on the familiar stalling tactics that had served him well in many a high-level briefing. "At this juncture, the most prudent course of action seems to be to continue looking for Marius in the local area as we have no credible intelligence indicating he would go to any other location."

"Ah-huh," Percy said. From the corner of his eye, he could see her half-grin, similar to Marius's crooked one. She was amused by him, by his military lingo. He loved her smile, quick and sincere.

Percy turned on the radio. Most of the stations were static, a few AM ones still broadcasting a mix of Country-Western music, religious fervor, and STOL—Rad punk for rad radicals. Percy tuned into the punk music and sang along. John enjoyed her impromptu serenade. They drove out of Crossroads and eventually turned off the paved road onto the long dirt road that led to the long gravel drive that ended at the Morning Star ranch.

Even at this late hour, there were people moving around. A shed had been designated as a lab back when John had first arrived. They had expected Marius to not be far behind and that he would need a space to work. The shed stood dark and empty, but the bunkhouse was abustle, with a few tents and RVs ringing it. The sounds of tired people settling down for the night filled the air with a constant murmur. It reminded John of many a staging site. Just a temporary rest before deployment.

But this time it wouldn't be to some far foreign shore, wrapped securely in the knowledge that 'we fight them here, so the good folks at home can shop at Wal-Mart and eat at McDonald's in peace.' This time the end of the driveway was the front line. This time the enemy might already be among them, brought in with a concealed wound or a forgotten cut.

John still questioned the wisdom of the Tenartiers' offer: All are welcome here as long as you work and you don't hurt others. At first it had only been one or two people, then a couple from New York, a family from

Albuquerque, but then more and more people showed up. They'd heard that there was a cure in Montana and had been directed to the Morning Star ranch with its AWOL cure. A few had left when they discovered Marius wasn't there, but most stayed. Where else could they go? No flights, no trains or buses, no gas for sale.

Some people moved into Crossroads itself, staying in hotels, and later abandoned houses. Most stayed on the ranch, which was up to fifty people, not counting the usual ranch hands and the Tenartier family proper.

Percy stopped near the red maple that grew in a circle of grass at the end of the gravel drive. She hopped out, her long ponytail bobbing as she hurried to the back to start unloading. As she passed John's window, she tapped on the glass. "You coming?"

John blinked and rubbed his eyes, nodded and stepped out into the cold, night air. He still wasn't used to the way the first inhale seemed to freeze his nose hairs. He hadn't realized that he preferred deserts to tundra.

"C'mon. Dad saved chili for us." Percy shifted the bags she was carrying as she climbed the porch steps, calling greetings to several people as she headed inside.

The house's first floor was barely recognizable as a family living area. Most of the furniture and all of the personal items had been removed. Milk crates lined the walls, filled with printouts on every conceivable topic. No one had known how long the internet would be available, so they'd downloaded guides to gardening, medicine, and more.

Annette's office had been turned into an infirmary, stocked with bandages, antiseptic cream, gauze, tape, insect bite and anti-itch creams, and a dwindling supply of antibiotics, antidepressants, and anti-anxiety pills scavenged from local pharmacies and abandoned homes.

While most Montanans were of a hardy disposition, possessing a determination that bordered on irrational obstinacy, a few families had heeded the governor's evacuation order and gone to the pickup points in Helena, Great Falls, and Butte.

"Here. Eat." Percy handed John a bowl of chili. John's hand brushed hers as he accepted it. Her hands were warm and a little rough, nails short and rounded. There was a thin pink scar on the back of her right hand. He wanted to rub his thumb over it, feel the tiny puckered flesh, imperfect in the perfection of her skin.

She cleared her throat.

"Thanks." John dug into the chili, which was both hotter and spicier than he'd expected. Percy dropped into the chair across from him. He could feel the weight of her gaze. He needed to say something.

"Your dad and I should talk about security."

"Dad's getting the herd in from the allotment, remember? He won't be back until tomorrow morning. I'm the boss of the ranch." She flashed her dimples in a forced grin. "So, let's discuss."

"Should we wait for your mother?" John asked.

Percy shook her head. "Thing is, my mom's not doing so great. She loves us all. I know she does, but Marius ..." She twisted her spoon through her chili, watching the meaty mix separate and fall in on itself again. "Him being gone again has really taken a toll on her. He's always been different, special. Not just smarter." She pursed her lips. "I'm tired of talking about Marius. Can we not?" Her face was so young, and yet so anguished. A few strands of hair brushed at her cheeks. John envied them. He wanted to wrap his arms around her and tell her that he would protect her from all things, that no one could love anyone more than they loved her.

She looked away and sighed. "Sorry. I sound like a callous jerk." She squared her shoulders, so small and delicate looking, yet so resolute. "Talk, oh wise Captain Courage. Tell me what we need to do to protect what family we have left."

"We'll find him." John said.

Percy grimaced.

Don't make it about Marius. John could practically hear her thoughts. He changed the subject. "There's a lot of natural resources on your property. The main thing will be safeguarding them and stockpiling what we can now. We'll need more of everything, but energy's going to be the big issue." He took a careful bite of chili and blinked back the tears. "With modern cultivation methods, I'm sure this place can do just fine, but we might lose that. We need backups."

Percy nodded. "SunQuest. If anyone still has solar panels, it'll be them."

"We'll have to get batteries and teach folks how to use what panels we can find," John said.

"Let's go tomorrow," Percy said. "Once Dad gets back, of course."

John frowned. "We need to get the new refugees settled and make sure the perimeter's secure. We need to figure out if any of those people can handle themselves in a combat scenario. We need to —"

"I'm going." Percy's chin stuck out, emphasizing the cleft in it.

John didn't hesitate. "I'll go with you."

Percy's Toyota pickup was a veteran of many a poorly maintained country road. Loaded with John's and Percy's go-bags and a rifle apiece, there was still plenty of cargo space in the bed. Percy leaned against the hood, a grey-brown cowboy hat with dark blue band tilted back on her head.

"I thought you military types were early risers." She looked at her wrist, devoid of watch.

"No excuse." John headed over.

The sun had just peeked over the horizon and the yard was washed in pale gold. It glittered off the frost that covered the tents and vehicles, making the place look gilded. A few of the refugees stirred. John suppressed the urge to stay and organize the morning's chow. They'd figure it out. Philippe was back to help Annette through her daze of worry and grief. Plus, Anatole, their younger son, could help while Percy was away.

Percy hopped into the driver's seat as John climbed in the other side. His knee was so stiff he could barely bend it. He rubbed it, waiting for the truck's heater to drive out some of the ache.

"And away." Percy spun the wheel, maneuvering around a tent and down the drive.

John had rehearsed a few conversation starters. Now as they bumped down the driveway, his mind froze like a private holding a grenade with the pin pulled.

It wasn't until they had passed the eastern edge of Crossroads, heading north that Percy broke the silence.

"So, tell me your life story in thirty words or less."

John caught her wry grin and sidelong glance. He stared out the windshield, watched the brown countryside whiz by. How long until they didn't have gas? How long until this trip would take days, rather than hours?

"Or don't."

"Sorry. I was just thinking. I'm not sure where to begin."

"Were you born? Or did the Army build you in a lab? That's what I heard."

That's what Marius said. Even now, his absence haunted them.

John decided to accept Percy's offered humor. "Built in a lab."

Her smile widened.

"And then?"

So, he told her about growing up, joining the military. He told her about various deployments. He talked and talked, words flowing out effortlessly as he watched her listening. After a while, he realized he was doing all the talking. She's going to think I'm an arrogant, insensitive jerk, he thought.

"Apologies for the rant." John paused. "What about you? Were you born on the ranch?"

"At the medical center in Helena. I want to hear more about your adventures."

"And I want to hear about you."

So, she told him about growing up on the ranch,

about her favorite horses and camping trips, about school in a small town with a genius nerd of an older brother. John told her about how he had nearly fired Marius the first time they met. He was getting to the fateful trip to Harrow Hall when Percy pointed out the windshield.

"That's an Army truck, isn't it? Don't they go in convoys?"

John leaned forward to look. A lone Humvee drove towards them. John blinked, rubbed his eyes, looked again. "Pull over," he said.

"What?" Percy slowed and flipped on the hazards.

John clambered out of the pickup and fast limped to the center line, waving his arms over his head.

The Humvee slowed and stopped a good standoff distance away. John smiled. It was good to see Torres hadn't lost any of her security instincts.

Chapter 19 – Marius

Morning Star Ranch, Crossroads, MT, U.S.A. -

Winter, Year 1

Torres was out of the Humvee before Marius realized what she was doing. For a second, he thought she was charging the red pickup parked on the side of the highway, emergency flashers on. Then he saw John get out and he recognized the pickup's driver.

Percy!

Torres ran to meet John and they hugged, John nearly lifting her off the ground.

Marius stumbled out of the Humvee. Percy practically knocked him over when she threw her arms around him.

"I can't believe you're alive." She sounded as stunned as Marius felt. "Where have you been? We thought you were dead until this group showed up at the ranch. They said you were in Portland?"

"What group? Did they have kids with them?" Torres broke away from John to join Marius and Percy. "My niece. I'm looking for her. Her name is Elfy. Did she make it? Is she okay?"

"The group with the Afghan woman had some kids." Percy looked at John. "I don't remember their names."

"A little girl. She's five. Six? About this tall." Torres held up her hand to show Elfy's height against her side. "Short dark hair. Latina."

"That could be her, but I don't want to say for a hundred percent." It was his turn to look at Percy for help. "We have records at the ranch."

"John tries to vet everyone, but that's not really doable with most of the refugees." Percy patted John's shoulder. "Drives him nuts, all those blanks on his questionnaires."

"Refugees?" Marius was still trying to understand how his sister and John were driving along the highway like nothing had changed, like the world wasn't on fire, and Toby wasn't dead in the back of the Humvee.

"I'll explain on the way," Percy said. She did a little skip of joy, beaming at Marius. "Mom and Dad are going to lose their dang minds! C'mon. You ride with me, brother mine."

Parts of Crossroads looked abandoned, but little had

been ransacked. Marius watched his hometown creep up, surround, and fall away from the truck. John was riding shotgun in the Humvee so he and Torres could bring each other up to speed and strategize. Marius had left Miranda in the back of the Humvee, her hand resting on the sleeping bag that held Toby's body. Dawn and Bailey huddled against the side wall. No one had spoken for hours until they'd run into Percy and John.

Marius didn't remember much of the trip through Crossroads other than that he didn't see any signs of the Infected or the Enlightened or bioformations. They passed the Jenkins's place and Percy turned the truck left, leaving the paved road. Marius couldn't remember the last time he'd been back to the Morning Star ranch. Gravel crunched under the tires. They'd be home soon, where people would expect him to have answers, a vaccine, a cure. They'd expect him to save them all. He stared at his hands, scrubbed clean of blood as if Toby had never been.

A make-shift fence had been constructed along the edge of the property with watch towers at regular intervals. It looked like something out of a Frontier Days style historic village complete with a moat-like ditch at least three or four feet deep and about six feet wide. A backhoe waited near one end of the moat as if they planned to continue digging soon.

Percy slowed the truck and stopped in front of a new gate made of unfinished boards reinforced with rebar. A pair of watch towers overlooked the gate from either side. They held a pair of kids who, until a few months ago, had probably been high schoolers. Each held a rifle and the girl in the western tower had a pair of binoculars.

On seeing Marius, the girl shrieked, "It's him. It's him!" She slid down the ladder and ran to open the gate. The boy in the eastern tower spoke into a walkie-talkie and waved to Marius, grinning broadly. They thought he was some kind of hero.

As the girl jogged down the road, Marius recognized Helen. She had attended a junior science fair he'd judged a few years ago. She came to a halt in front of the truck. "I can't believe it. You're home. This is so awesome."

John poked his head out of the Humvee and called, "I'm right here, Keith. Open the gate."

The boy clambered down to help Helen swing wide the heavy gates.

Percy waved to the pair as they drove through. To Marius she said, "Mom and Dad are gonna want to see you first thing."

Marius nodded. He'd imagined this homecoming so many times. It felt wrong to celebrate with Toby's body cooling in the Humvee. Would it be worse to take this moment of joy from his family?

The familiar turnaround with the maple tree in the middle came into view. And on the porch, lined up as if posed for a family photo, waited his family: Dad, Mom, Anatole, even Buddy, the golden retriever.

Marius didn't remember getting out of the truck. One minute he was sitting next to Percy, the next he was in his father's arms, his own arms around his mother and Percy with Anatole between them. Everyone was crying, laughing, and talking. Buddy, the family's golden retriever mix, capered around them, barking and play-bowing in excitement.

"Fuck ..." Torres said. Marius looked over the barrier of his family's arms. Torres's eyes were brimming with tears. Marius's stomach dropped, his mouth already filling with the useless 'I'm so sorry for your loss' phrase.

But Torres bolted toward a cluster of children who were playing in the side yard. One girl dropped the end of the jump rope she'd been holding.

"Tia Lourdie!" she screamed. She started to run toward Torres then stopped and yelled over her shoulder, "See, Washington. I told you she'd be back. She's a Cobra Commando!"

Torres snatched the girl up before she could finish speaking. She sank to her knees, arms tightly around the squirming child.

"Basta, basta." Elfy wriggled. "You're squeezing too much."

"Squeezing is what Cobra Commandos do bestest, mi sobrinita favorita." Torres buried her face in the girl's dark hair, her shoulders shaking with sobs.

"I'm your only niece," Elfy said, but she leaned into her aunt's embrace and patted her back. "More like a python than a cobra. Did you know pythons and boas are constrictor class snakes?"

Marius swallowed the lump in his throat. Annette's eyes brimmed with happy tears, watching the reunion of the Torres family.

"Let's give them some time," Philippe said. He put a hand on Marius's shoulder and walked him up the porch.

"I'll take care of everything out here," Percy said, lagging behind with John. "Don't start without me! I wanna hear the whole story."

Out of the living room windows, Marius watched his sister and John drive the Humvee and truck over to the side of the barn. They parked in a patch of torn up ground that looked like it was in the process of being turned into a parking lot.

The house itself was hardly recognizable from the comfortable home of his childhood. Maps covered the living room wall, the front office had been converted into an aid station, the dining room table was strewn with papers, rounds of various calibers, and bins they were being sorted into. It looked like a recreation of the headquarters of some band of resistance fighters during World War II.

In the kitchen, Annette took Marius's face in both hands, looked deeply into his eyes. "What happened? Where were you?" Her own grey eyes were bright with tears, but she hadn't stopped smiling since he'd seen her.

"We'd better all sit down," Marius said, and they sat around the kitchen table. Percy bustled in through the back door, pausing to kick off her boots in the mud room. Philippe made a pot of coffee and Annette set out scones with blackberry jam and clotted cream. The moment shockingly normal until Marius started his story.

He explained how he'd been kidnapped by the Infected and taken to Portland, where they'd tortured him and threatened his family to force him to try to find a way to stabilize the more advanced strain of HHV. He started to explain about the Enlightened when John arrived.

"Ursula's getting Miranda and the other two settled in the bunkhouse," he reported. He turned to Marius.

"Torres filled me in on Portland. Seems we have more enemies than we thought, but we've been getting folks prepared for all eventualities."

Marius couldn't resist smiling. Everything else in the world seemed to have changed, but John was still John.

"I can't thank you enough for watching out for my family." Marius shook the soldier's hand, then pulled him in for a hug. John patted his back awkwardly and stepped back, a smile on his own face.

Marius noted John's limp had worsened. Time to talk about that later, he decided. Philippe and Annette filled him in on the founding of New Avalon.

"It started with just the locals," Philippe explained. "They came here looking for the vaccine. Some stayed to help out and for protection. Most folks went down to Helena to try their luck with the evacuations. Some stayed on their land. You know how we are."

Marius nodded. The people of Montana were a stubborn, independent lot, shaped by the hard land they inhabited.

"Some of the kids put things on social media, let people know where we were and that we could help," Annette said.

Marius caught John's eye and smiled at the soldier's grim face. John would have hated that. Talk about a breach of operational security.

"The governor called and demanded we bring you to Helena, but by then things had pretty much fallen apart. We told her, 'You want him, send an army.' We're still waiting," Percy said. She gave Marius a quick hug as she passed behind his chair to take her own seat. "He's stupid and ugly, but he's ours."

"So, then people started showing up from further away. We had to refit the bunkhouse. Your friend, Dr. Rajiv, came all the way from Baltimore," Annette said.

Marius hadn't seen Rajiv since before he was hired by Chrysalis. They'd been roommates at Johns Hopkins, where Rajiv had specialized in immunology. They had kept in touch even when Marius let down their youthful ideals by working for a multinational pharmaceutical corporation. In the end, Marius had to admit, Rajiv's concerns had been well founded. He dared hope Rajiv could help with his mold project.

"We haven't had any serious discipline issues among the civilians. The scientists are going to be happy you're here. Still haven't gotten a vaccine they think'll work," John said. "Now, if you'll excuse me, I'm going to go check on Miranda." He slipped out through the mud room.

"I should go talk to them, see who's here, how we're set up for equipment," Marius said, the urgent need to work pressing him as much as Liam's boot ever had.

Annette frowned. "You just got back, darkling. Can't it wait a day or two?"

"The Enlightened are on their way. That seems pretty pressing, Mom." Marius took her hand and squeezed it as he rose from the table.

"Yeah, we heard about the Enlightened from some of the new arrivals. Are they different from the Infected?" Percy asked.

"As far as I can determine, the Enlightened are humans infected by the SAM-D strain. They retain higher functions and act as controllers for the other Infected, animals infected with SAM or any of the FOX-

H Infected. They communicate by using the bioformations like a network. I was able to destroy a nest of them in Portland." Marius paused at the tipped heads and raised eyebrows from around the table.

"All right, son," Philippe said. "Well, that sounds dangerous. What can we do?" Ever practical, his dad.

Marius explained about the mold, how it spread through the network. "By itself, it'll slow the Infected down. It's better than nothing. I had spliced an inhibitor into the mold I was working with in Portland. It spread through the city's network and brought the whole thing down after I set some on fire in the lab they had me in. Everything exploded. All the bioformations burned away. The ash fell for a couple days, at least." Marius didn't want to mention that since the explosion and the ashfall, he had yet to see a cloudless sky. If the effect from the explosion had traveled further than the Columbia basin, past the sightlines of Portland, how much ash might be in the upper atmosphere? Enough to trigger a long winter? Enough to cool the globe for years, like after Krakatoa's eruption?

"You need a hot bath and a rest. There'll be time to go out to the barn and check out the labs in a couple hours. C'mon." Annette directed Marius upstairs.

She paused, almost reverently, outside the closed door of his bedroom, her arms tightly crossed.

"Mom." Marius put an arm around her shoulders. She felt so thin and small, so vulnerable under his hands. He could no more protect her than he had been able to save Toby. It might be best if he left the ranch. That way the Enlightened or mercenaries like Liam wouldn't have a reason to threaten his family.

He drew a breath, smelled the familiar scents of home, the faint incense smell from Percy's room, the modeling glue from Anatole's, the ancient dusty scents of the attic, the cool air from the window at the end of the hall. His own room, when he pushed the door open, was as he'd left it when he'd moved to Baltimore. Reference books were piled next to his desk. The closet door was slightly ajar, as it always was, its monster far less frightening now than when he'd been a child. On the windowsill, a fat clump of melted and rehardened wax served as a stand for a single candle. The window was cracked open.

Marius looked at his mother. Annette blinked back tears and crossed to blow out the candle and close the window.

"So you could come home again," she said.

"Peter Pan," Marius said.

"My Neverland boy." Annette smoothed the long hair back from Marius's face and studied him for a moment before hugging him fiercely.

"I'm home." Marius hugged her back.

Marius hadn't intended to fall asleep, but it was pitch dark in the room when he woke, disoriented and alone. He bolted up and fumbled at his side for his revolver, but he'd hung the holster on the foot of his bed. He remembered the camping lantern Annette had placed on his nightstand before leaving him to rest and clicked it on.

Outside, people moved in and around the barn. The

windows had been covered with transparent plastic so it was hard to make out anything beyond vague outlines. Marius went to his desk and surveyed the documents John and Percy had collected for him.

With the knowledge he'd gained while working for the Enlightened in Portland, Marius understood the virus better. He now understood why the Chrysalis vaccine had only granted limited immunity. It was reactive, the enzymes keying to the receptors in each strain, excluding the other strain. What he needed to do was go back, not to the second-rate vaccine that Carmine created, but to the antigens within his own body, to the most basic form of the virus he could find.

But a vaccine would be hard to make with less than state-of-the-art labs at his disposal. If he could isolate the inhibitor again, anyone with access to its genetic code could stand against the Infected. No more trying to vaccinate individuals in the face of a global pandemic. The mold would neutralize the Enlightened's networks, killing many of them. The rest would devolve into Infected and be much easier to deal with. The trick would be to spread the mold faster and further than the virus could spread, make the cure more infectious than the disease.

"You're not coming to dinner?"

Marius jumped at the sound of his mother's voice. Annette leaned against the doorframe, a plate in one hand, a glass of milk in the other. How many nights when he'd been in high school had she brought him dinner while he worked? Indulging his genius, she called it.

"Hey, Mom." Marius smiled.

"Saving the world?" She set the food down and looked over his scattered papers and Post-it notes.

"Trying." Marius shook his head. "I'm not sure I can re-sequence the inhibitor."

Annette sat on the end of Marius's bed. "The other scientists said you can make a vaccine from your blood. That's what John said, too. He said you cured him after he was infected out East."

"But that's not a scalable solution," Marius said. He went to the window, which showed only his own reflection against the darkness outside.

"I don't understand," Annette said. "Can't they clone your antibodies or whatever they need? It doesn't have to be a direct transfusion every time, like with John, does it?"

"They tried that at Chrysalis." Marius turned from the window and paced the room. "The problem is me."

"You?"

"Yeah. Why am I naturally immune? I mean, there are people who are just immune to some diseases. We know that. But I shouldn't be immune to the base virus. It's not infectious. It took Rasmussen tinkering with it, using CRISPR to move stuff around before it started hurting anyone. Plus, I wasn't exposed to anything until Harrow Hall, but I looked at the m-RNA while I was in Portland. I've had this immunity my whole life. Unless my assumptions are wrong. I don't know why I would have antibodies to a virus that wasn't infectious."

Annette clasped her hands in her lap and stared at Marius. He'd never seen her study him that way. It worried him.

"What?"

"Do you remember when you donated your blood at school?"

"I remember you grounded me totally unfairly for being a good citizen." Marius tried a grin, but Annette didn't smile.

"I need to talk to your dad." She hurried out before Marius could say anything.

He got up and followed her downstairs. People were gathered around the kitchen table, poring over maps of the town of Crossroads and discussing what supplies they might find at what locations. John and Torres had a whiteboard on the counter, propped against the cupboards, and were working out a guard roster, from the look of the names, sectors, and times listed. Percy perched on a stool with a notebook in hand, pointing at people who gave her names and numbers.

The bustle of activity, the sheer number of people was almost overwhelming after so long with only himself or a few others for company. The last few weeks, traveling with first Torres and Miranda, and later the throuple, had been a good way to ease back into society, but watching the camaraderie of the group, Marius felt like an outsider to their easy banter, their earnest plans, their friendships.

I've become Other and strange, he thought, as if he'd been stolen away like some changeling child in one of his mother's fairy tales from her native England.

"Marius." John greeted him with a cup of coffee. The conversations around the room fell silent, all eyes on the scientist, as if he might announce that all was well and the Infected had been vanquished by the simple act of his return. Well, it wasn't Lord of the Rings. He'd been to Mount Doom and the Enemy still roved the land, just as dangerous as they'd ever been, if not more so.

"Hey, there." Marius sipped the coffee, tried to think of something to say. He knew they wanted him to be a hero, to have answers. What he had were more doubts than any of them. It might be possible to eradicate HHV by seeding their bioformations with mold, but New Avalon didn't have the resources to do that. The Infected could spread and regroup faster than a few hundred people in the middle of Nowhere, Montana could destroy their nests or lairs or whatever they had.

"They're in our base, killing our dudes," as Anatole would have said.

What New Avalon needed was a way to contact other survivors, other communities that had weathered the initial spread of the HHV pandemic. Folks who knew what it was, knew how to protect themselves from it. Vaccinate and expand, push the Infected back in an ever-widening circle because they surely would be trying the same tactic: infect and expand until only a few naturally immune people like Marius, and those like John and Torres who'd been exposed and vaccinated for both strains, remained.

"Have you been out to the labs yet?" Percy asked.

Marius shook his head. Without understanding the base virus, he'd have to make two vaccines, one for the SAM-D and the other for the FOX-H strains and that was assuming there were only two infectious strains and no major mutations had occurred since Rasmussen first released the virus at Harrow Hall.

"Son, can we talk to you?" Philippe stood in the living room, his arm around Annette's shoulders. Her eyes were red and puffy.

Marius bit his lip. "Sure, Dad. What's up?" He set his mug on the counter and left the kitchen.

"We have something to show you," Annette said. Her voice barely quavered, but Marius could hear the tears she was fending off.

"Okay." He followed his parents upstairs, down the hall past the pull-down ladder to the attic, and into their bedroom. Here, too, evidence of the new, more primitive life abounded. They had a bucket in the bathroom next to the toilet that served as a chamber pot. The windows were covered with plastic as insulation since there was no more central heating in the house. This far from the wood stove's chimney, it would be cold at night.

"Sit." Philippe patted the bed. Marius sat and his parents sat on either side of him as if he was a kid again. Philippe reached under the bed and drew out a worn satchel. It was stuffed with composition notebooks and a few loose papers, as well as some black and white photographs. Philippe handed it to Marius but didn't let go of it.

"We need you to understand we love you very, very much, son," he said.

Annette squeezed Marius's hand and sniffed.

"What's going on? What is this?" Marius looked from one parent to another.

"You ... you're ..." Philippe took a deep breath and stared out the window.

"Mom?"

"You're adopted."

"It was winter when we found you, almost Valentine's Day," Philippe began. "I was working for the CIA at the time." He ignored Marius's surprised expression. "That's how I met your mother."

"You were a spy, too?"

"No, I was a Literature professor. Your dad was loitering around the university, trying to pass himself off as a student. He was hopeless, but charming. Eventually, his duty took him to Spain. That's where we think you were born."

"Where you *think* I was born?" Marius bit his lip to stifle his questions.

"I found you in a ... well, son, it was a lab, basically." Philippe's hands moved over the leather satchel in his lap.

"A lab?" Marius stared at his father's face and felt a growing sense of unease. He wanted to deny what they were saying. He'd only just come home, and they were taking his family away from him. Again.

"After World War II, the US and the Soviets secretly fought over the best minds," Philippe said. "For decades, we brought former Nazis to America as part of Operation Paperclip. My mission was to find one of the doctors who'd been on the run. He'd been hiding in Spain for over forty years by the time I joined the Agency. He'd been involved in the Nazis' eugenics programs, an early geneticist if you can call it that. They were trying to create *Ubermensch*—a master race of superhumans—smarter, stronger, better looking. The next evolution of humanity."

Marius tried to focus, to follow, but he didn't want to go where Philippe was leading. Still, his curiosity won out. "And how do I feature in all this spy versus spy stuff?"

"We're not sure how Oskar, our original target, was getting the babies, but when we raided his lab, he had a room full. He'd been overseeing his son's experiments on them. Most didn't make it. He killed the rest, tried to destroy the lab. You were the only survivor."

Marius stood up and paced to the end of the room, looked out the window, returned to stand looking down at the people he'd always believed were his biological parents. He felt like a fool. The truth was as plain as their faces. Philippe's cleft chin, echoed in Percy's face, and less strongly in Anatole's, but not in his own. Annette's brown hair, silky and straight, like Percy's and Anatole's, not dark, thick and wavy, like Marius's. And there were less obvious things that any geneticist worth their Ph.D. should have picked up in a minute. Marius's bone structure was different. He was taller than his father. Even his skin was a different hue, olive tan where Annette was ivory pale and Philippe a ruddier shade, but still clearly of Northern European not Mediterranean ancestry.

"What happened to the other ... babies?" How had he alone been spared?

"That doesn't matter," Annette said.

"I'm not a child, Mom," Marius snapped and, for the first time, saw guilt in Annette's eyes.

"We agreed to tell him everything." Philippe took his wife's hand. He met Marius's gaze, his dark blue eyes so different from the younger man's jade green. How did I not notice? Marius wondered. *They do not see because they do not wish to see.* But the time had come when he must face the truth. Lies had led to the pandemic that destroyed the world, so he would bear the weight of what his parents had to tell him.

"Maybe the best thing to do would be to give you the files. After you've had a chance to read them over, then we can talk." Annette patted the satchel.

"Okay," Marius agreed. He wanted to eliminate the pain and fear from his mother's eyes. Grey eyes, he couldn't help noting. It was as if every minute difference between him and them had suddenly been outlined in fire with neon arrows pointing at it. His mother's widow's peak, the differences in their earlobe shapes, how his cheekbones were higher and finer than his mother's, his jaw sharper than his father's, and not just due to his youth.

With numb hands, he accepted the satchel.

In his room, he cleared an empty space on the floor the way he had when he'd been a kid trying to work out some problem or project. He needed to think.

Marius set the satchel on his bed and lifted the flap, pulled out a pile of loose papers and faded photographs. There were official-looking stamps on some of the documents. Others were scribbled pages that had clearly been part of a lab notebook. The photos had names written on the backs, lists of aliases from the look.

Marius flipped through the photos, feeling numb. These were the monsters the American government had not only forgiven for their horrible crimes, but had rewarded with new names and new lives, peaceful lives of relative anonymity and on top of it all, the ability to continue their work.

And I'm a part of all that—the product of a Nazi experiment.

Marius shuddered as if the faces staring up at him could infect him again, twist his soul as the virus twisted the body. He'd neared the bottom of the stack of personnel files when he froze. He recognized the face. It was several decades younger and about fifty pounds lighter than when Marius had known him, but it was the face of Dr. Karl Rasmussen, the man who'd captured Marius at Harrow Hall and injected him with both infectious strains of the Harrow Hall virus.

Karl was listed as the son of and assistant to Dr. Oskar Rasmussen, the man Philippe had been assigned to recruit. That meant Karl could have worked for Oskar when Marius was brought into the former Nazi's laboratory. Had Karl held him as a baby, experimented on him? Marius shuddered again.

A report was clipped to the younger Rasmussen's photo. It read:

```
Level 3 clearance has been
granted to Agents Keller and
Tenartier to redirect the
mission due to the death of
former VIP, Oskar Rasmussen.
New VIP: Karl Rasmussen.
Recruit and resettle per pre-
planned parameters with the
exception of annual salary,
```

which should be offered at
25% of Oskar's rate. Should
Agents deem it necessary,
they may provide a one-time
resettlement bonus of 50%
Oskar's annual rate. Agents
are advised they must file a
separate addendum justifying
any pay out of bonus moneys
or additional incentives.

A faded copy of Rasmussen's American passport and a New Jersey driver's license with his name and picture on it accompanied the report. And that was it.

Marius dug through the satchel, but there were no other documents referencing the younger Rasmussen.

Had Rasmussen known who he was when they'd met at Harrow Hall? How could he have?

Did Philippe tell anyone when he took Marius? Was his adoption even official? But it had to be. He'd seen his birth certificate ... a document that said Philippe was his father and Annette was his mother. Another lie.

He groaned. Whatever paperwork Philippe needed, he could have easily gotten using his Agency connections.

So, was it a coincidence that Rasmussen's business partner recruited Marius to work for him at Chrysalis? There had to be some other connection, some clue. Marius kept digging through the paperwork.

Was Rasmussen following me my whole life, waiting for his experiment to ... what? To unleash a disease that would destroy the world, whispered a deep part of Marius's mind. Like innocent Pandora, his very existence had ushered evil into the world.

The room felt close and small. Marius started to stuff the papers back into the satchel but caught himself. These were the only links he had to a past he hadn't even imagined. He smoothed out a crumpled sheet and set it carefully into a pile before putting everything neatly away.

Philippe and Annette were waiting for him in their room. Marius studied them, feeling detached, like the scientist he'd almost forgotten he was. It was as if he'd never really seen his parents before. He'd missed the quick intelligence in Philippe's eyes, thinking all his father cared about were cows and horses, hay and feed and vet bills. He hadn't seen the way Annette looked at him, measuring her love to ensure that her adopted son never felt left out or different from the children of her body.

For the first time, Marius looked at his parents and saw people with complicated pasts and hidden depths. His whole existence had been built on a lie they told him, on a secret they kept from him and yet, he couldn't fault them, couldn't believe for a moment that they didn't love him.

"Marius?" Annette held out a hand to him, worried by his silent appraisal.

"Mom ..." Marius said. And there it was. She was his mother in all the ways that mattered. He went to her and hugged her, marveled at how beautiful she was. The years had pressed crow's feet into the corners of her eyes, streaked her brown hair with grey, roughened her skin and spotted it with moles, softened her figure. She felt slight in his arms, and he wondered how much of her osteoporosis had stolen. Once she had seemed all-wise and eternal. Now she seemed so human, fragile despite her fiercely loving heart and the determination that had built a life for herself and her family far from her native land. What had it been like for her to follow her spy husband across the ocean with her stolen son?

Marius looked over Annette's head and met his father's eyes. He felt a swell of gratitude for the man who'd picked him out of the wreckage of a Nazi doctor's lab and decided, against all good sense and reason, to keep him.

"You must have questions," Philippe said.

"I do." Marius nodded. "But they can wait. For now, what matters is, I'm home. With my family."

Chapter 20 – Miranda

Morning Star Ranch, Crossroads, MT, U.S.A. –

Winter, Year 1

Miranda watched the last shovel-full of cold earth cover the shrouded corpse of Airman Tobias Airedale. Across the grave, Dawn hugged herself, her face blank even as tears trickled down her cheeks. Bailey stood at attention, hands knotted into fists at his sides.

We are gathered here today blah blah blah.

Because of me, Miranda thought. We are gathered here today because of me. Because I trusted Liam, because I trusted Marius, because I trusted John and Torres and all the rest of those military types to keep me safe. But they didn't. They didn't keep me safe or Toby or my dad.

Out of the corner of her eye, Miranda could see Marius, surrounded by his loving family, all of whom were alive and well. His jaw was clenched, his eyes welling. Like he had any right to feel bad, but somehow he always found a way to make everything about him.

Ha ha, jokes on you, Marius. It was all me. It was all my fault, no matter how much you want to be martyred over Toby's death.

The plan had been simple. Get Marius to Liam and the mercenary would do the rest. Miranda had taken it upon herself to sneak into the bunker while the others were reacting to her dramatic announcement that 'He took Marius! I tried to stop him' whimper, sob, and so on. She had uncapped the bleach, let it sting her nostrils as she walked into the closet Marius had filled with shelves to grow his precious mold on. It had been pretty, watching the mold curl in on itself. It had been nice, sending the message of comfort to the nearby Infected.

No need to worry about that icky mold. I've taken care of it. I'll protect you like they never protected me.

She hadn't planned to start the fire, but after she destroyed the mold, she realized that Torres would notice. The former Marine would wonder how Liam could have possibly known what it was. Well, Ms. Suspicious, no one will notice the missing mold if the whole place is on fire.

So, she'd gone a bit off plan. All for the greater good, like Liam said. No one would get hurt.

That had been the stupidest lie she'd fallen for.

"No one'll get hurt. I'll take Marius and leave you the map," the mercenary promised.

Liam had failed to live up to every part of his deal. Toby was dead, Marius was still free, and there had been no map waiting for her under the red rock at the end of the gravel drive.

Someone tapped Miranda's shoulder. It was Marius's little brother. She knew Anatole was seventeen, only two years younger than she was. It was strange how much older she felt when she looked into his innocent, hopeful grey eyes.

"You okay, miss?" he asked. For once, the boy wasn't wearing his favorite charcoal grey cowboy hat. Which was lucky for Miranda. She wouldn't have been able to keep a straight face.

As it was, she managed a nod and swallowed a sound that could have been a giggle but was probably a hiccup. Probably. It was best Anatole think her overwhelmed by grief. If he knew how the ball of rage in her gut churned, especially when Dawn hugged Marius. Hugged him when Toby would have still been alive if not for meeting the train-wreck scientist.

It's never him. Leave before you get killed, too.

Miranda jerked her attention away from the boy, wrapping herself in the Infected's comforting presence. She hadn't initially realized the Infected were in the area, but they'd reached out, swallowing her fear and shame in righteous fury. It was good to have someone on her side the way John had the security team, Marius had his family, or Torres had her niece and that Afghan woman.

As they walked back down the gentle rise towards the house, Miranda let her mind unspool, threading it out among the Infected's network. There were a few close to the ranch, mostly Littles acting as scouts. They could only stay a short time each because their tiny minds couldn't focus on even simple commands like SCOUT and DON'T ATTACK for more than a few hours at a time.

It was important the humans not be alerted to the others, to the hive. It grew inside the shelter of the abandoned quarry only a few miles away. Part of her yearned to find it.

If we can't have him, no one will.

Miranda smiled at the thought. She recognized its echo from her own girlish crush. Once she had only been able to see Marius the way everyone else did. Handsome, brilliant, the Dudleyest of Dudley Do-Rights with his earnest green eyes and his movie star perfect hair.

But we know the truth. Abomination.

Yes, he was, wasn't he?

As the rest of the good folk of the Morning Star ranch filtered back to their various tasks and groups, Miranda drifted away. To the west of the ranch house, the foothills of the Rockies started to roll up. It took only a few minutes walking to be hidden from view behind a swell.

Miranda stopped, listening to the prairie wind whine down from the mountains. She stepped forward, letting the tall grass brush her thighs. It reminded her of that night in Wiltz, alone in a field halfway around the world. When would be the next time she went that far again? Nowadays, biking was about the fastest mode of travel. No business class upgrades on a Schwinn.

Come. Come home. Don't be alone. Don't be lonely.

The sensation was the same, too. A pull, like she could sense a different gravity. The hive was—she turned slowly back and forth like someone looking for more bars on their phone—that way.

Without thinking, she walked. Once upon a time, there was a pampered preppie high schooler who preferred to walk no further than the distance of Rodeo Drive. But that girl was long gone. Miranda had spent the last weeks walking or biking and she was ripped. She smiled, feeling her own power as she moved.

Yes, it's nice. It's good to be strong. We are strong together. You will be even stronger with us.

Enough with the hard sell. I'm on my way, aren't I?

Miranda had never been big into meditation or any of the woo-woo stuff. Obviously, she did yoga—hot yoga and vinyasa flow mostly. Where else to show off her super cute lululemon outfits and expertly styled messy buns? But as she walked, following the pull of the hive, she fell into a trance-like state. She wasn't concerned about the mind-meld, more curious than anything. She didn't realize how far she'd gone until she stood at a rusty, half-open gate.

A nearby sign warned the mine was closed to the public and trespassers would be prosecuted to the fullest extent of the law. Judging by the litter of old beer cans, tobacco and marijuana cigarette butts, and used condoms, few of Crossroads' youth had been overly concerned. Past the sign, a narrow trail led over the edge and down toward the mine's main entrance. It was completely covered by bioformations.

In here. Come. Be one of us.

Yep, there was definitely a hive down there. Miranda could sense the Infected like little tickles against her mind. She paused, focusing. Something else was down there, too. A stronger presence, something with a true mind that could actually communicate more than just the basics. An Enlightened. It sat at the center of everything, the brain of the hive.

Miranda hadn't felt one this strong since Portland, since her dad had left her behind in a collapsing hospital while he was whisked off in a helicopter. How many family fights had ended the same way? Well, clearly not the whole collapsing hospital part, but the rest. Albert Viers, forever promising that 'We'll talk about it when I get back, Mandy' no matter how many times she'd screamed at him that she hated that nickname.

Yes, we know Viers. Come in. We can connect you to him. We can help you.

Miranda drew a curtain across her innermost thoughts. Not just about her father, but the fact that she wasn't about to go spelunking in some weird quarry, especially not one crawling with Infected.

Let me see you first, then maybe I'll come in. She caught an Infected's mind with hers. It used to be a goat and was coming back from spying on the ranch. It was easy enough to push her way into its teeny brain and ride along with it as it tripped nimbly down the rock face. As the Infected goat touched the bioformation over the entrance with its tentacles, the wall opened enough for the creature to wriggle through.

Inside, the air had felt close and heavy, filled with the smell of oil and dirt, the syrupy tang of spilled sodas and decaying snacks. As the Infected goat traveled inward, the temperature dropped. The air felt chalky as if it was filled with old dust. Along the sides of the tunnels, were bioformations ribboned with thick, dark reddish-purple veins that took nutrients where they were needed. Smaller, twisted bundles of nerves fired off messages. The hive's Enlightened could use the network to communicate to any point instantaneously. Any Infected linked to the bioformations would give and receive information as if it were simply an extension of the hive.

The Infected goat showed the hive all the delicious people gathered at the ranch. Only the Abomination was there.

I smelled him. He wasn't spreading the black stuff like before, but he was there. She could kill him for us.

Miranda flinched as the attention of all the hive's Infected pointed at her. The Enlightened gathered the Infected's wants like a choir director and sent them to Miranda as less chaotic musical notes. Still, she could sense their hungry little voices, so full of rage and ruin. It would be easy to destroy the ranch. She could set it on fire like the bunker. She could tip over a candle into a box of papers, printouts of how to build a forge or set a broken bone. After they were all dead, no one would need that information anyway.

She would walk away as they screamed. Some of them would burn. The Abomination. He would have to be burned. None of the Infected or the Enlightened wanted to touch him. Not after Portland.

But the rest, the helpless rest, so lost without him. Oh, the Infected would feast. They would gorge themselves. They would gnaw the flesh off and crack the bones. The children they would save for last.

Would you like to eat them?

The idea, the filthy rotten idea of eating children, as if that should tempt her, shook Miranda to her core. She stumbled back, feeling as if a stone had slammed into her stomach. She broke her connection, leaving the Infected goat confused deep within the hive.

The Infected reached for her, tried to pull her back and oh, it would have been nice to let them. To not be alone and scared all the time.

It's okay. Let go. Be one of us.

I will, but not yet. I have to go back to the ranch. I'll set them up for us. Don't worry, I'll take care of you, just like my dad took care of me.

It took every ounce of self-control Miranda had to hold the idea—*I'm on your side. I'll be back. I'm on your side.*—as she left the quarry. Each brush of the Infected against her mind threatened her concentration. Sweat broke out along her brow, her nerves stressed in the extreme. She took off her coat, keeping the placating assurances going while keeping the curtain firmly over her inner fears.

John's lessons about self-defense and making herself a hard target came back to her. She kept her pace steady and her mind calm. She didn't know how long she could fool the hive, but she didn't let herself think about it. Not until she was back on the hill overlooking Toby's grave. There were no Infected nearby. The scouts had left to hunt, and she could finally relax. She wiped her face, found a dried crust of blood. She didn't even remember her nose bleeding.

She desperately wished they cared about her, but they

didn't. They didn't love her, not even in the way she loved her father. They weren't her family. They were trying to use her, like everyone else.

"I'm gonna kill them all," Miranda muttered.

"Can we talk?" Torres had snuck up on her. Miranda frowned. She really had to figure out how to deal with the Infected without zoning out so much.

"Um." Miranda tried to conjure a tear, but annoyance and sorrow didn't mix easily. She settled for sniffing and dabbing her eyes. *See, I'm upset, not colluding with your enemy or anything.*

"I apologize for saying you were a spy for the Infected." Torres said. She sounded like she was reading off a cue-card.

Miranda crossed her arms over her chest. "M'kay."

Torres rubbed her neck. "Look, Marius was right. It's not your fault what happened to you or to your dad."

No, it's not. It's his fault. The Infected brushed her thoughts.

I need space. Miranda frowned, pushing them away.

"I guess what I'm trying to say is, I miss you." Torres gave a half shrug and looked over at the little cemetery. Other than Tenartiers, Toby's was the only grave there so far. How many more if the Infected came to the ranch? How many would never be buried at all? Miranda tried not to picture Torres's niece or those little Afghan girls being ripped apart for food or nesting materials. As a general rule, the Infected didn't recruit juveniles. Most were too fragile to survive the mutation. It was a waste to try.

"I've been really focused on getting here, on finding Elfy," Torres said. "I was not my best self."

From their vantage point on the hillside, the women could see a group of children gathering around a figure with a hand-knit scarf draped over their head. Soraya had started a school. She insisted, announcing that if children in war zones could do lessons, children on ranches should have no trouble paying attention.

"Not your best self, huh?" Miranda pursed her lips. "The word I was thinking of started with a B, too."

"Fair." Torres shoved her hands into her pockets. Under her coat she was wearing her holster with Jimmy's gun. It seemed weirdly sentimental that she didn't trade it in for one of the bigger guns that were a part of the ranch's growing armory.

"Do you have anything you want to say to me?" Torres prompted.

"Like what?" Miranda turned to face her, hands clenched into fists. "Like Marius did a really shitty thing to me and my dad and you're right there with him every step. I mean, what the hell, Torres? Is his dick that good?"

Torres froze, her eyes wide, her chest stilled in mid-breath.

Do it. Hit me. Do it. Do it. Do it!

Because if she did, Miranda could finally go. If Torres hit her it would prove beyond a shadow of a doubt that she had no place among these people. That she was right to keep quiet, leave, and let the whole valley get swallowed up by the Infected who were squirming and churning under the earth, waiting for the signal to attack.

"I'm sorry about that, too." Torres said. Her nostrils were flared and her eyes bright. Miranda could practically see the anger thrumming through her like a plucked string. "I know you had a cru—a thing for Marius. You two have been through a lot together and, in some ways, he's the only family you have left. He thinks of you like—"

"Like a sister," Miranda snapped. "I know. He told me. After I kissed him. Which I know he told you about. Did you have a good laugh?"

"No, Miranda." Torres's voice was soft and full of pity, which Miranda realized was far, far worse than if the other woman had simply hit her. "You've been through so much. Way more than anyone your age should have had to deal with. I keep treating you like you're a seasoned Marine, and you're barely out of high school. I haven't been fair to you and I know it."

Much as she wanted to fling back insults and disdain, Torres's words stilled some of Miranda's anger.

"It's been pretty shitty for all of us," she allowed.

"Understatement of the century. Local girl rates apocalypse 'pretty shitty'." Torres grinned as she mimed holding a microphone out to Miranda. "So, Ms. Viers, what else can you share with our viewers at home?"

Down the hill, the children had gathered around the Afghan woman for their lessons. Miranda cocked her head, considering. The kids, at least, deserved a head start.

"Well, Ms. Torres, the viewers shouldn't get too comfy because the Infected are on the way."

Chapter 21 – Marius

Marius stood in the kitchen doorway and watched his parents dipping candles from the huge soup pot, which usually only came out a few times a year at holidays. Philippe leaned over and murmured into Annette's hair. She snorted and swatted at him.

Marius coughed.

"Oh, hey there, son." His father looked over his shoulder as he held the dripping wicks over the sink.

"Coffee's brewing," his mother added. Was she blushing?

Marius smiled and shook his head as he poured

himself a cup. He settled at the table and pulled out a fresh notebook.

"Someone has questions," Philippe said.

"I do," Marius said. "So, my birthday. Is that just a random guess?"

"Not exactly," Philippe said. "I found a charred tag on your, well, I guess it was a crib. I didn't bring it back because there was only so much I could smuggle out and a baby was already stretching my limit."

Marius made notes.

"And you said it was February when you found me?"

"Yes. You were almost seven months old." Annette finished her candle and hung it over the drying rack before she sat down beside her son. "Your dad brought you to me on Valentine's Day."

"Still better than a puppy," Philippe said.

Annette sighed indulgently. "That joke was old the first 3,000 times."

"It explains my middle name. You are both terrible at naming people. Since we're being honest," Marius said with a grin.

The back door burst open, and Torres rushed in. Marius jumped to his feet.

"What?"

"The Infected," Torres said. "There's a hive in the quarry. Miranda found it. They're planning to attack us."

Miranda followed Torres in and nodded.

"I'll get John," Marius said. This was exactly what he'd been afraid of. The Infected would never leave him alone. Without the inhibitor he'd made in Portland or even the mold he'd cultivated in the bunker, what defenses did they have? Memories of the Infected attacking the people in the field outside Wiltz flooded Marius's mind. This was what he'd brought to his own family.

John was in the stable. By the time they returned to the kitchen, Soraya had arrived, passing her teaching duties over to her co-educator, Phineas.

Once Miranda explained that she not only sensed a hive, but an actual Enlightened residing inside, the six of them fell into a stunned silence.

"We have to go," Soraya said in the silence that followed.

"Go where?" Annette asked. "There's more than fifty people on the ranch. Even if we did manage to pack everyone in, we don't have enough gas to get very far."

"What about Crossroads?" Percy added. "Or the rest of New Avalon? They can't all leave, not everyone. If we're not here, the Infected will just attack them."

"We save the ones we can," Marius said, catching John's eye.

"That's crap!" Percy stood up so fast her stool would have fallen if John hadn't put out his foot and caught it.

"That's the world we live in now," Marius yelled back. Because of me. More than anything he wished he hadn't come home. The Infected wouldn't have a reason to attack if he weren't there. Back in Portland, he convinced himself that letting his family die would be worth it to stop the Enlightened. But instead of ending the HHV threat, he'd destroyed a city, and had nothing to show for it—just a few trays of mold in the shed and a set of instructions scribbled on notebook paper in case someone else needed to copy his methods. Even in the apocalypse, he wanted to make his findings available for proper peer review.

"So that's it?" Percy glared at him. "We just give up on everyone else and save ourselves? Marius, we invited these people here. We promised them we would help them."

"Percy, this is our best option," John said in his very reasonable voice.

"It's *an* option." Percy crossed her arms over her chest. Marius recognized the look. John would have more luck getting a deer carcass away from a pack of starving wolves than getting Percy to change her mind.

"Which means there are other options," Torres said. Percy threw her a grateful look.

Marius almost said, "Who's side are you on?" but stopped himself. Childish old habits came back quickly in his boyhood home.

"Even if they aren't particularly good ones, we should give them proper consideration," Annette said.

"There's the Air Force," Torres said. "Up north of here, in Great Falls, I mean. There's an Air Force base, right? And they've got ICBMs."

"Hold on there, Dr. Strangelove," Philippe said. "Sure, a nuke would solve the hive problem, but we don't want to end up like Pripyat."

"But if they have nukes, they must have other bombs, right?" Percy's eyes sparkled. "Like those bunker-buster ones. Would that work, John?"

"Probably." John rubbed his face. "It would depend on how deep the hive was under the ground and what the composition of the area around and above them was, but probably yes."

"He said yes. It goes on the board." Percy scampered

out of the kitchen and returned with her whiteboard. She wiped it clean and wrote:

OPTIONS

  - Leave :*(

  - Bombs :D

"I am concerned that the bombing might be unsuccessful," Soraya said. "Much as I appreciate the need to explore all possibilities, it seems to me that we may be wasting what little time we have remaining in pointless discussion, rather than preparing. The Infected could strike at any moment."

"They won't, though," Miranda said. Everyone looked at her. "I can feel them. They think I'm on their side. I could basically walk right into the hive. I'm a VIP."

"What about me?" Marius asked. The beginning of a plan was forming in his mind, and it involved infiltrating the hive.

"Uh, they totally hate you, so no."

"But if I could get close enough to the Enlightened, if I could get my blood on him, that would destroy the hive, right? It would cause another Flash, like Portland."

"Yah, but like, you can't get within a mile of the quarry without them straight up murdering you," Miranda said.

"Maybe we could send in one of those bomb robots with Marius's blood," Percy said.

"Sure, from Anatole's bomb robot collection," Marius teased with a grin, and Percy rolled her eyes.

"We don't have bomb robots, but I bet the Air Force does. I thought you were the smart one." She stuck her tongue out at him.

"That's not a terrible idea," John said. "We wouldn't

have to sacrifice our territorial advantage and we could minimize the risk to our personnel."

Percy wrote on the board:

Bomb-Bot & Blood ✓✓

"I would like to evacuate," Soraya said.

"We shouldn't divide our forces," John said. "Or our resources."

"Regardless." Soraya folded her hands on the table and stared straight ahead.

"We can keep everyone safer if we stick together," Torres said.

"I am sorry, but I have heard too many empty promises of safety and peace to trust another. I won't be staying and neither will my children." Soraya met Torres's eyes and held them. "No children should remain, in case any part of this unlikely plan fails."

"Elfy stays with me." Torres's didn't flinch.

"I merely offer to help my friend," Soraya said with a slight dip of her head.

"Let's take a break," Annette said. She stood and leaned forward, her hands braced on the table as she looked around. "It's always difficult to make rational decisions when your child is in danger. We are all doing the very best we can, and we all care about each other."

Marius went out to the shed. Between the plastic sheeting and the grow lights Anatole's school friends rigged up with suspicious ease, the place was a perfect little tropical zone. The mold trays were snuggled on three rows of shelves. Another day or even two and he'd be able to harvest this crop. Even without the inhibitor, when combined with his blood, it would hurt the Enlightened. Hopefully, kill it. Did they have that much time? Doubtful.

"Hey." Torres stood in the doorway. The shed was cramped with two people, so Marius stepped out.

"Walk with me," Torres said.

"I thought you'd have had enough of that for a lifetime," Marius said.

Torres didn't even smile. "I think she's right."

"Who? Soraya?"

"Yeah."

"Are you gonna go, too?" Marius asked. He stopped and grabbed Torres hand. When she didn't look at him, he gently lifted her chin. The pain in her eyes tore at his heart.

"I can't lose her again. I just can't." Torres's eyes brimmed. She jerked her hand away, swiped her eyes.

"I know." Marius pulled Torres to him. Her head fit perfectly in the crook of his neck, but she stood stiffly, her whole body quivering with tension.

"You should go." It was the hardest thing he'd ever said.

Torres wrapped her arms around him and held tight. She'd never clung to him like that before, like he was a buoy in a stormy sea. It was both exhilarating and terrifying to see her this way, so vulnerable and unsure of herself. He knew beyond any doubt that he would do whatever it took to be worthy of her trust in him.

Marius wished he could keep her safe in his arms forever, but the best he could do was to stroke her back as hot, silent tears soaked his shirt. He buried his face in her hair. No matter what else happened, he wanted to keep this intimate moment with him perfect and whole forever.

After a few minutes Torres pushed herself away, wiped her face on her sleeve, and glared at Marius.

"No."

"No?" Marius wiped his own face.

"No. I'm not letting you get killed in some stupid way. I worked my ass off keeping you alive for way too long. Plus, who's gonna rub my feet if you get turned into monster chow? I can't believe you're so freaking selfish."

"What?"

"There has to be another way."

"Lourdes, this makes sense. It does. I don't like it, either, but I get it. You just got your family back and so did I." Plus, though he didn't say it, there might not be another chance to set up another lab. "We have to do what we can to protect them. My family is staying, so I'll stay and fight for them."

"Then we'll stay, too," Torres said, but Marius knew her well enough to know when she was bluffing.

"Soraya's right. You said it yourself." Marius took both Torres's hands, stroked his thumbs over the backs of them. Her skin was so soft there, not calloused and rough like the rest of her hands. "I want Elfy to have her best chance, too." He lifted her hands and pressed his lips to them.

Torres grabbed him and kissed him fiercely. When they parted, she pivoted, pulled his arms around her and rested against him. He could feel her heartbeat against his chest. He leaned down, hooking her shoulder with his chin to draw her even closer.

"I can't pick," she said.

"I would never ask you to pick me over your family."

"Which is why I can't pick."

Marius kissed her ear and nibbled at it until she giggled.

"I'm saying I understand," Marius said. "I kept thinking that all I wanted was to be near my family, you know the people related to me by blood. But I found out something and it made me rethink all that."

"Like you suddenly don't like your family?" Torres half-twisted to look back at Marius.

"No," he said. "I found out that family isn't just blood."

Torres turned to fully study him, eyebrows raised. He told her everything, as best he could, about the Nazi experiments, his father's time with Agency, being born in Spain (which she said explained why he was so caliente), his parents faking his birth certificate, and that Rasmussen might have known who he was the whole time.

"Or not." Marius ended with a shrug.

"Viers could have known, too," Torres said. She snapped her fingers. "That would explain it."

It was Marius's turn to wait with raised eyebrow.

"Courage mentioned that they were going super hard on your recruitment. At the time I didn't pay much attention."

"That doesn't mean he knew, though. Maybe Rasmussen was pressuring him without telling him why." Marius bit his lip.

"Maybe we'll never know, and we got other shit to do right now," Torres said. She stepped away, shading her eyes against the late afternoon light skimming down from the western mountains as she looked back toward the main house.

People were heading back inside.

"Your dad is sneak-smoking," she said, taking Marius's hand and leading him toward the house.

"Yeah, but he's not good at being sneaky."

"Good enough to steal you from a Nazi," Torres said. He pulled her close and they walked together hip to hip, arms around each other.

As they reached the door, Marius drew Torres into a tight hug.

"Whatever you decide, I love you," he whispered.

She brushed her lips against his, then kissed twice along his jaw and whispered back, "I love you, too."

The kitchen looked unintentionally festive with all the candles and lanterns. The light hadn't failed yet, but inside it was already very dim. Philippe finished lighting a kerosene lamp and joined Annette at the table.

Marius began. "We've been talking-"

"Me first," Miranda interrupted. "I'll do it. I'll take Marius's blood to the hive. I can fool the Infected long enough to get to the Enlightened."

"Miranda, no," John said.

"John, take this as a compliment, but you're not my dad," Miranda said.

"If we wait a day, we might be able to have the Air Force bomb them out," Torres said. "Then no one has to go kamikaze the hive."

"Do we have that time?" Soraya asked.

"Don't know." Miranda shrugged. "But if you take off in some random direction with a van full of kids, you're probably gonna wind up eaten by the Infected or raiders. We met some dudes like that."

Marius shuddered, remembering the scalps hanging from the marauders' horses like trophies. He exchanged a look with Torres. Soraya's plan to run might be best in the short term, but when children outnumbered the adults protecting them, they had little chance of getting very far.

"You've all worked so hard for this place," Torres said. "This is your home, you're family and we are a family, too. I want to keep the kids safe and I want to never let Elfy out of my sight." She patted Soraya's hand. "I get it. I want to just run and keep running forever, but it's not good for the kids and it's not actually keeping them safer."

"We could conduct a limited, short-term evacuation," John said.

"What do you mean?" Percy picked up her whiteboard.

"Soraya and Torres could take the kids into Crossroads," John said as Percy added notes to the board. "That would give them a head start if things didn't go well here. We can advise Mayor Flynn to alert the rest of New Avalon so they know about the hive."

"Assuming Miranda's plan works," Soraya said, "we could return the following day. Phineas and I have been promising the children an excursion."

"That could work, except one thing," Torres said. "I'm staying. If something goes wrong at the quarry and the

Infected come here, we'll need everyone with any kind of combat experience, which is mostly us." She waved at herself and John. "I want to be with Elfy, and it's crap that we're in this position, but I'm not gonna hide away when my skills could swing the outcome here."

"Are you sure?" Marius studied Torres's face, the set of her shoulders, her clenched jaw. He could see she wasn't sure, but she was determined.

"Each of us can help but we can't all help the same," Torres said. "The kids need someone who can protect them and they need someone who can nurture them. I'm not really the soft and cuddly type, so Soraya," Torres turned to face the other woman, looking deep into her eyes. "Will you take my niece and treat her like one of yours and if I don't see her again will you love her as hard as you can forever?"

"I will." Soraya jumped to her feet and hugged Torres. Tears welled in both women's eyes.

"Um, are they like married now?" Miranda smirked.

"I think we skipped the whole marriage and messy divorce thing and went directly to co-parenting," Torres said with a weak smile. She hugged Soraya again before stepping back.

"What? Shut up. You're crying." She mock-glared around at everyone who was wiping away tears.

"Okay, cool. Now are we done planning the suicide mission or whatever? I'm hungry," Miranda said.

During dinner the discussion continued about how best to defend the ranch, protect everyone there, and warn the rest of New Avalon. Torres volunteered to take Bailey and go to the Malmstrom Air Force base in Great Falls. Hopefully, they'd get a radio call from Miranda, letting them know her plan worked. But, if Miranda's plan failed, a bunker buster would work. In case either or both Miranda's and Torres's missions failed, the family would prepare to defend the ranch.

They stayed up late into the night going over the details, figuring out what supplies should go where and which people should do what. Sometime around 2 am, folks wandered off to bed.

Marius sat on the stairs, studying the maps and plans on the living room wall, floor, and covering the TV. Torres sat next to him, her head on his shoulder. He was pretty sure she'd fallen asleep as he'd never known her to be that quiet or still for more than a few minutes.

He lifted his shoulder and she sat up, rubbing her face.

"Come up to bed," Marius said.

"Your parents are home," she said with a sly smile.

"They're very heavy sleepers." Marius ran his hand up Torres's side and leaned in so his lips brushed her neck as he spoke. He was pleased at the goose bumps that rose on her arms and the way her nipples immediately tightened.

"I'm gonna check on Elfy." Torres stood up, cracking her back and twisting at the waist.

"Will you be up later?" Marius leaned back on the stairs, offering her as enticing a view as he could present. He even flashed his eyebrows and made a little kissy face.

Torres snorted and shook her head. "I might," she said with a chuckle. "Go on, hashtag sexy scientist."

Chapter 22 – Torres

Great Falls, MT, U.S.A. - Winter, Year 1

Before first light, Torres lifted Marius's arm off her side and slipped out of his cozy bed. She dressed by feel and tiptoed out of the room. Let him rest for a few more hours. She and John had too much work to do for her to stay, no matter how adorable and sexy Marius looked when he slept. As every grunt knew, a good offensive started early. Zero dark thirty, right on time.

By the time the sun put in an appearance over the eastern prairie, the ranch churned and buzzed with activity, like a kicked hive. Torres frowned, trying not to think of the Infected. No point wasting time when there were tons of other things that needed doing.

A short line of vehicles that still had gas in them was lined up, doors open as they loaded people too young or too old to fight. Soraya was leading the evacuation. She and Percy bent over the hood of Percy's truck, studying a map. Soraya hadn't been back to Crossroads since arriving at the ranch.

Annette and Philippe had organized shifts of supporters—people who couldn't fight directly but were young and strong enough to cook or tend any wounded. John and Anatole were on horseback, riding around near the edge of the ranch. John picked out fighting positions and Anatole marked them on his map and wrote down what supplies John thought they would need at each one.

Torres was in the process of staging gear in the barn when Marius came in, still tousled and blinking with a cup of coffee in one hand and his lab notebook in the other. He kissed her deeply and wandered off to the shed, muttering about mold and the cure.

Dawn and Bailey took a bin of sorted ammunition from the house to the barn, where they could load it into magazines. Bailey trudged back to the house, but Dawn lingered. Torres handed her an empty magazine and a bucket of 9 mm rounds. She watched to see Dawn knew how to properly load, and went back to work, waiting for the younger woman to say whatever was on her mind.

"I want to go, too," Dawn said after a few minutes.

"To Great Falls?"

"To the hive," Dawn said. "I want to go with Miranda. She shouldn't have to go alone."

"It'll probably be easier for her to sneak in alone," Torres said. She was curious how far Dawn wanted to push the issue. It would be safer to have someone go with Miranda, but worse than going alone would be going with someone who shit the bed at first contact.

"Maybe, but it'll be more dangerous. I'm going, if she'll let me."

"What about Bailey?"

"What about Marius?"

Torres thumbed the last few rounds into a pistol magazine, which she slapped into the weapon before handing it to Dawn.

"That's it? I can go?" The younger woman blinked.

"You already said you were going. Why are you asking permission now?"

"I ... um ... yeah. I'm going, so, thanks." Dawn held the pistol gingerly as if it might bite.

"Safety's here. This is on. This is off." The former Marine pointed to the red switch on the side. "It's fully loaded but none in the chamber, so you've got fifteen rounds."

Dawn nodded, her eyes huge as she stared at the gun cupped in both hands.

"Like this." Torres adjusted Dawn's grip, showed her how to sight through the front notch and brace herself for the recoil. "Well, Tex, looks like you're ready for a showdown," Torres drawled. "Go get you some duds." She pointed to the pile of clothes and make-shift armor.

Dawn picked out some things and pulled them over her own outfit. She looked ridiculous in an oversized hunter camouflage jacket and matching pants. It could have only been worse if she had smeared her face with movie-style stripes of green and brown like she was a Cobra Commando.

"You're gonna be fine." Torres patted Dawn's back.

"What are you doing?" Bailey stood in the barn doorway.

"I'm going with Miranda," Dawn said. She put on a pack Torres had just finished filling.

"Five minutes, Zoomy," Torres said to Bailey. "Then we gotta hit the road."

Bailey went to Dawn, shaking his head. "You should stay here where it's safe."

"We discussed that." Torres squatted in front of the line of go-bags, which were repurposed hiking rucks or school backpacks. She put two granola bars in each, a roll of gauze and one of tape, a pack of bandages, which had been made from strips of linen sheets, and two road flares.

"If necessary, I can accompany Miranda," Bailey said.

"I need you to talk to the Air Force folks," Torres said.

"I'm not convinced that my presence is essential to convincing Wing Commander Patel that she needs to scramble any fighter jets," Bailey said.

Torres stood up and walked over to Bailey. He shuffled, and went to parade rest, which nearly broke the steely-eyed killer demeanor the former Marine was affecting. She sighed and tried to soften her tone. "I get it. Toby's gone and you don't want to lose Dawn." Torres lowered her chin and narrowed her eyes. "But if Miranda's mission goes sideways and we don't have the Air Force in our back pockets, the Infected are going to wipe out everyone here. Including Dawn. Have you ever seen someone get bitten? Turn into an Infected?"

Bailey slowly shook his head and held up a hand as Torres opened her mouth. "I don't require a graphic description, sergeant. I am well aware that it is horrific."

Dawn strapped on a pair of skater knee pads and joined Bailey and Torres. "I'm not just gonna hang out here and knit socks while you're out there risking your life. I can help Miranda. Someone has to watch her back. I've been on my own before, Bay. I'm not scared."

"Our emotions are irrelevant to the actual degree of danger the Infected pose!" Bailey snapped.

"You can't go with us," Miranda said. All eyes turned to her. She leaned in the doorframe, wearing a backpack and carrying the rifle Torres had set aside for her.

"I can't hide a lot of people from the Infected. Me and Dawn. We're gonna be like ninjas or whatever. In and out. So, go to Great Falls, where you can be, like, actually useful." She didn't wait for further arguments before spinning around and stalking away.

"I'm gonna go check on Marius," Torres said. She left Dawn and Bailey to make what peace they could with their choices.

She and Miranda were nearly to the shed when Dawn caught up with them.

"Ready for adventure," she said with the forced enthusiasm of someone recovering from a good cry.

Marius had reorganized the shed so there was a bit more space. A high school age girl and boy, each wearing medical gloves and paper masks, were carefully droppering amber liquid into travel shampoo bottles. A woman Torres recognized as having worked in the zoology department of Chrysalis peered into a microscope. Beside her was a bag of blood.

"Marius, how much blood is that?" Miranda stared at his inner elbow suspiciously.

"A pint." Marius crossed to a shelf filled with a hodgepodge of bottles. He selected four and added them to Miranda's pack. "And I'm leaving another pint with Karlien before we head up to Great Falls. Don't look at me that way, Ms. I'm going to face a hive of Infected armed only with bubble gum and a bad attitude."

"I have Percy's gun." Miranda held up the rifle.

"And my axe," Dawn added.

"What?" Torres glanced at her. Dawn didn't have an axe at all.

"Nothing. It's an internet thing." Dawn picked up a vial from a tray next to Karlien. "So, this is it, huh? The cure?"

Marius gently took the vial back and set it in the rack. "That's my blood. If someone's infected, it'll cure them if administered before they start to mutate. It'll also damage the Infected's network, which is the best we can do since we can't harvest the mold in the next fifteen minutes."

"If Miranda gets bitten, what do I do?" Dawn asked.

"Nothing," Miranda said. "I'm already vaccinated. But if you get bitten, I'll inject you with one of these and we hope for the best." Her brow furrowed and she turned to Marius. "Why are you rushing all the blood stuff? I thought you were staying here, Dr. Science."

"I did, too," Torres said. Leaving Elfy was easier knowing that Marius was safe with his family. She hated doing that math. It felt like trying to measure her love for each of them. And that was without the healthy helping of familial guilt that was twisted around and through everything that had to do with Elfy.

Marius shook his head as he slipped his battered first

aid bag over his shoulder. "If we're going to send anyone into a city like Great Falls that could be full of Infected, it should be someone like me. Besides, there might still be lab equipment at the university or at the Malmstrom clinic. I know what to look for."

Torres tried to think of a single good argument, but the truth was, Marius was as experienced or more experienced with the Infected than anyone else. She comforted herself with the idea that if he went with her, she would be able to keep a close watch on him and keep him from doing anything too stupidly heroic.

Miranda shrugged. "It's not a bad idea to keep him away from the hive for a day or two." She nudged Torres. "I think there's one of those horse lead things in the barn for him. You know how he likes to wander off."

Torres grinned. "Much as I might enjoy tying him up, I think we'll be okay."

"Eww, TMI!"

"I'll be good." Marius picked up a go-bag. "You be careful." He hugged Miranda briefly, waved to Dawn, and followed Torres out without a word.

The drive to Great Falls seemed like one of the longest and shortest of Torres's life. The lies she'd told Elfy clung to her like wet spiderwebs.

"Go with Miss Soraya. I'll be right behind you." She hadn't said they'd be safe, hadn't promised they'd be reunited with absent family. At least she hadn't lied that much. Instead, she'd stretched a wide smile across her face and infused her voice with careless optimism. "Just a short trip. You can play I-Spy with Wahida. Here, I saved you this." She pressed a package of sour gummy fruits into Elfy's little hand.

"Okay. See you soon, Tia Lourdie." Her niece beamed up at her. She's lost her first baby tooth while Torres had been gone. She started toward Soraya's van, then ran back and threw her arms around Torres's waist. "So, you don't get too lonely without me." Then she was gone without a backward glance.

The last Torres had seen of Elfy was her dark head bent together with Wahida's as the girls picked through the gummies. The former Marine had managed to keep her face happy and even wave as she'd turned back to Percy's pickup.

Neither Marius nor Bailey tried to strike up conversation as they drove north. In the back, three canisters of gas jostled each other. No guarantee of being able to refuel in Great Falls, so they brought their own. Their go-bags and guns rode closer to them. Marius had his first aid bag on his lap. It reminded Torres of being on patrol, never knowing when they might have to fight for their lives.

At the outskirts of the city, they left the seemingly endless sweep of gray-brown fields that had spooled out on either side of the road, and passed the Great Falls International Airport, descending into the valley of civilization. Pine trees clung to the hillsides. They drove by the small houses and motels found clustered at the edges of any city. Torres had expected the situation in Great Falls to be worse than Crossroads, but the plumes of smoke rising from both sides of the Missouri River reminded her more of a combat zone than a disaster area. On their right, a grassy hillside sloped up, crowned by the Great Falls Visitor Center. Their flag was upside down.

In the backseat, Bailey refolded the paper map of Great Falls. "Keep going straight. At the third light, we'll take Tenth Avenue across the river."

"Is that a checkpoint?" Marius pointed to a pair of trucks that had been parked across the intersection. On the roofs of nearby buildings, two gunners in Air Force uniforms wielded SAWs. They were not exactly aiming at the pickup, but they surely were not aiming anywhere else. There was no guarantee those airmen would shoot Americans, but Torres was not about to risk anything. Even loaded with only 5.56 rounds, a SAW would chew through the pickup. That's what machine guns were designed to do.

"Let me do the talking," Torres said. She stepped out, hands held up.

"Where's your pass?" A woman called. She stood behind a dumpster, not exactly hiding, but easily able to duck behind cover. She wore captain's silver bars on her collar and cap. Her nametape read: McCormick.

"Didn't know we needed one, Captain McCormick," Torres said.

"On your knees. Weapons on the ground," the captain said. They followed orders. Torres wished she'd left Jimmy's HK at the ranch. Watching it vanish into a box with their other weapons felt too final.

They were cuffed and bagged and put into the back of an Air Force security forces car. The ride was quiet, but short. Hands helped Torres out and guided her inside a building, placed her on a metal chair. She didn't hear

Marius or Bailey being brought in. Feet shuffled around, but their captors knew not to talk in front of her.

The hood was removed. McCormick sat across from her. The room looked like it had once been an office, a government office judging by the number of official portraits on the wall. A large wooden desk commanded the room, with the plaque that read Cascade County Sheriff's Office. Torres had been seated at a card table in the middle of the room and McCormick sat across from her. On the table between them was a newspaper with Marius's Chrysalis ID picture smiling up at them. "The Cure for HHV!" the headline proclaimed.

"Aren't I a lucky gal?" McCormick said.

"You can be," Torres said. She nodded to the paper. "But we both know OSINT isn't always a hundred percent."

"What's the deal you're looking to make?" McCormick rubbed her eyes. Her shoulders sagged with weariness.

"Airman Byron told us you had missiles and fighter jets. There's a hive of Infected near our base. You take care of it for us, we'll get your folks vaccinated. No one gets HHV. This isn't that half-ass Chrysalis vaccine." She pointed her chin at the newspaper. "He's the real deal."

"And if we just keep him?"McCormick raised an eyebrow.

"We can't stop you," Torres admitted. Why hadn't she thought of that? But at the time, leaving Marius at the ranch, within easy reach of the Infected had seemed a worse option. At least here, the humans wouldn't kill him.

A rattle of gunfire sounded from somewhere outside.

The captain didn't react.

"What's going on here?" Torres asked.

"The Proud Defenders of Freedom." McCormick sighed and shook her head.

"Civilian militia?" Torres guessed. In gun country, like Montana, it seemed like the obvious, if not the best, solution to many problems.

"Mostly," McCormick said. "A few deserters, too. More the longer we stay here. We lost our missile techs when one of the transports crashed just after take-off. The PDF captured our pilots."

"The PDF?" Torres snorted. "Really?"

McCormick gave a tired smile. "Let's just say, Mensa's not missing any of these folks. They're the ones who refused to evacuate. They've got this Irish guy spouting off all this 'our land, our birthright' nonsense and how the government's trying to trick them into leaving."

Torres's eyes narrowed. "Liam?"

"How'd you know?"

"Had a couple of run-ins with him before. He was trying to take Marius east to sell him or something. We were hoping the Infected would take care of him, but as my mom says, 'La gente fea nunca se mueren.' Ugly people never die."

McCormick leaned back, studied Torres. "Seems we have an enemy in common."

"Seems like what you need is an assassin," Torres said.

"You're an assassin now?"

"No, just a grunt with a bad attitude and not a lot of other options." Torres sat up straighter. "Here's my offer. You let us go, we'll take out Liam and get your pilots, and they get rid of the hive. But it has to happen within the next twenty-four hours. Our people can't hold out long if the Infected attack."

McCormick sat up as well. "Counteroffer: we keep Marius here as a hostage. You and Airman Byron get our pilots. If you want to kill the Irishman, that's on you. My main concern is my pilots. Get them back here and we'll discuss our options."

"No deal." Torres slouched back.

"I don't have to deal when I have all the cards," McCormick said. She sounded tired, not cruel.

"You do. Marius can make the vaccine, but he can also not. He's no good to you if he's not cooperative." Unless you realize you can just steal his blood. Torres hoped the other woman couldn't read that fear on her face. She hurried on, trying to redirect the captain's attention. "Look, ma'am, I want to work with you, but if we don't get help from your pilots, we're not gonna have a place to go back to. That means, the hive will be looking for a new feeding ground." Torres paused to let that sink in. "More importantly, Marius's lab will be gone. That's bad for everyone. We need action, not 'options'."

"We don't have any fighter jets," McCormick said. "Best we can do is some munitions left over from Iraq."

"Bunker busters would work," Torres said. "Can you drop from a transport?"

"We could try."

"Good enough!" Torres beamed.

All things considered, the night crossing went better than expected. With both the First and Tenth Avenue bridges out, Torres had to trust to a kayak and luck to cross the Missouri. A brittle layer of ice covered the river, but the sides still ran free. Under the thin light of a waning gibbous moon, Torres used a pair of ski poles to drag her light craft up onto the ice and then allowed her weight to break it so she could paddle forward a few feet. The trip seemed to take hours.

Although McCormick offered to let Bailey go with her, Torres declined. He wasn't a seasoned combatant, and she would feel better knowing that someone was with Marius.

Mist rising from the river shrouded the kayak. The riverbank was dark and still. McCormick had briefed Torres on what to expect. The PDF didn't patrol the land from the east bank of the Missouri to River Drive, just outside the base, a swath of nearly five miles. Behind her, on the west bank, faint lights pinpointed McCormick's scouts who patrolled to ensure that neither the PDF nor the Infected crossed the river.

As the kayak nosed up onto the frozen mud and dead grass of the riverbank, Torres hopped out. She pulled the craft half out of the water and tucked the paddle into the cockpit. At a crouch, Torres climbed the bank and squatted behind a tree to survey the route. It was a straight shot past the Extended Stay and across the road to the strip mall. From there, a catwalk—theoretically unguarded—led to the back of the Malmstrom officers' club.

Torres trotted across the strip of frostbitten grass to the edge of the hotel's parking lot. A few empty cars remained. The windows were unbroken. No looters yet, which could mean that the Infected had claimed the area.

Torres scurried to the corner of the hotel and watched the street for a few minutes until she was sure there were no Infected or PDF. Across the street, through a parking lot, over a sagging chain-link fence, and across railroad tracks that shone slick in the light of the crescent moon.

The back door of the strip mall wasn't even locked. Torres followed her planned route through the empty, echoing cavern of a building, pushing open the service access door and climbing the stairs to the roof. That door was locked and when a couple of good kicks didn't do the job, she wasted a bullet on the lock.

Across the catwalk, which was actually unguarded as McCormick promised. Torres crept down the exterior ladder on the back of the officers' club. Most of the base was dark and quiet. A few homes had faint lights flickering inside—candles or wood burning stoves. McCormick and Bailey had agreed that the most likely place for the PDF to be keeping the pilots was the security forces station. Torres had memorized the base's map.

When she arrived at the security forces station, she circled the brick building twice. No guards, no lights. Nothing. Maybe the pilots were somewhere else. Or maybe they were dead. She tried a side door. Unlocked.

Inside, she found that the militia had set up a headquarters in the biggest briefing room. Their maps and plans were taped to the walls. The maps were marked with areas showing where the Infected were and where the Air Force still held out. There were a lot of areas marked in red for the Infected.

There was also a copy of the same newspaper McCormick had with Marius's picture. Someone had written: "Wanted—Reward of ALL THE MONEYS!!!" in red ink under the photo.

Torres took a ring of keys from a large desk that sported a mug with an Irish flag on it. She pushed open the door to the detention area and found the pilots. There were five, two women and three men, huddled on cots with no blankets or cold weather gear in a building with no heat.

"Well shit," Torres said.

One of the women stood up and marched to the bars, glaring at Torres. "We're still not gonna fly for you. Tell Liam. We've all passed SERE and there's nothing he can do to break us."

Torres glanced at the woman's namepatch on her flight suit. "Okay, Bennet, but what if I told you I wasn't working with that IRA reject?"

"He's not IRA anything. He's an Ulsterman. He's told us at great length," Bennet said.

"I don't care." Torres began testing the keys to unlock Bennet's cell. "Just tell me where he is so I can kill the bastard."

"You're on the wrong side of the river, sweetheart," said one of the men. "Liam took a bunch to raid McCormick's base. They got information that their target is in town and they're trying to get there before the monsters get to him."

"Fuck." Torres froze, her mind racing. Marius was alone. Well, not alone. There was McCormick and the rest of her squadron, and Bailey. *But I'm not there.* The thought chilled her to her core. *I can't protect him.*

"Psst, honey," the man yelled. "Less staring, more rescuing."

Torres did some breathing exercises, forced her shaking hands to steady, and flipped to the next key. What she needed now wasn't panic. She needed a plan and a plan required information.

"How are they getting across the river?" Torres finished opening Bennet's cell and went to the man's cell.

"They've got speedboats, but they can also go across the dam," he said. "The water's low enough."

"Great. Thanks, pumpkin." Torres went to the next cell without unlocking Pumpkin's cell.

"Hey!" he yelled.

"Hey what?"

"You can't leave me here."

Torres opened the cells for the other two men and remaining woman then returned to Pumpkin. "I can, but I won't. We'll need all the help we can get." She unlocked the cell. "Let's go. We gotta warn McCormick."

Torres led the way out of the building, her stomach twisting. She swallowed back the bile rising in her throat. She would get to Marius before Liam did. She had to.

Chapter 23 – Miranda

Starling Union Quarry, Crossroads, MT, U.S.A. -

Winter, Year 1

This was a MISTAKE.

Miranda maneuvered one of the ranch's 4x4s around the outbuildings and turned west toward the foothills. Neither she nor Dawn were good riders, so Miranda drove. As they crested the first low ridge, she looked back. A lone car drove down the road, heading north towards Great Falls.

Okay, okay, I can do this. Miranda tried to calm herself. It was hard because her first instinct was to reach out to the Infected. They would take away all her fear and doubts. But they would also realize that she meant to destroy them.

All she had to do was enter the hive undetected and inject the Enlightened at its core with a vial of Marius's abomination blood. Sure, this could totally work.

Already, she could feel the Infected reaching out.

What's going on? When are you coming back? Come home.

Soon. Leave me alone or the other humans will notice.

There. Maybe they would shut up for a few minutes.

Miranda parked the 4x4 near the gate and got out. She left Percy's rifle in the little buggy.

"Once we get in there, that's not gonna be any use and it's heavy," she said at Dawn's questioning look.

"No problem," Dawn said. "I'm leaving this, too." She set the walkie talkie on the seat. If the plan worked, they would call the ranch and give them the good news. That way John could decide if they still needed the bombs.

The walkie talkie would be useless in the mines, not to mention dangerous. If it got accidentally switched on, the crackling would announce them like a siren. If things went bad, they'd have to hope they could make it out and call for help. Or at least warn the ranch.

Miranda walked into the quarry, wrapping her coat tighter, despite the sun trying to warm the air through the clouds. Whenever her mind brushed the Infected, she redirected them.

Don't look here. Nothing to see but us rocks.

"Oh hell no," Dawn muttered as the women arrived outside the biofilm sealed entrance. "Seriously?"

"Seriously," Miranda said. She reached out and touched the nearest node where both blood veins and nerves overlapped. *It's me, a humble scout.* She tried to mimic the way the goat Infected had communicated with the hive.

It must have worked because the biofilm thinned and retracted with a moist, disgusting squelch, like someone trying to slurp Jell-o through a coffee filter. Dawn made some pukey faces, but otherwise kept quiet and still, which helped Miranda hide them.

There were other scouts returning. Miranda could feel the hive connecting with them via thread-like tentacles that bored through the ground. Great. The Infected had their own high-speed landlines.

Inside, the women crept alone, single file. The tunnels had been narrow before the Infected had added squishy meat-walls. The dim beams of their flashlights did little as the darkness pressed against Miranda, filled with stalking Infected. It seemed like they'd been walking forever, the slimy humidity dropped over them like a drunk jock at a frat party.

"Are we close?" Dawn rasped, trying to keep both her voice and her panting breaths low.

"Yeah." Miranda lied. She wasn't really sure. Her understanding of the hive layout was jumbled, but she couldn't risk reaching into the heart of the hive because then the Infected would know they were there. Every Infected she misdirected added to her mental load. The strain was quickly becoming unbearable. Her head ached, the pain moving from the base of her skull to wrap around her temples and press down on her sinuses. She kept sniffing, hoping not to smell her own bloody nose.

"Which way?" Dawn shone her flashlight on the

ground between their feet. Ropey strands of bioformation twisted along the edge of the tunnel, climbing up the walls like carnivorous ivy. Miranda didn't have to see the ceiling to know it was choked with tubes and tentacles. How had this seemed like a good idea?

"Miranda?" Dawn tapped her elbow.

"Down." Miranda closed her eyes, straining to keep the Infected distracted from the void she was creating in their network. *Nothing to see here. One of the others is taking care of it.*

"Down?"

"I think so." Miranda bent over and tried to catch her breath. Her vision swam. The churning, rustling, whooshing sounds of the hive seemed to get louder and then quieter like someone was turning the volume up and down.

"We've been here for hours," Dawn sounded worried and a little annoyed.

Sorry the adventure isn't as stellar as you expected.
What adventure?

Oh shit! Miranda hadn't meant to think so loud.

Miranda? Where are you? We looked for you at the ranch.

"Miranda?"

Miranda whimpered. She held up a hand, begging Dawn to quit talking. She couldn't do it any longer; she couldn't juggle all the Infected's minds, plus the hive's network, plus keeping Dawn calm and updated.

"Are you okay?" Dawn put her hand on Miranda's forehead like a worried parent with a feverish kid.

She smells delicious.

"No. Leave her alone."

"What?" Dawn stared at her.

Miranda had said that out loud. Hadn't she? It was harder and harder to tell when she was talking and when she was just thinking to the Infected.

Dawn was close enough that Miranda could smell her, warm and slight hint of vanilla. Soap? No way she had perfume. Did she?

Taste her and find out.

Miranda's mouth filled with saliva at the thought of pressing her teeth against Dawn's soft, fawn neck. She would bite gently at first, like a lover, and then —

No!

Miranda clenched her fists. *Get out. Get out. Get out.*

"Hey, are you okay? You're freaking me out."

"Just. Shut. Up." Miranda hissed out the words, straining to keep her mind closed to the Infected. It was so much harder than when she agreed with them. Agreed that it would be so nice to be close to someone, to feel their skin against hers. But not Dawn.

That's not who we want. We want him. So do you.

Miranda shuddered. Tears of frustration tracked down her cheeks. No matter how hard she tried, she couldn't escape the Infected. They were a part of her as surely as the virus was a part of Marius.

You're perfect for each other. We'll bring him here and make him understand.

The hive sent a message to their scouts, the Littles that were close enough to still be in range. They abandoned whatever other task they were doing and turned toward the Morning Star ranch.

Which was bad. Miranda needed to distract them, to

keep them busy at least long enough for the kids to get away. Besides, Marius wasn't even there. All those people would die for no reason.

Since the Enlightened already knew Miranda was there, she broadcast her presence as a means of hiding Dawn.

It was a mistake to bring her. I sent her away. Now it's just us. I'm here to help you.

Miranda touched Dawn's shoulder and pressed a finger to her lips. Dawn's eyes were huge, terrified, but she nodded.

"First," Miranda grunted. "You go first. I can't."

Wordlessly, Dawn put Miranda's hand on her shoulder, taking the lead deeper into the mine.

Miranda watched her feet following Dawn down and down and down. The only sounds were the faint huffing of the woman's breathing. Any second the Infected would reach out of the void behind her and yank her back into the meatwall. She stumbled as the floor dropped a few inches.

The tunnel had changed into a wide, square passage. The ceiling and walls were striated with light and dark layers. An old lamp hung from the wall attached to a thick cable that ran away in either direction. The wall under her fingertips felt roughly organic - soft, warm, and giving to the touch. The air was humid and filled with a familiar smell, sweet and pungent, like a dumpster on a hot day. She turned her head slowly, not wanting to see, but needing to know.

Dawn's flashlight danced over the walls as her hands shook, making it hard to focus, but there was no mistaking the fleshy membrane with its branching network of pulsing purple veins. They were in the middle of a room with four tunnels spoking out.

More importantly, they were in the main chamber where the Enlightened rested. The bioformation pooled down from the wall into some kind of nest on the floor a few feet from where they stood. Veins from the meat wall ran into and out of the center. The sides of the nest were formed from the bodies of several dogs and from the middle of the nest, an Enlightened lifted its heads.

He had once been a human, like all the Enlightened, but he was small. Had he been young or just little? As he lifted his heads and turned his long, serpentine necks to face the women, Dawn gave a low squeal. She hadn't seen the Enlightened before.

The Enlightened curled back its lip and growled, but otherwise didn't move.

Welcome back.

The smaller, sensory tentacles that hung from the ceiling and walls detached and reached towards the women. Dawn shrank away from them. They brushed Miranda's hair and her shoes, sliding up her legs and over her hands, gently poking at her. Did they mean to keep her there, encased in a nest like the Enlightened?

No, no. Your father wants to see you again. There's much to be done still.

And I'm happy to help. Miranda held out her hands and stepped toward the Enlightened's nest. Just a few feet closer. She couldn't afford to miss.

The tentacles tightened around her ankles and wrists,

not restraining her—yet—but showing her they could.

We want to trust you. Can we still trust you?

Behind her, Dawn was whimpering. Miranda was honestly surprised she hadn't panicked and run.

I'm here, aren't I? I came back.

You did. But you're hiding something. You separated from us. Let us in, Miranda.

The tentacles squeezed harder, one slithering around her neck.

Dawn gasped, but Miranda didn't look. She couldn't spare an instant of thought for the other woman as the Enlightened probed her mind. She showed them Soraya's convoy.

See, here's the ranch and all the people and they're scared. They plan to leave.

Miranda took another step, allowed the tentacles to pull her to her knees. Only a few more inches and she'd be at the nest. She reached out to the network, commanding the Infected and they responded. She drew them back from her and Dawn. The Enlightened tried to resist her control, tried to turn the Infected against her. Miranda grinned as she flexed.

You thought I was weak. You thought you could force me. My father made me better than you, stronger than you'll ever be.

The tentacles retreated further. The Enlightened cringed back. Miranda could feel his fear and disgust through the bioformations at her fingertips. Her smile widened.

I don't have to use Marius's blood to get rid of you. I own you.

You dare bring the Abomination's blood here? Panic

and rage, instantaneous and so hot Miranda could feel it radiating through the pulsing purple veins.

The Enlightened lunged at Miranda, jaws filled with multiple rows of teeth snapping. Miranda shoved a vial of Marius's blood into the nearest mouth. The Enlightened bit down, tearing into Miranda's wrist. She felt the vial shatter, cutting her palm as the cool blood squeezed from between her fingers.

Dawn screamed.

The Enlightened reared back. Its tentacles caught Miranda and yanked her further into its nest. It was flailing. Trying to bite off her hand or get the shards of glass out of its throat, she couldn't tell. The soup of sludgy blood around them worked into a clotty froth. Miranda's feet skidded forward as the tentacles dragged her down. Her free hand fumbled in her pocket.

One, two, three vials of Marius's blood. She threw the first. Felt it break when the membrane nearby spasmed. The other two slipped out of her slime-drenched hand. She didn't know what happened to them.

Dawn's light vanished, plunging them into darkness. Miranda's own flashlight was long gone. She must have dropped it somewhere. But Miranda could navigate by using the Infected's network. She could sense her position in the hive in the same way she knew where her elbow was or how to wiggle her toes.

The Enlightened shrieked. It fell across her, reeking like warm, spoiled ham. She braced her feet and splayed hands, holding herself up enough that she could keep her head out of the muck in the nest.

Breathe.

The smell choked her even more than the pressing

weight of dead flesh. Her mouth filled with vomit. She gagged, struggling to get space to puke anywhere other than on herself.

A flash of light blinded her. A ball of heat washed over her, stealing her air, baking her skin into an instant sunburn. It was the same as the effect Marius had set off in Portland.

The Abomination is in Great Falls. Destroy him!

The Enlightened used the last moments of its existence to broadcast through the network. Miranda couldn't tell how far the message would travel. Out to the scouts, definitely. Were there other hives nearby? Were those flickers she felt Infected from farther away? She couldn't focus. Tried to command them—*Ignore*—but her head hurt. Couldn't think. She didn't remember hitting it, but the blood sheeting down across her face argued that she must have.

Miranda fell, too dizzy and weak to hold herself up. One nostril was in the muck. She gurgled, trying to draw in air not blood. Her lungs felt full of wet cotton batting.

Dawn was gone. She'd abandoned Miranda just like John and Marius had done.

Miranda closed her eyes, rested in the soft flurry of ash falling all around her. Her heart fluttered, slowed, fluttered again.

Am I dying?

We're coming, Miranda. I will never abandon you.

Dad?

Chapter 24 – Marius

Marius stood in front of the topographical map on McCormick's office wall. The captain had marked and dated the positions of the Infected and of the PDF. The Infected were pushing inward from the city's outskirts, while the PDF were retreating into the heart of Malmstrom base.

From down the hallway, drifted the low voices of Bailey and the rest of McCormick's folks. The captain had gone on a presence patrol. Those who stayed behind were debriefing the young airman. Would Bailey want to return to the ranch or stay in Great Falls with the remainder of the squadron? There was Dawn, but she might want to join him here rather than risk staying in New Avalon. Assuming the ranch was still there when they returned.

Marius bit his lower lip, tried to distract himself with next steps. Miranda would succeed. Torres would succeed. McCormick had agreed to help furnish a lab in exchange for vaccines once he could make them. He knew how to introduce the mold spores into the Infected's bioformations. All he needed to do was find the right mold and repeat his work from Portland. That would require time and a lab, but they could do it. If Miranda succeeded and Torres succeeded.

He hated waiting.

A door slammed. A shot rang out. Someone screamed.

Marius ducked behind the desk. Outside people were yelling, screaming, shooting. He should go, try to fight, or at least help the wounded.

But what if it was the Infected? What if they captured him again? He had barely survived and the memory of the pain he'd suffered kept him frozen behind the desk. The fractal scar pattern on his back seemed to itch and burn as if thinking about the Infected were enough to activate it.

The door burst open. From under the desk Marius could see three sets of feet. Air Force boots and two sets of civilian boots.

"I remember you right enough." Liam's voice sounded jolly. A loud smack followed by a thump as Bailey fell to the floor. Marius could see him from under the desk as the young man wiped his bleeding lip. One eye was already swelling and purple.

"I'm getting fecking tired of asking you. Where is Marius? We know he's in town."

Bailey looked at Marius, shook his head so slightly that the scientist almost didn't see it, then pushed himself up.

"He went with Torres."

"Went where?"

"Across the river."

More sounds of someone getting hit. The door slammed.

"Hey, get this lad back to the boats. Himself is on t'other side of the blessed river," Liam yelled, his voice muffled by the closed door.

Marius scrambled up. He might be petrified by the Infected, but he'd be damned if Liam were going to kill another of his airmen. His first instinct was to race after Liam, to trade himself for Bailey. He knew the Irishman wouldn't kill him, at least not right away. The same didn't hold true for Bailey.

But what would Torres do? Some sort of tactical maneuver where she could have her cake and eat it too. Marius didn't know what that might be, and Bailey didn't have time for him to figure it out. He paused, unslung his rifle, then hurried after the sound of Liam's and Bailey's retreating footsteps.

From outside came the deep whoop of a civil defense siren followed by more running feet, people shouting, and revving engines.

Marius yanked open the door and jogged down the hallway to the main door. Outside, a fleet of a dozen or so pick-up trucks and SUVs was parked. People dressed in civilian clothes were dragging Bailey and several other airmen to the vehicles. Others had taken position along the sides or in the beds of the trucks.

But none of them were looking towards the building. They were looking out into town, toward the noise that might have been the wind, but wasn't. Marius knew that prairie wind could sound haunted, but it wasn't any wind. The screeching, shrieking, moaning cacophony could only be one thing.

The Infected.

They climbed up the sides of buildings, charged down the streets, some even flew. Marius shuddered, remembering the bat Infected that had taken him to Portland. None of these flying Infected were large enough to pick up a human.

Behind the advancing wall of Infected, Marius could see pockets of the Air Force trying to hold them off. He was sure the word John and Torres would have used was 'overrun.' They'd been overrun. No wonder the PDF had been able to get into the sheriff's office so easily. It had been essentially undefended.

Three humanoid Infected grabbed the nearest PDF member and dragged him back. Marius didn't watch. Instead, he scanned the remaining humans for Bailey. If he could find the airman, they could get to safety—he hoped.

Liam stood in the bed of one of the pick-ups. Bailey knelt beside him. Both men stared at the onrushing wave of Infected. Two more PDF members were dragged away. The Infected were closing the gap and had already covered the driveway leading to the highway. The trucks could still make it across the shallow ditch if they went now, but no one was moving. They were shooting, not trying to escape. Marius was sure they would run out of ammunition far sooner than the Infected would run out of bodies.

Marius pulled out his pocketknife and sliced his palm. The Infected seemed to hate his blood, so it might give him some space. He raced across the parking lot and grabbed Bailey by the shoulder of his field jacket while the PDF was distracted.

Liam whipped his rifle around to aim at Marius, then his face broke into a wide grin. "Well, I'll be fucked."

"You're about to be." Marius jerked his chin toward the Infected. "We need to go. Now!"

Liam's eyes flicked up to the Infected, to the PDF, back to Marius, then narrowed. "Get in."

Marius vaulted into the bed of the truck and slapped the roof of the cab. "Go. Go. Go!"

The truck lurched into motion and everyone in back grabbed for the sides or fell to the bed. One of the PDF members nearly fell out, but Bailey grabbed him by the belt and yanked him to safety. The truck bounced into the ditch and out again. There was a smushing crunching sound as it ran over several smaller Infected.

An Infected that looked like a bull mastiff mixed with an actual bull charged the truck. It was on a collision course. Liam shot at it, but the rounds didn't seem to even register. It tried to ram the side of the truck, but the vehicle veered just in time. Instead of flipping them, the Infected only knocked the truck briefly up onto three wheels.

Marius didn't wait for the Infected to get enough room to bash them again. He squeezed his sliced hand until he had a palm full of blood and threw it into the

Infected's face.

The creature screamed and stumbled, shaking its enormous head. The nearby Infected scattered.

"I can see why they want you," Liam said.

"Want me dead," Marius said.

The nearest PDF member's eyes widened in shock.

"I'm of the opinion," Bailey said to the shocked PDF woman, "that we should endeavor to set aside our political differences with a view of saving all of humanity. If Dr. Marius doesn't surv—"

The truck zig-zagged, overcorrected, cutting off Bailey's words. It accelerated down the open stretch of highway. Marius hadn't spent a lot of time in this part of Great Falls, but he was familiar enough with the town to know they were headed out of town. Not a bad plan, but what about when Torres returned, with or without the pilots?

Marius couldn't imagine his life without her. She'd been his shadow since Chrysalis, but lately she'd come to mean so much more than the simple feeling of safety and comfort he got from her presence. He'd seen her heart, which she usually guarded so carefully. No matter what happened to him, he had to find a way to protect her, to keep her safe.

"Not necessarily." Liam braced himself in the corner. Two more trucks had made it onto the highway, but the Infected had dragged a third onto its side, chomping on the humans like spilled candies.

"Not necessarily what?" Marius tore a strip of cloth from his T-shirt and wrapped his hand.

"They don't necessarily want you dead like." Liam leaned up and took a shot. One of the flying Infected careened off, smashed headfirst into a hardware store.

"There's a deal to be struck," Liam said slowly. "If you're willing to take a bit of a journey, you can keep your family safe enough. Or you can try your luck with these." He took another shot, wounding but not killing an Infected. The three remaining trucks were starting to outpace their pursuers. Most of the Infected dropped back to attack the straggling PDF fighters or the Air Force holdouts.

"No!" Bailey grabbed Marius's arm from where he squatted in the corner of the truck bed. "Don't listen to anything he says. They're planning to trade you to the Enlightened. I heard them talking. They—"

Liam put his boot in the middle of Bailey's chest and pushed.

The young man somersaulted backwards out of the truck bed. He landed in the ditch and rolled. At first, he didn't move. Marius didn't realize he was on his feet until he felt the arms holding him, either restraining him or keeping him from falling, it didn't matter. All that mattered was that Bailey moved. That he got up. That he was alive.

Was that him? Yes, his head lifted then ducked down. Was he hurt or hiding? Where were the Infected? Had they noticed Bailey?

"Tie him up, boss?" asked one of the people holding Marius.

Liam cocked his head. "What'll it be, boy-o?"

"Go back for the kid and we'll talk," Marius said.

"That's it." Liam grinned. He knocked on the cab window and twirled his finger. "Round about and quick like, lads. It's a race now so."

Bailey had a concussion, maybe worse. Marius treated what he could from his first aid bag and got the young man settled in the bed of the pickup. Liam had directed his convoy of three into a truck stop and after a quick sweep of the area, sent most of the remaining PDF members to scavenge the few semis that were still in the lot, as well as the shop and diner.

"The lad wasn't wrong," Liam said. He leaned against the back of the pickup, tapping an empty cigarette pack against his thigh as he watched the road, the sky, the parking lot, everything.

"About trading me to the Enlightened?" Marius stared out over the river. Where was Torres? Would she have the good sense to keep away from the Infected? Where would she go with the pilots when she realized the sheriff's office was inaccessible?

The Infected had attacked the sheriff's office while he was there. He couldn't believe that was a coincidence, considering they'd never pushed so far into the heart of Great Falls before. Had Liam tipped them off? No, he'd lost a lot of his own fighters. He'd been genuinely surprised, which meant the Infected had known when and where to attack.

They're tracking me, Marius thought. Bailey groaned as he shifted uncomfortably.

No one will ever be safe near me.

He remembered Torres saying goodbye to the last of her family so she could guard him. How often had she risked her life for him? How often would she do so in the days to come? Was she even alive?

"Got it in one," Liam said. "I've been offered a chance at a preserve, like one of those safari jobs they have in Africa but for humans."

"What?" Marius frowned at the mercenary.

"Like with lions and gazelles and such. The Enlightened sent a runner. Little fellow, all tattooed up with black marks on his face and the like. He says there's a bounty on your head, which was not news to myself."

"So you came to collect?" Marius waved at the downtown area. In addition to the smoke from chimneys, there were several thick black plumes rising lazily into the air.

"Nothing so mundane. Didn't know you were about, but when I saw your man there," Liam hooked a thumb toward Bailey, who was glaring from his good eye, "I knew you was somewhere close."

"But we wouldn't be talking if you planned to hand me over." Marius bit his lip. What did Liam hope to gain?

"I'm still handing you over," Liam said with a grin. "One of these days you're going to pay off, boy-o. The human lotto ticket. Just gotta keep playing is all."

"And Bailey?"

"Now that's what we can talk about. I'm thinking you can help me. I don't want to become one of those." Liam waved toward downtown. "I know you can fix it so I don't. So, here's my offer: Make us immune and I'll let yours go. Free and clear to leave Great Falls. We'll work things out between us, the lovely captain and I. No need to interfere, eh?"

At the moment, Marius didn't really care what

fiefdoms Liam and McCormick divided Great Falls into. With so many Infected in the city, there probably wouldn't be much left to fight over by day's end. The immediate problem was getting Torres, Bailey, and himself out of the city alive and in one piece. The slightly less immediate problem was the hive. There was a chance Miranda had failed, that she was ... but, no, she was a survivor.

"There's a hive near my family," Marius said. "Torres is bringing out pilots. You include them, I'll give you the vaccine." An easy offer to make. The scientist would have vaccinated any uninfected human regardless of who they were. If not for his medical ethics, there was the simple math of fewer unvaccinated people meant fewer possible Infected later.

"Done." Liam held out a hand. Marius had to chuckle at the absurdity of the situation, but shook the other man's hand.

Liam reached into the cab of the truck and pulled out a satellite phone. He dialed a number and when a voice sounded on the other end said, "Got your target." He listened briefly then said, "Better make it a sight faster than that unless you want to be stitching him back together like a jigsaw." He listened again, then hung up.

"You have a phone?" Marius felt a wave of envy. How long had it been since he'd used a phone? The global landlines and cell towers were probably down and wouldn't be repaired in his lifetime, if ever. At least the satellites continued their mindless orbiting.

"And a jet or helo or something that flies," Liam said. "Not like that lot." He pointed at the flock of flying Infected circling the downtown area. "Any road, they've noticed us and if that eejit Carmine faffs around too much, there won't be enough of us left to bury in a matchbox. It's gonna be a fecking nightmare to get to the airport."

The Infected had picked up their trail and were advancing again. They were joined by other Infected from the edges of town. Liam yelled for the remaining PDF members to drop what they were doing and get their arses back to the trucks.

Marius climbed into the bed of the pickup and settled himself where he could keep an eye on Bailey. He tried not to think about Toby, bleeding out in the back of a Humvee.

Bailey squinted towards the Infected then looked at Marius. "There appear to be significantly more now."

"Yeah," the scientist said. His brain raced through possibilities, coming back again and again to a road strewn with the bodies of the uninfected. Bailey had to survive. Torres had to. The pilots had to, or the ranch would die with them. But the pilots wouldn't survive if they crossed the river and ran face first into thousands of Infected.

Marius grabbed his first aid bag and jumped out of the truck bed. He jogged to the cab where Liam was directing the PDF members to redistribute weapons.

"New deal," Marius said. Liam's eyes narrowed, but Marius went on before he could say anything. "Here." He pulled out the travel shampoo bottles filled with pale amber liquid. His HHV antibody rich blood. He held them out. "The vaccine. Take it now. Give it to them." He waved at the humans. "Take Bailey and get out of Great Falls. The Infected aren't interested in you. They're here for me, but they'll kill you if they have the chance."

Liam took the bottles. Marius held up a syringe and showed him how much to inject.

"Not that I'm not eternally grateful, but why?" the Irishman asked.

"Because I'm going to the airport by myself," Marius said.

"Don't be daft."

"They want me alive. If not, they would have told you to kill me. They wouldn't be sending something to get me."

Liam poked his head out of the truck cab and the two men assessed the approaching waves of Infected. The first flyers would be there in minutes, the faster runners shortly after.

"This is probably more than I'll ever see from Carmine." Liam waggled a shampoo bottle. "Tell you what I'll do. I'm gonna take your man with us out of town and send him on his way with a gift."

It was Marius's turn to narrow his eyes suspiciously.

"Ah, go on with ya. Nothing bad like. Just some mold I picked up from a half burned out laboratory in Portland."

Marius was stunned. It felt like he couldn't breathe. If Liam had the mold from Portland, with the originally spliced inhibitors it would be far more effective than anything the makeshift lab at the ranch could ever produce. It was the difference between his family barely surviving on a tiny patch of uninfected territory and them being able to actively push the Infected back and reclaim the world. Or at least central Montana. Start small, he reminded himself.

"Unless you don't want it?" Liam cocked his head.

"No!" Marius gasped. "No, I mean yes, we definitely want it. Give it to Bailey. He'll know what to do with it."

"Do you want to say your goodbye, then?"

"I'll let him know what's going on." Marius trotted back to the bed of the truck.

Bailey was sitting up, head hanging, looking like he might throw up.

"Okay, here's the deal," Marius started. He explained the plan, ignored Bailey's entirely reasonable protests, and only a few minutes later stood alone in the middle of the road, watching the three trucks zoom away.

He turned to face the Infected and started walking.

Epilogue

Torres stood at the window of the bunkhouse. Light streaked the eastern horizon, but no one else was up yet. Winter had finally loosened its death grip on the Montana plains, although it refused to leave the mountains. The air was chilly in the bunkhouse, even in Torres's sweats and thick, hand-knit socks. She breathed out, watched her exhalation cloud the glass. With a finger, she wrote: ¿Donde estas? Under that she added: Mi amor.

Through the glass, Marius's childhood house stood dark and still against the lightening sky. But the person she most wanted to see wasn't home.

"Hey, boss," said a voice from behind her. Torres wiped the window with her palm before turning to face Andy. He was one of the newer ranger recruits, an accountant from Chicago who had a way with horses.

"Morning," Torres said. She ran a hand through her hair, ruffling it into spikes. Almost time to cut it again.

"Dawn wanted to let you know they're ready," Andy said.

"Is Bailey sitting this run out?"

"Yep. Percy's got him on radio detail. So far nothing."

Of course nothing. Who would be left to broadcast within their range? Over the past several months, the few ham radio operators they'd made contact with had gone silent one by one. Maybe it was the unusually cold and long winter. Maybe it was the Infected. Maybe it was

...

"Anywho," Andy said, half-turning to leave.

"Yeah, thanks. Remind Dawn to update the board before she heads out the gate," Torres said. She pulled on her coat and headed out to face the day. The sky was showing patches of pale blue, a good sign after a winter of worrying that the clouds wouldn't clear. Before the radios had gone quiet people had reported unusually heavy clouds from all over the world. Were they from nukes? Or from folks destroying nests of Infected? Or both? Or something else?

Using the ranch's radio, as well as Mayor Flynn's at Crossroad's town hall, they broadcasted that they'd had luck using mold to fight the Infected. If the message ever got to anyone who could use it, they never knew.

But those were bigger worries than the folk of New

Avalon could contend with. The scope of their lives had shrunk after Great Falls. The Enlightened had kept their word and the Infected had left the city, scattering out through the mountains and across the frozen plains. Thanks to Miranda, the hive in the quarry was burned out and the Infected didn't seem keen to push into their territory. For good measure, the Air Force had dropped a bunker-buster on the quarry before flying off eastward. They'd gotten word to rally at an Air National Guard base in Duluth, Minnesota. Whether they'd made it there or found anyone alive and uninfected upon arrival was a matter for the Magic 8-Ball.

With the breathing space New Avalon had gained, the survivors could focus on longer-term problems like the abrupt end of supplies from and communication with the wider world. Torres tried to bury herself in the work, tried to think of this time as a deployment, a time to work and not mind that she was separated from Marius. On good days, she could pretend that he would come back. On bad days, she remembered finding him in the ruins of Portland, fresh scars on his back from the Infected. She told herself they wouldn't kill him and tried to convince herself that was good, that they weren't torturing him, that he would be able to find a way to escape and come back to them.

There was nothing she could do, even if the winter hadn't been one of the worst in living memory. Where would she go to find him? Bailey had reported seeing a tactical helicopter as he left Great Falls. There was no way to know where they had taken Marius or even who 'they' were. Miranda tried to find him using her connection to the Infected, but after her betrayal and the destruction of the hive, there were few in the area and none willing to communicate with her.

But fretting at home like a lovelorn school kid was not Torres's style. She needed to get out, to do something, to keep moving, keep busy, to strike some kind of blow on behalf of humanity. Which had led to the creation of the New Avalon Rangers.

Sitting around the kitchen table, late one night a few weeks after Great Falls, Torres had suggested that they needed scout teams.

The lamps were lit, mirrors propped behind them to cast more light into the room. John was cranking the ancient grinder Torres had found in an antique shop, filling the room with the warm and acrid smell of freshly roasted coffee beans. Philippe was knitting, his brows drawn together in concentration as he followed the pattern in the book spread on the table before him. Annette watched him, her own knitting still in her lap. Percy perched on her stool with her whiteboard across her lap, marker dangling from her lip like an unlit cigarette, as she calculated supplies. Outside, the wind had dropped and Torres could hear the occasional crunch of footsteps in the snow as folks moved between the bunkhouse, the barn, the outhouse, and the other smaller outbuildings.

"By spring, we'll need some long-range recon teams," Torres had said.

"Rangers," John said. He tapped the side of the grinder and cranked some more.

Torres rolled her eyes. "Recon."

"Marius liked Tolkien's rangers," Percy said, which Torres thought was a cheap ploy, but did settle the naming question.

The mission of the New Avalon Rangers was to scout the area around the ranch in an ever-widening spiral, to find and help survivors, and to re-establish lines of communication. So far, they'd made it into Crossroads three times and halfway to Great Falls. No one had been to Helena, but it was on the board as a 'Needs Done' mission.

Dawn and her party of three rangers were leaving to assess if the mountains were passable, and if so, they would go out to Running Rabbit. There was plenty of good gear still there, not to mention communications equipment.

"Boss!" Helen, who moonlighted from her work in the mold growing operation, rode toward Torres, waving her hat. She pulled her horse up and let it turn in a tight circle as she talked.

"There's a rider at the gates. She's from Great Falls. She said they need our help." The girl pulled up her mount and vaulted off with an ease Torres would never have, she was sure. Helen held out the reins and Torres clambered up on the horse, which danced under her.

"Go let Percy and John know. Have them come down to the gate," Torres said. She kicked at the horse, which laid back its ears and sidled sideways before setting off in a bone-jarring saunter toward the gate over a mile away. Torres hoped her teeth wouldn't rattle loose by the time they arrived.

At night and in her quiet moments, the Infected came

to Miranda. She felt them like an amputee with phantom limb pain. An ache, an itch, something that was more than a little yearning.

In daylight, when busy, it was easier to block them out. And truthfully, she didn't have to block them out as most of the Infected in the area had died with the hive. The rest had fled. Only occasionally would some pass through New Avalon territory, their questing minds ever-seeking a connection with the bioformation network.

What they found instead was Miranda. A mind that had been tainted, stained, scarred by the Infected. Whether she liked it or not, she had been twisted into something they recognized, something they gravitated towards, something they called to.

Miranda didn't remember how she and Dawn had gotten out of the hive. All Dawn would say was that she'd dragged the other woman out and that it had been gross. When Bailey returned, dazed and damaged, from Great Falls, Dawn had fussed over him for all of three days before joining Torres's newly established Rangers. Bailey didn't seem hurt by her easy abandonment.

"Her involvement makes sense," he'd said as he and Miranda sat together on the porch swing, watching their breath plume out around them as they huddled under a blanket. Winter had painted the world in glittering white that seemed to stab at the eyes and up into the brain.

"Does it?" Miranda didn't know who she resented more: herself for being afraid to go out again and face the Infected or Dawn for doing it so effortlessly after everything she'd been through. The soil over Toby's grave hadn't had time to pack down before it froze. On clear days, the mound was visible from the barn loft, where the Rangers roosted, organizing their supplies and divvying out their weapons and ammunition.

"Of course, it does." Bailey sounded surprised that he should have to explain the obvious. He often sounded like that. He reminded her too much of Marius sometimes.

"How?" Miranda pulled her feet up, kicking off her boots to tuck them under her. She liked being curled tight like a little pearl safe in its shell.

"Dawn was out there." Bailey waved vaguely around. "Before she ever found us, she survived threats that I still have difficulty truly comprehending. And yet, despite the horrors she's seen, she seems exhilarated by the challenge of it. Frankly, it seems like a poor adaptation to me, but perhaps our group survival depends on individuals who are willing to sacrifice themselves for the greater good."

Like Marius.

But neither of them said it. After all his promises, he'd left her. Again. He'd left them all.

Miranda had hoped that severing her ties to the Infected, that turning against them at the hive would be enough, that it would buy them some time and some peace. And it had, in a way. At least it had gotten rid of the ever-present scratching at the back of her brain. Other than the occasional pull of the stray Infected passing through, she was alone in her mind.

She watched Torres and John teaching the Ranger recruits the basics of marksmanship. They had little ammunition, so they did a lot of practicing before anyone got actual rounds. How long before they'd all be back to bows and arrows? Torres and John talked about setting up some sort of smithing operation to make new bullets. All they needed was to find and bring back the right equipment and supplies, which seemed as likely as Miranda finding a functioning Starbucks.

"Kentucky."

"What?" Miranda glanced at Bailey.

"What?" He frowned at her.

"Nothing." She shook her head. It had been months since she'd felt an Infected as strong or as coherent. It reached out to her, but didn't push, didn't try to force its way in. *This one has manners and shit,* she thought and felt it agree.

What do you want? She knew it wasn't wise to engage, but she was curious and lonely.

Your father wants you to join him.

The Infected passed her an image. The mouth of a cave, a faint bioluminescent glow emanating from within. A sign beside the concrete stairs read "WELCOME TO MAMMOTH CAVES."

Akeem hadn't seen the sky in over a year. When he'd arrived with his older sister and her new husband, his hand clutched tight to the back of Jamila's coat, they'd been rushed down a set of concrete stairs into the cave system. Akeem wished he'd known then. He would have stopped, held up the line for a moment, risked letting go of Jamila just to look up, to see the expanse of the heavens one last time.

He couldn't remember if it had been early or late, if it

had been cloudy yet or not. He didn't think so. The ones who came later talked about the clouds, but Akeem didn't remember any clouds. Had it been evening? Would he have seen stars?

At rest time, he drowsed in his hammock, squinting his eyes so the light from the glow worms in the ceiling and walls of his sleeping quarters sparkled through the haze of his unshed tears. It could be starlight, but it was a low blue-green. He remembered the stars. They had twinkled warm yellows and reds, stately golds and silvers on clear nights when his father had taken him and Jamila far out into the fields near Hawija. They had helped his uncle harvest watermelons. After, they had sat on the ground, hands and faces sticky with sweet juices as they laughed at Abu Omar's stories of Cousin Omar's adventures at the American university.

Most of the time, Akeem was too busy to miss the light, the sky, the stars. Everyone in the Mammoth Cave hive had duties and everyone who wanted to stay on the right side of the Enlightened performed those duties with enthusiasm. At twelve, Akeem was too young to be given truly difficult tasks, so he spent his days processing the reclaimed items brought to the great hive. In the beginning, most of the things were the baggage brought by people like Jamila and her husband. They had believed they would be chosen. They had passed the blood tests, hadn't they? Akeem had been too young to test, but the Enlightened had assured them that he would be well cared for and as soon as he was old enough, he would be allowed to test.

That time stalked closer with each passing day as Akeem's limbs stretched, his hands and feet seeming too big for the rest of him. He'd found the first hairs of manhood in formerly smooth places and, although he diligently plucked them, they returned with friends.

At first, Akeem had believed Jamila when she promised him that he'd be able to join her. "We'll all be one. We'll never be alone again. The Enlightened will bring us all together as one being, and not just humans. All creatures." Her face had been luminous, the way she talked of her wedding. And how had that turned out? Not the grand affair of her girlish dreams. No, she had married in a cheap dress before a magistrate and a pair of Cousin Omar's school friends who had both been drunk and giggling the whole time.

Small consolation that those men were probably dead or Infected now. Akeem had ceased looking for people he'd known among the Infected. He couldn't even recognize Jamila anymore and he'd watched her change. No chance he'd be able to recognize two men he'd only seen once for twenty minutes on a hot July day when the Los Angeles outbreak had been only a whisper in the news.

The only way Akeem had found to keep track of time was to ask the new people coming to join the hive, but these days there were precious few of those. The Enlightened said that it was a good sign. Most people had either ascended to Enlightenment, joined the Infected, or like, Akeem, would do so soon.

"We could run away," a girl had whispered once a few months ago. She had a puffy parka and heavy boots. She told Akeem that people were starving. The winter was too long and too cold. There was no power and no heat. People were going south and the Infected were waiting.

The girl had been brought in by Enlightened and left to scream in a cell for three days. When she'd finally begged for water and promised to be good, Akeem was allowed to tend her.

Akeem had shaken his head. He pointed up at the bundles of tentacles and webs of bioformation. The network knew everything. There was no point in trying to leave the cave. Where in the world could they go that the Infected didn't control? Jamila had had the right idea, even if things hadn't worked out for her. A chance at ascension was better than death, better than being turned into nesting material, better than being one of the simple Infected who wanted only to fight and eat.

But the girl hadn't believed Akeem. She had tried to escape, had stolen a knife and stabbed an Enlightened before she was torn apart by the Littles. Akeem still remembered the sound of her scream, cut off half-finished when her throat was ripped out.

Sometimes the memories crowded in so much he felt he couldn't breathe. The air was always warm and moist, thanks to the bioformations. Akeem slipped away from the packs and bundles he was supposed to be inventorying and ran.

Not out. There was no out.

He ran in and down. Mammoth Cave was a massive system of tunnels and caves, some of which could have housed multi-story buildings or soccer fields. Even with all their spreading and spreading, the Infected hadn't used up all the space. There were lower parts of the cave system, where murky water dripped from tooth-like stalactites to their reaching stalagmite mates below.

Here the air was cool and stale, but it didn't have the

meaty reek that underlay everything about the Enlightened. Akeem followed his feet, having long since gotten used to moving though the darkness. He had a flashlight, in case, but he didn't want to turn it on. Someone might see it.

Ahead, a faint blue glow. Akeem slipped sideways, barely able to squeeze through the narrow passage, his shirt catching on the rocky walls, but not tearing, as he wriggled out. The room was egg shaped, with a wide, shallow, circular floor and curving walls reaching to a narrow point high above. There was a chill to the air and a scent, earth and roots, and something like pine. Did the chimney go all the way up to the surface?

But Akeem didn't spend long considering the chimney question.

In the middle of the room was the source of the soft blue light. A tube, like a tanning bed stood on one end, but made of transparent glass or plastic. The tube was filled with liquid that emitted a faint bioluminescent glow.

But it wasn't the tube that captured the boy's attention, either.

It was the man.

He floated in the liquid, eyes closed, face slack as if deeply asleep. The man's hair floated around him in a dark halo. His tawny skin was only a few shades lighter than Akeem's. And he was naked, except for all the tubes running into and out of his body. Some tubes were deep purple or nearly blue, while others were pale pink, yellow or bright red. Thick tentacles held the man's wrists, ankles, waist, and neck.

Akeem crept closer, his hand out to touch the tube.

"I wouldn't." A man's deep voice startled the boy. Akeem jumped and turned.

Behind him was one of the Enlightened. It was a point of vanity among them to retain their human features or to only have adaptations with obvious benefit. The Enlightened despised the chaotic nature of the Infected with their many sets of teeth, their duplicate and often useless eyes, their uncontrollable tentacles, and their insect-like feelers.

This Enlightened had kept most of his human features. In the blue glow from the tube his skin had a greenish hue, moist and shiny, with thick veins of slowly pulsing blood just under the surface layer. He was bald, but still had a human shaped head and ears. His eyes gleamed in the darkness. Many of the Enlightened's retinas changed, becoming adapted for low or no light environments as if caves had always been their destiny.

"Do you know who I am?" the Enlightened asked. He moved into the room and Akeem saw that his bottom half was all thick tentacles, like an octopus. They moved almost gracefully across the floor so that he seemed to glide, rather than the jerky up-and-down of a human's walk.

Akeem shook his head. "No, Revered, I don't know. I was just..." He couldn't think of any good reason to be here. The Enlightened would give him to the Infected. He was too young to ascend. He would be nesting material, like the girl who tried to run away. Tears welled up and he bowed his head miserably.

"Do you know who this is? Why he is here?" The Enlightened slithered past Akeem, right up to, but not touching the glass.

"N-no, Revered." Akeem sniffed. He too stepped forward. If he was going to die, he might as well have a good look at the man in the tube of blue goo.

"He took my child from me," the Enlightened said. From below his ribcage a second set of withered-looking arms reached for the tube as if they wanted to smash it open and break apart the man inside. The Enlightened frowned and with his main set of arms pushed the second set down impatiently.

"Why not use him for nesting?" Akeem asked. His voice sounded loud and echoey in the great empty chamber with no bioformations to dampen the sound.

"That was my intent when I had him brought here. I thought if I had him, my daughter would follow, but she did not. So, I meant to kill him. Half a year ago he created a sickness that threatens all our hives and networks. But as I started the process, I found that filtering our blood through him removed the sickness." The Enlightened rolled back, leaning into his tentacles as if he was a businessman in an expensive office chair. He waved one of his main arms at the floating man. "Go see his back."

Akeem walked around the tube, studying the man from every angle. He was young, barely older than Jamila's husband, maybe late twenties or early thirties. He was handsome, like a movie star. On his back were the black swirling pattern of tattoo-like marks Akeem knew were caused when the Enlightened tried to turn someone and the ascension failed. He'd never seen someone live through a failed ascension. A few had become lesser Infected, but most just died horribly.

Somehow the man in the tube's body had halted the

ascension process, had rejected Enlightenment. Akeem felt hope flutter in his belly for the first time since Jamila had left him with a kiss and smile.

The Enlightened was watching the boy closely as he rounded the tube, returned dutifully to his place, his face carefully blank, cursing his fast-beating and traitorous heart that seemed bent on alerting the world to his rebellious fantasies.

"Can you imagine how much that must have hurt?" The Enlightened's voice was filled with greedy relish. He enjoyed the idea of the man's pain.

Akeem shook his head.

"Did you notice there are layers of scars?" the Enlightened pressed. "We kept him suspended for weeks, trying to get him to fix what he had done, but in the end, Carmine was right. We could never trust any cure that came from him. He proved that in Portland. So now he serves in other ways."

"We all serve the Enlightenment," Akeem recited.

The Enlightened glanced at him, as if sensing he was perhaps not as sincere in his platitudes as he could have been.

"And I should get back to my duties," Akeem said.

"Indeed, boy. Be off," the Enlightened said. "If they ask where you were, tell them you were with Viers."

"Yes, Revered." Akeem started to leave. He paused at the door for a final look at the man who floated in a dreamless sleep and who contained the power to destroy the ones who had destroyed the world.

The End

About the Author

M. K. Martin is an author and editor. Her work appears in literary journals, in several anthologies, and in her debut novel *Survivors' Club*. Martin is a restless world traveler who started writing young. She was an exchange student to Paraguay, joined the US Army, got deployed to Afghanistan and to Iraq, and currently lives in Ireland. Martin has a BA in Psychology, another BA in Linguistics with a minor in Creative Writing, and a deep love of tea. Find out more at mkmartinwriter.com

Special Thanks

Special Thanks: Once again, I am deeply indebted to my writing community. Whether it was workshopping a piece or providing overall feedback, they have been a source of encouragement and helped me refine this book.

My long-distance writers' group:
- Kristin Ammerman – whose high standards ensure I always bring my best writing to the page, even when that requires writing tough, emotional scenes.
- Polly Irving – who helps me figure out how to say what I mean because no one has telepathy
- Sarah Shipley – whose delight in my stories is very motivational
- Paul Tallman – who has a gift for naming things and world-building and meta world-building

To my VCFA alumnx:

- Erin Stalcup – whose workshops provided me with so much craft info
- Sara F-ing Stancliffe – who is finding her truest true self and is brave enough to share that wonderful person with the rest of us. When do we get your magnet poems?
- Virginia Boothe – wise and generous soul who's found a way to turn challenges into opportunities and who loves with an open heart and a strong back.

To the amazing editors who polished and pushed this story to be the best it could be:

- Karen Eisenbrey, for final edits and proofreading (any remaining typos are clearly immortal, so just ignore them).
- Oren Ashkenazi, who correctly pointed out so very many issues with the early draft, including that Miranda should actually be in the story.

Finally, to Aaron, my muse and enabler. None of this would be possible without you, partner. ♥